AUTUMN NIGHTS

13 SPOOKY FALL READS

CASS KIM AMANDA STOCKTON MARTIN SHANNON
JACOB FAUST S M ROSE TARA JAZDZEWSKI
DIXON REUEL MANDY LAWSON MEG HOLEVA
MATTHEW CESCA ALANA TURNER NICOLAS GRAM
K A MILTIMORE EDISON T CRUX

Edited by
A W WANG

CONTENTS

FOREWORD

Dear Readers:

When my good friend Cass Kim, the author of Wilders and a new star of YA fiction, mentioned doing a Halloween Anthology for charity, I jumped at the chance to be a part of it.

She has assembled a group of thirteen plus one authors to contribute a short story to celebrate all that is spooky about Halloween. Each of these wonderful writers are up and coming talents, who bring their own unique flare and creative twistiness for those who appreciate this time of year.

This book is for those who love black cats. For those who love autumn leaves, spiced rum, and pumpkins. For everyone who loves Friday the 13th. And for those who love tales well told.

These thirteen plus one stories span the different genres from historical to scifi, from horror to comedy, from LitRPG to romance - all with a Halloween flavor. In them, you'll find scary darkness and unexpected humor, happy endings and sad ones, good people and evil beings, and mystery throughout.

Thank you for reading this anthology. You'll have a great time, and it's for a good cause.

Enjoy the spookiness of October 31st, and prepare to be entertained!

Best regards,
A.W. Wang
Author of Ten Sigma

BLOODLINES: A SAGE ROBERTS STORY

BY CASS KIM

"Look, Delphie, I know you hate the rain, and the dark, and pretty much anything else in the world that's even a little bit not safe and cozy, but if you don't go outside right now and pee, you're going to be holding it all gosh darn night." Sage Roberts tugged on her dog's leash, inching the shaggy mutt closer to the back door of their house. At almost eighty pounds, the dog was difficult to drag. It was no small feat for the teenager to coerce the reluctant dog toward the dark, damp yard, his paws scraping across the tile floor.

With a sigh fit to shake the eaves, she dropped the leash, flung the door open even wider, and danced out into the rain. Sage threw her hands high above her head, tilting her face up. She skipped and twirled in the patchy moonlight, reveling in the slow cold drops splattering her face. She knew if her parents were home, her mother would be yelling that she'd 'catch a cold' for such behavior. That knowledge made it just a little more fun. As it happened, her parents were away on a twentieth wedding anniversary cruise. Which was also serving as Sage's first trial of staying home alone for an entire week. They'd left yesterday, and so far she'd stuffed her face with pizza then had ice cream for breakfast before school.

"Come on, Delphie!" She leaned down and patted her thighs. The dog crept forward, belly scraping the ground, ears low. Adding extra sweetness to her voice, Sage clapped her hands between sentences. "Delphie! Who's a good little scaredy-cat dog? Who's the worst guard dog in the history of dogs ever?" The dog perked his ears up just a little. He stood now in the threshold of the door, nose lifted and sniffing. Despite living in a quiet subdivision with large yards and well spaced houses, all relatively new and well maintained, the rain always brought out the scent of something… different. It was worse in the fall, with the chill, heavy rains that heralded the colder weather of winter. You could smell it in the spring, sometimes, but the softer mists didn't bring the smell up the same.

It wasn't the sickly-sweet smell that made one think of pumpkin spiced lattes and candy corn. The scent was a darker, deeper odor. Ashy, and tangy like something decaying. The kind of scent that stayed in your nose even after you'd gone back indoors. The smell never really bothered Sage, but it was one reason that several of the houses were now empty in their neighborhood.

With a cackle, Sage darted forward and snatched the leash, tugging Delphie out and into the rain. He peered at her dolefully before giving in and snuffling at the ground.

"Look, Delph, we can just stay in the yard tonight. I know it offends your puppy-doggo sensibilities to smell like wet dog, so do your business, and it's straight to bed." She glanced down the street that wound behind their home as the dog lifted one leg and took her advice. The family in the house behind them had moved out a few months ago. Without the aid of the house lights, the streetlamps couldn't quite keep the darkness at bay. Unlike her dog, Sage had never been spooked by the dark in their neighborhood. It was a subdivision, after all. Did it get safer than a quiet subdivision? Not in Sage's sixteen year old mind.

Once Delphie finished peeing, they went back inside, and Sage dried his wiry curls with an old towel. She, too, was not a fan of wet dog smell. Sage gave him a small biscuit, which she knew her father would not approve of, because 'we have to keep his weight down for his health', but she thought he deserved it. The last storm before her parents left, her father had literally had to carry the shaking dog out into the night to pee. At least that had not been the case tonight.

Sage turned the TV off and paused midway to the stairwell. Something felt… wrong. The house was too quiet. No newspaper rustling as her dad caught up on the day's news before bed. No soft clink of plates and cups as her mother put away the dried dishes from dinner. Just the soft, fading patter of rain on the roof.

Last night she'd created a dance party with Delphie, then gone to sleep with her phone still playing music. Tonight, the silence felt heavy, ominous. Padding up the carpeted stairs, dog at her side, she shrugged her shoulders and brushed off the strange feeling.

"Delph, you're rubbing off me, you coward!" Sage patted his head, ruffling his ears from side to side, and leapt into bed. It was a well-known fact that once you get your feet off the floor and pull the covers up high, you're safe from all sorts of monsters. She'd just have to brush her teeth longer tomorrow morning.

SAGE WOKE to the sound of her phone clattering to the floor, still buzzing with incoming texts. Delphie hopped off the bed, mouth open in a grin, panting in excitement for breakfast. With a groan and stretch, Sage flopped her feet down and scooped up the phone before standing. Sunlight filtered into the windows; the dawn had washed away the clouds hours ago.

"Ugh." she swiped her phone open, skimming through sixty new text messages. Group texts with her friends always went so crazy, so fast. She scrolled through the bulk of the conversation, half reading, as she followed Delphie downstairs.

Let's go to the pumpkin patch!

Yeah!

Totes!

I'm in!

I can't.

I'll drive! I'll take the van and pick us all up!

Is Sage still sleeping? Saaaaage! Saaagey!

The last message was from Sage's best friend. Of course Evvy would want to make sure Sage came to the pumpkin patch too. They'd carved pumpkins together every year since fourth grade. Delphie nudged her legs with his nose, panting up at her. It was well past his preferred breakfast and tinkle time.

Yeah, cool, what time? She tapped into her phone before plugging it in and dropping it on the counter. She fed Delphie and cracked open a seltzer water. While he crunched through his kibble, chasing the stainless-steel bowl across the kitchen floor, she returned to her phone.

3pm?

I can't, Joe's soccer game starts at 2. Mom said I have to drive him and his stupid little friends.

Sage ignored the new texts. Her schedule was open for today, so she'd just chime in when they picked a time and go from there. Though she should probably clean the bathrooms. Even thousands of miles away, her Mom would somehow know if Sage skipped her weekend chores.

After walking Delphie up two blocks, around the small pond, and back, she checked her phone again. Forty new messages. At least it looked like they'd settled on a time.

It's open until dusk.

Well what time's dusk?

Weather app says sunset is at 6:00 tonight.

They have a hayride! Can we do the hayride too?

Sure.

Get there at 5:00? Get our pumpkins?

Eat a donut!

Hayride last! It'll be spookier at sunset!

Jay, will your brother's game be done by then?

Yeah. I'll start with Evvy and work my way around. Everybody be ready by 4:30. You ain't ready, I ain't waitin!

Sage rolled her eyes and snorted. Of course Jay wanted to pick up Evvy first. Everybody in the school knew he had a ridiculous crush on her. Evvy'd turned him down when he'd asked her to the Homecoming dance last month, but Jay clearly still held out hope.

I'm in. Sage replied in the group text. Almost immediately a message just between her and Evvy popped up.

Sagey, yaasss! Can I come over and make him pick us both up together? He's so weird how he won't give up. We'll carve the 'kins tonight and watch scary movies. Tradition!

Only her best friend would type a novel for a text. Sage sent a grinning emoji to match the smile the text had put on her real face.

Yes! Tradition lives!

When they'd first started the tradition of carving pumpkins together and watching scary movies, Evvy's parents were going through a divorce. Sage's grandma babysat the two girls after school three days a week. She'd started the annual pumpkin patch and subsequent carving tradition with them as a way to distract Evvy from all the changes at home. It was something she could count on staying exactly the same each year, as Sage's grandma had promised.

Granted things had changed a lot in the seven years since

they'd started. Back then, Grandma Rosemary had still been alive, and filled with energy. The scariest movie they watched was Hocus Pocus. Now, the girls shared a mug of hot spiced cider in honor of Grandma Rosemary and watched much bloodier horror films.

It remained the best part of Fall; that hadn't changed. They'd never missed a year and planned to pass the tradition on to their own children someday. Sage checked the cupboards to ensure they had spiced cider packets and pulled a few of the better slasher films from the DVD drawer, stacking them haphazardly on the tiled counter that separated the kitchen from the living room. She blasted her "Halloween Dance Party" mix through the wireless speakers tucked high up on the cupboards and bounced around the house preparing. Once the old newspapers were stacked, and the carving kits with little serrated knives and large plastic gut scrapers set out, she ate a quick sandwich.

Sage finished cleaning the bathrooms, one per floor, just in time to shower and do her hair and make-up. She was sure Evvy and Gemma would both blast the pumpkin patch trip all over their social media. When the doorbell clanged thirteen fast chimes in a row, Sage was just running the mascara wand through her lashes for the final time. Delphie howled and dashed toward the door. Laughing at Evvy's use of the unlucky number, Sage capped the mascara and raced down the stairs after him.

"Evvy, you look too cute for a pumpkin patch!" Sage was only half teasing, as Evvy had arrived in a maroon and gold dress, a little too short for bending over and picking up pumpkins. Her long black hair was perfectly flat-ironed and smooth, cascading around her shoulders.

"Sagey! You look too casual for a girl-boy outing that's literally meant for canoodling." Evvy gave Sage's jeans and sweater a long judging stare before winking. After brushing into the house, she bent over to grab Delphie's head and give him a big smooch between the eyes.

"There will not be any canoodling. It's not like we're going to a movie," Sage retorted. Delphie danced along behind them, the curls on his head now gleaming with a red lip print from Evvy's sticky gloss. Sage reached down to wipe it away.

"Oh wait! He looks too cute, let me take his photo." Evvy squatted in front of Delphie, mindless of her short skirt. She tapped the floor to get him to look down for a perfect shot. After snapping the picture, she stood back up, right back on track. "And, there will *so* be canoodling. Why do you think the guys wanted to be in the back of the hayride as the sun sets? How much more make-out perfect could it get? Chilly, spooky, dark. I swear Sage, you don't even want a boyfriend."

Sage snorted before replying, "You think? I've told you about seventy-million times I'm waiting for college. No offense, Evvs, but the guys here are just..." Sage sighed then shrugged. "I just think I want to meet somebody I haven't known since I was three."

"Yeah, yeah. But a little practice dating, a kiss or two, wouldn't hurt, ya know?" Evvy tugged her skirt down and checked her phone. "Looks like Jay is dropping off the last soccer kid. Should we walk Delph before we go?"

"Yep."

The girls took Delphie the normal route, up around the pond and back. While Sage picked up Delphie's waste, Evvy took photos of the trees. The rain had knocked quite a few of the colorful leaves to the ground, leaving naked tree limbs to stretch into the sky, spidery fingers reaching for the distant sun.

Jay pulled his parent's van into the drive just as they got back.

"Heyo!" he shouted at them from the open window. "Hurry up! We gotta get Gemma and Sinclair too. And stupid Max couldn't get a ride into town, so we gotta jet out there to get him, which sucks, man. So, let's go!"

"Jay, you're being rude AF!" Evvy hollered back, putting an extra sashay into her hips with a wink at Sage.

"Uh," the gangly boy swallowed, his adam's apple bobbing. "Sorry. Can you guys put the dog inside and hop in?"

"Do you have to tease him like that?" Sage muttered to her best friend as they locked up the house, backs turned to the van.

"Half of flirting is the teasing." Evvy shrugged carelessly.

"It's mean, since you're never going to give him a chance."

"Then he shouldn't be rude. Call it justice."

"I swear, you're going to get into a bad situation one day with that attitude."

"Uh, Sagey, haven't you heard of the 'Me Too' movement? You sound like some old white dude."

Sage rolled her eyes. "I'm saying that you know it's not fair, and you know Jay has a temper, so why taunt him?"

Evvy just clucked her tongue and walked to the car, climbing into the far back. Sage patted Jay's shoulder as she climbed in after her.

Jay called Sinclair's phone while they drove, and the guys hollered back and forth about the latest football game. Maybe Jay was finally taking the hint. Evvy scrolled through the photos she'd taken, starting her Instagram campaign for the day. Every once in a while she'd nudge Sage to get an opinion about a filter before posting. The photo of Delphie was especially cute.

"Hey, can you text me that one?" Sage rested her head on her friend's shoulder, watching her work her editing magic on the photos.

"The Delphie one? Shoot, I'll print it and frame it for you. You know your Mom will want to hang it on the stair wall." That was probably true. The wall along the stairwell at Sage's house was covered in a cascade of still life photos from their childhood. Sage watched as Evvy flipped through the photos from their walk, amazed as photo editing magic made the red, orange, and yellow of the leaves pop into crimson, fire, and gold. Evvy's fingers were fast and sure as she cropped, filtered, and posted. She had over fifteen thousand followers on her Instagram and posted at least twenty photos a day.

"Hey, wait! Take that filter off for a second." Evvy's fingers paused before she tapped the 'undo' arrow.

"What?"

"Look at that." Sage used two fingers to zoom in on the photo. A single red leaf floated on top of the pond.

"Yeah, it's really pretty right? That's why I took the picture."

"No, like, why is the water clearer in the back of the pond, but so murky here? Like, you can see the leaves under the water in the back. But you can't see anything but black here, by the red leaf. That's weird."

"What do you mean it's 'weird'? It's called shadows, Sagey. That pond always looks kind of gross anyhow."

"No, but...wouldn't the shadows be more like the tree branches in shape? Like sticks and stuff?"

"Maybe it was a cloud?" Evvy shrugged and returned the photo to its normal size as the van pulled into Sinclair's drive.

"I'M NOT GETTING on this hayride first. The crowds in the pumpkin patch were annoying enough for photos. I want the furthest back seat!" Gemma tapped her foot, gesturing for the other kids in line to go first. Sage felt her face flush in embarrassment. Were her friends always this rude, and she was just now realizing it? They'd run around the pumpkin patch, the guys completely unaware of families and small children. Gemma and Evvy had spent more time posing for photos than looking at pumpkins. Well, at least Evvy had gotten serious about finding the right one for carving after a little while.

Gemma, with freshly dyed blond hair and a tight little dress, had focused more on selfies, and never even ended up with a pumpkin loaded in the back of Jay's van.

Normally Sage would have been posing with her friends or taking some of the photos in good humor. For some reason, she felt different this time. She'd hung back, wandering through the rows of pumpkins, drawn to the edge of the field. There was a heaviness in her heart, a feeling of pressure. Maybe it was just from thinking about her grandma. Or being home alone all weekend. When a bell had chimed for the final hayride of the night, she'd picked a large pumpkin and headed back to the group.

"Hey, Sage! Earth to Sage. Hop in." Sinclair reached down a hand to help her into the back of the trailer, stacked high with bales of hay. She forced herself to grin at him as she grabbed his hand and was hauled up. Of all the guys, he was the least immature today. At six foot one, he was one of the best athletes in their small school.

"Thanks, Sinclair." She patted his arm as she squeezed past and sat further up, giving Gemma her preferred back edge seat.

"Ugh, this hay is so prickly!" Evvy tugged her dress further down before sitting, trying to protect her legs from the coarse pieces sticking up. Sage resisted the urge to say 'I told you so' and watched as Gemma used the scratchy hay as an excuse to sit on Sinclair's lap.

"You can sit on my lap, uh, if you want to Evvy." Jay's topaz eyes, his best feature by far, darted down to his lap then back up.

Evvy glanced at Max for a long moment, waiting to see if there would be a better offer. When there wasn't, she shrugged half-heartedly and sat in Jay's lap, pulling her hair over her cleavage. After frowning at her friend, Sage deliberately looked away.

Without a word, the old driver climbed onto the tractor they were hitched to and the enormous back tires began grinding across the dirt path. Sage's body jerked with the sudden movement and she heard Gemma make a snide remark behind her. Readjusting on the bale, Sage kept her gaze resolutely forward. She wanted to enjoy this ride – she'd always loved these traditions. The sway of the trailer as it made its way out of the fields and toward the dark woods soothed her frustration with her friends.

Giggles floated up from behind her, but Sage barely heard. Adrenaline danced up her spine, chasing away the moment of calm. Two scarecrows were standing guard at the front of the wooded trail, pointing toward the sinking sun. Blue flannel shirts hung, buttoned around straw-stuffed bodies, and burlap sacks with crudely sharpied faces stared out from under baseball caps. Sage couldn't quite see where they were anchored to the ground. Drawn to them, she held the black button gaze of the nearest as it followed the progress of the big John Deere. She swore the mouth quirked as the trailer of giddy teens rolled slowly past.

Rubbing the chill from her arms, Sage attributed the strange notion to the wind. Surely, the wind had made the burlap fold and twitch a bit. Behind her, Gemma let out a small scream, then giggled.

"It's so dark out here. Sinclair, hold my hand!" Gemma's voice carried clearly, her flirting just this side of desperate. Sage remained resolutely forward facing. The last thing Sage Roberts wanted to do was look back and see her friends in various states of making out. The dirt path wound away from the open farmlands. Soon, they were surrounded by trees, the dying light of the sun a deep orange glow flitting between branches.

The first few twists and turns were quiet, peaceful again. The path was smooth, the crunch of the large tractor tires soft and even. Sage was able to relax, peeking back to exchange grins with Evvy. Her friend could be a little selfish sometimes, but no matter what, she'd have her back. In her heart, Sage knew if she told Evvy she felt weird, her friend would shove her phone in her pocket, notifications turned off.

As if sensing her thoughts, Evvy hopped off Jay's lap and plunked down on the straw bale next to Sage. She made a face as she tugged her skirt again and shifted to try to avoid the pokiest pieces.

"Sagey, are you feeling okay?" Evvy pressed her shoulder against hers, peering into her eyes. The sun had kissed the horizon goodnight moments ago, leaving pink and orange streaks quickly fading across the sky.

"Yeah, I just. I don't know. I'm not feeling the group thing, I guess." Sage shrugged, avoiding Evvy's gaze.

Evvy leaned closer, so she couldn't be avoided. "We'll ditch these guys as soon as we can, okay? It'll be just pumpkin tradition after this."

When Sage met her eyes, Evvy crossed hers then bumped her nose to Sage's, like they had when they'd pretended to be pony sisters back first grade. Sage couldn't keep the smile from tugging at her lips.

"Yes! I knew I'd make you smile. Now, let's get spooky up in here." Evvy gazed out into the darkness of the forest. She raised her voice in a wail, "OooOOooOOoo."

Gemma screamed again, making the driver turn and scowl.

"Yer gunna make me take the shortcut home, you keep being so loud. Be respectful of the young 'uns on this ride." His glare shifted to Gemma. "And get yer own seat. This is a family ride."

He rotated back around, his shoulders hunched, muttering words Sage couldn't quite make out, as he increased the speed of the tractor, causing the trailer to sway and wobble.

Evvy raised an eyebrow at Sage, her expression unusually serious.

Pushing up against Sage's ear, Evvy whispered, "He gives me the creeps. Sage, I didn't want to make a big deal of it, but he was staring at us before we got on. Like, really staring hard. I think he's a total old man creeper."

Gemma made her way huffily over to the girls and laid Sinclair's sweatshirt over the bale before sitting. "Sinclair said I should just follow the rules. Can you believe that?"

Sage bit her lip to cut her snark before replying, "I think he's probably right. It's like, what, ten more minutes or something?"

Gemma rolled her eyes and finger combed her hair. She had always been more Evvy's friend. Maybe it was just Sage's mood, but Gemma was acting rude even for, well, Gemma.

Evvy elbowed Gemma, "Gemms, you gotta chill. This is supposed to be fun, remember? Like, group fun, not like finally-get-Sinclair-to-make-you-his-girlfriend fun."

Sage looked off into woods, trying desperately not to get in the middle of things. Evvy and Gemma had gotten into some serious cat fights at school. Never really physical, but some of the things they said probably hurt worse than a shove anyhow.

"Oh shut up, Evvy. You're no better. You're no better at all, throwing yourself at Jay in a desperate attempt to get some attention from anyone." Gemma's voice dripped sweetness as she looked between the guys and Evvy.

"Gemma—" Evvy's voice held a hard warning.

"You don't even like him. I remember when you called him a...what was it? 'A skinny Momma's Boy' right?" Gemma stared Evvy down as she quoted her, daring her to deny it.

"Gemma, don't be such a bitch. I said that like...two years ago." Evvy gritted her teeth, and Sage scooted a little further back.

"Oh?" Gemma shrugged her shoulders, face a picture of innocence, "I could have sworn it was after he asked you to homecoming."

Jay stood up, his face red. Sage thought she saw the glint of tears in his eyes, but it was dark enough she couldn't quite tell. He stepped forward as the trailer thumped over a large rock in the path, tipping sideways. The sudden jerk tossed Jay, one foot still in the air, over the side of the bales.

Evvy and Gemma screamed. The driver slowed and then stopped the tractor. He grabbed a large flashlight, cursing loudly. The trailer froze in silence. No sounds came from the ground.

Sage felt sick to her stomach.

Jay still hadn't stood back up.

He'd fallen headfirst.

"What the hell did we hit?" The driver was grumbling, limping back along the trailer. "There's not a damn rock on this path. Been driving the thing all day."

Sage held her breath, slowly rising on wobbly knees. She could see the top of Jay's head now, as he worked his way to his feet, shaking out his hand.

"You good, man?" Sinclair hopped down to check him out.

"Yeah, yeah, just caught myself with my hand, man."

The driver approached Jay, one shuffling step at a time.

Exhaling slowly, Sage let her gaze drift back further, to the dark shape in the path. Though the sky was clear, there was no moon out to light the forest. Only the ambient light of the stars, and the bobbing yellow glow of the flashlight revealed the shadowy lump in the path.

The clump of darkness on the trail moved. First a small twitch. Then a bigger spasm. It wasn't a rock. The driver was right. They'd hit something else entirely. Something alive. Maybe close to death, now. In horror, Sage wondered if they were sitting there, watching its death spasms, doing nothing. Nausea rolled up her throat. She had to get off this trailer. Immediately.

Tumbling past legs and crunching over feet, Sage dove off the back end of the trailer. She hit the ground running, her heart driving her to the dark form. Skin tingling, hairs on the nape of her neck crawling, she sprinted past the yellow glow of the flashlight, to the black lump.

It was a cat.

Sage knelt down, afraid to touch it. She had to see it better. She had to know how to help. A whistling breath wheezed from the creature. Whipping out her phone, she thumbed the flashlight on. Illuminated in front of her dirty jeans was a black cat, with slick dark fur, and bright green eyes. Sage reached a tentative hand toward it, taking in the ripped right ear. It looked like it had been torn long ago, now just a scarred and jagged edge.

The cat scrunched its eyes into slits, blood trickling from its mouth. Setting her phone down, she placed a hand gently on its body. It met her gaze as they both panted. Unable to control her body, Sage froze, her hand warming in its fur. Her stomach roiled as nausea surged again. Sage's arm spasmed, hand leaving the cat, as she reflexively turned away to retch.

When she turned back, the cat was up and staggering into the woods. Unthinking, Sage trailed after it, oblivious to the shouts from the trailer, oblivious to the footsteps following her.

In a haze, Sage followed the cat around trees, dodging old rotting logs, heedless of her phone still sitting, flashlight on, in the middle of the dirt path somewhere behind her. When the cat sped up, so did Sage, feet pounding in a rhythm matching her wildly beating heart. Eyes glued to the bobbing tail, a deeper shadow in a sea of shadows, Sage stumbled when she burst into a clearing.

Hitting the ground hard, sharp pain yanked her out from the fog clouding her mind. Crawling slowly to sitting position, she looked around. The cat was nowhere to be seen. Sage was at the edge of a clearing, perfectly round, and strangely easy to see. She looked up; the moon was still absent. With not one tree in the circle, Sage could use the starlight to make out the moss-covered forest floor.

Warmth soaked into her jeans. She was bleeding. Shaking, Sage held her right hand out in front of her. Fat drops of blood rolled across her palm and soaked into the rich, velvety green forest floor. She gasped and stumbled to her feet, clutching her right hand to her chest. Footsteps crashed through the woods. Off to her left, Evvy was shouting her name, voice hoarse with fear.

Gazing around the curves of the clearing one last time, searching for the cat, Sage backed from the circle. She turned at the boundary and came face to face with the scraggly, smelly beard of the tractor driver.

"You shouldn't be here." He reached around and clamped a hand around the back of her neck in a vise-like grip. The man pulled her toward the road, steering them around trees and dragging her over fallen logs. His grip never once loosened. His stringy hair swayed as he marched on, hunched and limping, and unusually strong. As he pulled her out of the woods, he bellowed to the others, "get yer butts back in the trailer or stay out here til dawn."

Evvy ran over and wrapped her up in a tight hug, scolding her in words that ran off Sage's buzzing mind, finding no purchase. Evvy used the sleeve that Sinclair tore off his hoodie to wrap Sage's hand tightly. The tractor driver cranked the engine and got them all back to the farm within a few minutes. There, he handed them another waiver. Sage numbly signed the second paper, exactly the same as the one they'd signed before lining up for the hayride, ignoring Gemma's protests about suing. She just wanted to go home and pretend the weird night had never happened.

WHEN JAY DROPPED the girls off, Evvy insisted on taking Sage to the hospital to see if she needed stitches. Sage refused. Her parents would never leave her home alone again if she had to go to the emergency room the second night they were gone. Evvy, undaunted, barged in and helped her bandage her hand. Even if they couldn't carve pumpkins with Sage's hand, they could still have hot cider and watch a scary movie.

After they took off the makeshift bandage and washed it with soap and water, the bleeding had slowed to a mere ooze. The cut was large enough that a normal band aide wouldn't fit, but the big ones made for skinned knees worked well enough.

"Alright, should we make the cider first, or pick the movie?" Evvy unzipped the hoodie she'd thrown on to take Delphie for a quick pee while Sage changed out of her dirty jeans and sweatshirt.

"I don't know if I can watch a scary movie. That cat getting hit really freaked me out."

Evvy nodded, frowning. "That was the weirdest thing. I mean, we weren't going *that* fast, so how did we even hit it? Cats are quick."

Sage hugged her own wrap sweater tighter around her body and stared at her reflection in the dark kitchen window. "I don't know. There was something weird in the woods. I could feel it."

Evvy snorted and started filling the kettle with water. "Sagey, you know you can't scare me with stories, right? Remember when we first started the carvings? Grammy Rosemary would tell us those old witches' tales?"

Sage tore her eyes away from her pale, floating window face and turned to Evvy. "Oh yeah. Some of those were really creepy. Remember that time my mom got so mad at her?"

"Oh yeah! That was so weird, right? Like, she didn't let her babysit us for a few weeks after that, until Halloween was over that year."

"Huh. I never really thought too much about it before but… can you remember what story she told us?" Sage tapped the cider packets to shake the powder down while Evvy turned the burner under the kettle to medium high.

"I think it was something local. Like one of the old town tales, but from before the lumberjacks and the museum stuff." Evvy tilted her head, brows furrowed in thought.

Emptying the cider mix into two over-sized mugs, Sage tried to picture that night. "Wasn't that the year before we turned thirteen?"

"Yeah! It was! Because she was saying how once we turned thirteen everything would change."

"Almost like she knew she'd get sick."

"Yeah." Both girls were silent for a moment, lost in memories. The soft bubbling of the kettle changed into a low whistle. Evvy flipped the burner off and grabbed the kettle before it could turn into a shriek. They poured the steaming water into the cups, and each stirred the powder into warm, cinnamon goodness.

In unison, they walked to the living room and settled on the couch, mugs cupped in hands, inhaling the aroma.

"You know... I think that was the year she was reading those old books." Sage pictured the worn journals her grandma had brought out that year. They'd been filled with spidery handwriting, scrawling across worn, crinkled pages. The dog-eared covers had no titles, no writing of any sort across them. Just some kind of stamp she couldn't quite picture.

Evvy nodded, her memory jogged as well. "That's right! That's so weird. I feel like I totally forgot those books even existed until now."

"Yeah..." Sage sipped at the hot liquid, brows furrowed. "Me too."

Evvy's mouth turned down at the edges, the hot cup forgotten in her hands. "What was the story about? All I remember is your Mom being, like, super mad. I can't remember the story. Just that Grammy Rosemary said it was a true story."

Sage paused, mug held at the edge of her lips, as a single line came back to her. "It all started with the new moon." Her voice was strange, hollow. As if the words bubbled up from her chest, rather than trickling down from her brain.

Evvy's phone buzzed and broke the spell, both girls blinking slowly before Evvy set her cup on the end table and answered the call.

"Hey Mom." A pause, "No, I'm at Sage's." A longer pause. Evvy rolled her eyes and sighed. "Yeah. Okay. I will." Her eyebrows rose along with her voice, "Yes, Mother. I heard you. I'm leaving now." She tapped the red button to end the call and took a large swig of her cider.

"Sorry Sagey. Mom just checked my grades on the school's parent's website. I'm guessing it'll be a few days until we can do a pumpkin carving horror fest." Evvy made a face, then shrugged. "That'll give your hand time to heal anyhow. You sure you're okay?"

"Yeah, yeah, I'm fine." She forced a small smile at her best friend, "I'll probably just walk Delphie and go to bed in a bit anyhow."

"Alright. But call me if you need anything!" Evvy downed the last of her cider and carried the mug back into the kitchen. Sage heard the thunk as she set it in the sink basin.

With a groan, Sage rose from the couch, her legs stiff from her mad sprint through the woods. She walked her friend to the door, the click of Delphe's nails on the wood floor accompanying them down the hall.

Evvy paused at the door and gave Sage a big hug. "I'll text you later – after the lecture I'm about to get!" She ruffled Delphie's ears and she dashed out to her car. After the door swung closed, Sage tumbled the lock in place, listening to the car engine rumbling to life then fading into the night.

She turned to Delphie, who gave a half-hearted tail wag. The house was once again too quiet. The dog followed as she clicked on the TV to some laugh track sitcom and sipped at her cider, standing in the middle of the living room. *It all started with the new moon.* She turned the phrase over again and again in her head. Was that even the start of the story? Or had her brain just made something up? Where had her mom put those old journals anyhow? Surely she hadn't donated them or thrown them out when she'd cleaned out her grandma's old house before selling it. Or maybe she had.

Sage polished off her cider and settled the oversized mug in the sink next to Evvy's. Her cellphone sat on the counter, dumped there by Evvy when they'd first gotten back to the house. Frowning, she wiped at the dirt that still clung to the upper right corner.

It all started with the new moon. Well, what was a new moon anyhow? Sage wandered back into the living room, typing the term into the phone's internet and tucked her legs under her as she settled into the couch.

"Delph," she said as she skimmed the search results, "Did you know that a new moon is when the moon is completely dark?" She scrolled through the pages, "I guess it's like, once a month."

Delphie settled into a curled up position and closed his eyes, entirely uninterested. Sage read on in silence for a while then became lost in flipping through Instagram photos, before watching a few video clips from celebrities.

Before Sage knew it, it was eleven and Delphie was nudging her to go out before bed. She stretched and yawned, tossing her phone on the couch cushion beside her.

"Alright, buddy, let's do this." She clicked off the TV then slid her feet into a pair of flats. Flicking on the light over the backdoor, she then clipped Delphie's leash in place. At least it wasn't raining tonight.

Holding the leash carefully in her left hand, she led the dog out into the night. The old lantern-shaped wall sconce beside the door cast a caged glow a few feet into the yard. Delphie, nose buried to the ground, began his circuit around the edge of the lit area. An owl hooted off in the shadows, stopping Delphie short in his sniffing. He froze, nose raised, snuffling. Tentatively, he stepped further down the yard, pulling Sage just past the lighted area. She yawned, looking up at the stars.

As they made slow progress toward the street, Sage scanned the sky. Still no moon. She twisted, turning to see if maybe it was behind the house, peeking out at them from around the roof. The little hairs on her arms stiffened. This was too great a coincidence.

"Come on Delph, go potty so we can head back." She started tugging the dog back toward the pool of light in their yard, suddenly concerned about not locking the door to the empty house behind them.

They were halfway between the street and the lighted yard when Delphie froze, staring into the darkness, tail straight and alert. Sage's stomach clenched as she peered out, following the dog's gaze.

In the shadows between street lamps, just past the empty house beside hers, her straining gaze caught movement. In the darkness, a cloaked figure surged forward, one leg lifting and hunching forward, the other dragging, scraping the foot along the sidewalk.

The thick hair along Delphie's spine rose and puffed. The figure continued its disturbing, effortful progress forward, slipping in and out of the shadows.

She looked over her shoulder to judge the distance to the door, the light there warm, bright, and so very safe. Looking to that glowing beacon was her undoing. When Sage turned back, her eyes were no longer adjusted to the night beyond her yard. Following Delphie's rigid glare, Sage strained, but could not pick the dark shuffling figure from the shadows created by the dancing tree branches.

He could be anywhere now.

Heart pounding in her ears, she tugged frantically at

Delphie's leash. He did not budge. Digging her heels into the soft dirt, Sage yanked with both hands, tears forming in her eyes as she tore the cut in her hand back open.

"Damnit, Delphie!" She exploded, whipping her gaze along the sidewalk, through the nearby trees. Finally, the dog turned, running for the door, pulling her off balance and ripping the leash from her hands.

Sage scrambled for footing, limbs panicked and uncoordinated. She lurched forward, a mere foot from the safety to the lit yard, when a hand gripped her ankle.

It dragged her back.

Dirt crowded under her nails as her fingers dug furrows through the soil, marking the path toward the pond.

Lurch. Pause. Forward surge.

Sage sobbed, clawing at the earth, twisting and flopping along the ground.

And still, the grip on her ankle remained iron.

Lurch. Pause. Forward surge.

Soon, the soil she dug her broken nails through turned softer, moist. It reeked of decay. The rot clogged her throat, stifling her screams.

Lurch. Pause. The hand dropped her ankle, and Sage flipped on her back, staring up at the bearded face of the hayride driver. The black cat stood, feet tucked together, back curving gently, at the edge of the pond.

"Don' try to run. I'll jus' catch ya, and I'll be less kind the next time."

Sage stared, speechless. She gasped for breath, hands shaking, one finger bent at an odd angle.

The hunched man leaned closer, peering at her hands. "Cat! I got a job fer you."

The black cat slinked forward, eyes luminous despite the lack of light. It slid up to her, head brushing past her crooked finger, tail wrapping along her arm. Nausea rose again as warmth cascade through her hands.

When the cat stepped away, tail bobbing in pleasure, her hands were clean, whole. There was a dull ache, but no true pain.

"What the—"

"Ah! I don't recommend ya say that word on this night." The hayride driver cut her off before she could utter the curse. "Ya don't need to be drawing any unwanted attention from that realm."

Sage gulped.

"I thought I'd not find ya. After last year… I thought I'd spend another century waitin' for the right descendent. Year after bloody year drivin' that awful hayride. Each year ya kids getting worse and worse acting."

Sage swiped at the tears on her face. She had to be dreaming. Surely she'd wake up soon. Dropping her head back to the ground behind her, she'd never wished for her alarm to go off more in her life.

His lank hair swayed as he shook his head. "Ya don' know nothing." He sighed, muttering under his breath about failed teachings then raised his voice, "Cat. I got another job for ya."

The cat sauntered over, a purr echoing.

Sage's eye caught on the torn right ear. It *was* the same cat from the woods.

It climbed up on her, settling to lay on her torso, front paws just below her chin. It rested its whiskered cheek against her jawline.

Images flooded into her head. Thirteen young women sitting in a circle, candles lit, full moon over head. The same thirteen holding hands, nude, on a spring morning. A journal, new, carefully written in. Passed to another.

An angry man yelling in a church building. A town gathering, faces shuttered and angry. Cheeks gaunt, clothes baggy.

The young women, older now, torn from homes. A hidden child in the last home, unknown to the surging mob.

Each woman put on trial. The women separated.

One, slowly crushed as rock, after heavy rock was placed on her body.

One, tied to a long pole, with dry brush piled below.

The images moved faster, the cat purring harder on her chest.

One, caged and left in a dark forest. Abandoned, and trapped.

One, tied to stones and dropped in water.

Faster, still, images of horror, flashing by too fast to process.

And finally, the hidden child. Stumbling through the woods. Following a small black kitten away from the town.

A flood of simultaneous images, the child growing, the cat fighting off a dark creature, its ear torn and bloodied in the process. The child, a woman now, raising her own family. The cat watching through windows, sneaking through towns and forests, always following, always protecting. Generations flew by, always a new daughter. The journal, worn and weary, passed from mother to daughter. And always, the cat, alone. Waiting. The journal shoved into a box by an angry woman. Dimly, Sage recognized the woman as her own mother. A quick image of her mother and her grandmother arguing over her crib. Both with arms waving and faces shuttered. The last image Sage processed was of her own home. Her, face upturned, dancing in the rain before pulling Delphie into the night.

The cat pulled away and ran off into the woods.

"Ya done good, cat!" The hunched man crouched awkwardly before her. "It hurts him still, to think on those days. These many years of loneliness."

"He's….hundreds of years old?"

"We both are. They ain't been kind to us, neither." He settled back on his heels, movements stiff. "Ya have the gift." He continued. "Long, they've been waiting, the thirteen. Tis only by your blood, freely given, under a new moon, that the curse may be broken. Then the cat and I can take our leave of this place."

"What are you talking about? What gift? What curse?"

"When they was taken, they knew. They knew twas a demon. The sisters created their own spell, bound to those of their blood. Ya have their blood."

Sage shook her head in denial, shoving down the images the cat had shown her.

"Ah yes. Ya do." His weight shifted toward her.

"I—I'm just a normal high school kid. I'm nothing special."

He reached out and grabbed her hand, holding it palm up. "Ya got a lot to learn. But for now. Look." He dragged a gleaming silver knife across her palm.

Sage yelped and tried to yank her hand back. He held her firmly.

"Look."

Sage followed his gaze, to where her blood was dripping. Small, white flowers sprang up, spotted with crimson. Sage fought as the haze began to descend again. She did not want to do things she couldn't control, like earlier, in the forest.

"I knew then, when I saw ya in the meadow. Their meadow. Ya didn't see the flowers. But I did. Cat almost ruined everything, the way he did it. Thought we'd never get ya away from that friend of yours this night."

Sage fought the clouding of her mind, feeling as though she was looking at her body from a distance, watching this scene play out. It kept her calm, quieting her terror.

The flowers were undeniable. She knew she should ask questions. She just…didn't know where to start.

"Ya don't believe me. I don't blame ya. Ya should have been taught long ago. Ya should have known your destiny from the day you were born." He swiped his greasy hair back with one hand, letting go of her wrist.

Sage stared up at him, forcing her lips to move. “My…destiny?”

“Aye. Born to the new moon. Born to the descendants. Born with the gift. We had one once, a few generations before ya. A rare younger sister. Died in a freak accident. I reckon was a demon generated accident. Cat was locked out of the house, unable to protect her. Never even got ta free a one of them. They’ve been waitin’ a long time.” He paused, breathing heavily, as if speaking so much in one turn was an effort he was not accustomed to.

Sage swallowed, thinking of the dark creature the cat had fought off in the visions. The haze remained, but her thoughts seemed to be adjusting to it. Filtering slowly through.

“Tonight, we free the first. I’ll show ya how. After, you an’ the cat will find where each was sacrificed. Thirteen day’s journey apart. The places lost now, with time. Ya got to find that journal. The clues were written in, years yonder.” He shook his head, pausing.

“How…how do I? I mean, what happens when I free them? How are they trapped?”

“Their souls must be reunited through the blood of the chosen descendant, to leave this world. That demon what possessed them townsfolk knew the secret. Spread them far. Trapped them, to use their energy to stay here in this world.”

“They…they’re keeping a demon here?”

“Aye. Against their will. Being fed on, piece by bitty piece each time he needs the power.”

Sage’s stomach dropped in horror. She felt a sickness deep in her soul at the thought. To be murdered, ripped from your sisters, and then trapped with your soul being eaten year after year. With no escape. But, what would it cost her?

“How much blood? And what happens to them when it’s done? Will this… this demon try to kill me too?”

He stared at her in silence, as if weighing his response.

"There be no knowing what will happen once the demon finds out about ya. But every sister you release is a sister he can't be usin' for strength. Tis a lot of blood. Almost too much." He rolled the knife hilt between his hands. "And the sisters. They'll be free. As will I. As will Cat." He looked up, his eyes eerily bright in the moonless night. "We need ta be freed."

She took a breath, the haze retreating, helping her shove her doubts down deep. "I'll do it. Tell me how to save them."

He nodded, face grim. "It'll take a lot o' blood. Ya can't do but one per month, for that reason. And that's if ya find the next by the new moon."

He handed her the knife. "Ya cut hard, and deep. Nice and clean. Concentrate on the purpose – the freedom. This pond, it used ta be a lake. This is where Virginia was drowned. Cat knows this spot, and only this spot. He was hers, first. So, ya start here. Then, ya find the journal."

Sage gripped the knife he offered. Her hand shook as she breathed deeply. This was insane. It couldn't be real. But if it was… If it was, she was the only one who could help these women.

"How will I know if it worked?"

He clenched his hands. "We won't. Not til tha full moon shows us."

"Shows us what?" The knife hilt was worn, smooth in her hand.

"A Telling Tree will sprout." His head whipped to the side, then up to the sky. "Hurry now, girl. Tha next day has almost begun. Ya got to do it now."

Sage swallowed hard. She gripped the knife, fitting perfectly in her petite hand.

As instructed, she focused on the image of the woman he'd said had died here. Virginia. Tied with heavy rocks. Dropped into a small lake. The nausea rolled through her, followed by unnatural heat. Her mind followed the image this time, rather than flashing away. Panic stirred in her stomach as Virginia sank down, below the surface of the water. Sage felt her own lungs begin to burn, her eyes tearing at the lack of oxygen. The haze clouded her mind again, calming the adrenaline.

She drew the knife, slowly, deliberately across her hand. Deeper than he had.

SAGE WOKE WITH A START, in her bed. Warm, cozy, with a bit of a headache. The kind she usually got when she tossed and turned, having a hard time sleeping. Of course. She always tossed and turned when she had weird dreams. *It was just a crazy dream.*

Sighing with relief, she reached over to her buzzing phone. Evvy was sending a string of text messages, the count past seven now. There was slight ache in her right hand as she stretched the fingers, recalling the strange dream of cutting her palm. She was glad to see her hands were whole, with no mark on the palm. Just a faint crease from curling it in her sleep.

Delphie whined and nudged at her arm. Judging by the sunlight streaming through her window, he must be very hungry for breakfast. She yawned once more, cracking her jaw, before shoving the covers off.

Sitting up, Sage froze when she saw the black cat curled up at the foot of her bed. *Oh shit.* As she carefully moved the mound of covers, he looked at her, revealing his torn right ear.

ABOUT THE AUTHOR

Cass Kim is short, sassy, and loves hoodie weather. Few things make her happier than crunching through colorful leaves and sipping hot spiced cider while curled up with a book. She's best known for writing the "Wilders" series, which can be found on Amazon, and free with Kindle Unlimited. Following publishing the final book in the Wilders series at the end of 2019, Cass plans to begin the Sage Robert's series.

If you want to connect with her, you can follow her on Twitter: (@CassKim_writes).

FADE TO BLACK

BY AMANDA STOCKTON

INVISIBLE GIRL

Her father said there were too many ghosts back in Seattle. Too many shadows around every corner that reminded him of her mother. It had been six months since she died, but it was Katy who felt like a ghost, an unseen thing left to the trenches of her mourning; alone and just another shadowy reminder of what her father lost.

Portland was supposed to be a fresh start. A new beginning. Even if it just felt like running away from something that cannot be outrun. Pain has a funny way of finding you no matter how well you hide. Shadows lurk still when the sun is highest; they do not merely dwell in the dark.

It was a new town and that meant a new school and new teenagers Katy would inevitably have to interact with. Starting, of course, with every teacher's favorite student torture: "Please introduce yourself to the class."

"My name is Katy, and I'm new here, obviously." Her less

than enthusiastic participation in Mrs. Asher's spotlight practice in humiliation generated a few snickers.

"Hi, Katy," several of the other students replied, as if it were some kind of underage support group rather than third period history.

"Why don't you tell us something about yourself. What brings your family here?" Mrs. Asher was digging for the point of red-faced confessions.

Katy grit her teeth and looked Mrs. Asher right in her wrinkled, white-browed face, "My mother died six months ago and...crippled by the loss of his wife, my father cashed in all our savings and moved us down here, just so I can answer these kinds of stupid questions."

Mrs. Asher's face turned a shade of pure crimson that twisted a satisfied smirk on Katy's face. The old lady cleared her throat and beckoned Katy to take a seat.

Choosing the empty spot at the back of the class, Katy collapsed in the chair and quietly basked in her victory. Well, for a moment anyway. Until the words she'd said caught up with her and heads turned to take a better look at the girl with the dead mom. She shrunk, sinking down in the chair, and wrapped her arms around her middle. A victory over the teacher wasn't worth all this attention. At least not this kind.

She ducked her head, silently slipping on her earbuds for the remainder of class. When the bell rang, she snuck out the door with haste, deciding the best thing she could do was finish the school year as invisible as she was at home. It was only October, and there were still more than seven months left to hide.

"Hi." A girl with the most ridiculously perfect, long blond hair collided with Katy. "You're the new girl, huh?"

Damnit. "Yeah. I guess that's me," Katy replied.

"I like your hair," said the mystery blond, touching Katy's hair, which was bottle-dyed black. The coloring was something Katy did before her mother died, but everyone only wanted to notice it and its so-called 'implications' after she was half-way an orphan.

"Thanks. I guess."

A second girl with bobbed, rose gold hair approached. "Ew, Anabelle, don't be gross. You can't just touch people."

Her shoes were those ones all the suburban moms wore. The ones with the man's name . . . Cal's? Or was it Pat's? It didn't matter. What was obvious was these girls were a very specific type, one Katy knew well. And depending on how the next few sentences went, they would dictate how the seven months of her decided invisibility would turn out.

"Sorry about her. My name is Scarlett. Scarlett Farside. And that is Anabelle."

"I'm—"

"Katy. I know. I was in Mrs. Asher's class," Scarlett said.

Shit. "Oh. Right. I thought I saw you in there." Katy lied but Scarlett didn't need to know that.

Anabelle's face ignited with greedy anticipation. "Your mom really died?"

"Jesus, Anabelle, take a sensitivity class." Scarlett wrapped an arm around Katy's. "You really nailed the old hag. I didn't think she even had a pulse before that."

"Yeah, I probably shouldn't have…"

"No, she had it coming. Lady is a real bitch ever since her husband left her a few years ago. I'm guessing she's so dried up he couldn't even find it anymore."

Anabelle laughed. "Yeah, and Scarlett has hated her since she failed her last year."

"Messed up my whole GPA. I was honor roll. I swear if that old bag is the reason I don't get into my top five I will break her neck."

"But I thought we had a way to…"

"Cram it, Anabelle."

Katy stayed quiet. It was the only thing she could really

think to do. She wondered how long they would make her stand there, wading in awkward silence under the weight of their judgement. That was until two boys barreled down the hall and scooped Scarlett and Anabelle into their arms with no more difficulty than plucking daisies from a sodden field. Scarlett screamed. Not the kind of scream someone does when, for instance, they find their mother dead on the couch. No, this scream was hollow, playful.

Katy tried to slither her way out from the eye of the storm while the two girls were busy tonguing their letterman-clad beaus.

"Hold it, new girl!" Scarlett yelled.

Son of a... "Yes? Sorry, I didn't want to interrupt. I have another class and another teacher to humiliate with awkward honesty."

"Or you could come with us." The looks of wanting painted on the faces of these tumultuous seniors sent alarm bells off in Katy's head. While some small part of her wanted to continue as planned and retreat to the shadows, another more eager part, desperate for a sense of something normal, wanted to see how much trouble they could really be. Once the taste for rebellion was out of her system, the quiet isolation at home would embrace her. What harm could one day really cause?

"Come where?" Katy asked, trying not to sound too concerned.

The boys smiled. According to the machine-embroidered lettering on their jackets, they were named Dave and Michael. Typical Americana boys. With shaggy hair, purposefully made to look unkempt. Well, Katy assumed it was purposeful. Dave kissed at Scarlett's neck, and Katy tried hard not to roll her eyes.

"Mission Manor," Scarlett said.

"What's Mission Manor?" Katy started to wonder if it was all a big joke. The popular kids initiating the newbie with some bit of local lore.

"It's our local haunt," Dave said with a toothy smile.

Scarlett rolled her eyes. "It's a haunted house. Used to be some missionary house or something. Anyway, a bunch of people died there, back in the eighties. They say it's haunted. We go there to drink."

Anabelle finally came up for air from Michael's mouth. "Yeah, you should come."

"Unless you're afraid of the goblins." Michael wriggled his fingers in front of his face animating feigned terror. The others laughed and waited for Katy to reply.

She looked into their expectant faces. Eyes wide with presumed inevitability. Meanwhile, other students walked by without looking up. No eyes glanced her way even if they did flick toward Scarlet and the other three. Katy remained wholly unseen by everyone else. She couldn't deny there was something pleasing about being seen, about being invited, about even the thought of being wanted. What choice did Katy really have?

"Sure. I mean. Ghosts aren't real. But yeah. I'll go."

Scarlett's face lit up. She wrapped her arms around Katy and dragged her toward the door just as the fourth period bell rang.

THE RED DOOR

Katy followed the other four up a street in the middle of her new neighborhood. She almost hadn't noticed when they came upon her house, her dad's old red pickup parked in the driveway. By instinct, Katy shielded her face from the windows, hiding from some off-chance her father would be looking outside at that very moment.

They came to a gravel driveway a few blocks up the street. Did those actually still exist in the suburbs? The old black mailbox hung open like a slack-jawed head on a spike. The others walked down the drive. Katy stood, unsure, questioning the plan for the first time since leaving school.

"Come on, Katy!" Scarlett yelled. "It's down this way." A smile spread on Scarlett's lips. Not in earnest. It was what someone does when they think they're supposed to smile. When they are trying to convince even themselves that they feel something genuine.

The red truck lingered near the edges of her vision, standing as a beacon, should Katy need it.

"Katy!" Scarlett called again from far down the gravel drive. Katy whipped her head around and ran to catch up with the group.

"So, what do you guys do down here? Drink beer or something?" Katy kicked a large rock out of her way.

"Beer?" Dave asked. "Who drinks beer anymore?"

I dunno, literally millions of people. Katy chuckled. "Isn't that like a Portland thing? Microbrew and flannel?"

"Yeah, if you're on that stupid show," Michael laughed.

Anabelle slapped Michael in the chest. "I love that show, shut up."

"Oh, right. Yeah. Me too." Michael went for another kiss, but Anabelle raised her hand, blocking his mouth. She scoffed.

"So, what is Mission Manor? Really," Katy asked.

"Used to be some kind of missionary headquarters or some stupid thing," Scarlett said with a smirk. "They like recruited people there for holy endeavors of saving lost souls. Whatever. One night, one of the missionaries went crazy and killed everyone who was in the house. Claiming the shadows made him do it. He was still carving up the last victim when one of the recruits showed up and knocked on the door. But it was locked. And the victim couldn't get out."

"And then they got killed, too." Dave's toothy smile widened with far too much enthusiasm.

"Obviously. The story started with 'everyone got killed.'" Scarlett remarked.

Katy nodded. "So what about the guy who did it?"

Scarlett shrugged. "I dunno. He died too, I guess."

"The shadows claimed him for the darkness." *Again, Dave, too much excitement.*

"You're such an idiot," Scarlett laughed.

"But you love me."

"You wish." Scarlett and Dave went back to whispering sweet nothings in one another's ears. Scarlett giggled in fractured bursts, her cheeks calling her name in color.

Despite her concerted efforts, there Katy was, all alone. A very awkward fifth wheel in a caravan headed toward an allegedly haunted house. *Great work, Katy. You absolute genius.*

The group rounded a corner of trees—Mission Manor finally coming into view and bringing the surround sound of lover's snipping and quipping to a sudden stop. For as large as the manor was, there was something else altogether small about it. Katy wasn't sure if she had imagined something different, or maybe it was the situation in whole that she found to be lacking in experience.

Mission Manor, the bronze crest hung by the red front door. A soft green patina weeping from the letters like toxic tears spilled over the decades of loneliness. If a building could be lonely, Katy imagined this one was. Dilapidated and likely barely standing, the old house's white paint peeled from its wooden siding. Black shutters hung askew, giving the whole place a very architectural 'walk of shame' vibe. A graffiti tramp stamp scrawled along its side completed the look: "your dead already." *Why was it that these self-proclaimed street 'artists' never made it through second grade grammar?*

Katy gazed at the house like it were a real thing. Not cold and empty. Not like a house. She imagined something beautiful in the framework. If only someone had taken the time to love it, care for it. If only someone were able to actually see *it* rather than only the stains of death.

Something grazed Katy's ankles. A black cat weaved itself between her combat boots like a silken figure eight that left stray strands of fur embedded in her laces. Katy reached down to inspect the feline's mangled right ear. It purred against her touch, nuzzling her hand with a cold, wet nose. But Michael threw a rock at the kitty, sending it scurrying somewhere behind the manor.

"Go on, Katy." Scarlett was no longer giggling. Each one of them held the same flat expression.

"Wh-what do you want me to do?" Though she had an idea, she also thought it was a terrible one.

Dave nodded toward the door, a wolfish smile permanently emblazoned on his mouth. *Seriously, no one smiles that much.*

"You're the new girl. Knock," he said.

Katy grit her teeth. She may not have believed in hauntings or ghosts, but something foul was at play. And that made the hair on the nape of her neck stand on end.

"You're not scared are you, new girl?" Michael teased as Anabelle still refused his advancements.

Katy sighed. "Why would I be afraid of a door?"

"Go on, then." Scarlett pushed Katy forward, sending her stumbling toward the decaying front steps. Katy tested them one at a time, pressing her foot down on the wood, making sure they would carry her weight. She did the same as she crossed the front porch, approaching the door with careful reluctance. Should a bucket of pig's blood or some other terrible cliche fall from the rafters, she might have time to dodge it.

Nothing came by the time Katy reached the door. Despite the persistent shine of the candy-apple red paint, the door was freckled in chips exposing the aged wood underneath. Rocks gathered around her feet told the tale of those wounds. Ignored and battered, Katy's heart felt for the house more than ever. She extended her hand, ready to knock and face whatever these kids had planned for her.

She pelted the door with her knuckles. Knocking out "shave and a haircut" on the old oak.

Two thunderous beats answered her from inside.

Katy whipped her head around. Scarlett and the others still stood in the driveway. Eight eyes stared back at her, more white than iris.

"Funny," Katy yelled. "How'd you do that?"

"That—that wasn't us," Scarlett stammered.

The door's handle shook. A wild, violent force pulled at it from inside. Katy took a step back. If all four of them were still there in the gravel then who--

"Katy…" a whisper called against the grain of the other side of the door.

"Stop it."

But the whole door shook, threatening to rip off the hinges. The framing rattled against its nails.

"Stop it!" she screamed.

The door flew open. "Gotchya!"

Katy lurched backwards, her heels dipping off the top step. She caught herself in time for Scarlett and the others to break out into a chorus of laughter.

Standing in the doorway was no monster or ghost, it was-- Just. Another. Boy. A boy wearing a black leather jacket and visually pleasing well-fitted jeans. His dark hair, cut in that fashionable way all the hipsters get credit for even though it originated sometime in the twenties. His hard jawline coated in a beard that couldn't quite figure out how to be a beard yet. His eyes, oh Katy could not pry herself from those cold blue eyes. They were like ice given a breath of life. She swallowed hard, trying her best not to gawk at one of the conspirators.

As the others walked by and filed into the manor, Scarlet chortled, patting Katy on the shoulder. "You should have seen your face." Scarlett nodded to the leather-clad boy. "Oh, Katy, this is Jason Chase. Jason, *this* is Katy." Scarlett pushed by Jason and joined the others.

"Hey," Jason said. "Sorry about..." he motioned toward the door. "...all that."

Katy brushed her hair behind her ear. "Oh! Yeah. Right. Well, I knew it was a joke."

"Still got you pretty good though." Jason smiled.

"Okay, well. Maybe a little. How'd you know my name anyway?"

"Scarlett texted me on your walk over."

Katy smiled and nodded her head. *I knew it.*

"Welcome to Mission Manor." Jason opened his arms wide with welcome and offered an exaggerated bow.

Katy replied with a mock curtsey. "Oh, why thank you, my good sir."

Jason laughed and closed the door behind them.

MISSION MANOR

There was, in fact, no beer waiting inside the manor. Just a broken staircase that kept them grounded on the first floor and enough dust to choke the dead.

Jason and the others had stocked a cooler with bottles of stolen liquor. The stale air of the manor combined with Dave's ear-bursting music threatened to churn Katy's stomach. Even if the only thing in her belly was alcohol, something wild and ragged wanted to come up if she didn't get fresh air and fast. But the front door—black on this side—was locked to keep any strangers from intruding on their party. Katy couldn't remember who had the key, so instead she went to a window. It stuck in the jam. Despite her efforts and every last ounce of strength she could summon, the glass would not budge an inch.

"Can I help you with that?" Jason asked.

Katy pressed her lips into a hard line and motioned with her hands toward the stubborn window. *By all means, give it your best.*

Jason wriggled his brows and rubbed his hands together for effect.

Katy twisted her mouth into an amused frown. *Cute. Very cute.*

He pulled against the window, trying to force it open. Still, it would not give. *Probably hasn't opened since the Reagan years.*

"Ouch. Defeat," Katy teased.

Jason, not one to be outdone by an inanimate object, removed his leather jacket and wrapped it around his fist.

"What are you doing?" Katy asked.

Jason winked at her. Then he punched a hole in the window. The glass shattered, hitting the old wood floor in a hail of sparkling sharp edges.

"What the hell, Jason?" Anabelle yelled, having spilled some of her drink.

"I like this idea." Scarlett crossed the dusty floor to where Jason and Katy stood. She picked up a stray brick from the fireplace and hurled it through the remaining glass. Dave laughed and grabbed an old chair, smashing it against the broken the window with a cacophony of exploding glass and splintering wood.

Katy shielded her eyes, taking several steps back, while her peers wrecked the last of the glass from the window's frame. Her head started to spin, and before she realized she was falling, Jason was there, catching her. He held her in his arms for what could have been forever. His chilling eyes stared into hers. The room spun behind him, but Jason Chase's face stayed in focus, keeping Katy grounded.

"You okay?" he asked.

"I am?" Katy didn't mean for it to come out sounding like a question, but Jason smiled anyway. *Oh, Katy girl, pull yourself together.*

"Are you?" Jason's grin only exacerbated her feelings of awkward failure.

"Yes." Katy pushed herself back to her feet and from Jason's arms. "I am. Yes." Before she could manage another bout of self-embarrassment, Katy stepped back to the destroyed window, finally able to take a deep breath of fresh, crisp air. It was only then that she'd realized it was dark. How could they have been inside the house for so long already? For just a moment Katy thought about her dad. How he must have been worried or angry or whatever combination of emotions parents feel when their kids don't come home from school. She checked her phone but there had not been a single text message. She shoved the thing back into her pocket and sighed.

"What's that about? You sure you're ok? You feel off." Jason put a hand on Katy's shoulder.

Sly. Very Sly. "I feel *off*? And that's based on knowing me for exactly half of a day, is it?"

Jason shrugged. "Call it a sixth sense."

I'd call it game, but nice try.

"Don't believe me?"

"Not even a little." Katy laughed despite herself and doubly so when Jason feigned a wounded heart.

In unison, the alarms on everyone's phone—aside from Katy's—blew up. Michael cut the music, and quickly, the only sound in the manor was wind blowing through the broken window.

"It's time," Scarlett said, practically salivating with desire. The others grabbed bags from the corner of the room.

"Time?" Katy shook her head, confused. "Time for what?"

No one heard her, however. They were all busy with their

bags. Pulling out random assortments of candles, feathers, chalk, and was that a jar of...blood?

"We have to draw the circle by exactly twelve-fifteen." Scarlett took the chalk and scrawled a circle on the wide planks of the floor. She scratched the crumbling utensil into the aged wood, stretching intersecting lines across the plane. Five lines made five points. A star. But more than a star, Scarlett drew a pentagram.

"Whoa...wait. Are you guys"-- Katy shook her head and snickered--"Are you guys really trying to cast some kind of spell?"

Anabelle and Scarlett stopped their preparation while the three guys picked up the pace.

"It's just for some fun." Anabelle crossed the room.

"Yeah," Scarlett agreed. "And now that we have a sixth, it might actually work."

"A sixth? You think that I'm going to participate?"

Scarlett took Katy's hands. "Well sure, Katy. Look, we all have something that we want more than anything else in the world. That's all we're doing here. Just invoking a power to ask for a few simple wishes."

"Wishes? Are you summoning a genie?"

"Something like that." The way Scarlett replied sent a chill racing down Katy's back. She looked again at the front door, and knowing it was still locked did not grant her any kind of mental reprieve.

She did not believe in things like magic or wishes or pentagrams or any of this nonsense these kids were slinging at her. Truth be told, Katy didn't think any of them believed in it either. More than likely, this was just another prank.

"What do I have to do?" Katy didn't want to look like the scared little girl once again. She could play along and earn their respect. Or she could demand they let her out of the house and almost certainly spend the last seven months of high school not being invisible but a target.

WHEN YOU WISH UPON THE DEAD

Scarlett and Anabelle finished the chalk markings inside the circle. Dave and Michael placed feathers and small bones in supposedly coordinated sections of the pentagram. And Jason? Jason was in charge of the blood. Sheep's blood.

The whole scene resembled something out of a movie. It looked ridiculous. But being nearly Halloween and given the alleged history of the manor, Katy guessed it was all a normal local affair.

"So, now what?" Scarlett asked. Which Katy found somewhat surprising, considering up until this point it had seemed as though Scarlett was in charge.

Jason opened a book bound in dark tattered leather with pages thick as papyrus. "Each of us stands at one point of the star."

Scarlett, Dave, Michael, and Anabelle each took positions around the pentagram, while Jason stepped to the fifth point.

Katy didn't want to ask where she was to stand. Or maybe given the fact that they had obviously been planning this for some time and didn't even know Katy existed as of that morning, she could get lucky and not be involved at all.

"Katy, you stand in the middle," Jason said.

Shit. "The middle? That sounds rather...ominous."

"We need someone who has been touched by death to stand in the middle."

Touched by death. The five of them, standing in their circle, stared at her with expressionless faces. *Son of a bitch, they only brought me here because of my dead mother.*

Jason broke the circle. He grabbed her hand, his ghostly blue eyes piercing her. Leaning in, his lips grazed the lobe of her ear. When he spoke, the heat of his breath chased butterflies into her stomach. "I need you, Katy. I have been waiting for you for so long. You will be safe. I promise."

Something in the way Jason spoke rang with honesty. Katy would be the first to admit it just felt good to be told something so profound by…well, anyone. Even if he didn't mean it, even if it was a lie, it felt good for the moment and that was a moment longer than what she'd felt in months.

Katy nodded. She walked to the center of the pentagram. "Do I need to do anything?"

"Just think about the thing you want most in the world," Jason replied.

"Harvard," Scarlett whispered, squeezing her eyes tightly shut.

Katy looked around the circle. Everyone's eyes closed. Dave, of course, had some kind of ridiculous smile crusted on his face. Katy figured she should close her eyes too. She tried to focus. Think about something, anything. What did she want? It was an interesting question. She'd never given much thought to her future. Nothing with the kind of hope that Scarlett had.

Her mother came to mind. Something Katy had adamantly tried not to think about ever since she came home from class that sunny Thursday afternoon. Finding the body sprawled out on the couch…the body, not even a person anymore, just reduced to nothing. A husk of dead flesh emptied of all that made her mother real. A stroke had taken her early in the morning. She didn't even have a chance to drink her coffee.

Jason started chanting something indecipherable. It almost sounded Latin. Or at least what Latin sounded like on TV.

Katy wasn't sure if she was supposed to keep her eyes shut or if she should still be thinking about what she wanted. But then the others chanted along with Jason. Katy opened her eyes.

Jason opened the jar of blood, dipped his fingers into its wide mouth, and painted a crimson stripe down the center of his forehead. He walked around the circle, proceeding to anoint the others in a wash of red. When Jason came back to his place at the pentagram, he focused on Katy. His eyes had darkened from their regular light blue.

Jason smiled and whispered, "This is only possible because of you. Thank you."

Katy stared at Jason with wide, unblinking eyes.

He dipped his fingers, again, into the jar and drew a line across Katy's lips with the blood. She tried not to seem squeamish when she pursed her lips to keep the putrid liquid from entering her mouth.

Everyone continued the chant. Everyone besides Katy. She studied them: blood smeared on their faces, speaking in a dead language, completely surrounding her. Katy wrapped her arms around herself, desperate to keep from trembling. It didn't matter what she believed or did not believe. These kids certainly appeared to hold belief in what they were doing. Just how far were they willing to go to see their wishes granted?

"Answer us," Jason yelled. "Answer our calls!"

"Your sacrifice has not been made." A voice carried through the wind. Katy stiffened, a wave of goosebumps spiked across her skin. Her lower lip quivered. The voice called again. *"Your sacrifice must be paid."*

Katy expected perhaps a seventh person was hiding in the house somewhere, making the voice. But then came the pounding from under the floor. Pounding like fists of someone in the grave. But it wasn't just under her feet. It wasn't just under the chalk. The entire floor shook with the thrumming of desperate escape.

Katy's arms squeezed her middle until she could no longer breathe.

"A sacrifice must be made," the voice demanded. Icy tendrils

slithered down Katy's back and into her spine. She could feel it. Wriggling around inside of her. Echoing off her rib cage and aiming for her heart.

"What is that?" She finally managed to utter words, but they were curt, direct, and full of fear.

Jason reached behind him, pulling a knife from his belt.

Katy froze. Her body too rigid to shake. "What are you doing?"

"You heard the voice," Jason said. "A sacrifice must be made." He stared at her. His eyes now faded to an empty blackness. Jason extended his hands, the knife clenched in his grip. Katy stumbled backward into another pair of hands that held her secure in the middle of the pentagram.

"No!" she screamed. "This isn't funny. Joke's over." She pleaded with them over and over again, but they remained void of mercy.

Jason brought the knife before Katy's face. A glint of light caught in its silver blade causing her to look away. But just as she did, she thought she caught a glimpse of someone, perhaps a seventh person in the room. But they were little more than shadow. Katy screamed again. Jason slid the knife across her arm.

Then he did the same to himself and passed the knife around the circle. Scarlett, Dave, Anabelle, and then Michael all took their turns opening a vein and spilling drops of precious blood over the chalked symbol at their feet.

The pounding under the floor stopped.

Wind blew through the room like a hurricane in a bottle, whipping Katy's hair into her face. The strategically placed feathers lifted and spun around the circle of bleeding teenagers.

There it was again, the shadow person, standing outside the swirling mass of air and feathers. It stepped closer until it loomed just behind Jason. Katy screamed and ran for the broken window. Shards of glass dug at her palms as she hoisted herself through the wall. Her shoulder caught her fall into the rocks outside, and Katy yelped in pain.

The gravel shifted under Katy's panicked feet. The jagged edges of the rocks dug into her already gashed hands. Air and fear choked her throat. All she could do was squeak in pain as she pulled a rock from her open wound.

A chorus of screams broke through the empty window behind her.

Katy finally found her feet and skirted down the gravel driveway as fast as her legs could carry her until the screaming was snuffed out by the night.

BE CAREFUL WHAT YOU WISH FOR

The front door slammed behind her. Katy threw her back against it, as though she expected some tide of wind to oppose her escape, fighting to drag her back to the manor. She held her hands out, despite the tears blurring her vision, she saw the blood dripping down her palms to her elbows. Her body slid down the door to sit on the floor.

Katy sniffled. Every part of her shook. She went to wipe her face, but her hands were covered in blood and muck. So she pressed herself once again onto her feet and crossed the front room with a sheltered grace, looking for signs of her father. He'd fallen asleep on the couch again. Per usual. Even in a new city, a new house, a new bed, he couldn't bear the idea of that empty pillow next to his.

To the left was the bathroom. Katy closed the door before turning on the light, old habits of keeping herself invisible. The switch clicked when she flicked it, and she had to shield her eyes from the onslaught of light. Slowly, she opened her eyes and threw herself backwards at the sight of a darkened figure in the mirror. Katy stumbled into the shower curtain, clinging to it to keep herself upright.

She blinked. The darkened figure in the mirror was only herself.

"Okay, there Kay. It's not a monster. It's just your own lovely self."

Upon closer inspection of her reflection, she rethought the last part of her statement. *Yeesh.*

She turned to the mess she'd made of the shower curtain. *Shit.* She pulled it down. Her father used the shower upstairs anyway. She could replace it without him ever noticing.

After turning on the sink, Katy ran her hands under cold water, prying glass from her palms. Along with her hands, she wrapped the knife wound on her arm in some gauze before pulling off her soiled t-shirt. The shoulder she'd landed on was already turning a nefarious combination of black and purple. But there was no blood. *Thank God for small victories.*

Katy grabbed a fresh shirt from the dryer across the hall and then headed into the living room to shut off the television. She grabbed a blanket off of the chair beside the couch and dropped it, stifling a scream that threatened to burst from her lips.

It was her mother. Laying on the couch with black sunken eyes. Lips shriveled around her teeth. Bony fingers stretched out across her emaciated belly.

Katy snapped her eyes shut. When she opened them again, her father laid on the couch, asleep. Over him through the open curtains of the window, Katy caught a glimpse of that same black cat from outside the manor. After yanking the curtains closed, Katy took a deep breath.

Pull yourself together. It wasn't real. It wasn't real.

She bent over to retrieve the blanket she'd dropped. Before she could stand, Katy's father grabbed her arm where Jason had cut it. His eyes were lost in darkness. "The sacrifice has been made."

"Dad!" she screamed, pulling herself away from his grip. Katy ran for her room. Her father's confused ramblings followed, calling her name, asking what was wrong. But how could she possibly explain it?

It's just that I met some kids at school and we summoned the devil at an old haunted house. If it wasn't haunted before, it certainly is now. You know, typical high school stuff.

She leapt into her bed, pulling the covers over her head, and cradled her favorite stuffed elephant.

CONSEQUENCE

Morning came with both the dreaded feeling of being much too soon and the overwhelming flood of relief to have made it out of the dark without another incident. Nothing more than the sounds of a cat meowing outside her window until dawn broke through the night. The alarm rang with an annoying, tedious beeping. Katy slammed her bandaged hand on its off switch.

School. The idea of actually going seemed like a terrible one. But Katy couldn't stand the thought of staying home and possibly having to talk to her dad about last night. So she showered and got ready for another day of twelfth grade. And for the most part it was just that. She hadn't caught sight of Scarlett or the others in any of her classes. Good blessings could come after all, or so she thought.

After lunch, Katy went to her locker for her math book. She stuffed the barely bound, very out-of-date text into her backpack and shut the locker door with a clang. And there, waiting on the other side...was Scarlett.

Shit.

"Hey there, Katy." Scarlett purred. "Didn't get to say goodbye last night. You ran out in such a hurry."

"Yeah. Not really my scene." Katy slung her backpack over her shoulder. *Just get to class. Just get to class.*

"You know, we should thank you. This morning, I got my acceptance letter from Harvard." Scarlett giggled. "Oh, and did you notice the substitute in today for Mrs. Asher?"

Come to think of it, Mrs. Asher had been gone that morning. Katy thought nothing of it. But the dark, elated look smeared on Scarlett's face implied something more sinister than the flu.

"A true tragedy, really," Scarlett said through her bared teeth. "Seems she took a little stumble down the stairs. Broke her neck. Her head, they say, was twisted clear around."

"Like an owl," Anabelle laughed.

Katy pressed her lips together.

"Sometimes wishes do come true. With a little...push." Scarlett closed what little gap there was between her and Katy. "Jason went looking for you, you know. Said he was really looking forward to breaking you in. Kinda makes you wonder what he was wishing for, eh?"

The bell rang, and Katy pushed herself between Scarlett and Anabelle.

"Watch out for the shadows," Scarlett called. "You never know what may be hiding there."

"Yeah, like your dead mom," Anabelle added.

Katy halted, reversing her escape. She turned on heel and sent a balled up fist right into Anabelle's left cheek. She and her perfect blonde hair slammed into the lockers. Scarlett swore something at Katy, but she didn't stick around to hear it. Instead Katy bolted for the doors. She shoved her way through them so hard crimson stains bloomed on her bandage-wrapped palms.

She didn't know where she would go. It didn't really matter. As long as it wasn't home, school, or least of all Mission Manor.

A tight knot wound itself in Katy's stomach. It wanted to burst out of her in a fit of rage and, also likely, vomit. She felt every bit of the fool she had tried so hard to avoid. Everything went wrong from where she'd hoped it would have gone. She closed her eyes, the sun's glare beating down on her like a bad cop movie's interrogation lamp.

Closing her eyes offered no relief, only the flooding of shadows cascading through her from the pits of a living nightmare. Her insides quivered with the images of darkened reflections on a knife's edge and pounding beneath her feet.

Just then, something hard crashed into Katy. Or rather, she had crashed into it.

She opened her eyes, and of course, it would be none other than Jason Chase.

"You have got to be kidding me," she spat.

Jason reached out a hand to try and steady her, but all she could think of was that damned knife. Katy pulled away.

"Hey, look, I know last night got a little...wild," Jason said. His eyes had returned to their normal icy blue.

Katy looked away from them. "Wild? Yeah, you could say that. What the hell was that?"

"Did you get the thing? What you wanted?"

"What I wanted?"

"Your wish? It was to see your mom again, right?"

The air turned thick and pulled out of Katy all at once, leaving her unable to breathe or even remember how.

"Yeah, that's what I thought. Look, Katy. I'm sorry you got dragged into this. But I needed you. He wouldn't stop."

Katy stood in silence. Still not breathing.

"My dad. He beat my mom up all the time. And me. I just...I just had to make him stop."

Katy nodded her head. "Yeah."

"So, I'll be seeing you then?"

"What?" Katy came out of her daze at the implication she and Jason would ever be speaking again.

"Well yeah. Of course." A satisfied grin painted itself on his face. Jason turned toward a brand new luxury car, one of those where the doors open up instead of out, and got into the driver's seat. He rolled down the window. But if he had driven there, their collision would not have been an accident.

"Did...did you know I would be here?" Katy asked. Which, considering *Katy* didn't even know she would be in that spot, on that street, seemed thoroughly suspect.

Jason leaned through the open window. "I couldn't just let you ghost me like that. So, I added to my demand."

"Added to your demand?"

"I'll always be able to find you, Katy."

"You put some kind of paranormal lojack on me?"

Without an answer, Jason's car thundered to life, and the tires squealed as he drove away.

"What the fu—"

A PENNY GAINED

The rest of the week went about as well as Katy could have expected. *If one could consider watching your back and looking around every corner for a nefarious group of demon worshipping sociopaths as going well.*

Without fail, Jason and his demonauts would show up no matter where Katy went. Even at the cafe on the opposite side of town, the one with the really bad online reviews but free wifi. Scarlett came out of nowhere and *accidentally* spilled coffee on Katy's white shirt.

"Whoops, guess I didn't see you there. Seeing as you have a way of just...disappearing." Scarlett grabbed Katy's coffee off the counter and left with it.

Tires screeched and Jason's obscene car skid down the street.

As much as Katy didn't want to believe it, and although she was seeing a trend in this fruitless desire, she couldn't help but admit to herself that what happened in Mission Manor held some weight in truth. She shook her head. Reality was a hapless bitch.

When Saturday finally came, Katy didn't leave home. She spent the day in front of the TV or behind a book. She forced conversation with her dad, which, thankfully, did not include any mentions of Katy being covered in blood and screaming through the house in the middle of the night. She assumed either he'd thought the episode was a dream, or just decided to ignore the whole situation. Like he did everything else about her. But really, it was just another normal Saturday. The demonauts didn't even show up at her doorstep to taunt her. For the first time all week, Katy felt normal. She felt like Mission Manor really was just a bad dream.

"Want some popcorn, Katy-Matey?" her father called from the kitchen.

"Oh! Great idea. Extra butter," she replied while putting on the movie they decided to watch. Katy couldn't even remember the last time the two of them had actually just sat down and watched a movie together. The whole idea made her kind of giddy.

The menu screen for the DVD came across the television, and Katy checked to see how her dad was handling snack duty. The microwave was humming while her father poured himself a drink. Scotch. At least it wasn't tequila again.

Taking the standard pre-movie precautions, Katy continued down the hall to the bathroom. She closed the door, encasing herself in darkness. Before she had the chance to reach for the switch she saw it. The shadow person was looking at her from the mirror. Katy lifted her hand, but it betrayed her, refusing to move any further.

The shadow walked out from the mirror, inching closer.

Every part of her tried to scream, to run, to hide behind her father. But she was frozen. Unable to do anything but watch as the shadow drew nearer. A hot tear rolled down her cheek.

"A debt must be paid." The same voice from Mission Manor crept through her body, and this time the icy tendrils didn't just aim for her heart, they speared right through it.

The shadow person pressed into Katy, climbed inside of her gaping maw, keeping Katy's screams only for itself, contained within the darkness.

CIRCLE

Mission Manor appeared much in the way it was that one and fateful night: a circle of children paying their debt and making their sacrifice to fulfill a wish. Little did they know, the true prize of their sin and the true value of their offering was not theirs to own.

"All things come with a cost," Katy's voice echoed in the dusty old room.

Scarlett fell to her knees, blood and chalk nipping at her jeans.

"You have been gathered. A penance has yet to be paid."

"What are you talking about?" Scarlett groaned. "Katy—"

"You asked for death. Did you not find it?"

"None of us asked for this!" Scarlett's words were cut short. Her damp mascara-stained face went blank as she too fell into the circle, silenced, alongside Anabelle, Michael, and Dave--that damned smile finally wiped from his mouth.

Jason's lip quivered. "Please. I di-I didn't mean for this to—"

"Shhh."

"Katy."

"The only thing that you did not mean was to be just another foolish, arrogant, little boy who thought his might to be broader than the cosmos. And you are"--Katy's finger tapped on Jason's nose with each word--"Just. A. Little. Boy."

Jason's bright-blue eyes looked up, wide and glassy, reflecting back Katy's staring face.

"Oh, how those eyes made Katy quiver."

"You are—"

Laughing at some unheard joke, she said, "Poor, sweet girl. She looked for her future, and she saw nothing. An empty hollow of"--she drew a deep breath--"hopelessness. Katy saw no future for herself because that future already belonged to me." Katy's fingers wrapped around Jason's chin, forcing him to look into her face. "What you misinterpreted in that missionary's silly little book is that the only wishes I grant are my own."

"I—I'm sorry. Please…I'll do anything," Jason begged as the front of his pants darkened with moisture.

Katy's hand gently caressed Jason's cheek. "Yes, you will. Now, keep those pretty eyes open while I perform my next trick."

The dagger sparkled a wet crimson shine, and another lifeless clump of flesh was added to the pile. Blood pooled within the chalked circle, seeping into the cracks between the floorboards, until every last drop sank into the earth below. From the depths rose a darkness. Shadows swirled through the room, a scentless black smoke pulling from the ends of another plane.

Stop this! Please!

"Oh Katy, dearest. Do not dwell on these souls. They are nothing more than kindling for the fire. What we will accomplish together is so much more important. So much bigger than what these parasites could ever have imagined." She walked to the front door. The black knob turned itself and opened the room to the clear Sunday morning sky. "Look outside. The sun is shining. And here, shadows lurk, even when the sun is highest."

Her boots hit the gravel driveway, and the black cat leapt to her shoulder, rubbing its mangled ear against her cheek. "We do not merely dwell in the dark. Not anymore."

AMANDA STOCKTON

ABOUT THE AUTHOR

Amanda is of mostly human ancestry. Her hobbies include napping, drinking too much caffeine, and running into the sea. Also, she writes and makes art.

Check out her website: batwordsmedia.com

Follow her on social media: @batwomanda

MAGICIAN'S WEEKEND

BY MARTIN SHANNON

I took a deep breath and tried to shake off the smell of Cathy's duffle bag in the back seat. My daughter had just wrapped up the week at a late October sleep-away camp in the mountains of northern Georgia. The poor kid was in a whirlwind this weekend—finishing camp, then meeting her mother and brother at the airport for a quick jaunt out to Kansas City and some time with the in-laws.

I reached down and turned up the radio, letting eighties music flood the Dad Wagon with the rich sounds of awesome.

Dad's Weekend!

I drummed on the steering wheel as the Mazda roared onto the highway. The family was safely at the airport and bound for the Midwest, which meant I was free: free to drink beer, ignore basic hygiene, and perhaps even take the weekend off from Magick.

My name is Eugene Law and I'm a Magician. I don't do card tricks or kid's birthday parties. I deal in real Magick, the cosmic powers of the universe, and all the crap that comes with.

An idiot stopped short in front of me, forcing me to throw on the breaks and bringing back a vivid reminder of the last week. I rubbed at my neck and the dull ache that had returned to roost between my shoulder blades. It wasn't unexpected—five nights of tracking a particularly malicious poltergeist, which had culminated in a complex and dangerous exorcism, had been an unpleasant way to spend the week.

But all that's behind me. It's Dad's Weekend!

I merged into traffic, my butt jiving along with righteous guitar riffs of my teenage anthem, while my sore shoulders did their best to rock out against the seat back—spirits be damned.

The wind whipped through my hair from an open window, and I let my open hand float on the breeze to the groove. There might have been a little more gray in my short locks than when I'd originally belted out the words to the song, but that didn't stop me from doing it again, or from ignoring the odd looks from passing motorists.

We need beer.

My brain reminded me that no Dad's Weekend was complete without a trip to my favorite brewery, so it was without hesitation that the Mazda and I pulled off the highway just outside of Ybor City north of Tampa to cruise in and pick up a little nectar of the gods.

"I'LL NEED a six pack of Unholy, please."

The young lady behind the bar was more than happy to take my cash and send me on my way with an icy cold package of the glorious Tampa Trippel. I set the beers next to my daughter's duffle, the dirty bag's smell almost overpowering the joy of a free Magician's weekend. I smiled at the beer—well, almost.

Adult beverages secured, the Mazda and I were back out on the surface streets, and navigating the narrow asphalt back to the Law estate, beer and the biohazard bag in tow.

I hit the button and pulled into the garage of a pale green

bungalow Porter and I had lucked into early on in the marriage. After having two kids, we'd had to make a couple of additions to the place, but it still held a little of that old Tampa charm. The Dad Wagon safely back in its spot, I hopped out and practically danced my way around to the passenger door.

My wife's voice came back to me the instant I grabbed the handle of our teenage daughter's disgusting bag.

Don't forget to wash Cathy's clothes.

"No sense in doing today what you can put off for tomorrow," I said to the six pack dangling in my other hand. "These aren't going anywhere." I tossed the bag on the washing machine, letting it clang against the metal lid before promptly forgetting about it all together.

"Now, Mr. Beer, where were we?"

I lovingly carried the bottles into the house, and navigated my way around the toy trucks and blocks my son never seemed to get the hang of putting away until I reached the kitchen. I found a note from my wife on the counter.

Gene, by now you have forgotten about the bag. Put the beer down and wash Cathy's clothes. See you Sunday night. -P

I folded up the note and shoved it in my pocket. The clothes could wait; there were more important tasks ahead. I placed the beers in the fridge and pulled out my phone, my fingers dancing across the tiny glowing display.

"Mark's Pizza."

"Yeah, I'd like to get a..." I stopped, remembering there was no family this weekend. "I'd like to get a large Man Pizza with double meat."

"Anything else, sir?"

"No, but is that sausage, pepperoni, steak, and—"

"And green peppers, sir," the young man said, his words mixed with the sounds of a busy pizza joint.

"Can you nix the rabbit food and add… I don't know, is there a meat left?"

"Ham, sir?"

"Perfect."

I wrapped up the order, then fished sufficient cash out of my wallet and placed it on the counter.

"Well, Mr. Beer," I said, checking the clock. "It's beverage-o'clock somewhere."

The hands of our large kitchen clock confirmed it was actually closer to seven, and given that it was mid-October, the sun was already quickly vanishing.

"Don't want to miss happy hour." I opened the fridge and let the cool air wash over me before selecting a single bottle to kick start the Dad Weekend.

Only heathens drink from the bottle.

"Ah ha!" I said, discovering a handful of dusty glasses in the cabinet behind an arm of kid's cups. "This'll do nicely."

It was right about this point then I realized that the dull ache between my shoulder blades had wormed its way up to my neck. I twisted my head from side to side a few times and tried to shrug it off, but that only exacerbated it further.

Pop. Fizz...

The beer poured gloriously, like majestic gold. The bright liquid filled my pint glass and left a narrow band of foamy head across the top.

You really should be hydrating if you have a headache.

Porter's voice in my head was right, but since when was my wife being right going to stop me?

"Beer is mostly water," I said to no one but myself.

I retreated to the living room, high-stepping over Kris's toys until I reached the couch, then unceremoniously deposited the kid junk that had consumed those cushions onto the floor and took a seat. I popped on the TV and let the mind-numbing laugh track of yet another recycled sitcom wash over me. We hadn't made it deep into the second act before the door bell rang.

Pizza!

I set the glass on the counter and scooped up the cash.

"Mark's Pizza," the young man on the door step said, holding the oversized box in his hands. "That'll be—"

"Here you go," I shoved the wad of cash into his hands. "Keep the change."

"Hey, thanks." The kid tucked the greenbacks in his jacket. "You got a cool cat, man."

"Huh?"

Sure enough, pressing against the young man's legs, was a black cat—its right ear torn like a cheap paperback and its nose clearly loving the smell of meat pizza.

"I don't have a cat."

"Oh," the kid said, not sure what to make of the stray pressing against his shins. "That's weird."

I shrugged my shoulders. "Cats."

The pain in my neck was ramping up, but I figured the pizza would help with that.

The feline made a motion toward the open door, and I pushed it back with my foot. "Nope, no cats in here."

Hiss!

The cat took a swipe at my shoe, but its claws didn't make it past the leather. "Go! Get out of here."

"You sure that's not your cat?"

"Positive," I said, frowning at the ornery animal sitting on my front porch.

"Odd."

"Whatever. Thanks for the pizza." I slammed the door and took my double-meat masterpiece back to the dining room table. For a second I contemplated getting a plate, but the blessed aroma of pizza and beer was too much. I opened the box and removed a slice.

"See this, Mr. Beer, this is double-meat—"

Meow!

The cat was perched at the sidelight window of my front door, its stupid clipped-ear face pressed up against the glass.

Meow!

"Go!" I shouted, putting the pizza down and feeling the full extent of the building headache. It had now solidly taken root at the base of my skull and was clamping down just behind the ears, constricting the blood flow to the important decision-making bits.

Meow!

"Damn cat." I banged on the glass. "Get out of here. Go!"

Chirp!

My cell phone chirped on the counter, pulling my attention away from the retreating tabby. It was Adam, my apprentice, an early thirty-something young man with a flair for Magick, but also a decidedly frustrating inability to grow up.

Gene, my Wizards and Warlocks group needs a place to game tonight. Mom kicked us out. Can we come in?

I had my fingers in motion drafting a resounding no when I noticed the second half of his message, then looked up to see the pudgy, bearded man waving through the same sidelight the cat had been in only moments before.

My headache immediately ramped up five notches.

"ADAM," I said, the door opening the moment after I remembered I'd given him a key and made sure all the protective incantations I'd placed on it would allow him through.

Damn it.

"What are you—"

My apprentice jingled a felt bag of what sounded like dice. "Gene, thank you so much for… Holy crap, is that double-meat Man Pizza?"

"Yes, I was going—"

"Hey everybody, Gene got us pizza!"

No, no, he most certainly didn't.

My apprentice gestured to a small group of equally ragtag individuals, introducing them one at a time and directing them into my house with what I hoped were their character names. "Okay, Gene, this is Amanderous the Flowing," he said directing my attention to the petite redhead.

She hid behind a pair of red and black horn-rimmed glasses and offered only a modest wave. "Hey."

"It's nice to meet you, but I'm not sure I have time to—"

"Amanderous is a sea-elf ranger. She's hella proficient with her Bow of Agility and Short Sword of Gleaming Might."

"Night," the young woman said, pulling out a seat at my kitchen table.

Adam tilted his head. "What's that?"

Amanderous pulled off her backpack and drew out a set of papers. "It's the Sword of Gleaming *Night.*"

That doesn't make any sense... Stop, Gene, you need to take control before this gets worse.

The redhead lifted the lid and snaked a piece of Man Pizza from the box. "Thanks for getting pizza."

Too late, it has officially gotten worse.

My headache jumped up a couple more notches. The pounding at the base of my skull had now staked out new territory behind my ears. "I—"

Amanderous waved me off. "I don't need a plate, it's cool."

No, no it's not cool.

"Gene," my apprentice directed my attention back to the door. "This is Edvilandia."

The lanky young man stooped his shoulders to fit under the eve. "Hey."

"Uh, hi. Listen, Adam—"

"Edvilandia is a cleric of the dark gods."

"They have better spells." The young man slid my pizza box

around and took a seat next to the redhead. "I mean, I get tired of healing all the time."

My scathing glare should have burned Adam to a crisp where he stood, but somehow my apprentice remained blissfully ignorant of the veins protruding from my neck.

"And last but not least, I want to introduce you to Jacster the…"

"Vengeful," the diminutive young man said, shucking his immense backpack on my floor like an overworked Sherpa. "I'm going with Jacster the Vengeful."

"Not the lawyerly?" Adam asked.

"No." The shorter man drew a few eye rolls from the rest of the pizza-eating party crashers. "Vengeful."

"Got it." My apprentice pointed to an open chair.

Jacster the Vengeful took his spot and immediately enacted his mighty vengeance on my Man Pizza, folding a particularly large slice and sticking the business end in his mouth.

"Adam." I fought back against the headache now crawling up the back of my head like a piton-driving mountaineer. "May I have a word with you?"

My bearded apprentice nodded, then placed his own backpack below the table and slid down the zipper of his hoodie to half-mast. "Sure thing. Let me get my Cavern Master's screen up and get things ready."

"Is he playing?" Amanderous pulled her hair back in a pony tail. "We need a rogue."

Edvilandia's lovestruck eyes glazed over. He was clearly a tad bit enamored with the sea elf sitting next to him. "That's a great idea."

"Yeah, that would be awesome. Gene, you don't mind taking a pre-made character, right?"

"I don't know what—"

"Pinkersty the Plucky." Jacster, the motley crew's bag man,

removed a thick stack of books and papers from his pack. "Here you go."

Adam accepted the paper for me. "All right, I'll explain all of this, but for the moment you just have to get up to speed on the basics."

"Adam."

"This is Pinkersty the Plucky. He's a halfling rogue with a peg leg."

"Adam."

"I know what you're thinking, peg leg doesn't make sense for a thief, but I'm telling you, with a fifteen in agility and a sixteen in likability, Pinkersty is a force to be reckoned with."

"Adam!" I cried, grabbing the young man by his hoodie and dragging him into the kitchen. "Stop talking."

My apprentice's mouth hung open, his eyes as wide as the plates no one at my dining room table was presently using. "Okay."

I had a hundred things I wanted to say to him, but the lot of them couldn't decide which one would make it out my mouth first. It was like a checkout lane on Black Friday—all my choice words were too busy fighting each other rather than taking out their frustrations on the bearded kid directly in front of me. "Gah!"

Adam smiled and nodded, then placed a hand on my shoulder. "It's cool, man. I know you don't do role-playing games, but I can totally vouch for you. I'll keep it simple. Don't worry. In fact, I'll do the first few rolls for you."

I let go of his hoodie—I had to—the headache had made its way to the crown of my head, and I could feel each of my hairs. "Ugh."

"Gene's in," my apprentice cried, rejoining his band of merry misfits. "Anybody want a beer?"

No!

My apprentice opened the fridge and retrieved my Dad's

Weekend five pack and placed it on the table. The bottles disappeared like puddles on a hot day, the resident sea elf providing a key-chain opener.

"So, where were we?" Adam pulled out the seat at the head of my table and set up a folded paper screen.

Jacster consulted the materials in front of him like my accountant at tax time. "Edvilandia was getting firewood, and we were going to camp for the night. You had told him to roll for ingenuity."

Clunk!

The heavy plastic dice rolled across my table, the noise exacerbating the already throbbing pain between my ears.

"Fifteen," Edvilandia the Lanky slammed his palm on the table hard enough to rattle my already unhappy neurons. "Hot damn."

Adam consulted his paper screen, his pudgy fingers running down a chart on the inside. "Success. The fire is lit and providing you warmth."

"I stand away from the flames," Amanderous said, clicking her pen in rapid-fire and highly grating fashion. "My sea elf doesn't want to risk drying out."

"Right." Adam nodded.

Jacster splayed out another book like he was field-gutting fresh game. "I use my perception and check the forest."

Perception? You failed, all of you failed.

"Roll," Adam said, his hands gripping the top of that paper screen.

"Sixteen." The small man's voice was giddy.

"You use your barbarian powers of perception to see deep into the forest and find something hiding in the brush."

"What is it?"

Adam turned to me. I was still leaning against the counter in the kitchen trying to fight through the darkening edges of my fading vision. "Let's let Pinkersty try. Would you like to roll?"

I'd like to roll all of you out my door.

"You can do it," I said, the sound of my words like a cheese grater against my cerebellum.

"Eighteen." Adam's cry elicited an excited table banging from the rest of the nerds and sent my head spinning. "You see... a troll!"

A hush descended over the table, only to be quickly replaced by Jacster's furious page turning. "I draw my Double-sided Battle Axe of Righteous Destruction and step in front of the fire."

"Amanderous, Edvilandia, what about you?" Adam the Cavern Master asked, rattling dice in his hand.

"Hey, Pinkersty." The young woman popped up and pointed to something by my door. "I think your cat wants inside." The sea-elf didn't let me finish before she slipped out of her seat and opened the door, letting the black ball of fur shoot past us into the living room.

Adam raised an eyebrow. "When did you get a cat, Gene?"

I wanted to respond, but the headache had made it to my temples, and had taken up jack hammering them like a teamster. "I…"

"I prepare a spell." Amanderous circled something on a paper in front of her.

"Which one?"

How about Leave House...

"I'm going to prepare to summon a Blade Mistress." The young woman rolled a few dice and totaled up the numbers. "It's going to take two rounds."

"The troll lets out a wild yell and smashes the closest tree," Adam cried, his words grating my already sensitive skull. "A piece of tree hits Pinkersty, knocking him to the ground and taking"—a die shot across the table—"five life points!"

Boom!

I hit the ground like I'd reached the end of a roller coaster and forgotten to put on my harness. Standing on the other side of the counter I'd just been leaning against and peeling back the broken drywall and shattered wall studs as if they were crepe paper was a very large, and very real Bridge Troll. Its round head and stucco-like skin were covered in tiny flecks of what had must have been a really nice part of the living room.

Adam rattled dice in his hand. "So, Pinkersty, you ready to roll for initiative?"

I CLUTCHED my head and tried to figure out how a Bridge Troll had made it past my Magickal defenses. "Adam, get down."

"You got it." My apprentice tossed a die across the table, oblivious to the troll tearing his way through what remained of the kitchen, "Pinkersty jabs his dagger at the troll's kneecap." The multi-faceted plastic rattled against the crumbly remains of what had been my Man Pizza. "Ten. That's a miss."

The Bridge Troll's massive body pushed past my sink, tearing the recently remodeled metal like a candy wrapper, before tossing it into the far wall where it crashed to the floor next to Edvilandia the Skinny.

"Is my champion summoned yet?" Amanderous doodled little swirls on her paper while a very real Bridge Troll grabbed my legs with both catcher's mitt hands.

Adam shook his head. "Nope, one more round. Jacster?"

The pint-sized bookbarian said something I couldn't make out against the backdrop of being dragged across the broken tile floor.

"Adam, snap out of it." I swung my arms and tried to get the bearded Cavern Master's attention.

"So you are going to try a Wild Yell Raging?" my apprentice asked, consulting his paper screen.

"Yeah."

The Troll had me by my shirt and inches from his oversized face. Its thick skin lay piled like badly poured concrete, holding two angry, deep-set eyes.

I tried to keep my pounding brain from oozing out my ears and spoke to the Troll in measured tones. "We don't have any issues. Just walk out that door and we'll call it even."

The Troll hesitated.

Please?

Jacster grabbed a handful of dice and shot them across the table. "Eight, plus my proficiency bonus and my magical Loin Cloth of Girding gives me fourteen."

"I'm sorry." Adam shook his head. "Your attempts to inspire strength and confidence in your party backfire and send the troll into a murderous rage."

Oh, hell.

The Bridge Troll's dark eyes flashed the instant before its fist hit my chest. For the second time today, I hit the hard floor, this time expelling just about all the precious air that had been in my lungs.

"Edvilandia, it's your turn. Pinkersty is down five life points. Do you heal him?"

I coughed at the dust and did my best to suck air back into my lungs.

That would be nice.

"No, sorry, Pinkersty, I'm calling on the dark gods to bring their fury against the troll."

Of course you are.

Adam leaned over the cardboard shield like a kid at Christmas. "Roll."

"What the hell is wrong with you guys—"

"Fifteen." The string bean pumped his noodle arms in the air. "Yes!"

The lights flickered, and a swirling mass of unholy darkness appeared between me and the Troll. I squinted my eyes at the brilliant flashes of purple and green emanating from that cloud of hovering evil.

"Not so fast." The Cavern Master consulted his infernal chart, giving me time to back away from the malevolent black hole quickly filling the space between my kitchen and dining room. "The troll's natural magic resistance gives him an advantage against the dark gods." Adam rolled a die behind the cardboard cover. "Twenty!"

"Show me!" all three of the players shouted.

I might have wanted to see it too, but in that moment black tentacles had begun to reach out of the reality bending hole opening up in what had been my dining room. "Adam!"

"Damn." Jacster consulted his books. "Perfect strike. So, what happens?"

"I can tell you what happens," I said, kicking back at the vile octopus like appendages reaching for my legs. "You four get the hell out of my house and take whatever it is—"

"The dark gods turn on you. Their evil tentacles reach for you, hungry to crush your bones into dust."

"Whoops, sorry guys." Edvilandia's face fell.

"Son of a… That's it," I reached for my Magick. I'd had just about enough of all of this. It was time to hit back. I didn't know what sort of enchantment my apprentice was under, but I figured I'd swing first and ask questions later. "Ledo," I shouted, willing the well of cosmic power in my body to break the tentacle's grasp on my leg.

Nothing happened.

Oh, shit.

Adam shook his head. "Remember, you can't use magic. Pinkersty is a rogue. Sorry, Gene."

"What the—"

"Amanderous, it's your turn." The Cavern Master pointed to the redhead twirling her pen.

"Is my champion ready?"

Black and slimy tentacles reached for my legs. "Please no, guys! Just stop. I can't take much more of—"

Adam nodded. "You bet. The skies open and a beautiful Sword Maiden charges down on a moonbeam. She's the most stunning woman any of you have ever seen. Her armor shines with the brightness of the sun, and her sword glows with the righteous fire of the great warriors of old."

Amanderous scribbled something on her paper. "Kick ass. I tell her to attack the old gods and the Troll."

"You tell her what?"

Porter?!

Bedecked in shining armor that certainly was meant to attract the eye far more than protect its wearer from edged weapons, my wife stood behind me, broadsword in hand and flexing muscles I didn't remember her having. "What the hell?" she said, letting her sword dip so she could examine the undersized silver chest plate barely keeping a comically well-endowed bosom covered. "Is this how you see me?"

"Yes, but I'm far more concerned that this is how Adam sees you."

The valiant heroine removed her ornamental helmet, "Oh... now, that's just creepy."

The headache advanced past my forehead. It squeezed down on my eyes so much that I was fairly certain they'd pop out and roll across the floor if I made any sudden movements. Sadly, the dark gods didn't feel the same way. The black tentacles trapped my arms and legs, then dragged me across the floor. I rolled over the broken tile directly toward the yawning portal to madness. "Porter!"

"What do I do?" my wife cried, pushing the helmet back on her head.

"The sword. You swing the damn sword!"

"You don't have to yell at me."

More tentacles wrapped my legs, while somewhere behind

the portal to insanity, the Bridge Troll had figured out how to take the long route back to me and smash his way through the other side of my kitchen.

"Just swing the—" My words were cut off by the slimy blackness of string bean's dark gods.

Slash!

My wife, the Sword Maiden, swung her blade in a wide arc, and sliced through the dark god's tentacles. The gleaming metal narrowly missed removing my leg in the process.

"Hey, this is kinda cool."

"Watch out," I cried, spitting the tentacle from my mouth.

"Huh?"

I was too late. The Bridge Troll's massive fist collided with Porter's head, sending my heroine and her sword crashing into our coat rack.

"Your Sword Maiden takes twenty life points." Adam scribbled something on a sheet of paper. "How many does she have left?"

"Porter!"

"I'm okay." My wife pushed her gleaming, armored chest and bare legs out of the pile of broken wood and once-a-year winter coats.

Amanderous scrunched up her face. "Twenty? She's got three life points left."

Porter collapsed back into the splintered boards, blood suddenly flowing from newly discovered wounds, and her once shiny armor now laying bent and misshapen against her petite frame. I scrambled toward her, but Edvilandia the Lanky's dark gods and the Bridge Troll had other ideas. The former wrapped its tentacles around my neck, while the latter hooked my legs in its granite-crushing grip.

"Pinkersty," Adam said, looking up from his screen and twirling a pencil in his fingers. "It's your move."

I clawed at the tightening appendages of the inky black dark gods, while at the same time kicking out my feet in the hopes I could separate from the Bridge Troll—I wasn't making any headway with either.

"Do you want to use your dagger?" the Cavern Master asked, the rest of the motley crew leaning in to hear my response.

"I..."

The pain in my head had now come full circle, its vise-like pressure squeezing what brain cells I had left into an increasingly tighter space. If I still had my Magick, it had found a way to escape my every attempt to use it. The power I'd called upon to escape an almost countless number of scrapes was nowhere to be found, and Porter lay just beyond me, her once-gleaming sword faded and tarnished.

None of this made sense, but when Magick was involved things rarely did. Still, this entire experience was surreal even for me.

"Meow!"

Darkness encroached on the edges of my vision while that damn stray cat scratched at the door to my garage.

There's a cat in my house. Why is there a cat in my house?

"What do you want to do, Pinkersty? It's your move."

It might have been my move, but the dark gods and a very zealous Bridge Troll had already worked more than enough moves of their own—realigning my spine in unique and non-traditional ways.

"Meow!"

Why is there a cat in my house? And what does it want in the garage?

My head rolled to the side as the darkness closed in, leaving me with Adam's words and a view of Porter's sword.

It's your move...

The sword, just reach the sword.

"Gene, I mean, Pinkersty it's your move. If you don't know what to do, I can help you."

Adam the Cavern Master was doing his best, but the blinding pain in my head was stronger. Flashes of light and starburst vision sparkled around the silvery blade.

Just a little closer.

My fingers grazed the sword's edge, even as I felt every one of my heartbeats.

Almost got it...

"Okay, I'll just have Pinkersty use his advanced rogue subterfuge skills and escape detection," Adam rolled a few heavy plastic dice across my table. "Eighteen!"

"Nice work, Pinkersty." Jacster flipped through one of his many rulebooks. "It looks like he should be near undetectable for the current round unless his opponent succeeds in a thwarting throw of more than two times the current distance divided by the—"

"It works," the Cavern Master said, brushing off the pint-sized barbarian.

"But the—"

Adam leaned over his cardboard screen and made eye contact with the younger man. "It works."

"Well, that's not how the rules indicate, but I'll allow it." A clearly annoyed Jacster closed his book.

Thump.

I wasn't expecting to hit the ground, and for a moment I was sure I'd survived the impact—that was until the hot flash of pain lanced its way through my skull. "Ugh."

"Gene," Porter said, pushing herself up against the coat rack. Her skimpy armor splattered with blood. "Where are you?"

I sat up to find my wife's eyes searching the room frantically for me. "Here."

"I can't see you."

She might not see me, but the Bridge Troll could see her, and that was never a good thing.

"Look out!" I cried, but she didn't stand a chance. The living mountain of poorly laid concrete had her in its beady sights.

Porter raised a gauntleted wrist, but the Troll's fist was like taking a wrecking ball at close range. My Sword Maiden rocketed across the foyer and skid over the broken tile before slamming into the front door.

"Porter!"

"The troll takes"—Adam rolled a die—"one life point—lucky."

"Meow!" The feral cat continued to scrape its claws down the door to my garage. Her claws left faint marks in the white paint.

Amanderous pushed up her glasses and leafed through the papers in front of her, then paused to lean over and whisper something to Edvilandia. Based on the look on his face, she'd just inadvertently become the first woman not named mom to place her lips that close to his ears.

"Let's do it." Edvilandia grinned.

I was convinced she could have told him to clean the gutters and gotten the same reaction.

I grabbed Porter's sword. It was surprisingly heavy—but then again I'd never held a two-handed broadsword before today. Blinding flashes of pain lanced through my head. I tried to blink them back, but the room continued to pulse in time with the beating of my heart.

"Edvilandia and I are working together. I'm going to cast 'Bleeding Hearts of Inspiration' while the servant of the dark gods here is going to send the spirit of… who was it again?"

The string bean jumped up. "Morganus the Vile. I'm going to send the avenging demon Morganus the Vile into the Sword Maiden. That will boost her agility and her strength—"

"Life points go up by fifty," Jacster said, consulting one of the many volumes splayed out in front of him. "Nice work."

The Troll's back was to me. Just a few more feet and I'd be there. Porter's sword dragged along the tile, its blade too heavy for my tired shoulders.

Come on, you can do this!

"Sounds like a plan." Adam ran his fingers through an unkempt beard. "Roll."

"Sixteen," the duo said, excitement in the voices.

"It works!"

"Meow!"

The Troll's back was right in front of me. All I had to do was raise the sword and deliver a killing blow, but before I could get the silvery steel at the ready, a black and pulsing blade of pure evil tore through the Troll's thick hide.

"Porter?"

"Hardly," came a voice from my past on the other side of the dying monster.

"Morgan?"

Wearing dark, skintight armor laced with black roses and malevolent skulls, my ex-girlfriend's flaming black blade cut the Bridge Troll in two, and left a blue-blooded mess on my foyer floor.

"Gene, it's so good to see you," Morganus the Vile said, her eyes hungry with unholy malice. "I'm going to enjoy this."

Adam sat back behind his screen. "The troll is dead."

"Woohoo!"

"But." He leaned forward again, letting only his eyes peek above the screen. "Morganus the Vile summons an army of vampire zombies from the surrounding forest. Did you forget that this was the Dead Woods?"

The table plunged into silence, the excitement of defeating the troll vanishing instantly with this new revelation.

Crash!

Clawing undead hands shattered the sidelight of my front door and reached for us.

"Oh, for the love of all things—damn it, Adam," I fought to get Porter's sword off the ground. "Really?!"

The black flames of Morganus's cold steel cast a dark radiance against my wife's blade. "This is your end, Eugene Law."

Clang!

The black fire weapon cut the air in a wide arc and caught on the chandelier my wife had insisted on hanging when we first moved in. I'd been dead set against it at the time, but I hadn't counted on it being useful for edged weapon defense.

Adam checked the results of his last roll. "Morganus the Vile misses. Now, let's see how the vampiric zombie horde did."

I stumbled backward, trying to keep the sword maiden's blade between me and a heavily armed ex. "Son of a—are you serious?"

"Meow!"

Crash!

"The vampiric zombies attack"—our Cavern Master tossed a die across the table—"and get a… one?"

Pale white arms and bloody fangs broke through my front window, only to bunch up against the frame like over-zealous preschoolers on free ice cream day.

"About damn time," I said, my back making contact with the door to the garage, the impact sending a fresh wave of pain through my skull. "Argh!"

"Meow!"

Boom.

Morganus the Vile's evil blade broke free of the chandelier and sent it crashing to the tile.

"Aw, hell."

My ex was on me in an instant, her dark armor flooding the house with an eerie purple light. "Now I'll end what you started all those years ago, Gene." She pressed the cold steel of her blade against my neck. "I'm going to enjoy watching you die."

Behind the demonic woman, the vampire zombie horde forced their way through the jagged remains of my front window. Pale white claws and bloody fangs filed into my house like spawning salmon.

"Meow!" The feral cat rammed its head against my knee, then resumed scratching at the door.

What the hell do you want?

"Morganus the Vile swings her sword to separate Pinkersty's head from his body—sorry, Gene, it's just a game." Adam shook the dice in his hand. "If she gets a sixteen or better, Pinkersty is toast."

Hatred, abject and pure boiled in the eyes of my ex. "It's finally over, Gene."

The plastic die rolled across the table, bouncing off the now empty pizza box and clanging against half-drunk beers.

Morganus's evil blade pressed against my neck, while something else squeezed my lower back.

The knob...

"She rolls a—"

"Meow!"

I dropped Porter's sword and closed my eyes. My fingers found the handle to the garage and gave it a turn.

"Fifteen!"

The door opened, and I fell backward, my demonic ex's blade missing me by scant inches as the garage floor raced up to greet the base of my skull.

Bright flashes of light erupted in my head, followed by gut-churning pain. Like a puma on the hunt, the cat leapt on to my workbench and sent half-repaired toys crashing to the ground along with an expertly sorted jars of screws. The room spun, the walls melting into a blurry watercolor of faded colors, but still the cat continued undaunted on her collision course with my daughter's faded bag.

Hiss! Scrape! Squeak!

The sound of claws on fabric and the high-pitched cry of a cornered animal were the last things I remembered before my world faded to white.

*P*URR...

I opened my eyes to find myself face to face with the bright golden eyes of that damn one-eared porch cat.

Thump.

She dropped one very dead and rather iridescent lump of wet flesh on my chest, then resumed her rather self-satisfied expression.

I pushed myself up, surprised to find my head no longer pounding.

"What's this... A Cerebellix?"

The now dead brain rat lay harmless on my chest. Native to the questionable decision-making states, the infuriating creatures possessed a penchant for causing hallucinations and, with enough exposure, madness. It must have made its way into Cathy's bag before she left Georgia.

I tossed the bloody lump aside and ran a hand over the cat's head. "Uh, thanks, buddy."

"Meow."

I dragged myself up and wandered back into the house, overjoyed to find it exactly the way I'd left it. There was no gaming group eating my rapidly cooling pizza, and the beers in my fridge were still unopened and waiting for what I hoped might be a salvageable Magician's weekend.

Knock! Knock!

My apprentice's face appeared in the sidelight, along with

the faces of his buddies. “Hey, Gene, can we use your house for our—”

I immediately turned around and walked back into the garage.

"Hey, guys. I think he's going to open the garage door."

I opened the sprinkler box and turned them on, then smiled to myself at the sound of Adam and his friends making a run for their car.

“So, cat,” I said, returning to the house and finding my beer exactly where I’d left it. “How do you feel about Man Pizza?”

“Meow.”

“I couldn’t have said it better myself.”

MARTIN SHANNON

ABOUT THE AUTHOR

Martin Shannon's been using his imagination to avoid weeding since he was in short pants. Magician's Weekend is the first published short story in the "Tales of Weird Florida" series. His first novel, Dead Set, is due out in early 2020 and continues the thrilling adventures of Gene Law, his wife Porter, his apprentice Adam, and the rest of the crew that call this strange state home.

Interested in learning more? Check out www.martin-shannon.com where you can get another short story and sign up to his newsletter to stay up to date on all things Weird Florida.

HANNAH AND GREGORY

BY JACOB FAUST

Paper decorations covered the halls from floor to ceiling. Pumpkins, full moons, werewolves, purple mushrooms, black cats, and a witch had recently taken up residence in the school. They stood guard as waves of kids left class and rushed to the exits, talking of candy and costumes while the teachers tried fruitlessly to control the noise level. Even the adults couldn't help but smile and laugh, touched by the excitement of a holiday weekend.

"I hate Halloween," Gregory grumbled, adjusting his backpack strap.

Kevin bounced around, trapped in the confines of the narrow corridor. "Why? Halloween is awesome! You get to go trick-or-treating, and it's on Friday this year. That means you can eat candy all weekend!" It didn't take much work for Gregory to conjure up a mental image of Kevin lying in bed in the onset of a sugar coma. The kid got wired from eating a single Oreo.

"I don't get to go trick-or-treating," Gregory said. "My stepmother thinks it's stupid so we don't get any candy."

"I love my stepmother," Kevin said. "I got, like, all the questions wrong on the math test, but she wasn't even mad. She's gonna take me trick-or-treating! What kind of costume are you going to wear?"

"I'm not wearing a costume. Are you even listening?"

"I'm gonna be Spider-Man!" He shot pretend webs at the ceiling and smacked into a door frame. Down he went, only to pop right back to his feet, still wearing a goofy smile.

Gregory shook his head. He didn't need to be reminded of Kevin's happy family or how much fun his weekend was going to be or how he wasn't punished for poor test scores. Some people had all the luck. Gregory absently rubbed at his still-sore cheek.

Outside, he sat by the curb and waited with his chin in his palm. It was nicer here, less cluttered and crazy. There were fewer excitable kids stomping around. The only set of footsteps that approached him was calm and quiet.

"Dad's late?" Hannah asked.

"What's new?"

Hannah dropped her backpack on the ground and sat next to him. "Why does he have to work so late? I wanted to go costume shopping."

The chilly air nipped at his nose. "You don't get to wear a costume, remember?"

She nudged a stick with her shoe. "I know, but... I hoped it would be different this year."

Gregory shook his head. "She didn't let us last year, she won't let us this year, and she probably won't ever let us. We're getting too old for it, anyway." There was a pause. Gregory felt bad for her, but she had to understand the way things were now.

"I miss Halloween," she finally said. "It was always so much fun."

"It was. But that was before—"

"Her?" Hannah pointed.

Swallowing, Gregory followed her finger. Sure enough, the

showy red car belonging to their stepmother headed toward them. She parked, and when the kids didn't teleport inside, she honked. Gregory and Hannah grabbed their bags and hurried into the back seat. Dad must have been in here recently; it reeked of alcohol.

Their stepmother pulled away, and all was quiet in the car. It was a harsh, unpleasant quiet, but Gregory preferred it to the alternative. He mentally willed it to stay. It didn't.

"Why are you picking us up, Regan?" Hannah asked with just a trace of venom in her voice.

Regan's lip curled. "Oh, it's not by choice, believe me. I would rather be at home, but your father is too busy *working* to take care of his own kids. So here I am. Honestly, that man sometimes..."

Gregory gave Hannah a sideways look, telling her to be quiet. She ignored him.

"It's not his fault. He's just trying to make enough money."

"Money wasn't an issue when I married him. Now all he does is work and complain about working and spend time with you ungrateful little gremlins, who *waste* all that money he makes."

Through the windshield, the back of the car in front of them rapidly approached. Gregory grabbed Hannah's arm and gave a wordless shout. Regan swerved, missing the other car by an inch. It was her fault—she was the one who wasn't paying attention—but that didn't stop her from laying on her horn.

"If I had known how things were going to turn out," she said, not bothered in the least by the close call, "I would never have bothered with this sorry little family."

Gregory squeezed Hannah's arm tighter, warningly.

"It's your fault," she snapped. "It's your fault we have no money. I wish Daddy never met you!"

"Hannah, *shut up*," Gregory hissed.

Regan glared at them through the mirror. "Why don't you both shut up?"

The harsh quiet returned, and Gregory could almost breathe easy. They were just a few minutes from home. Once they got there, they could go their separate ways.

As their house came into view, Regan took a sharp turn down a side road. Gregory and Hannah exchanged glances but didn't dare speak. They were soon leaving the border of the small town. Buildings were replaced by colorful trees, streets by dirt paths.

"Where are we going?" Gregory forced himself to ask.

Regan didn't answer, but her knuckles grew white on the wheel and the car picked up speed. She went down dirt road after dirt road, weaving through places that were more forest than trail, slowing only to avoid low hanging branches that threatened to scratch her precious paint job. When they came to a particularly dark, drab part of the forest, she stopped the car. The only spot of color was a small patch of dirty, misshapen pumpkins

"Get out." The doors unlocked. When neither kid moved a muscle, she raised her voice. "Get out! I am *done* dealing with you! Get out of this car, right this instant, or so help me..." She raised her hand threateningly. Gregory stared at her image in the mirror. How could someone who looked so much like his mother be so vile? He got out, Hannah following his lead. "I hope I never lay eyes on you nasty children again." The car sped off, leaving them alone in the silent woods.

Hannah turned in a circle, taking in the endless stretch of trees and hills. Gregory gave her a minute to process what was happening, walking to a pumpkin and giving it a kick. It was hard as stone.

"Greg." Hannah's voice was high and thin. "W-what do we do?"

"Follow her tire tracks," he said with forced calmness. "It shouldn't take too long to get home."

She nodded, came to his side, and they began walking. He wouldn't admit it out loud, for his sake and hers, but he was glad he wasn't alone in this creepy forest. Her closeness and her body heat on his arm were comforting. Hopefully his presence had a similar effect on her.

"Why did she do this?" she asked after a couple minutes.

"She's evil," Gregory responded simply. "She's a mean and wicked person who likes doing mean and wicked things." The gravel spun up by the car crunched under his shoes.

A bird flew from a tree. Hannah jumped and took Gregory's hand. "Why would Daddy marry someone like that?"

Gregory didn't answer.

Hannah squeezed his hand so tight it hurt and stuck so close to him it was hard to walk. She shivered. Whether it was from the autumn chill or from fear, Gregory wasn't sure.

"Do you remember last Halloween?" he asked. He needed to get her mind busy and distract her from their predicament.

"Yeah. We were stuck at home and didn't get any candy."

"No, before that. The last time we actually *had* Halloween."

"Oh."

"Weren't you a fairy, or something?"

"Tinker Bell."

"Ah." He had remembered that, of course.

A smile crept onto her face. "And you were a pirate, and your sword kept falling out. You tripped on it and spilled your candy!" She giggled.

"I still ate it all, though."

"Eww!"

"It was all clean! Everything was still in the wrappers."

"Boys are gross."

"It was candy! You can't waste candy." They both laughed.

An owl hooted, cutting them off. The sound echoed through the woods.

"Greg... are we lost?"

"No. We're following the tracks, remember?"

"Yeah, but... the tracks kinda zigzag, and I can't always tell which way is forward."

"It's easy, you just..." He studied the ground, voice failing him. Hadn't they gone over this track already? "Um." He chuckled. It sounded fake to his own ears. "We'll find our way back."

"We will?"

"Yep!"

As the sun set and the shadows stretched into night, Gregory doubted his claim. If he was correctly reading his watch in the fading light, it was already past ten. If not for the full moon, the woods would have been pitch-black. But even as his heart beat faster and tears threatened to well in his eyes, he kept his smile and periodically said they were getting close. His mood wasn't helped by how dead everything looked in the moon's blue glow, from the scraggly trees to the dry dirt and wilting bushes.

With a gasp, Hannah pointed. "Greg, look!"

He squinted. Just over the hill, the dark roof of a house peaked over the tree line. "See?" he said as confidentially as he could. "We must already be back to town."

"'Already'?" Hannah ran toward the house, practically dragging him with her. They went around a clump of thickly-woven, barren, stick-like trees and found themselves in a small clearing that faced the hill and house.

"Uh... Greg? What kind of house is that?"

He craned his neck. "A, uh... Halloween house?"

"Is that why it has chicken legs?"

The house, indeed, stood atop a pair of stick-thin bird legs that dug into the ground with massive, taloned feet. They were smaller around than Gregory's own legs, yet they held the house aloft without visible strain. The building itself was no more than a ten-foot cube of wood with a small porch. He edged away, trying to remember where the tracks were. There was a certain foreboding *something* to the structure. The sooner they got out of here and back to safety, the better.

"Should we knock?" Hannah stayed planted, oblivious to Gregory's discomfort.

"I think we should, uh, keep moving. Now."

She tilted her head. "How would we even knock? Climb the legs? Throw a rock at the door?"

"There's no one here. It's just for decoration." *Curiosity killed the cat, Hannah.*

"Why would they put decorations all the way out here?"

"For adventurers like us. And they did so good! Now let's go home." Something rustled the trees in the distance. Gregory jumped about a foot. "C'mon, we gotta go home! You're afraid of the woods, remember?"

"I bet we'd be safe in the house. We could stay until morning, then keep looking when it's light out. Bears and wolves and stuff come out more when it's dark, right?"

She was being surprisingly logical. Gregory gaped at her for a moment, trying to find an argument. Something rustled again. Probably a squirrel or something. A really big, really fat squirrel, maybe. "Dad will worry if we don't get home soon."

That got through to her alright, though not in the way he had intended. Her face scrunched in a mix of anger and sorrow. "No he won't. He doesn't care about us anymore."

"What are you talking about? Of course he does."

"Then why does he let Regan be our mom? Can't he see how bad she is?"

Gregory didn't know what to say. How did you explain something so complicated, especially when you yourself didn't understand it? Dad sobbing late at night, talking to himself, breaking things for no apparent reason, juxtaposed with his rare moments of clarity, tenderness, and compassion...

"Hannah—"

Whatever brotherly wisdom Gregory was about to come up with was interrupted by a low, quaking roar that shook the earth. It shook Gregory to his very bones, making his brain flop against his skull and heart pound his ribcage. He was reminded of the roar of a tiger from the zoo: big and loud even from a distance. Only this was louder and more guttural and was almost human. The woods trembled again, maybe a hundred feet away, and rippled toward them.

“Hannah!"

She rushed to his side. He took her by the hand and ran. Behind them, something ripped through the tree line and hurried toward them, ground trembling beneath the weight of its heavy feet. Its putrid breath was hot on his neck. Gregory dared to glance over his shoulder. The sight was so terrifying his scream caught in his throat. His feet went numb, and he would have tripped if Hannah hadn't yanked him to the side. They tumbled behind a line of dead trees, the titanic shape rushing past, but not without swiping at Gregory's leg. Its claws ripped through his jeans and raked his flesh. He yelped, tears springing from his eyes. The pain was hot and throbbing and worse than anything he could think of, tracing up to his thigh and down to his foot. He clenched his teeth as hard as he could to keep from whimpering as he searched for the beast. It wasn't hard. The moonlight was cut off by the wall of skeleton-like trees, but even through the darkness Gregory could plainly see the abomination as it plowed through a chunk of the forest, trunks snapping like gun shots, before managing to slow itself. The dark form was at least ten feet tall and almost as wide. Six legs shaped like a horse's, covered in sleek black fur and ending in massive paws, sprouted from its thick underside. The upper body could have passed for that of an exceptionally hairy man's, if not for the cat head and clawed hands. It shuffled its feet and raised its panther-like nose to the sky. Big, floppy ears swiveled as it sniffed, probably picking up the scent of the blood dripping from Gregory's leg. It grabbed a small tree and, with a growl, ripped it from the ground. After giving the air a few experimental jabs, it turned toward Hannah and Gregory and broke into a gallop.

They scrambled to their feet sprinted forward, blindly weaving through the dark shapes of the forest and jumping over holes, getting cut and scraped by branches and thorns as they darted from one broken spear of moonlight to the next. That thing kept coming from behind, thudding nearer and nearer and breaking everything in its path. Gregory could hardly stay on his feet from the searing pain each step sent through his leg, made worse by the way the ground quaked beneath the beast.

They crossed over a ring of large purple mushrooms, and Gregory's stupid, numbing foot tripped over one. He knocked Hannah over, and the ground jumped up to slap him. The hulking monster was on top of them, raising its tree like a spear. It stabbed at Gregory's head.

A ring of pale yellow light shot up around Gregory and Hannah, rising from the mushrooms. The panther creature was thrown back and stumbled over its feet. It snarled, the sound piercing Gregory's eardrums, and inched toward the intrusion. In the pale glow, the monstrosity's features were starkly visible. Huge, jagged ears twitched and swiveled. Thick grimy yellow teeth gnashed together, a steam of sticky-looking saliva pouring out. What really made Gregory's blood run cold were the beady, bloodshot, hungry eyes that glared at them. They were primal, animalistic, predatory, and, worst of all, strikingly human. Just what *was* this thing? It swung a massive paw, giant claws extended. When the blow met the light, skin and fur sizzled, and the huge cat withdrew its hand with a petulant hiss. Undeterred, it stalked around the ring, looking for an opening. All the while, it stared hungrily at Gregory. It licked its lips and, faster than Gregory could hope to react, thrust its spear forward. The wood burst into flames, disintegrating completely before reaching him. The beast stamped its feet like a child throwing a tantrum.

"These humans sure are stupid, aren't they?" a voice asked.

"Why are they here, wandering around during the dark?" asked a second. "Don't their kind know better? They look so young and weak..."

"Hmm," said a third. "Say, they aren't stupid. They're babies." A small orb of white light floated up from a mushroom and hovered around Hannah's head. "Perhaps we have a chance, after all."

"Who let their babies wander loose in the forest?" the first voice asked. A harsh red orb rose from between Gregory's feet.

Hannah pulled Gregory close. "Who are they?" she whispered.

"I-I-I..." The salivating beast still pacing and eyeing Gregory made it difficult to think. "What are you?" he asked the lights.

"What are you, it says!" cried the first. "Can't it see our faces?"

Another ball of light, this one a gentle blue, drifted into the air. "Maybe not."

The white orb hummed. "They're quite different from us, these humans. Maybe their eyes don't work like ours."

"So mysterious, aren't they?" asked Blue.

Red bobbed like a fishing lure. "They can't see us! Then what good are they?"

"What good?" Blue echoed.

"All life is valuable, little ones," White chided.

"I'm not little!" said Red.

"It would not do for the leptaur to make a meal of them. Such bravery is rare." White hovered closer to Gregory, studying him.

"Bravery?" Red dashed side to side like it was shaking its head. "Stupidity is more like it."

The beast swiped again, more cautiously. Gregory threw

himself over Hannah, but the barrier of light stopped the attack once more.

White continued. "They are braving the night to return home, protecting each other all the while. If putting those around you before yourself is not brave, what is?"

"Whatever..."

"We have need of bravery, do we not, my children?" White pulsated, and the beast's eyes dilated, even more drool pooling out of its oversized mouth. It backed up, turned, and trudged away. "How fortunate for us all you humans found our ring. We can protect you from the leptaur and other dark beasts of the forest, but we must ask a favor in return."

"A favor? Oh, yes," Blue asked, glowing excitedly. Red danced through the air.

"A favor?" Gregory rasped. His foot grew cold even as the rest of him grew hotter. "What are you talking about?" With the great beast gone, he felt a hundred pounds lighter, but these colorful, talking orb things put him at almost greater unease.

"What the heck is a lept tire?" Hannah blurted.

"It doesn't know what a leptaur is?" asked the blue orb. "How strange..."

"A leptaur," White said, "is a magical beast from faraway lands. It and many other terrible things were brought here by the witch Baba Yaga."

"What kind of witch is named Baby Mama?" Hannah asked.

"Baba Yaga," Gregory numbly corrected. "Like from the fairy tales and folklore stories."

"You nerd! How do you know that?" She was letting her curiosity again distract her from her obvious danger they were still in.

"Doesn't matter," Gregory gritted out. "What does matter is that these weird little balls of light want something from us."

"We are fairies," White said. "We, too, are magical beings. This forest used to be filled with our people. Alas, since the witch landed here, many fairies have gone into hiding lest they be used in one of her atrocious spells." It sighed. "We are fearful and scattered and weak. That is why we need you, brave baby humans, to help us."

"We don't want to help you, we just wanna get home." Gregory wiped sweat from his brow.

"Oh. But we saved you from the leptaur. It is now your turn to aid us, don't you agree?"

This was all happening so fast. His mind spun as it tried to process everything from being abandoned to being almost mauled to talking with little "magical" balls of light. Gregory opened his mouth, but all the came out was a pained gasp. A hot, stabbing pain replaced the numbness in his foot. He curled up, pulling his knee to his chest. Red spots danced around his vision.

"Greg?" Hannah grabbed at him. "Greg, what's happening? *Greg*?"

"It must be the beast's venom," said White. "Allow me to see."

Hannah swatted at it. "Stay away!"

"Do not strike me, baby, I only wish—"

"I'm not a stupid baby!"

"I apologize if I caused offense, but allow me to see the wound. I may be able to help."

Hannah glanced between Gregory and the orb, biting her lip. She shuffled out of the way but kept her hand on Gregory's shoulder. Her touch was comforting, but there was only so much it could do against the wracking pain. White floated to the puncture wounds and hummed.

"The damage is not too bad. It would be simple to fix it..."

Gregory ground his teeth as liquid pain pulsed through his veins. "But?"

"You must agree to assist us."

"With what?" Hannah asked. Her fingers were icy even through Gregory's shirt. His skin was so hot...

"There is not time to discuss it. The venom in this human's blood grows stronger even now. We need your word to assist us immediately. But be warned: an oath taken in a ring of purple mushrooms cannot be broken without dire consequences."

"Hannah," Gregory forced out. "Everything about this is just weird. We can't do anything they say."

She averted her gaze. "We'll do it."

"Excellent," White said. It glowed brighter and expanded, pouring into Gregory's gashes. A tingling sensation spread up his leg.

"Hannah!" he yelled. "I told you—"

"Greg, shut up!" she fired back. "I had to say yes. After Mom left us, and Dad started acting all weird, you're all I have. I'm not losing you."

Gregory stared at her, speechless, as the tingling spread through the rest of his body, flushing out the pain and sickly heat and knitting up the damaged skin. He stretched his leg experimentally. Not a hint of discomfort anywhere.

"Thanks," he mumbled. Hannah removed her hand from his shoulder.

"Now, brave bab—human peoples," White said, a hint of fatigue in its voice. "We need you to save my husband and father of my children, the king Oberon, from the clutches of Baba Yaga."

"You have a king?" Gregory asked.

"Oh, yes. He is the greatest of us all. He is the only one powerful enough to stand up to the witch. But alas, she tricked him and captured him in a flask, rendering him powerless. If our Seering is correct, Baba Yaga will use his soul in a spell to uncover great riches. She will perform this spell at exactly midnight tonight, the day humans call Hollow's Knight."

"Halloween," Hannah corrected. "Why don't you go get your king by yourself?"

"Because," Red said like it was obvious, "Baba Yaga's hut is warded from the outside against fairy magic. It's hard enough to *see* inside, much less physically go there. Besides, she's dangerous. Now hurry up and help us already. I miss my father."

"I don't care if you saved us from the luh-lept-leptaur, you can't just..." *Miss my father*? she mouthed. She turned to Gregory, brow furrowed. "We're helping them." The fairies' lights pulsed stronger and became more vibrant. Their happiness spilled over them like warmth from a fire.

Gregory felt his eyes widen. "We're going to help them save their king from an evil witch?" he asked slowly, numbly.

"That's right."

"But t-that's crazy! We can't—w-we just got *done* with a dangerous adventure. We can't just—"

"It said it misses its father, Greg. I miss *my* dad, and I know you do, too."

Sometimes, Hannah, while not riled up and oblivious to the world around her, was annoyingly kind. She wanted to spare these fairies from a similar fate they had suffered through these past few years. It was hard to say no to that, but...

"I have to protect you, Hannah. I'm your big brother! I can't protect you if we go chasing after a witch."

She crossed her arms and looked away. "Well, I'm going. If you want to protect me, you have to come, too."

Gregory groaned. This sister of his... "Fine! But if things get dangerous, we are *out*, okay?"

She smiled and, after hugging him, looked back at the fairies and nodded. "Ready."

Moving in unison, the fairies twirled around them in tight circles, going faster and faster. The world flashed once, twice, and they stood in a familiar clearing. Towering above them on chicken legs was a small house.

"Whoa." Hannah grabbed Gregory for balance.

"Did we just teleport?" Gregory asked. "You things really are magic."

Blue laughed, the sound light and melodious. "Things? Are we just things?"

"We are not things," Red said. "We are fairies. Call us *things* again and I'll call you *babies*."

"This is the den of the beast," White said. "Inside are Baba Yaga and our king. You have until the stroke of midnight to find and prevent him from being used in her spell."

"What kind of spell?" Hannah asked.

"She plans to use his soul to enchant a treasure map. With the correct spell, the map can lead its holder to great fortune. Unenchanted, it will lead only to misfortune."

Hannah chuckled. "We should take the map and give it to Regan."

Gregory wasn't in the joking mood. How lucky it was for the fairies to find a pair of kids to rope into this barely an hour before midnight. What other kinds of magic were at work tonight?

"I hope her nasty cat isn't around," Red said, darting around restlessly. Blue nodded.

"The hut has a password, I believe you humans would call it," White said. "It can only be said by a female. One of you is a girl, correct?"

"I'm a girl," Hannah said with a roll of her eyes. White drifted closer to her and whispered in her ear. Hannah edged closer to the house, growing suddenly pale, and spoke:

"Oh cabin of great magic,
thou art so tragic"

The house's enormous legs vanished, and the house dropped to the ground at Hannah's feet. She shrieked and fell back.

"Are you okay?" Gregory ran to her side. She was frozen, staring at the door, waiting for someone to emerge. No one ever did. "Maybe she isn't home?" Gregory ventured.

"We can sense her." Blue floated around Gregory's head. He was pretty sure that was the first thing Blue said that wasn't a question. "The magical aura around Baba Yaga grows. The witch is beginning the spell."

Gregory pulled Hannah to her feet. "Hannah, this is crazy! What are we doing here? We're kids! We can't stop a witch." He squinted at his watch. "We only have forty minutes!"

"Are considering breaking your oath?" Blue was back to its questions.

"That would be a shame," Red said.

White pulsated disappointingly. "Indeed. These babies are a long way from help. It just wouldn't do for the leptaur to find them again..."

Gregory swallowed and glanced at Hannah. She looked about how he felt. "Guess we don't have a choice," he said.

She shook her head. "We don't have to *stop* the witch anyway, right? We just have to run in, grab the fairy, and run out. Easy."

That sounded incredibly unlikely, but Gregory nodded. When did his little sister get so brave? Maybe she was only pretending for his sake, just as he did for her.

"If you release the king," White said, "he will be able to deal with the witch, who will no doubt be weakened from conducting the spell. It will be simplicity itself."

"Pfft. Yeah, sure," Gregory said. He grabbed Hannah's hand. "Let's go save a fairy."

This close, the house's blood-red paint job was apparent, chipped and faded in places but impossible to ignore. Gregory's legs turning to jelly, they crept inside, the squeaky door snapping shut behind them. The first thing Gregory noticed was that the hut was *much* larger on the inside. He had expected a single room, sparsely decorated with archaic and ritualistic symbols, maybe a hay pile in the corner to serve as the witch's bed. Instead, they walked into an entry room that led into a long hallway, dotted with dozens of doors on each side. At the far end was a winding wooden staircase that led out of sight. The walls were plain wood, bare of any decoration or ornamentation. There were no light bulbs or sconces or anything else to provide light, yet everything was adequately—if a bit dimly—illuminated, leaving not even a trance of a shadow.

"So," Hannah said, stepping forward, "how do we start?"

Gregory wanted to say "By getting out of here" but held his tongue. The entry room was empty, save for a black end table that held a flask of dark purple liquid. "I guess we check each door, one at a time. We'll find Oberon eventually." He couldn't believe how matter-of-factly he was speaking about this mess.

"What if Oberon is with the witch? What if the witch sees us?"

"Uh, w-we'll think of something. For now, let's start with the first door on the left."

He moved forward, but Hannah put her arm out. She swallowed and squared her shoulders. "*I'll* start with the left side," she declared. "You go right."

"That's stupid. We have to stay together."

"There are tons of doors. I want to get out of here soon, and splitting up will be a lot faster."

"That's not safe!"

"None of this is safe! If the witch finds us, one *or* both of us..." She shrugged. "We can't stop the witch either way. Being fast is our best chance. We'll still be right across from each other, anyway."

Gregory hated that she thought that way and, worse, that she might be right. "Fine. But be careful. If anything happens, call for me. I'm not gonna let Baby Mama hurt my little sister."

Her laugh warmed his heart. Together, they walked into the hallway. She went through the left door. He went through the right.

The room looked like a library. Four cluttered bookshelves wrapped all the way around the room. Gregory still didn't know where Oberon was, but he suspected it wasn't in a battered copy of "One Thousand, Three Hundred and Thirty-Seven ways to Fly a Broom," so he went back to the door. Only, the door wasn't there. The wall it had occupied was covered up by the bookcases. He felt around, searching for a hidden doorknob or a book or something that might let him out. Nothing.

He opened his mouth to call for Hannah when a different, foreign voice rang out.

"Was that you who just came in, Miss Fortune?" Gregory just about jumped out of his skin. The words came from every direction, impossible to pinpoint, and were as loud and clear as if spoken directly into his ear. More strange magic was at work, but at least the speaker wasn't in the room with him. "I didn't realize you ever left. Were you visiting that little bar of yours again?" The voice was scratchy, phlegmy, and brittle. It was hard to judge, but it sounded like it belonged to a woman.

After the surprise of hearing the voice wore off, Gregory redoubled his efforts to find an exit. Who was Miss Fortune? Was there someone else here? He needed to get to Hannah *now*. He ran a circle around the room, searching for something, anything. He tried to yank the shelves off the walls, kick in the floorboards, jump at the ceiling. With a wordless yell of anger, he smashed his fists against the wall.

"While you're here, Miss Fortune, fetch that map for me, will you? I seem to have misplaced it. The ritual is almost ready." The floor lurched, almost knocking Gregory off his feet. It took him a second to place why: the house must have stood back up. Gregory felt more isolated than ever.

In desperation, he threw a book at the wall. The ancient paper crumpled and floated to the ground in a sad heap. He reached behind him for another book, and his fingers brushed against something stiffer. He grabbed it and held it to his face. It was a yellowed piece of paper filled with dozens of little drawings and figures. At the top right corner was a small red X, and in the center, near what looked to be a hill, was a house with legs. It had to have been the map he kept hearing about. He folded it and tucked it in his back pocket. If they couldn't find Oberon, maybe they could at least steal the map to keep the witch from using it.

The floorboards outside the door creaked. Gregory sucked in his breath, straining his ears. *Hannah,* he thought. *Please be Hannah. Open the door and let me out.* A section of wall swung open. Standing there, looking up at him with startlingly intelligent, probing eyes, was a black cat. Its fur was sleek and shiny, in sharp contrast to its torn right ear. Gregory exhaled. "Oh, good. A cat. I hate cats." He had all the luck today.

"Is that any way to speak to a lady, dear?" the cat asked.

Without missing a beat, Gregory laughed. "A talking cat! Why not?" If fairies and witches were real, why not talking animals?

"I believe you have something of mine," the cat said, sniffing around his leg.

Ignoring it, he tried to walk around the cat, but it twisted and turned, getting underfoot and making him stumble. "Get outta here, stupid talking cat, I'm busy!"

It squinted at him. "Care to rephrase that?" It leaped straight up, hitting him in the chin and knocking him down. Before he could gather his wits, the cat had its paws in his pocket, fishing out the map. It clamped the parchment in its teeth and scurried away.

"Hey!" Gregory immediately cursed himself for yelling but took off after the cat. "I need that, give it back!"

The cat darted up the stairs, three at a time. It disappeared around a corner up top before Gregory even reached the first step. The stairs creaked under his feet, threatening to give way under his weight. At the top was another branching path at which Gregory went right, after the cat. There were no doorways this time, just a straight shot to a room at the other end.

He saw no one. Not the witch, not his sister, not any Miss Fortune lady. Unless Miss Fortune was the stupid cat...

Someone spoke, and he skidded to a stop. It was too late.

"Oh, look what the cat dragged in!" Along the wall, hunched over piles of paper and a glowing glass jar, was the spindliest, wartiest, most hunchbacked woman Gregory had ever seen. At her feet, map still in its furry jaws, was the cat. The woman patted its head. "Nice work, Miss Fortune. After we find our treasure, we will have child stew!"

She raised her hand, sparks flying from her fingers. The world flashed, and Gregory sat in a small, metal box. In front of him was a window through which he saw the woman's scaly legs and the tip of the cat's remaining ear. There was a noise like flames crackling, and the floor of the box heated up. It was an oven.

He was being cooked alive.

HANNAH DIDN'T THINK she would find Oberon in "Magic-House-Cat Care: Basics" but checked anyway. It's not like there was anything else to do in this room. All it had were cat things: scratching posts, food and water bowls, a big ripped sack of catnip, a poster of an eye patch-wearing cat hanging from a tree with the caption "Hang in there," a currently dirty litter box, and a single computer mouse. The first two rooms had been boring, but at least they hadn't smelled like cat pee. Flipping through the book's pages, she found no fairy king, though there was a mention of fairies being a delicacy for some feline breeds. Maybe that was why the fairies of the forest had been too afraid to stand up to Baba Yaga: her pet cat, wherever it was.

Something creaked above her. The cat in question, a pretty black thing, stretched on top of a shelf. It had a torn ear, which twitched as it watched Hannah.

"Aww! Aren't you just the cutest little kitty?" Dropping the book, she dashed to the shelf. The cat was just out of her reach. So tantalizingly close. She wanted to hug it and squeeze it and save it from this mean witch's hut. Their dad never let them have pets, but—

"Don't touch me," the cat snipped, flicking her tail.

Hannah froze. "I didn't know cats could talk. Are you a magic cat?"

"If I say yes, will you leave me alone?"

She very much did *not* want to leave the cat alone. It was so tempting to stay and play with her and learn more about magic cats. Time was of the essence, though, so she supposed she would have to leave before she lost track of time. What were people always telling her? Curiosity killed the cat?

The strange voice from earlier returned. "While you're here, Miss Fortune, fetch that map for me, will you? I seem to have misplaced it. The ritual is almost ready."

Just like before, the voice seemed to come from right next to her, but it must not have been able to hear *her* if it thought she and Gregory were this Miss Fortune lady.

The cat stood, stretched, and hopped to the floor. "Excuse me, child," she said, "my oh-so lovely *owner* needs me." As much as Hannah didn't want to see the cat go, she didn't protest. The cat sniffed the air and walked straight through the door. Hannah rubbed her eyes and did a double take to make sure there wasn't a cat door or something. Shrugging, she followed it out, using the doorknob as intended. The cat, standing on her hind feet, opened a door on Greg's side of the hallway. Maybe he would get to meet the cat, too.

Hannah went to the next door in line. This was already the fourth, but there were so many more. With a sigh, she walked into the strangest room yet. Where all the others had been covered in bookshelves or cat accessories, this one was covered in doors. There were three on each wall. They were all the exact same design and size, spaced about three feet apart. She tried one on the left side. It opened to a brick wall. The two adjacent to it, however, revealed entirely different rooms. She walked into one, and it, too, was covered in doors. How did Baba Yaga find her way through this place, Hannah wondered, walking a circle around the room. How would *Hannah*? Did she search these new rooms, or did she keep checking the doors along the main hallway?

"Oh, look what the cat dragged in!" the witch's voice called out. "Nice, work, Miss Fortune. After we find our treasure, we will have child stew!"

What was that witch going on about? Busy checking all the doors, Hannah almost didn't process her words. "Child stew?" she muttered to herself. Fingers of ice squeezed her heart.

Greg! Where was he? Did the witch have him? She spun on her heel and ran for the exit. Only to realize she didn't know which door *was* the exit. How did she get to him? She didn't have time for this! She picked a door at random and sprinted through it, only to wind up in a room with even more doors. Each wall had six or seven, and when she tried to backtrack, she found the door she came through was gone. *No no no.*

She ran, throwing open door after door, sprinting through room after endless room. This was ridiculous! Greg was about to be turned into child stew, and she was stuck running through stupid *doors*. She was going to be trapped here forever, opening doors until she was eighty and the witch was rich from her treasure. Another door opened, another room revealed. She ran through it into another room, chose another door, and... she was out. Panting and sweating and panicked, she was right where she started. Finally. Freedom. But now what? Where was Greg? She looked helplessly around at all the unopened doors. If he was behind one of these doors, she would never find him. With how limited time was, it was pointless to even try. She needed something different.

Aching lungs and legs protesting, she ran the length of the hallway and flew up the stairs, only to be presented with yet another choice: the path to the left or the path to the right? There was no time for any more wrong decisions. Listening to her gut, she ran right. Another long hallway led to a circular room, where a low, throaty voice spoke. Hannah slowed to a creep just outside. A voice from inside covered her skin in goose bumps and made her hands quiver. *I can't do this, I can't do this, I can't do this.* This was so so bad. She was just a little kid! What was she trying to do acting all brave for the fairies? She wanted to run out and go home. But her brother needed her to save him. And that was that. It was only fair, right? Hannah couldn't keep her big fat mouth shut, and that was why Regan left them in the woods. This whole thing was Hannah's fault, so it was only just that she be the one to fix it.

Holding her breath, she peeked inside the room. A freakishly tall, misshapen lady stood in the center of a weirdly-drawn circle with a bunch of symbols and candles set on it. Against one wall was a small black stove, a small fire lit on stones beneath it. On a shelf near the stove was a straw pile upon which rested a glowing jar and the black cat, who winked at her. But inside the stove, visible through the glass, was her brother. A sob caught in her throat. Even from here, she could see sweat dotting his face. But he was moving. He would be okay, but only if Hannah got them out of this place.

She switched her attention to the witch. The bent-backed, gray-haired woman paced the circle, waving her glowing hands. At the center of the circle, sitting unassumingly on the floor, was a single piece of paper. *The map.*

Hannah tensed her legs and waited. Her heart pounded her ribs, its reverberation seeming to carry through her and into the floor. *Don't cry, don't cry.* The witch made two full revolutions, Greg's face going redder and redder. Baba Yaga turned her back on the doorway to chant at a candle, and Hannah slunk into the room, treading of the balls of her feet. She went as fast as she could while staying quiet. Just as she reached Gregory, the witch turned. Hannah ducked behind the stove. The fire made her skin writhe, but she didn't dare move.

"Ten minutes to midnight," the witch's awful voice said. "Just ten minutes, Miss Fortune. Then you'll have all the catnip and mice you want. Oh, it would be a shame if something were to interfere, wouldn't it?"

The cat yawned. "Something like a pair of smelly humans?"

"Why, yes, that would be just terrible."

Hannah's vision swam in circles. She reached a shaky hand around the side of the stove, low to the ground, searching for the handle. She knew she made an unbreakable oath or whatever to the fairies, but right now, she cared more about freeing Greg and getting out than finding the fairy king. If she could just find the handle, they could run out of here. Between the hot metal and the crackling fire and the witch's eyes, there were so many things that could go wrong. She had half a mind to forget stealth and try a speedy approach.

"How *ever* would we handle such a thing?" the witch asked sweetly.

The cat purred. "It's been a while since you've turned anyone into a frog."

"Would you like that, Miss Fortune? I know there aren't as many little fairies around for you to chase. Yes, maybe a frog would be just the way..."

Hannah's fingers brushed against something wooden. With a bit of effort, she wrapped her shaking hand around it. She gave it a pull, and the world grew around her. The stove was hundreds of feet tall, and the walls stretched up higher than she could see. She tried to scream, but all that came out was a croaky groan. Reflexively, she tried to grab her throat. Only, she couldn't lift her hand on account of it being massive and green and webbed. She would have thrown up if her stomach wasn't empty.

The ground quaked as a massive figure stomped over to her and picked her up. The witch's hands were cold and coarse, even to Hannah's own cold and coarse frog skin. Baba Yaga threw back her head and laughed. "Look at this, Miss Fortune! It's hideous!"

"Is that a new species? Very nice." The cat licked her lips. "Such a shame there's only one. It looks good enough to eat."

Baba Yaga released Hannah. She expected to break every bone in her new warty body, but the impact with the floor was as soft as if she'd landed on a pile of pillows.

"Have fun, my precious, but not too much fun! We leave as soon as this map is charmed."

Miss Fortune leapt from her spot on the stove, landing just in front of Hannah. The cat waited with hungry, playful eyes, daring Hannah to make a move. "As the clock strikes twelve," the cat said in a sing-song voice, "into the next life you shall delve." She bared her teeth and crouched.

Hannah made a break for the stove's handle. She took one step and tripped over her spongy toes. A giant, black paw swooped toward her. She tried to get out of the way, but her heavy body wouldn't respond. The paw struck her chest, sending her flying into the leg of the stove. The metal was hot, but strangely it didn't bother her. Which was good, because the wind was knocked out of her and she couldn't move. Miss Fortune crept closer and poked at Hannah's body. The paw was so strong, and the little jabs squished Hannah's organs. Thousands of feet above, the witch resumed her chanting. Each footstep rattled Hannah's tiny, fat body.

Miss Fortune mewled, and Hannah's breath came back just in time. The paw came again, now with claws extended. Hannah flopped onto her stomach and pushed off the ground with all her might. She jumped forward, straight over the paw and onto the floor behind the cat. She ribbited in triumph before the cat's jaws clamped around her. *This is it.* The cat would eat her. The witch would eat Gregory. Oberon's soul would be used in the spell. Regan would be thrilled to never have to see her stepchildren again, and Dad probably wouldn't care.

With a flick of her head, the cat threw Hannah into the air and readied her claws again. Hannah braced herself for impact with the ground again, but she stuck to something. She glanced at her feet, above her head. Her webbed toes were suctioned to the bottom of a bookshelf.

"Miss Fortune," the witch chided, "you shouldn't play with your food."

The cat hissed and leapt at Hannah, falling just shy of reaching her. "Come down," the cat growled. Another jump, another close miss. Hissing, she looked around for some higher vantage point before making her way toward a nearby bench.

Hannah frantically searched for anything that might help. Unless she could somehow figure out a way to defeat the cat with stacks of ancient books, she was out of luck. This wasn't how things were supposed to go. How had her good deed for the fairies gone so wrong? Wait, fairies? Hannah looked at the glowing jar on the shelf. Inside, an orb of royal purple darted around, bouncing harmlessly off the glass. Hannah pushed off the shelf and landed on the straw bed. Being a frog was easier than she thought.

"I believe you did *too* good a job with this one," the cat complained from a hundred feet away. Baba Yaga didn't answer, too busy with her spell. The strange woman's labored breathing filled the room. Before Hannah had a chance to do anything with Oberon's jar, the cat joined them on the straw. "You'll make a nice appetizer to your littermate," she purred. Tauntingly, she raised her paw over Hannah, claws stretching. Quick as a whip, she brought it down toward Hannah's head. Hannah leapt straight up, nearly brushing the cat's paw. As she descended, she saw the cat's wayward strike knock Oberon's jar to the floor. The witch let out a guttural, bone-chilling scream.

"You idiot cat!"

"Oops," Miss Fortune mumbled.

Air whistled by Hannah's ear holes, and she landed by the stove's handle. Next to her, Baba Yaga knelt next to a pile of glass, eyes wide and mouth open. "Did you EAT him?"

"I'm hungry."

"I gave you a frog!"

"Fairies taste better."

"You... you—*Spit it up*!"

It was now the cat's turn to run as the witch chased her all around the room. Seizing the moment, Hannah attacked the stove's handle. She managed to balance on her hind feet just long enough to place her clumsy front feet on the wood and push. Despite how easy these legs could launch her around, they couldn't even budge the handle.

Behind her, a sound like a stack of books hitting the floor made her jump.

"Why are you glowing?" Baba Yaga yelled. "Oh no, *close your mouth, he's getting out*!"

The world flashed oncc, twice, and Hannah was back in her body. She wanted to cry and hug herself, but there was no time. She threw open the stove, grabbed Greg's feverish hand, and yanked him out. "Greg are you okay?" It sounded like a stupid question, considering he was just in a stove. Breathing too heavily to speak, he nodded, sending drops of sweat flying everywhere.

Footsteps rushed toward them. The witch was chasing the cat which was chasing the fairy. Hannah jumped out of the way, pulling Gregory with her. The cat jumped on top of the stove, and the witch tumbled straight into it. Her long legs stuck awkwardly out, kicking the air futilely. Hannah stared at the stove, numb, knowing she should do something. Gregory, covered in red marks and blisters, lunged forward and fought with the legs until he could slam the door shut. Inside, the witch screamed with wordless fury.

Oberon floated over to Hannah's shoulder. "Thank you, baby human, for freeing me! If you had come a few minutes later, I shudder to think what may have happened. Though I fear we aren't safe just yet." Miss Fortune glared at the three of them, malice in her eyes.

"It's just a cat," Hannah said. "What's she gonna do?"

"What indeed?" the cat growled. "Strike you with lightning? Fill you with poison? Summon a leptaur?" Hannah's limbs filled with lead. Somehow, she didn't doubt the cat was capable of these things.

Baba Yaga banged on the stove. "Miss Fortune, you let me out right this instant or I'll make a rug out of you!"

The air turned purple as Oberon pulsated. The cat bared her teeth. "Don't you try anything, fairy."

Gregory tugged on Hannah's sleeve. "Get the map," he whispered. Being as inconspicuous as she could, Hannah crept backward.

"See!" the cat said, assuming a lunging position. "The girl has the right idea. Run. Not that I'll let you."

The cat jumped, Hannah scooped up the map, and the world turned purple.

They stood outside the hut, where they had left the fairies. Red, White, and Blue whirled around them.

"I didn't think the babies could do it."

"But they have! They've done it!"

"They've truly done it?"

"I have returned, my family!" Obern declared. "These human babies have freed me from my imprisonment!"

Hannah's head spun as the four balls of light danced around each other, cheering and speaking, dipping in and out of English and a strange, musical language.

"Hannah," Gregory said tentatively, as if afraid to believe this was real. "Did we—"

"You're not leaving!" Baba Yaga materialized in the middle of them all, glowing hands raised. "I'll sacrifice all of you for the spell!" She exuded as much malice as ever, but even Hannah could tell how weak she was, panting from exhaustion and heat exertion.

"It's over, Baba Yaga." Oberon drifted toward her, and his family followed. "Hollow's Knight has passed. It is a new day. You may have scared my people away with your devilish cat and threats of rituals, and you may have tricked me into that jar, but we will not be pushed around any longer. Now, my family!"

As once, the fairies glowed brighter. Their colors overlapped into a radiant rainbow-hued sphere. A heavy breeze picked up, almost pushing Hannah off her feet. She and Gregory held onto each other. The magic crackling around Baba Yaga's fingers grew weaker and strained.

From inside, Miss Fortune's voice carried over the wind. "I'm coming! I'll eat that fairy yet!"

"Hurry, my family," Oberon said. "What manner of spell should we use?"

"Turn her tongue into a snake."

"Turn *her* into a chicken."

"A chicken? Yes..."

The rainbow sphere expanded and shot toward Baba Yaga. The witch hesitated for the briefest of moments before the waning magic faded from her fingers. With a yelp, she vanished. The sphere cleaved through the air she had occupied and crashed against a barren tree. Instead of breaking or toppling over, the drooping tree straightened. The first signs of leaves appeared on its branches.

The hut's door opened, and the black cat ran out. She perched on the edge of the porch, fur raised. "Oh good, more food!" Just as she tensed to pounce, giant chicken wings sprouted from the house. In a flash, the shack was in the clouds, winging its way over the forest. "*Nnnooo*!"

"It's gone," Gregory mumbled. "She's gone." He pulled Hannah into a tight hug. She'd never self safer.

"We did it," she said.

"Can the rest return?" White asked Oberon.

"Yes, my lovely wife. Yes they can." He floated high in the sky and sang a song. Hannah didn't understand the words, but the king's voice was beautiful and full of emotion. It was a tale of loss, of pain and sorrow, of inner strength. Of love and family. Of unity.

Little balls of light—more fairies—came from across the sky. They descended and joined the celebration and lent their voices to the song. Before Hannah knew it, the forest was a living rainbow. Even as she watched, life returned to the prickly trees and to the brown mushroom rings and the dried up bushes. Green returned to the dreary world. Even the night's darkness lightened. It was everything Hannah envisioned when she thought of magic.

The fairies were home.

Oberon returned to them, as the dozens, maybe even hundreds, of other fairies danced and sang and celebrated. "This is all thanks to you, you brave, brave babies. How can we repay you? Anything at all, if it is within our power, will be granted to you.

Hannah surveyed the magical and immediate restoration of the forest. Now that the fairies stood united once more, there probably wasn't much that was beyond them. Gregory touched Hannah's hand, the one that still clutched the uncharmed map. She understood. "I think we already have what we need," she said.

"What would that be?" the fairy king asked.

She smiled. "A present for our stepmother." She couldn't wait to see the look on Regan's face when they walked through the door.

"I see. If you change your mind, you know where to find us." He raised his voice. "Now, then, my fairies! Let us return these brave heroes home. Search their hearts and find where they must go."

Rainbows filled Hannah's vision. The world flashed, and they stood in their front yard. Their father's car was parked in the driveway, right next to Regan's. He was back. Had he even been bothered that his children hadn't come home? She didn't care. All was quiet. All was safe. All was well. Hannah held the map tight in one hand, and with the other, she held Gregory.

"You know," her brother said, "we almost died about a hundred times tonight, and my favorite pair of jeans is ruined. But I can't remember the last time I felt so free." He smiled. Ready?"

"Let do it. Together."

Hand in hand, they walked inside.

JACOB FAUST

ABOUT THE AUTHOR

Jacob Faust is a stalwart author, voracious reader, and lifelong teller of stories. He lives in Deerwood, Minnesota, writing in the company of his many furry friends. If you can't find him there, he's probably lost in the clouds.

Find Jacob at:

Twitter: @Jacob_Faust2

Email: jacobcfaust6@gmail.com

THE TELLER TREE

BY S.M. ROSE

FIONA

The tree had not been there forever because everything has a beginning as surely as everything has an end.

But it had certainly been there as long as anyone in the town could remember. Fiona had even asked the old man who owned the drugstore where she and Sabrina liked to get milkshakes, who was rumored to have been living there since the very founding of the town. Even he could not remember a time when that patch of earth was bare.

He said that the tree had gained a few more knots over the years, was looking a bit more gnarly, and had a few more crows nesting in it, but that it had never really looked young.

Fiona couldn't imagine the tree as a sapling any more than she could picture the man as once being a young boy with scabby knees. As far as she was concerned, they had both come into the world wrinkled and wise and a little odd.

She loved that tree, even as a child when all her classmates whispered that it was haunted, that its roots would drag you into its center if you passed it unawares after sunset, and the crows would peck out your eyes. That the ghosts of the tree's former victims were always looking for another heart to join them, because even the dead grew lonely

It wasn't that Fiona was fearless or anything. There were plenty of things she was afraid of. The tree just wasn't one of them. Something about its presence was comforting, and she would spend her afternoons stretched out below its branches, whispering all of her hopes and dreams, all of the secrets that she couldn't tell anyone else.

And sometimes, if she was lucky, the tree would tell her secrets of its own.

ROGER

He frowned at his girlfriend as they stood outside the school. The game started in just over an hour; he didn't understand why she was leaving just to come all the way back.

"I'll be there," Fiona promised him, twisting a strand of her fiery red hair anxiously around her finger. "I just have to take care of something first."

"What about the campfire?"

Her perfect, bow-shaped lips turned downward. "I don't know..."

"Come on Fi," he said, heart sinking. "It'll be fun." Fiona always played it safe. She'd happily accompany him to the movies or dinner and go watch his football games, but the second he suggested something a little more daring, she shied away.

Sometimes he felt like she was always shying away.

"An illegal fire by the woods at night? Yeah. Super fun."

"You know I won't let anything happen to you," he said, putting an arm around her shoulders. "Besides, I thought you liked spooky trees."

Fiona leaned into him, smiling. He liked keeping her safe. Liked to keep her close. She felt so distant all the time. She was a quiet, close-lipped mystery before they had started dating. After, nothing really changed. Fiona talked to him, sure, but she never *told* him anything.

If he saw her crying, she'd brush it off, saying it was just something stupid. If she was abnormally quiet, she'd just say she was "thinking" and not tell him what was on her mind. He didn't understand it.

It seemed as though Fiona only trusted her secrets to the haunted tree on the edge of town. When Roger had suggested it was possessing her, Fiona just laughed at him.

"Fine," she said finally, pulling away from him. "I'll be there. See you after the game."

He leaned over to kiss her goodbye, but she had already turned away.

FIONA

It wasn't that Fiona didn't love her boyfriend; it was just that she didn't really understand why he was interested in her. Why the quarterback had gone for the quiet girl with her nose in a book.

He joked that she was a puzzle to solve, a mystery to crack, but Fiona hoped he really was joking. She didn't want to be a puzzle. She was a person. She was just a quiet one.

She knew he wanted her to confide in him more. But why should she confide in people? People lied and whispered. People talked.

Her tree kept all her secrets for her. It was the most faithful friend in the world.

She had been worried Roger would be angry with her for not wanting to go to the campfire. For not going right with him to the game and watching him warm up. He got angry a lot. She knew how that sounded, but he never hit her or anything. He rarely even raised his voice.

Even when he did yell, Fiona knew it didn't change anything. He loved her. You don't get angry at someone unless you love them. Only the people you love have the power to hurt you.

Fiona stretched out underneath the tree with a book propped in her lap. Her nose was running in the cold, so she wrapped her scarf a bit tighter around her chin and stared up into the branches.

The leaves were turning the golden-yellow of early fall; a few were already shifting to orange. Before long they would become a deep, blood-red, and then crisp away into brown, dead things that crackled in the wind.

Fiona closed her book, unable to focus on the words. She never could, when she had a secret to tell. The tree was always hungering for it, trying to pull it from her. She would get no peace until she whispered it into the knots. She had told many secrets to the tree, but this one she had kept close. Clutched it to her chest all summer, afraid to tell anyone, even the tree, because speaking it would make it true, and then it would be a betrayal.

But she had been holding it so tightly that it was starting to hold her back, constricting her ribs and making it hard to breathe. The tree could take that from her.

So Fiona whispered to the tree, and in the rustling of the branches and the quivering of the leaves, Fiona listened to the tree tell a story in return.

SABRINA

Sabrina was not what one might call a "fan" of football. She didn't watch the professional games like her dad and had never really cared about the sport all that much. But Fiona's boyfriend was the quarterback for their school, so she always tagged along. It was easy enough to sit in the bleachers with her friend for a couple hours, eating popcorn and hotdogs and pretending to care when Roger made a good throw.

Besides, the cheerleaders always looked cute in their uniforms. Especially Rebecca.

"Please tell me you're coming tonight," Fiona pleaded to her as Roger started to run across the field.

Sabrina nearly snorted into her steaming cup of apple cider. "Hang out with drunk seniors near a fire? Not likely. Besides, it's illegal."

"The lumber company has plenty of wood, and Roger chops half of it. They can afford to lose a few logs."

Sabrina noted that Fiona sounded doubtful herself. Likely, miss goody-two-shoes was just repeating the exact words Roger had said to ease her own misgivings.

"Thanks, but I'm gong to curl up beside my nice legal fire with a book."

Fiona rolled her eyes. "Come on, Brina. Rebecca will be there."

Sabrina glanced up and saw a flicker of triumph light her friends eyes as she realized she had convinced her. She sighed and relented. Let Fiona think it was for Rebecca, but she had been planning on going anyway. She was hardly about to let her best friend partake in illegal activity with a bunch of drunk seniors in the middle of the night—at least not alone.

"Fine. But if they start to summon demons, I'm out."

"Not everything plays out like a bad horror movie you know."

Considering the company of moronic seniors that would be there, Sabrina thought this was likely to do just that.

The stands erupted with cheering as Roger ran the ball into the end zone, securing the win with only thirty seconds left on the clock. Fiona looked up in surprise.

Sabrina grinned. “Miss his big play?”

“Don’t worry,” Fiona said, a smile on her face. “I’ll get a blow-by-blow replay after the game.”

Sabrina thought this sounded awful, but her friend was grinning like Roger’s manly enthusiasm was the most adorable thing in the world. *Boys.*

FIONA

As predicted, Roger spent the entire walk from the field to the lumber yard on the outskirts of town reliving his glory moments of the game. Fiona did her best to follow along, but mostly made impressed-sounding noises at what she thought were the appropriate times while going out of her way to step on every crunchy leaf that blew across her path.

The walk should have taken about fifteen minutes but took closer to twenty because every once in a while Roger would stop to illustrate a particularly good play he had made. Fiona would have to stand there pretending to be the defensive player, and Roger would demonstrate in slow motion how he had narrowly avoided a tackle and broken through the defensive line for thirty-plus-yard run to the end zone.

Fiona didn’t mind the long walk, though. It was her favorite kind of evening, and when Roger wasn’t demonstrating his best moments for her, he was holding her hand with her backpack and its fifty pounds of textbooks slung over his shoulder.

She loved how perfectly their hands fit together. So different but still matching.

By the time they reached the lumber yard, everyone else was by the edge of the trees,, piling scraps of wood into a small pit they had lined with rocks.

It was a perfect night for a campfire; the sky was full of clouds, but the stars peeked through the gaps and the moon occasionally shone its face upon them. The air was chilly, but Fiona was more than comfortable in her scarf and Roger's letterman jacket, and the slight breeze carried the scents of autumn to her noise.

Fiona had always loved the smell of autumn, rich and earthy. It was the smell of dying things, she knew, and maybe that should have bothered her, but it was always a smell that brought her comfort. A reminder that time was passing, that everything was changing, along with the leaves hanging above their heads.

Soon, the fire was crackling pleasantly, and Fiona shed Roger's jacket before she started sweating. They were all seated on logs they had rolled over from the piles, in something loosely resembling a circle.

"I heard something about scary stories?" said Sabrina, giving Fiona a meaningful look from across the fire. She had managed to seat herself next to Rebecca, who was still in her cheerleading uniform.

"Yes!" Roger said excitedly. "S'mores and stores."

Fiona gave her boyfriend a look. "Huh?"

"Like stories? But shortened, to rhyme."

"That makes no sense. We're not at the store," Rebecca said.

"It's—whatever," Roger mumbled, cracking open a beer and taking a few liberal gulps. "Someone start."

One of Roger's teammates heroically took up the role of first storyteller and tried to frighten them all with a grisly tale of murder in the woods. Fiona was not impressed. The premise was frightening enough, but Brad had no idea how to actually tell a story. He also paused dramatically every few seconds, which meant that a very short story took him nearly half an hour to tell.

"Next!" Rebecca announced, the moment Brad fell mercifully silent.

"Come on Fiona!" Sabrina called. "You always tell the best stories."

Fiona stared into the embers of the fire, thinking. She did tell good stories. But they weren't always hers to tell because she didn't know if they were true.

The tree had told them to her. It was years before the tree talked back, and Fiona at first thought she was imagining it. But in the whispers of the leaves and the creaking of the branches, the tree told her stories of the beautiful and terrible things it had seen.

The tree kept her secrets, though, and she didn't think the stories were hers to tell. So she twisted and changed them until they were strange and new and something closer to her own creation—yet she could never think up such wonders on her own.

"Once," she began finally, her voice quiet, and the others fell so silent they stopped moving. "Many years ago, when this town was nothing more than a few cottages on the edge of the wood, there lived…"

A GIRL AND A WOODSMAN

The girl traveled through the wood twice a week to deliver bread to her grandmother. In those days, there were no proper roads, and the quickest way to her cottage was through the woods. Otherwise, she would have to walk around the outskirts, a day-long journey at best.

Her mother did not like her to travel through the woods because they were fraught with wild beasts, wolves and bears as well as less natural creatures. But if ever the girl grew afraid, there was a place in the woods where she knew she would always be safe.

A twisted tree older than any in the forest was never far from the girl when she walked. No matter where in her journey she was all she need do was run a few paces and she would find herself at the tree. She would hide among its gnarled roots that wrapped around her protectively or climb high into its branches, far beyond the reach of the woodland beasts.

There was one day, an hour into her journey, that the girl heard the sound of footsteps behind her. Every time she turned, however, she saw no one.

Finally, she ran.

"Stop!"

Surprised by the sound of a voice so deep in the woods, the girl clutched the basket to her chest in fear. She could see the tree; in her need, it had appeared, but it was a few paces away. She edged back toward it as the man who had spoken approached. He was large and bearded, with a wolfish gleam in his eyes.

"What are you doing alone in the woods, little girl?"

"I am bringing bread to my grandmother."

"So kind of you," he said, his voice low like that of a growl. "I have long been hungry."

Something in his eyes told the girl that it was not bread he hungered for. She stepped back at the same time that he lunged forward. As she screamed, branches from the tree shot out, forming a wall around her and lashing out at the man as she continued to scream.

When she could scream no longer, the branches receded, and the man was gone. The girl ran the rest of the way to her grandmother's house.

Her grandmother was disturbed upon hearing what had happened and did not want the girl to return through the woods. "There are more kinds of wolves than one," she cautioned her granddaughter, "and they hunger for the hearts of the pure."

But the girl had to return to her family, for they needed her around the shop, and she knew that the tree would protect her. She bade her grandmother farewell and returned to the shadowed wood.

It was not long before she encountered the woodsman again. There was a large ax in his hand, the kind meant for cutting wood, but the girl knew it cut could flesh just as easily.

This time the girl did not hesitate. She just ran, kicking up sticks and stones and leaves in her wake. But no matter how far or fast she ran, she could not find the tree. Her foot caught on a root, and she tumbled to the ground.

The woodsman was looming over her laughing, and it was only then that the girl realized what she had tripped on—not a root, but a stump. A stump wider around than four men, with rings from many years, twisted and warped and old and kind.

She was alone in the wood with a wolf before her, ready to eat her heart. In fear and anguish, the girl let out a terrible scream—

ROGER

A scream split through the night, and Fiona jerked her head up, frowning at whoever had the nerve to interrupt her story.

Roger cast his eyes around the group, trying to figure out who had made the noise. His head was fuzzy from the beer. He had only half-heard Fiona's story. Something about a wolf and the heart of a girl. Something about a tree. He'd ask her to tell it again when he was sober.

The scream came again, but this time, the accompanying flashing lights made it clear it was sirens.

"Cops!" Roger shouted, jumping to his feet and cursing as his head spun from the alcohol.

"Fuck!" said Sabrina.

"Run!" screamed Rebecca.

"Come on, Fiona," Roger cried, grabbing her arm. The last thing he wanted was for her to be alone in the woods at night; he'd keep her safe by his side, which was where she belonged.

But Fiona hesitated, looking at him with fear on her face. It was a moment before Roger realized it was *him* she was afraid of.

She mouthed a single word, so quiet he was barely able to hear it over the sound of the sirens. "Wolf."

Fiona yanked her arm from his grasp and vanished into the woods.

FIONA

For the briefest of moments, the firelight gleaming in Roger's eyes had made them seem golden and wolfish, and Fiona was afraid. Usually, Roger made her feel safe, protected. Even when he was angry, she was never truly afraid of him because he kept her safe from the rest of the world. If he was the only threat, it was one she could handle. She preferred keeping all of the dangers in one place.

But in that moment, Roger had seemed scarier than the cops and far scarier than the dark, lonesome woods.

Fiona had thought she knew where her tree was, but everything looked so different this late at night, and she had never approached the tree from the lumber mill before. There were plenty of old trees in this wood—but none of the ones she passed were hers. None of these would keep her safe from scary wolfmen who wanted to eat her heart.

She liked trees in general, but that didn't mean she wanted to be lost among them late at night and all on her own.

A screech emanated from the shadows, and for a wild moment, Fiona thought the cop cars had followed her into the woods. She took a moment to laugh at herself, then screamed as the noise came again, and a large black creature shot out of the underbrush.

A panther! She thought, but this was far too small to be a panther. It was a cat black as the night around them, with a jagged scar over one eye and a torn right ear. He gave her a small *mew,* so quiet she barely heard it, and trotted away with his tail held high. Upon realizing she was not following him, he turned back and gave her a frown that for a moment made him look shockingly human.

"Mew!" He insisted.

"Okay, okay," Fiona said, scrambling after him. It was not as though she had any better ideas.

It was not easy following a black cat through the woods at night, but Fiona managed it. The creature was patient as she stumbled and crashed along the forest floor, and finally he stopped at the base of a tree, licking his paw and looking quite pleased with himself.

A moment passed before Fiona realized it wasn't just *a* tree, it was the tree. Her tree.

"Thank you," she whispered, and although she did not think she was being followed, she climbed the low-hanging branches until she was halfway to the top, and nestled in a spot where one of the fatter branches met the trunk.

The tree's leaves rustled in the night breeze, hungry for another secret. For another piece of Fiona's heart, which she had been giving to it steadily over the years.

But Fiona just lay there in silence, gazing at the few stars visible between the maze of branches above her head. She had given in such a dangerous, terrible secret that afternoon that she had nothing else to tell.

Sometimes, she had said, *I'm afraid of Roger.*

SABRINA

They had all only narrowly escaped getting caught by the cops Friday night, and Sabrina still heard a rant from her dad about breaking curfew. So Saturday, she laid low and hung around the house brooding, wanting to text Fiona but not really knowing what to say.

Sunday, her friend had called her instead and dragged her along pumpkin picking since it was a beautiful sunny day. It was only her love for Fiona that had gotten her to agree. She had nothing against pumpkins in general, but there was little more she detested than the hype that surrounded them every fall—pumpkin spice *everything*. In the great pumpkin-apple debate, Sabrina was a die-hard apple supporter, while Fiona picked pumpkin every time.

It was truly a wonder they were still friends.

Fiona was clearly in a bad mood, so Sabrina did her best to humor her. She hated seeing Fiona frown. It was like a dark storm cloud sweeping in and ruining a perfectly sunny day.

"What about one of these?" she suggested, plucking a pumpkin from the hay-strewn ground of the farmyard. It was no bigger than her head.

"That's a sugar pumpkin," Fiona said, snorting despite her mood. "It goes in pies. We need proper pumpkins that we can carve."

Sabrina threw her hands in the air. "Fine. Lead the way. You're lucky I love you so damn much." She regretted the words as soon as she said them and nestled into her scarf to try to hide her blush.

Fiona only smiled. "Don't let Rebecca hear you say that."

Sabrina shrugged nonchalantly. Rebecca was cute, sure. Especially in her cheerleading outfit. But Sabrina didn't really know her. And her smile didn't do the things to her tummy that Fi's smile was doing right now. "I'm not all too concerned," she said carefully as she followed her friend further up the hill.

"Things not go well Friday?"

"She's cute, but…not really my type. She was just kind of…there."

"You haven't heard anything from Roger, have you?" Fiona asked, bending down to inspect a particularly ugly, lopsided pumpkin. She had always insisted the weird, malformed ones were the most interesting to carve.

"He's your boyfriend," Sabrina said with as normal a tone as possible. She didn't like talking about Roger. Didn't like thinking about him either, when she could help it.

"He hasn't been answering my texts." She sounded so hurt and confused that Sabrina was torn between sympathy for her friend and an increased resentment toward Roger.

"He was kinda pissed Friday," Sabrina offered tentatively, prodding the side of Fiona's pumpkin.

Fiona frowned at this revelation. "Pissed at me?"

"He was upset you ran off on your own. Didn't stick with us. With him. Something about you believing your own stories too much."

Her friend was silent, but her face seemed paler than ever against the strands of fiery hair blowing across her cheeks.

"What do you see in him, Fi?" Sabrina asked gently. She had been wondering all summer. She didn't hold much stock in boys anyhow, but Roger seemed like a particularly odd specimen. Especially for someone as wonderfully odd as Fiona.

Fiona furrowed her brow, looking as though she were choosing her next words with the utmost care. "He's friendly," she offered finally. "He's actually geekier than he looks. Likes to read, sometimes. A big dork for sci-fi. And…well, he's *interested* in me. He wants to learn about me, which is pretty endearing."

I should hope he wants to learn about you and not just make out with you all the time, Sabrina thought dryly.

It was clear Fiona didn't want to talk about this anymore, so Sabrina let it drop. But she couldn't help thinking about her own words regarding Rebecca, and if they could be applied to Roger, too. Maybe Fiona had been sad, and lonely, and Roger had been *there.*

I was there, too. You just didn't see.

FIONA

That evening, Fiona tried reaching Roger one more time.

She tucked the phone between her shoulder and her chin as she unwound her braid.

He picked up on the third ring, and Fiona nearly let the phone clatter to the floor in surprise. She hadn't really been expecting an answer.

"Thank God," she said. "You haven't been answering me, I was worried!" She tried to keep the reproach out of her voice, but it wasn't easy.

"The police came to my house today."

Fiona felt the blood drain from her face. Shit. "What? Why?"

"Why do you think? Trespassing, arson, the expected accusations."

"But how did they know—"

"My jacket."

It took Fiona a moment. Then it hit. Wearing Roger's letterman jacket on the walk over because she was cold. Stripping it off as they sat by the fire and laying it on the ground. Not grabbing it when she fled at the sound of sirens.

When she fled from *him.*

"Fuck, Roger, I'm sorry."

Silence.

"Are they charging you?" she asked, voice soft. Maybe this wasn't the end of the world. Maybe it would all—

"No."

Thank God. "Thank God," Fiona said, echoing her thoughts out loud.

"They figured me losing my job was punishment enough."

Shit shit shit. Roger had worked at the lumber yard since his freshman year. It was how he had been saving for college. He was supposed to work there until graduation and then through the summer.

"Roger," Fiona began, with not the faintest clue of what to say next, of what could possibly begin to make this right. "I—"

He hung up.

Fiona's mind was a mess of guilt and regret, but as she ran her hand over the bruise from where he had grabbed her, one thought jumped for the forefront of her mind. She was grateful this conversation hadn't happened in person.

ROGER

Thunk thunk.

The tree was old, and large, and stubborn.

Thunk.

But years in the lumber yard had made Roger strong.

Thunk.

And patient.

Thunk.

And more than anything, Roger was angry.

Thunk thunk thunk.

Angry at Fiona, for losing him his job. But mostly, for running from him. For never telling him a damned thing.

Thunk.

He thought of what he remembered of the story that night, when his mind was addled with beer. The girl had run from the man in the woods—run to her tree. The tree had driven the man away, so he had cut it down. When he saw her again, there was no tree to keep them apart.

Thunk.

Fiona had run from him, away into the woods. Had likely run to her tree after calling him a wolf. Did she think him the villain of her story? He didn't want to eat her heart. He just wanted it to be his.

But it was the tree that had it when it should have belonged to him, wholly and completely. So he would get rid of the obstacle, and when there was no tree, he would be the only one she could run to. The one to whom she would tell her secrets and give her heart.

With every blow of his ax, the tree spilled another secret. Some were Fiona's, while some were the voices of strangers long dead.

I never want to go home again.

Another whack.

I killed her. Oh god, I killed her.

Another and another.

I think I'm in love with her.

I don't think I can do this.

Then, with one last mighty swing, the ancient tree creaked and slowly tilted toward the ground. It slammed to the earth in a bone-jarring collision of wood and dirt and stone, and Roger heard one last secret as it fell.

Sometimes, I'm afraid of Roger.

Roger sat down on the stump, laid the ax across his lap, and waited.

FIONA

Fiona felt the impact in her bones, a tremor that started in her feet and shivered up to the tip of her skull. She knew what it meant.

That didn't stop her from running as if her life depended on it, as if it wasn't too late.

As if that crash wasn't the end of everything, and she could still put it right.

She knew what she would see when she dashed into the woods, but a cry still tore from Fiona's lips.

"Fiona," Roger said, getting to his feet. She noticed he still held the ax in his hand.

"What did you do," she whispered. It wasn't a question. She knew what he had done. She just couldn't comprehend it.

"I've rescued you," he said triumphantly, and his eyes were more wolfish than she had ever seen. "Your heart doesn't belong to that twisted *thing* anymore. It's mine alone."

"It doesn't work like that." She didn't know how it worked, really, but she hadn't been trapped by the tree. Hadn't belonged to it. Had she?

"It does," hissed Roger, and he sounded angry now. "It took you into the woods that night, away from me. I could have kept you safe, but it pulled you into danger instead. You ran from me because the tree twisted your mind. But it's gone now. For good."

Fiona shook her head. "You didn't hear the end of the story. You didn't hear what happened to the woodsman. You didn't hear what happened to the tree."

"I did," he snapped, slamming his ax into the stump where it stuck, quivering. "The woodsman cut it down because it kept him from the girl. Once it was gone, the girl's heart was his."

God, she had known Roger was drinking that night, but he really hadn't understood a thing. The beer had blurred his mind, and his own screwed up ideas had done the rest. He had taken her story and twisted it into something different and awful, something that he had wanted to hear.

"No."

"It doesn't matter. It's just a story."

"Nothing is ever just a story," Fiona said. "They all start somewhere. And some aren't meant to end."

Roger wasn't listening. His eyes were clouded with the remnants of the rage that had driven him to pick up the ax and the sense of victory that had allowed him to put it down. As far as he was concerned, she was his now. Her heart, and her secrets were his alone.

But there must always be a keeper of secrets, and there must always be a tree in the wood.

Fiona stepped forward and kissed Roger gently on the lips, then stepped back and screamed.

For a moment, nothing happened.

Then everything happened at once.

The roots of the tree still burrowed in the ground shot up through the earth and twisted around Roger in a suffocating embrace. He started to scream but was cut short as a root wrapped itself around his mouth.

He was dragged back to the stump, and Fiona watched in a detached horror as the roots devoured him. His legs were bound together into a trunk while his outstretched arms and fingers twisted and morphed into branches.

In no time at all, the roots swallowed him whole. The result was a small tree, barely taller than Fiona, but it still looked old. Every bit of it was twisted and warped, and moss grew upon its bark.

It held all the same stories, all the same secrets, passed from one tree to the next.

But it would get no more of Fiona's. After one last, lingering look, Fiona turned on her heel and left. She did not look back.

SABRINA

Bench.

That was all the text from Fiona said, but Sabrina knew what her friend meant. God only knew how many benches were in their town, but the girls only ever sat on one. They had sat there after Fiona was afraid to go home and show her parents the C- she got on a test; Fiona had held Sabrina there as she cried when her grandfather passed away.

It was where Sabrina found her friend now, looking pale and exhausted, her eyes red and puffy as though she had been crying.

Sabrina sat down next to her, and ran her fingers gently along a bruise on Fiona's forearm.

"What's this?"

Fiona didn't look up. "From the other night. He didn't mean to."

Sabrina's blood froze over. "You never said he hurts you."

"He never means to. He just gets angry or frightened, and... holds too tight."

"Fi—"

"It's over, Brina."

"What?"

"With him. He's...gone."

Brina arched an eyebrow. "Gone? That sounds awfully...suspicious."

Fiona didn't seem to hear her. "Do you believe in fairytales? In stories?"

"Parts of them. I think the stories come from somewhere. That's not to say that I believe in fairy godmothers or midnight kisses breaking spells or—"

"What about happy endings?" Fiona interrupted. She looked

up, finally, her green eyes meeting Sabrina's own. There was something to read in those eyes, but Sabrina couldn't decipher the language. "Do you believe in happy endings?"

Sabrina nodded as Fiona's fingers intertwined with hers. "Yes," she said. Then neither of them said anything for quite a while.

EPILOGUE

Fiona stopped telling her secrets to the tree. It had enough of them, and it wasn't really her tree. Not anymore.

Instead, she started to confide in people. She told her parents a few things here and there. She whispered her favorite stories to the scar-eyed, torn-eared black cat that followed her to and from school everyday. But mostly, she told her secrets to Sabrina because she discovered she didn't want to keep anything from her, even the things that scared her.

On the way back from school every afternoon, the cat trailing them like a shadow, they would take the long way home. They would skirt along the edge of town to the border of the wood, hand in hand. They would not stop; would not talk to the tree. Often times, they didn't even look at it.

Mostly, they were too busy looking at each other.

Fiona did not know if a part of Roger was still in the tree. If he could hear or see or feel what went on around him.

She did know three things:

There will always be a woodsman hungering for a heart of a lonely girl.

There must always be a tree to tell the tales of ages past and to hear the secrets of that lonely girl and keep her safe.

She was not that girl anymore.

S.M. ROSE

ABOUT THE AUTHOR

S.M. Rose is a Boston-dwelling writer with a love of all things spooky, but not scary. (Black cats, ravens, and ghosts? Yes. Clowns? Stay away). Their favorite color is not black, because the world is a cruel, cruel place and black is not a color. They are a writer of all things fantasy, and the owner of many swords. Some might say too many swords. Those people are wrong. *The Teller Tree* is SM Rose's first published story.

FROM HELL

BY TARA JAZDZEWSKI

It wasn't quite like flying. Although it had been many years since she had flown with her mother, Katherine remembered the sensations like it had been just yesterday. The feeling of the wind against her skin, gently lifting her russet hair as they moved through the night. Never having been taught how to fly on her own, Katherine used more creative ways to get out of her second story bedroom.

Instead of trying to find a way to climb down in the dark, Katherine dropped from her bedroom window. Unsure what the experience of falling so far would feel like, she braced herself as the ground rushed up to meet her.The soft earth of the expansive garden surrounding the mansion absorbed the majority of the impact.

Looking up at the second floor and the bedroom window, Katherine was glad she couldn't see what she had been doing; if she had been able to see how far down it was, she was convinced she wouldn't have followed through with her plan. Looking around to make sure none of the servants had woken up, Katherine slipped around the side of the house into the breezy night. The moonlight cast the garden in a silver glow that danced across her favorite plants: rue and feverfew, sage, lavender, mugwort, comfrey and chamomile. Medicinal herbs always spoke to her, just as they had to her mother.

Katherine paused at the rose hips, reaching out her delicate fingers to caress them. The softness of the leaves sent pangs through her. Her mother had taught her about all the herbs in the garden, but the rose hips had been her mother's favorite. It had only been six months since she had fallen sick and crossed to Summerland, and Katherine missed her deeply. She felt so alone now; life as an only child had been lonely enough, but with her mother gone, Katherine had been left to be raised by her aunt, while her father buried himself in his work at his shipping company.

Katherine's Aunt Josephine had never approved of Emily, Katherine's mother. Josephine was disgusted and outraged with her sister-in-law's charity work; women often seen as lowly or of ill repute frequented her brother's house, where Emily treated them for a number of maladies with her knowledge of herbs and magic. Once, when Katherine was young, she had asked her mother about her aunt's disdain. Emily smiled, explaining that it was their duty to help those worse off because they were in a position to do so.

Looking back to the dark house, Katherine sighed and rushed toward the back garden wall. Knowing that the gate would squeak when opened, Katherine sprinted for the last few feet and expertly jumped the low fence. Landing softly, she slinked through the lane towards the cobbled street which led to East London.

The gas lamps hummed as Katherine moved further and further from the security of her home and into one of London's well-off neighborhoods. She did her best to slide between the shadows and stay outside of the lamp light. Her heart pounded anytime she heard footsteps, and in particular, the sight of a man with a top hat and cane gave her pause. There had been rumors that Jack the Ripper was a surgeon or other man of wealth and status, like her father's friends. She hadn't admitted it to anyone, but Katherine worried he could be a man in her social circle.

HER HEART RACED as she slipped through the shadows and ducked down the alleyways. Being out late without a male escort was thrilling as well as terrifying for a young woman of her social standing. The chill night air bit through her dress, and Katherine pulled her cloak tighter, lifting the hood gingerly around her hair and tugging it closer to her face. She was thankful she had thought ahead and worn her hard-soled boots. At first, she thought her softer slippers would be best since they would make less noise on the cobblestones, but as she drew closer to White Chapel, the refuse of the city piled up in many of the alleyways. Pursing her lips, she held the handkerchief to her nose as she crossed yet another suspicious looking puddle.

Edging through White Chapel, Katherine felt the hairs on the back of her neck and arms stand up. Tension lay thick in the air. Successfully navigating the fog-thickened night seemed like a monumental task. Buck's Row was where they had found the body of Polly, the first girl. It was a rundown old thoroughfare into the Eastern Section of White Chapel. Why she had agreed to gather dirt from there in the dead of night was beyond her comprehension, but she dutifully ducked down and scooped up a handful before retreating back into the dark. Breathing heavily, she slipped away from Buck's Row as a police constable turned to make his rounds. Sticking to the shadows, Katherine prayed to the Goddess to guide her path and mumbled spells of protection between her pleas.

After reaching the pub, Katherine sighed in relief and opened the heavy oak door. Warmth caressed her face when she dropped her hood. The place bustled with the familiar sounds of patrons, and she took a deep inhale of the smell of spirits and stepped inside. Something soft bumped against her leg. Her coven's familiar, a black cat with a docked right ear, headbutted her leg again before slinking through the crowd toward the stairs in the back.

Following the cat was a challenge. Drunk male patrons sized her up as she crossed the room.She kept her head down, smiling demurely whenever someone spoke to her directly. The barmaids circled knowingly; every time one of the men thought of starting a conversation with her, they swept in to snare their attention, freeing Katherine to edge her way to the back of the pub. Whispering a spell under her breath, she sprinkled some dried herbs in the fireplace on her way by. The male patrons, shifted by an unseen force, cleared her path as she made her way down the steep flight of stairs in the back.

The black cat sat at the bottom of the stairwell. It appeared the cat was overseeing the preparations that were occuring in the large cellar below the pub. Katherine paused next to the cat, watching as her covenmates bustled around, setting up the ritual. Not paying attention to her surroundings, Katherine unexpectedly felt a prickle behind her and stepped out of the way, just before Tabitha crashed into her.

"Goddess, child, whatever are you doing standing there in the dark? Hurry, hurry. Get that dirt to the altar! It's almost time!"

Katherine hurried to the center of the large circle that had been sketched on the cool concrete floor of the cellar, examining the runes surrounding it as she made her way to her place. Eleven other women settled around the circle as Tabitha finished preparing the altar.

Anxiety welled up in her chest; heart racing and hands sweating, she hurriedly wiped them on her dress. Time stood still as she thought about the women who had visited her mother while she worked as a healer and midwife. Gleaning information from the papers and with some sleuthing on her part, Katherine had gathered the spectres they were slated to summon were the age of her mother. It was possible she would be faced with a woman she had met or helped her mother tend to. She prayed to the Goddess none of the victims tortured souls would be a familiar face this night.

Turning outwardly to face the women, Tabitha raised her voice. "Ladies, covenmates. We are gathered here to do our part. To protect our city from these unspeakable crimes. This has gone on too long! Four murders have been committed here in White Chapel. Mr. Lusk just received a letter from this so called Jack the Ripper."

The women exchanged looks. Usually Tabitha's monologues were comical, but today there was a heavy weight in her words. A hush settled around them.

"The letter was addressed *From Hell*. It is time that we come together and reached out to the other side. This Ripper must be stopped! The police have had many false leads. Tonight we summon those poor women and put to rest once and for all the identity of Jack the Ripper!"

The women clapped solemnly as Tabitha began her chant. Walking the circle deisul, her athame outstretched, Tabitha cast the circle around the coven, cut a door, and closed it behind her.

She gazed over the circle and warned, "Remember ladies, we cannot break the connection through the veil, it is tenuous at best. No matter what happens we must push on and get the answers we seek! No matter the cost! We cannot risk leaving a hole in the veil for spirits to cross here."

Slowly, she turned, and the chanting rose around her. The woman weaved protection charms around the space. The energy around the circle buzzed and hummed as webs of gossamer thread criss-crossed and created a bubble of protection. The protection spells in place, Tabitha turned and began invoking the four Watchtowers. She called Elementals and Ancestors, before drawing down the Lord and Lady. Katherine knew this spell was a massive undertaking, and its magnitude weighed heavily on the convenmates.

A howling wind filled the cellar. Katherine furrowed her brows. This wasn't right. An unearthly wail rose, and a shimmery blue light filtered through the veil between the worlds. The apparition looked like no spirit they had summoned before. A silver slash carved into her wavering form, her glistening blood shining in the eerie light. Her mouth did not move, but her form howled.

Tabitha spoke, her voice rising above the otherworldly din. "Polly, walker of the night," she said, "we are here to aid your spirit into rest. We plead with you, give us a description of your killer!"

The spirit's eyes searched the room wildly, hands gesturing.

"My killer? You would have me describe him?" She shook her head. Her mouth didn't move, but her voice filled the room anyway, as clear as the scratching of nails on a blackboard and as comforting as a spider dancing on your skin. "No. I cannot."

"Why not?"

"Because he'll hear me!" Her whole form shook with terror, and her voice railed again. "No no no, he's here now, he's watching, he's watching EVERYTHING."

"Polly! What...?" The unearthly blue light brightened, the smell of rotten eggs spilled into the room, and the distant sound of a baying hound rose above even the spectre's own howls. Polly's form wavered and disappeared.

The coven members glanced around at each other, confusion etched across their features. Uncertainty flashed across Tabitha's face as she readied herself to call the next spirit. Katherine could tell the others were concerned that they would repeat the experience with the next victim's apparition.

Tabitha quickly called forth the spirit of the next victim,

Annie Chapman. The room became so silent they could hear a pin drop. Katherine studied the others as she waited to see Annie's spirit. Suddenly it was as if all the air was sucked from the room. Katherine's eyes widened as she worked to fill her lungs. The others struggle to draw in breath as well. A thick white fog rolled across the floor of the pub, sending icy stabbing pain into the feet of the women. The rafters groaned and creaked, shattering the silence.

Inhaling, one of the women across the circle from Katherine called out "Annie, walker of the night, can you hear us? We seek to aid you and bring your killer to justice!"

The fog thickened, but no sign of Annie's apparition appeared. Feeling eyes on the back of her neck, Katherine looked toward the ceiling. Suspended in mid-air and upside down was the prone form of Annie, her soulless eyes bore into Katherine. Staring as if caught in a trance, Katherine held back tears, Annie had been one of the women her mother had treated right before her death.The wounds on Annie's neck and abdomen mirrored the ones she had seen on Polly. Katherine studied Annie's face, wondering if the poor woman recognized her.

The coven familiar hissed, its black fur raised high along its back, tail switching and docked ear pressed against its head. All around her the women murmured to each other, no one noticing that Annie and Katherine were locked in a mutual trance. Katherine caught movement out of the corner of her eye and looked to the rest of the women.

Shifting restlessly, the coven elders rearranged themselves while Tabitha joined the circle. Another elder, Mary, moved to the center of the circle and began to summon Elizabeth, the third victim. The temperature of the room shot up, the biting cold replaced by stifling heat. Suddenly, a loud bang reverberated throughout the room as a bright light flashed and blinded the women. Rubbing her eyes to clear them, Katherine screamed. The figure of Elizabeth rushed towards her with blacked-out eyes, nose, and no mouth. The specter raced around the room and randomly rushed at coven members. Enraged Tabitha aimed her athame at the racing specter.

"Begone! Away from this space!" she roared, silver spindles shooting from the ritual tool towards what should have been Elizabeth.

The air cooled immediately. Tabitha stood near the center, chest heaving. Bile rose in Katherine's throat; the circle remained broken, both Tabitha and Mary standing in the center. Normally this was no cause for concern, but it felt like a sign of foreboding.

The women shook, visibly uncomfortable. Katherine could tell that many were fighting the urge to object continuing the ritual, but Tabitha's warning hung in the air around them. Mary and Tabitha joined hands and confidently summoned Catherine, the latest victim. The energy around the circle tensed as everyone waited for the last specter to appear. The air did not change. The mood and the room stayed the same. Slowly, almost shyly, the apparition of Catherine appeared. She hung just inches from the ground, the gory wounds at her neck and abdomen apparent.

"Catherine," Tabitha's voice faltered. She steadied herself on Mary's hand. "Catherine, walker of the night, we seek to aid you. Please, we implore you, give us a description of your killer."

Catherine's apparition bobbed as she gazed balefully about the gathered group. A hollow voice filled the room.

"It is not a man you seek but a beast. A horrid creature of the underworld. He has used our organs to feed his hounds. He stands taller than any man I have ever witnessed. His eyes shone red with malice. And his breath can freeze a room. Just being in his presence causes fear..."

A low, mirthless laugh reverberated over the space. Catherine's apparition wavered, terror frozen across her spectral features. She blinked several times before fading from existence. The baying of hounds once again flooded the room;.

Katherine felt like a thousand eyes were on her. She raised her eyes. The apparition of Annie still stared down at her. Warm spittle caressed Katherine's hand as though she had been licked by a large dog before hot breath poured over the nape of her neck and something flicked the back of her ear. A long, sharp nail traced along her exposed skin as an icy, otherworldly voice boomed from behind her "End them now!"

Shrieks filled the room as the three specters of the Ripper's victims began terrorizing the convenmates, and the bellowing of the hellhounds drowned out Katherine's thoughts.

A putrid smell invaded her nostrils, and her head got heavy. Just as the surroundings darkened, a bright white light flared from the center of the room. She tried to focus her eyes on it as her head filled with cotton fluff. Her vision dimmed, and her knees buckled. As she felt her body slip towards the floor, she felt strong hands catch her.

"You have the power to stop this all."

The voice echoed in her head as she began to rouse. Looking around, Katherine was surprised to find herself in her room. She sat up, nothing appeared amiss. How did she get home? She could not remember what happened after the white light filled the pub's cellar. Worrying about the safety of the other coven members, she scrambled out of bed and raced toward the dining room, hoping to catch a bit of news.

Her aunt looked up from breakfast reproachfully as Katherine skittered to a stop before curtsying and hastening an apology.Josephine curtly accepted Katherine's apology. She inquired, as respectfully as she could, if her aunt had heard any news of the night before.

This question caused her aunt's face to sour.

Too late, Katherine realized that her aunt must think she was inquiring if there was another Ripper death instead of seeking the latest gossip in the debutante circles. Mumbling about her duties, Katherine turned to leave.

"Tis a shame about your mother's people, I was never quite sure what she saw in them, but each to their own."

Katherine quickly searched for an out to retreat away from her aunt's hawkish stare.

OVER THE NEXT SEVERAL DAYS, Katherine tried to focus on her role as a young lady of society. She attended teas and luncheons. However, as her fingers worked on her needlepoint, her mind replayed the events of that night over and over, shifting information around as though trying to piece everything together in a way that they hadn't fit before. After exploring every scenario possible, she realized nothing provided a logical explanation to the seance. That voice echoed in her mind, tumbling through her memories. She tried to figure out what the voice had meant.

Samhain was nearing, and Katherine knew in her heart that Jack had meant she was special, that only she could control him and find his true name and true nature. She would try and summon Jack on her own after all the evening's festivities had died down. Katherine felt Jack's voice had been sincere. The more she thought about that night the more the malice left his voice, and the more daring her to come to him was replaced with comradery. She buried her nose in her books and spent as much time as she could gathering supplies. The voice had said *she* had the power to stop this. *Not* the coven. She was capable of doing this alone. Her coven, decimated from Jack's attack; the few remaining survivors were severely injured.The coven had underestimated her Goddess given powers. Katherine believed the voice was telling her to do a naming ceremony. Once a being's proper name was discovered, a witch had power over it. No one else had assumed that letter to Mr. Lusk could possibly be that literal, but because of what she had seen that night with the coven, she now scoffed at that fact.

Jack the Ripper was not human at all.

Usually, Samhain was Katherine's favorite holiday. This year, however, she could not get into the spirit. She anxiously waited for the day's events to unfold and pretend to enjoy going through the motions that her aunt expected of her as a young lady in a certain station in life. The coven typically gathered for a Samhain celebration, but Katherine's aunt would never allow her to go, and with a lull in the Ripper killings, everyone had become wary. Complacency could lead to one being caught unawares.

After what felt like far too long, her aunt retired for the evening. Quickly and quietly, Katherine worked her way through her house to gather up her needed supplies. After closing the door to her room, she let out a sigh of relief and got to work creating a summoning circle. She carefully drew each symbol and took each step with the utmost care. This was Katherine's first attempt at summoning alone, and things had to be correct in order for her to maintain her safety.

When she finished, Katherine sat back on her heels, satisfied, and took several deep, calming breaths.Spreading her hands out, she chanted, drawing the power and magic to and through her. The air crackled with power, and the hairs along her body rose. Katherine knew without a doubt that this summoning would be successful and Jack would be ensnared in her circle.

Katherine opened her eyes, and a hazy form came into focus before her. Excited, she worked hard to maintain her concentration; her voice, enhanced by the electricity around her, booming into her ears.

"The one known as Jack the Ripper. Show yourself. I bid

thee come to this space and give me thy name! I command it! Give me thy name!" Her voice echoed, full of power, and her eyes flashed as she gazed at the form now crouched in front of her.

"Hello, my dear Katherine."

The words sent a cascade of cold down her back, as if someone had dumped a bucket of frigid water over her head. Jack laughed, casually throwing a shock of electricity, like a tiny, mocking of jolt of lightning at her, collapsing some of her protective wards. Katherine thought, he shouldn't be able to attack her from the summoning circle. Yet since he clearly could, why hadn't he killed her? Something was wrong. Something was very wrong. Katherine knew she was strong enough to handle it, and squaring off her shoulders, she strengthened her resolve. Her hair rose in a cloud as her hands directed power toward the circle. Ribbons of green magic encircled the being's arms and wrists, locking into place like chains. The thing in front of her did not struggle. Exhilaration from her power surged through her, buoying her up and erasing all doubts as to her strength.

Katherine again demanded the creature give her his name. When she finished, Katherine sat back on her heels, satisfied, and took several deep, calming breaths.Surely he had the capability to answer. What was stopping him from giving her the information that she wanted?

"The being known as Jack the Ripper! Name thyself! Where is it you hail from? Give me your proper name!"

With the last word, she focused all her might into sending more magic down the chains connecting her hand to his arms. He did not even flinch as the waves of magic hit his body. She gasped as he turned and tugged effortlessly on the magical chains, breaking them free from her hands. Horrified, she stepped back as his foot rubbed out the runes on the ground and he casually stepped outside of the circle.

An uncomfortable sense of nausea and general unease crippled her as her magic hurtled past. His movements seemed predatory, as if a wolf had caught a weakened deer. Each step slow and deliberate. Dread crawled up her spine, and Katherine trembled uncontrollably. She prayed to the Goddess that if he killed her it would be quick and painless. Images of his victims flashed through her head, and she dry heaved.

Doubled over, she didn't care how weak and exposed she was. His shadow crossed her line of sight, and she held her breath instinctively. Hot breath tickled the nape of her neck, and she fought off a scream that erupted up from her core.

"How DARE you try and summon me, girl! To think that you had the power, the capability," The last word came out as a hiss. His anger was palpable. His words flung toward her like daggers. "I will tell you *nothing*. You greatly underestimate me child! This was not what I meant when I told you that you had the power to change things."

The heat radiating from his body threatened to suffocate her. she smelled the sickly sweet combination of clove and cinnamon overlaying a stench akin to the rotting of flesh mixed with waste and vomit. Katherine sucked air through her mouth in slow, deliberate breaths, willing herself not to taste anything. His voice rang out again, pulling her thoughts away from trying to piece together the strange influx of information that assaulted her senses. "You will pay for your insolence, girl," his said, his voice dripping with venom.

Everything had stilled. Katherine cautiously lifted her head and looked around. There was no sign of Jack anywhere. Her summoning circle was in ruins. The remnants of the ingredients she had used smoldered to the side of the summoning space. This had not gone according to plan, and it took everything she had to not verbally berate herself as she began cleaning up the mess.

After erasing all evidence of the attempt, Katherine was not sure how to feel. She sat up late replaying the night's events in her mind. What had she done wrong, and how had things gotten so complex so quickly? Curling up under her duvet, she was surprised to see the coven's black cat was cleaning itself by the large mirror near her vanity. Crying softly at the mess she had made, Katherine wrapped her arms around herself, fingers playing with the lace around her nightgown. His voice reverberated in her head. Something bad was going to happen.

IN THE DAYS following her failed naming ceremony, Katherine couldn't help but hold her breath every time one of the servants brought news to her aunt or father. The more time that passed the more uneasy she felt. Given how angry Jack was, Katherine knew it was only a matter of time before he struck again, and it would take everything in her power to not blame herself for his next victim. Many times she had debated whether she should go to the Mother Coven's elders and tell them what she had done, but there would be no forgiveness over her cheeky and presumptuous decision to summon and name Jack alone. Hoping that she could avoid any punishment from the coven, she buried her worries deep into the furthest recesses of her mind.

Just before 11:00 am on November 9th, her father's footman rushed in to the study where she sat with her father and breathlessly shared that the Ripper had struck again, killing a woman named Mary Kelly near one of her father's holdings out in Spitalfields. The footman looked at Katherine before suggesting that a conversation of this gravity not be held in the company of a young lady. After glancing at her father, Katherine took her leave and promptly slipped down the hall to eavesdrop on their conversation from a more discrete vantage point. Her hand fluttered to her mouth as she heard the details of the gruesome murder and she turned, closing her eyes, willing herself to continue to listen. The horrors those poor women had to endure at the hands of Jack.

Racing to her room, Katherine shuddered at the story still playing in her head. As she plopped down at her vanity, something jerked in the large mirror next to her. Twisting to gain a better view, she saw nothing but her reflection. Shaking her head, she tried to clear her thoughts and closed her eyes to take several deep breaths. Her eyebrows knit together. Nothing should sound like knocking in her bedroom. *Tap tap tap*. There it was again. It sounded as if something was tapping on glass, but she was on the second floor. Opening her eyes, she looked around. Nothing seemed out of place. The window was clear of any flora or fauna, no person stood there. Clearly the events of the morning were making her hysterical. Turning back to fix her hair, once again she thought she saw something out of the corner of her eye pass in front of the large mirror.

Standing up, she shook her hands to rid herself of her anxieties. She stepped to pace and stopped in surprise. The familiar was perched on her sewing chair. It seemed completely unperturbed at the events occurring around her, further solidifying in her mind that she was making herself hysterical and that what she was seeing couldn't possibly be real.

Sunlight fell over Katherine as she sat down opposite the cat. She pulled her embroidery into her lap, hoping the repetitive task would help clear her mind. While she focused on the needlework, she hummed softly. Besides the occasional lick coming from the familiar cleaning itself, the room was so quiet she could hear the needle piercing the silk fabric. Things seemed peaceful, and she calmed, confirming in her mind that she had sent herself into a fit of hysterics earlier.

THE GRANDFATHER CLOCK in the hall chimed loudly, shocking Katherine awake. As the gonging continued and she looked around the pitch-black room in confusion. She dropped the needlework into a glowing pale-blue puddle on the floor and scurried to find her oil lamp. Fumbling to light it, she frantically checked the room. The familiar was gone, and the last dolorous notes of the gong reverberated with an ominous echo. The air was still: not even the flame flickered and a heavy cloak of tension hung over the room.

Stepping into the hallway, Katherine couldn't shake the feeling that something was terribly wrong. Within steps, her fears were confirmed. The grandfather clock just outside of her room stood motionless, the pendulum frozen in place. The clock face still read minutes before noon. She couldn't piece together how the clock had woken her up.

Her heart leaped to her throat as the hair on the nape of her neck stood up. If the clock was still sitting at a few minutes to noon, she hadn't fallen asleep, and the thought filled her with dread. Long ago, Katherine's mother used to tell stories of this place, this *In Between*. She had thought they were just dark tales meant to scare children. She tapped her chin and desperately willed herself to recall more of what her mother had said.

Lost in thought, her eyes unfocused, and she no longer saw the clock face. It was easy to lose oneself in the silence of the *In Between*. An idea came to her, and Katherine wondered if she could access the ritual herbs stored in her bedroom, drying after being picked from the garden. A loud groan spilled out from somewhere down the hallway. Katherine's heart skipped a beat. There should be no noise. It was impossible. Then the clatter of dozens of paws came from behind her, and a sudden panic shook her shook her into action. She raced to her room.

Her hands were slick with sweat as she fumbled with the door knob. Blood was pounding in her ears as the door finally came open. She rushed inside and slammed it closed, pushing her back against it, panting. When her breath recovered she looked for her supplies. She hurried over to her vanity and froze, her whole body going rigid and cold, until her brain processed that the creature in the vanity mirror was not standing in the center of her room. A sinister smile curled his lips upward.

"Jack," she breathed his name out, barely above a whisper, terror gripping her soul.

Her mouth dropped open as his voice rang throughout the room and in her head; omnipresent and impossible to escape.

"I told you Kat, you have the power to stop this. I brought you here to offer you a chance, to stop the murders, and save London from the infamous Jack the Ripper."

Her blood ran cold as she understood what he was offering. How could she stop the killings? He kept mentioning she had the power to make all of these changes, yet she felt incredibly inept. What could she possibly do to make him stop? She had failed at summoning him and could not even keep him within the confines of the summoning circle. He didn't speak, almost as though he was waiting her out.

"How can I stop the killings?" Her voice sounded strong and confident, the complete opposite of the terror she felt inside.

"I am here to offer you a trade. I am offering your soul for theirs. Can't you see Katherine, all of this has been drawing you closer to me. I was angry at you for your insolence, yet I was able to forgive you after that last woman's death. Her sacrifice sated me enough to clear my head and bring you back to me."

Katherine's heart dropped. She should have let go of her arrogance and her fear of punishment. The Mother Coven would have been able to help her. Now it might be too late. "My… soul? So you aim to kill me then? What good would killing me be? How does this satisfy you?"

"You misunderstand child. I am not asking to kill you, I am asking to take you with me."

"Take me with you?" She paused, thinking carefully over what he meant. "I go with you, and you stop the random killings?"

A faint chuckle reverberated off the walls. Her skin erupted in gooseflesh as the temperature around her plummeted. The house rumbled.

She contemplated his words. Could she make that decision? Would he stick to his word and end the killings if she went with him? Her mind raced through the possibilities. A single thought rose above the others. Mum. Oh what a thing to have to think about. She had been content knowing that one day she would rejoin her mother in Summerland. If she believed that Jack that he would stop the killings and she left with him, she would have to give up the thought of ever seeing her mother again. She mulled over her choices, trying to decide if this was a decision she could live with for eternity.

"Tempus fugit, Child."

She smiled wearily. "Yes. Time flies."

For the first time since waking, Katherine felt like she had the upper hand. Decisions needed to be made. The possibility of stopping the killings was too great. It was her duty to protect London, a way to honor her family name in a way that was empowering to her. Standing tall, she set her shoulders and looked the creature square in the eye. A smug grin spread across his face.

"I accept your offer. I will go with you. And you will stop killing women." Her voice never wavered.

Knowing her words rang true and a deal was struck, Jack's malicious laugh rang through the room as his hellhounds bayed in delight. A hand reached through her vanity mirror. Her brain fought to flee from regrets about this choice, but she knew it was the right decision. Although her fingers trembled, she stepped forward resolutely. Slowly she climbed onto her vanity and met the outstretched hand. Longing for a sense of peace,

Katherine resolved to take in every last sensation her body experienced on this plane. Taking a deep breath, she let go of control and felt the hand tugging her forward.

The mirror swirled as her fingers made contact. She was not sure what she was expecting, but the glass was icy and strangely viscous. A sharp tug from Jack pulled her nose within inches of the mirror. Katherine took one last deep breath as he pulled her to him. The mirror was dark, she hadn't quite expected not to see. Thinking something must have gone wrong, she began to struggle against the sensation of the air being crushed out of her lungs. Her limbs writhed in protest. She fought to keep her mouth shut, unwilling to inhale the viscosity around her. Jack's sharp fingers clenched tight around her wrist, she felt the icy grip with painstaking detail. Her body screamed to take a breath, to fight, to live. With one final thrash, her body accepted its fate, and Jack's arms surrounded her, bringing her home.

TARA JAZDZEWSKI

ABOUT THE AUTHOR

Tara was born in a moonbeam on the blackest of nights and has spent her life sharing joy and desire with everyone she meets. She's an active part of the twitter writing community (@JazdzewskiTara) and is working on several projects, including two memoirs and fiction novels. Currently she resides in Western Washington and enjoys baby bats, playing with her children, and historical research.

CONSTELLATION BOY

BY DIXON REUEL

"To grieve is to carry another time."
- Matthew Salesses

When Captain Finch Turlow jolted awake only a third of the way through his sleep cycle, he felt every month, week, and second of the thousands of years it took for *The Kapernic* to fulfill its objective. Billed as mankind's "Journey of 200,000 Years" from first ape to star travelers, the ship's mission was to build Earth's first colony on a planet beyond our solar system.

That slogan stuck throughout *The Kapernic*'s construction and launch. It stuck through the initial three years its crew traversed the solar system, throughout the long stasis-sleep that followed as they travelled into deep space. Into the space beyond the Oort Cloud and the Hydrogen Wall. *The Kapernic*'s crew, when they finally entered orbit of the Planet Deka in Alpha Centauri, woke from stasis to a prerecorded message from Earth, which praised the 200,000 years it took humanity to make it this far.

As soon as Finch relived the accident in *The Kapernic*'s

thermal outlet that took his son's life, once nightmares came of heat and screams and firebreak hatches that would not open, Finch knew to just get out of bed. No more sleep this cycle. Even though Apec died three years into *The Kapernic*'s voyage through the solar system, just before the crew went into stasis, Finch dreamed as if Apec died yesterday. The slam of the thermal outlet against a teenager's still-growing bone. His boy's shriek. The hissing flush of heat into the outlet, preventing any rescue until cleared. No more sleep this cycle.

His bare feet welcomed the cold floor as Finch stood and left his sweaty, rumpled bed. When Finch decreased the opacity of his quarter's windows, the blood-orange curve of Deka dominated his room. He ignored the fuming planet. *The Kapernic* would enter orbit and begin the landing phase of their mission soon enough. Finch already grew tired of looking at Deka.

In the tiny bathroom afforded to a mission captain, he splashed ice-cold water on his face. As the water ran down his stubbly chin and soaked into the collar of his sleepshirt, Finch remembered the handwritten note stuck to his mirror.

"I am not my mind," Finch felt like an idiot as he read the affirmation aloud. But if the ship's neurals did not hear him say these words within a few minutes of a disrupted sleep cycle, it would mean another visit to their doctor. After so many appointments with that AI console and the mission so close to its end, any more doctor visits would jeopardize Finch's captaincy. He knew, from accessing his medical records in secret, that he teetered on the edge of another crew member being woken to replace him.

So, he pressed on.

"I am not my mind. My mind and my thoughts are products of an organ that can misfire, just like any other." Finch's pulse thumped in his throat as he spoke. Loss, grief, tempered and categorized as merely a misfired organ. If Earth did not see him completely deal with Apec's death, Finch would be pulled from the mission, put into stasis, returned to Earth once *The Kapernic*'s colony eventually founded and flourished. And they remembered his static body. Finch splashed his face again and gasped at its iciness.

"My thoughts are products of an organ that can misfire. Just like any other."

Apec's body, too. Not to be buried in this new, Deka world. "Corpses back to Earth", that was a footnote in the mission brief. Why people could not be cremated or shot into space, Finch had no idea. Even in their Arctic training for this mission and further training on Neptune's polar base, a corpse was always treated as a storage problem. Maybe the new colonists would have a different attitude towards death than Earth. Finch stared into his bloodshot eyes. Maybe they would allow burials on Deka yet.

He spoke the affirmation aloud again and again, until he gauged that his "misfiring brain" got the message. And the ship's listening neurals. Finch saluted his reflection and left his quarters. Since he had been such an obedient boy by enduring the theatrics of his affirmations, Finch reasoned that a visit to the freezer–only the second visit this week–would be okay.

"My constellation boy," he whispered to the lifeless face behind the container's window. There had not even been a wake. The neurals would not have allowed such grief-wallowing.

Apec had not time to outgrow a teenage boy's too-long eyelashes before his death. A little black cat lay tucked against a faintly-stubbly cheek, a stuffed toy from childhood. Limp grey threads hung from the gaping spaces in its worn face where the eyes had once been. Now sightless. The ear hung to the side of the cat's blank face, never to be resewn

A dynasty, such an arrogant thing to want, Finch admitted as he stared at Apec. Finch and son exploring space together, founding colonies, one day pairing Apec with a Deka colonist. A frontier dynasty nicely planted for the ages and Earthlings to come. Then Finch could die in peace. That had been the dream. But now Apec's makeshift coffin nestled in *The Kapernic*'s freezer, alongside shelves lined with the frozen embryos of future colonists. The little black cat stared, unseeing, at Apec's not-yet shaven cheek for eternity.

No mother; Finch decided to have a son without any of that or getting married. He would have raised his son to adulthood. Raised him beyond any of Earth's expectations. Finch's thoughts wandered as chilled air nagged at his lungs. A son to follow in Finch's footsteps as not just an astronaut, but an explorer. On an interstellar, galactic scale. The Turlow family name written in the stars.

"Captain Turlow?" Lieutenant Danaher's voice sounded from the mic inside the freezer, "You're up?"

"Yes, Danaher, I'm up." He waited for her to scold him.

"Captain, come to the main console. There's–"

Finch waited. When no further explanation came, he frowned and tapped the mic. "There's what?"

"Just come," she said, her usually cheery voice deep and somber.

Then added, "Hurry."

"The planet's not empty." Lieutenant Danaher looked up from the main console as Finch climbed into the front bay.

Deka's enormous surface blazed below them, as if made of fire. But no, its warm-hued, dusty surface only bounced light from the nearby star, the red dwarf Proxima Centauri. Vibrant yellow and orange storms swirled across the front bay's windows.

"I'm sorry, what was that?" Finch blinked as her words filtered into his brain. He looked about for the other two: Lieutenant Caffrey, who had awoken from stasis to replace Apec, and Lieutenant Sewell. Finch slid into the seat at the main console's enormous curved screen. As he sat, exhaustion flooded through his limbs. "Say that again?"

"Sewell and Caffrey are still in their sleep cycle. It's my turn to stay up overnight." Danaher tapped the screen in front of him. She enlarged their proposed landing site. "There's something down there. Deka's not as barren or empty as we thought."

Finch's heart made an odd flutter. From lack of sleep. From Danaher's news. From a sightless black cat. Finch did not know. Their mission turned on its head–really, a tiny part of him was secretly surprised they had even made it to the Alpha Centauri star system and lived. Surprised to be here at all.

As he sat there, his limbs felt oddly attached to his frame. His brain conjured more flashes of Apec's accident. Deka's dust no different to the dust from the accident in the thermal outlet. Finch felt out of touch, warped and tired. His captain's training took over and formed words and responses despite his exhaustion. "Something down there, like a rock formation, a geological feature? There are ancient ice flows on Deka that are long barren. They can look manmade, especially since we're entering orbit. What does telemetry say?"

"No." An edge in Danaher's voice cut into his babbling as she tapped the screen again. "Something living. One thing alive on the whole of Deka."

The damp collar of Finch's sleepshirt hugged clammy against his throat. *I should have dried my face better,* he thought.

"Captain Turlow?"

Finch realized he stared blankly into her face. A deep well of concern had grown within Lieutenant Danaher ever since the crew woke from stasis. Finch always had to be extra careful around her. Danaher, out of the other two who were awake, she was the one closest to pulling the trigger on his captaincy. Out of pure concern for his well-being, of course. Finch blinked through the blankness that enveloped his brain and focused his attention back onto the screen.

"What do you mean *something living*, Lieutenant Danaher? There's quite the spectrum - you mean something large and walking, or bacteria? We would have never been sent here if the former was the case. Even if the powers that be on Earth knew Deka held life–any life–we would have been briefed. And we would have brought the equipment we'd need, whatever that might be..." he babbled as he read the telemetry report that trailed across the bottom of the landing site's footage.

Danaher did not answer. She pinched a section of the screen with her forefinger and thumb. It zoomed into Deka's surface. The image blurred for a moment, then sharpened and showed Deka's lone life sign.

A Grim Reaper–a proper Grim Reaper of Earth lore, resplendent in flowing black robes hanging from a fleshless skull–floated right above the center of their landing site's coordinates. It did nothing, but waited.

"The fuck?" Finch jumped.

"I know."

"What the fuck?" Finch gasped and maneuvered the ship's camera. It swung around the grim specter and built a 3D profile. Finch automatically, out of training, diverted the camera feed into the ship's neurals so it could come up with an explanation.

"I know, I've..." Danaher straightened from the main console. Her uniform's smooth navy fabric bunched and wrinkled as she wrapped her arms around her middle. A deep line furrowed between her eyebrows. "I noticed it about an hour ago. And I've been staring at it ever since. It has to be fake. But it's not." She hugged herself tighter.

"This thing is really down there?" Finch asked as all sensation drained into his toes, leaving the rest of his body cold and numb. *Mission over, mission over, mission over,* his brain screamed as he watched the screen in disbelief. This ghost, alien, or whatever, would undo *The Kapernic*'s entire mission. The whole journey for nothing.

Danaher nodded. "Ship seems to think so."

Finch studied the floating specter. As he ran through every corner, paragraph, and pocket of the mission briefing, his mind stalled on one of its captain-only chapters, titled *Encounters. Is there a chance to complete the mission, despite this...effigy,* he wondered?

"Captain Turlow, what do we do?" she said, voice trembled.

"We are ordered in the mission brief to make contact," Finch said and realized that *The Kapernic* might just have been a suicide mission all along. Had Earth known? Had they been sent to Deka to make first contact under the guise of "boldly going" to found a colony? Had they really sent him and his boy on such a lengthy star-journey of exploration, only to be martyred?

"Make contact ... with that thing?" Danaher spluttered. "How? From, from afar? *The Kapernic* doesn't have a microphone, a speaker system, not to the outside." Tears dropped down her cheeks. She gasped an astounded laugh as her arms squeezed tighter around her middle. "Why would it?"

The hooded specter stayed still in the camera feed. Finch could easily claim first contact with an alien, he realized. That would be quite the feather in his cap. But that was not his mission objective. He had come to Deka for a different reason entirely.

"I suppose…" Danaher said after a long silence. "We could flash some of the exterior lights at…whatever that thing is. It can't be the Grim Reaper. That just, it can't. That just doesn't make any sense."

"No. Not contact from afar. We need to disembark," Finch said as the text of *Encounters* filled his brain. "First contact has to be one-on-one contact, as much as possible. To eliminate misinterpretations." Roughly another week before they would receive a transmission from Earth, wishing them luck right as *The Kapernic* was supposed to land on Deka. Throughout his entire career Finch had been trained for the bizarre, the unknown, for life not as they knew it. But not for–

"The familiar," he murmured and watched the Grim Reaper float.

The Reaper turned as if it heard him and stared up, sightless, into the camera.

FINCH, as captain, would stay behind.

If this were the normal course of their mission, Finch would have remained aboard *The Kapernic* anyway, until he got the all-clear from the initial ground crew regarding Deka's environmental suitability, that the surface levels of solar radiation were as calculated. And until he got the all-clear, that their colony pod had safely deployed and was entirely self-sustaining, with the first wave of embryos already gestating and the colony air farms flushed, errorless, into life. Only then could the captain disembark *The Kapernic*.

He had not been jealous of Danaher when he learned of this mission protocol. Indeed, Finch had felt quite the Michael Collins of Earth's first lunar landing. He was content to stay onboard while the other crew first entered the alien world. The captain would supervise the fully-automated initialization of the colony pod from *The Kapernic*.

But now, with that specter abroad, he itched to approach it.

They had to wait several aching hours for one of Deka's dust storms to pass before it was safe to land. Finch and Danaher stood outside the airlock, with Lieutenants Sewell and Caffrey inside, the team of two ready to disembark. The pair along with Danaher, who would follow Sewell and Caffrey once they were safely outside, wore full-coverage exploration suits, replete with noisy filtration systems and thick thermal conduit padding, all encapsulated in flex cladding.

The Kapernic handled their descent to the surface automatically.

"By how much did you move the new landing site?" Finch asked as the ship took them down from orbit.

"Not far. Only a few hundred meters. We'll park up on a new spot that's pretty much right alongside that … that thing…" Danaher finished putting on her suit and installed Deka's environmental update from *The Kapernic*'s neurals. There was an awkward pause, then she piped up. "I know we can't keep asking ourselves what's out there. But you all should know that I ended up dubbing our new landing site 'Star Harbor.'" Before she lifted her helmet, Danaher grinned into the airlock at Sewell and Caffrey, then turned that prideful grin on Finch.

Despite his sleep-deprived state, Finch blushed at the hankering for adventure that shone clear on her face. Despite everything, her smile disarmed him. Danaher rounded off her grin with a muffled giggle as her helmet went over her head and slotted into the rest of her suit. The giggle sent a tingle through Finch's veins.

Danaher spoke with such hope, as if their whole mission were still possible. The final heat transfers from their descent flushed through the ship's cladding. As he listened to the transfer's hiss, Finch realized that, since Apec's death, he had just gone through the motions without experiencing such hope or joy. He had thought they would see the journey through but would probably all die before landing on Deka. Finch heeded the gravity fluctuation warning lights and grabbed the nearest handhold. He still wore his sleepsuit and had trailed after the other three, like an unwanted younger brother that tagged along, while they prepped and suited up to disembark. A harbor meant safety, Finch thought as he clipped himself into place on the handhold beside the airlock door. It meant hope.

"Star harbor," Finch could only fuzzily repeat her words as his tired face broke into a smile for the first time in ... well, he could not even remember.

"Sure, why not?" Danaher answered over their mics.

Inside the airlock, Sewell tightened the suit straps around Caffrey's waist and cinched them both into neighboring handholds alongside the outer door.

"Deka's gravity checks out. No tethers needed." Danaher noticed that the two inside the airlock lacked the long cable that usually slotted between the shoulders of their suits.

"No. No need to tether them for reasonable gravity," Finch agreed, "You'll all move faster without a tether, anyway. Either towards that thing, or away from it."

The tremors of their descent intensified. As captain, he was glad for the self-piloting aspects of this mission. Apec had been devastated he would not be able to watch someone manually pilot *The Kapernic*, but Finch was delighted they would not have a pilot. The less chance for human error, the better.

"Hey, Danaher?"

"Hmm? Yes, Captain?"

"Whatever you're all about to meet out there, just..." he said to the black reflectiveness of her helmet. Already, Finch struggled to remember her brown wavy hair. Suddenly, he wanted nothing more than for Danaher to remove her helmet and for everybody to laugh at how her hair would remain frizzy for several hours after being squashed beneath the inner cloth cap. *Star harbor indeed*, he thought.

"Just be careful."

After making Earth history as the first ship to land on an extrasolar planet, Danaher, Sewell, and Caffrey left *The Kapernic*. Finch, still in his sleepshirt, returned to the front bay to monitor his crew, to watch that ghoulish specter that paid no heed to the people leaving the airlock. The Grim Reaper only stared right back through the camera with empty eye sockets.

Finch thought of that little sightless cat tucked against Apec's cheek

He recalled a song that he once, in a fit of ancestry tracing, recovered from the Turlow family archives: a recording of his great, great, many–great grandfather singing an old Irish tune.

"Where old ghosts meet," Finch muttered as he watched Sewell and Caffrey leave *The Kapernic* and approach the landing site. Danaher followed shortly after.

WHEN ONLY FINCH WAS LEFT, when Sewell and Caffrey died–their minds dismantled by the effigy so they ran screaming towards the nearest line of cliff and flung themselves into nothing, when Danaher clamored back inside *The Kapernic*, Finch finally left the front bay.

"Something's wrong! Seriously, seriously wrong! Some kind of hallucination!" Danaher pulled off her helmet as she scrambled through the still-opening airlock doors and pushed past Finch.

"Did you see Sewell and Caffrey?" she screeched as she dropped her helmet and ripped off her spacesuit's cladding and oxygen cases. "A kind of hysteria, Captain. Something must have leaked in *The Kapernic* when we landed!" Helmet off, Danaher's wavy hair stuck to her sweaty, flushed face. Danaher hurried into the next pod, into environmental control, and inspected the array of smooth switches set into a wall of consoles.

Finch frowned. Her helmet came to rest against his foot. He did not follow Danaher into the pod, only stayed just outside its door and listened to her rattling and fussing.

"Sewell just approached that specter, greeted it, then the next thing I know he's flung himself off a cliff. Caffrey with him. We're hallucinating. At least you and I have the presence of mind to realize that. We might be able to get away."

The airlock had two doors. From where Finch stood in the tight corridor, the windows in each airlock door lined up and let him see the Grim hovering outside, a few hundred meters away. Deka's yellow dust clung to its robe's tattered hem. *No, it's really there,* Finch noted. It remained in the middle of their old landing coordinates, its stare boring right into the ship at him.

He shivered/he shrugged/he turned away.

"If that thing is a Grim Reaper or whatever–" Danaher went on as she checked the air integrity, "–couldn't he just float right inside this ship? Why is he just in one spot? See? Makes no sense."

"Maybe it's a recording?" he suggested. Despite Sewell and Caffrey's deaths, Finch felt calm. Tired. Sure, a part of him screamed they should hit reverse and begin the long return to Earth, or get as far away from Deka as possible. But another part of him felt completely serene, as if all of this were perfectly logical, and they just needed to accept it.

"Maybe it's like a hologram of some kind? Left by an old civilization?" he wondered, out loud. Nothing in his body panicked. Finch was startled at the ghoul's presence at first. But now, even with the loss of Sewell and Caffrey, he just let Danaher's words wash over him.

Finch peeked into the pod of consoles and found Danaher performing a syringe flush of one of the decontamination filters. "What did you mean by 'get away?'"

She sat back on her heels from the enormous slatted vent that housed the filter. Danaher spoke deliberately at him, as if there was no other possible course of action to take or other interpretation for their situation. "Get away–" she waved her tools around, "–from here."

Finch frowned. "As in, we return to...?"

"Earth." She resumed the flush of the decontamination filter.

"But we can't go anywhere if we're hallucinating Grim Reapers!" Danaher thumped the filter's display with her gloved fist. Its readout showed *The Kapernic's* air toxicity levels operated at perfectly normal levels. She cursed and removed more of her suit's arm cladding for easier access to the filter's narrow chambers.

Finch waited in the doorway, just glad she did not demand his help.

Danaher flung aside more pieces of her spacewalk suit and hauled off her inner cloth gloves with her teeth. She spat them aside as she continued to work on the filter. "That thing out there has obviously taken a form that most people from Earth's culture would recognize. That we meet a caricature of death? Out here, on Deka? In space? Come on, Finch, think. It's too perfect, too suspicious. That thing is designed to make us go away."

"Maybe it's just lonely," he muttered. Finch glanced out the airlock window again. Death had not moved.

"It's not real," Danaher barked and flung her empty syringe into the corridor at him. "How can the Grim Reaper appear on Deka? Because it isn't really there. We're the ones who're sick, Captain!"

When she called him captain, something flipped in Finch's chest. Yes. He was captain. Trained. Pulled every string to get his son on this mission. First colony away from Earth. He and Apec. With Apec's death, his thoughts of legacy and lineage had drifted away between the blackness of the stars. But he could admit this, now that they were landed and safe, that there still remained a chance at founding something on Planet Deka, a landscape that was so far unsullied by all that Earth had become. Was hope possible even with that thing outside?

"You know… you know, Captain?" Danaher eyed him as she worked. "We are not our minds," she told him, pointedly.

Cold washed through his veins when he recognized her

words. Danaher watched him with that ever-present concern of hers. *To see if I snap and go crazy, too. Like Sewell or Caffrey.*

"Excuse me?" he asked.

Danaher's lips pressed into a firm, flat line as she tried another syringe flush of the decontamination unit. "I know that you had unauthorized access to your medical files. That was Apec's doing; he found you a backdoor into the neurals."

Not that it mattered right now, but Finch could not help but feel slighted at her intrusion. "You read my records?"

"You mean, you read your own?" She glared. "When you, of all people, really should not. But, anyway, we are not our minds, Finch. Our minds can misfire. That's exactly what's happening right now. We're hallucinating. Probably a firmament breach, or a thermal fluid vent is backed up and leaking. Although *The Kapernic* should have alarms blaring right now. We're the only two conscious to experience this. We must lock this leak down because we cannot wake any more of the crew. They'll only be affected too, infected. That'll endanger the whole colony, all the embryos."

"And the whole mission. We are not our minds," he chimed in, although he still chafed that Danaher knew about his medical files. Those stupid affirmations.

"Exactly," Danaher went on. "We're the living proof right now that the human brain can misfire just like any other. Imagine mission control receiving our message, that we've encountered the Grim Reaper on Deka? They'll detonate the ship."

"Detonate?" he asked in confusion. But then realization hit Finch. Of course, mission control would have a remote self-destruct on *The Kapernic*. Of course, they would. The moment Earth countered anything unsavory–*bzzt*–nuke from orbit. Finch nodded as her words rang true.

"You didn't know this, as captain?"

"So, what do you propose we do?" Finch hated the notes of pity in her voice.

She sat back on her heels again, the soles of her boots flashed bright yellow, caked with Deka's dust. Danaher lifted her arms and dropped them in resignation. "Abandon plans to settle the colony. Ignore that thing out there. Return to Earth with the colonist embryos safe. At the very least."

"Return to Earth? Do you know how long that would take? How long we would have to go back under stasis?"

Danaher wiped away a sudden tear and sniffled. More tears spilled again when she nodded. "Initialize the auto-tow. Return to Earth."

Finch eyed the empty syringe that had bounced off his shoulder and now lay at his feet next to her helmet. Without the usual metal needle of a medical syringe. No, to flush thermal fluid called for a thick polytrinium tube, rather than a sharp needle. He could incapacitate Danaher in other ways, though.

"Astronauts must always return home or drift away into the black. I suppose," Finch muttered.

Danaher stared at him through her tears, face red and blotchy. A tiny smile appeared as she sniffled and continued working on the filter. "I didn't realize you were a poet."

Finch shrugged and found the strength to smile too. "I suppose a good old hallucination is what's needed for poetry and songs."

Her chuckle at their impossible situation soon broke into chest-wracking sobs.

Finch watched her cry. And he wanted to crawl through the very plating of the ship to escape her sobs. His fingers found the red button on the control center's door. Danaher's final look to him was one of pity, pity that they should have to try and flee, pity that it would probably be their valiant fate to fail.

Finch knew he did not have an ally in her for the future he wanted.

He pressed the button, let the ship's neurals read his captain's fingerprint. He stepped back as the door slammed. Its inner seal hissed shut. Dampening vapor flooded the room and quenched its oxygen, as if to contain a fire. With only a blank expanse of grey door in front of him, Finch felt the slam of Danaher's body as she tried to get out. He only heard the sound once.

Then, and only then, did Finch leave *The Kapernic.*

HE WAITED until the next dust storm cleared. Then Finch trudged the few hundred meters across Deka's saffron-yellow surface, to the site of their old landing coordinates. The Grim Reaper finally moved again. It did not leave its spot. It merely turned in a surprisingly delicate motion to watch Finch's approach.

"So. Fucker. What are you, then?" Finch shouted several meters away from the thing, breathless from exertion. He gripped the heavy transformer box on his tether that attached him to *The Kapernic.* Sewell, Caffrey, they had not had this lifeline when the apparition decided to send them running over the nearest cliff. But Finch would be well–moored. Their fate would not be his. Finch had a colony to found. *What had Danaher called their landing site,* he thought. *Star harbor?*

"What are you?" he shouted again at the pristine skull floating in a cloak of black.

-When the very last thing on a planet dies, what happens to its gods?-

Finch startled.

He had not expected English. The familiar. Honestly, he had not truly expected a response at all. He felt as if he stood before a sphynx, his very soul in the balance. Before he continued, he tightened his grip on the tether.

"I guess..." Finch's brain scrabbled about for a suitable answer. He had not been outside *The Kapernic* since Earth. How strange to stand on a planet rather than in the artificial gravity of a ship. His body could tell the difference. Even his tongue felt heavy, jaws exhausted as if through too much talking. He chewed his lip before answering. "I suppose ... then ... that would make you the loneliest god?"

-No one left to reap. In a silence. Until you.-

If Finch wanted to initialize the colony setup on Deka, he would have to resolve this specter. Make it go away. Finch grimaced. He did not think his helmet microphone picked up the specter's words correctly. Or if it did, it was his own brain that incorrectly interpreted the Grimm's odd, slanted words. When he swallowed, his throat felt dry and so very small.

"And, are you really here?" Finch asked as his lips trembled. "Or am I imagining all this?"

-There is no difference.-

Despite everything, Finch had to laugh. "Oh, I think mission control back on Earth would have something to say about that!"

The Reaper's demeanor changed.

It delicately tilted its head, as if considering his words.

I should not have mentioned Earth, Finch realized, *nor mentioned that there was another planet of people to shepherd into an afterlife.* Then he understood. If the Grim Reaper stood before him, spoke to him, that meant–

"So there's a heaven?" he gasped, "There's ... life... something ... after our deaths?" Apec's forever sleeping face with his toy cat tucked against his cheek. Finch opened his mouth to ask, but the Grim spoke:

-After your lives, there are the revolutions of the Heavenly Spheres. A planet's motion affects what is seen in the heavens. The rules of Nature are not yet developed enough to prove correct. This will be proven correct when more of you come. From Earth.-

It floated almost sadly, the breeze blowing yellow dust from the tattered ends of its long black cloak.

Finch could not make head nor tail of the words that came into his ears. But the creature he spoke to did indeed communicate back and forth with him. And it seemed to pose no threat. It just seemed lonely. Finch stuck his feet firmly into Deka's soft, silt-like surface, stood taller in an attempt to rally his own gumption.

Let's communicate then, he thought.

"Do you know them? Do you know our dead?"

-I have not shepherded from Earth. Only this one.-

A sadness almost drowned Finch. He had hoped, even just for a moment, that someone else beyond Earth's reach knew of his Apec.

-You have lost?-

"I have lost–" he answered its question, then words failed Finch.

He gazed at the yellow dust beneath his feet. *The Kapernic*'s crew had, of course, trained in all conditions imaginable for this mission. But nothing could ever compare to this vermillion–orange landscape. His streamlined boots touched the alien planet, and Finch concentrated on how the tiny particles of dust powdered his boot soles. If Finch wept right now, tears would puddle against his eyes and he would not be able to see clearly anymore. He would have to return to the ship to fix it. In an effort to stop the tears from crying, he inhaled deeply, until his lungs hurt. Danaher's final thump of her body against a door, he heard that final sound deep in the thump of his own heart.

"A graveyard at the edge of the world is still a graveyard with the best view, I suppose," he muttered. His great-whatever grandfather, the singer, would no doubt be proud of his lyricism. He coughed and managed to say after a while, "I... have lost everything."

"My son, Apec, died on the voyage here," Finch spoke more.

"He was supposed to be one of us, one of the initial exploratory crew. Part of my team," he explained and glanced at the deep blue belly of Deka's sky. *What a background to think to.*

-Here-

Finch could not tell if it asked a question. He just nodded. "Yes, we came here. We ... humanity, whatever you want to call us, we finally charted every nanometer of our solar system. Then, after smug satisfaction, we came here. It's not good to explore every inch of home. We need to explore beyond home. There's an innate, deep need within us. To boldly go, right? We didn't go anywhere for such a long time, only muddled around on our planet, then eventually, later, the solar system. I watched logs of my grandfather chart the final valleys on Pluto, the discovery of four more planets–rocks merely!–beyond its orbit. We charted those rocks too. All the nooks and crannies of the solar system."

Finch watched the horizon and thought of those expeditions. The jagged line of faraway pastel peaks that touched the alien sky looked no different to his training grounds on Earth. This part of Deka could be Arizona, Death Valley, the Atacama. Anywhere. How could *The Kapernic* take them this far from home, only for it all to look so familiar?

-You never found it, other life?-

"The whole place was empty!" Finch ranted as words leaked from him. "Do you know what that does to a race of monkey-creatures? Nearly drove us all insane that we were alone. That's why, upon this expedition, I was going to be ready. I would bring my son. And where is he now to see this new world, to see our first alien? Dead in the freezer of that ship. Dead. A journey of 200,000 years," Finch muttered.

-We am.-

"I don't understand." He sighed impatiently. Finch just wanted to go to sleep. He felt so tired, bone tired. Just let him sleep. "That's not grammatically correct, what you just said. Explain again."

-We am.-

So, he thought in cold realization as the Grim continued to repeat itself in response to his demands for clarity, I am indeed hallucinating. At the end of his patience, Finch grasped stone and dust in his thickly gloved hand. Frustrated beyond words and sense, that Danaher had been right, that this was all in his head, he flung it at the demon. The stone made a beautiful yellow arc across the yellow sands. The dust faded as Finch turned and walked away. The stone had fallen through nothing.

IN ORDER TO found the Deka colony–to create Deka's dynasty of explorers–Finch began by first deactivating several programs within *The Kapernic*.

Specially, the running timer on the two other crew members. Those two would automatically wake from stasis sleep should Earth not receive a message in return to theirs, which would congratulate a successful landing. Then, if Earth received no response and those two crew never made further contact, meaning they never awoke, Earth would know *The Kapernic* had probably disintegrated upon entering Deka's orbit. Finch supposed all this as he ignored the Grim and climbed inside *The Kapernic*, down into its freezer.

The next interstellar mission would do better. That next ship, *The Gresham*, already under construction on mission control's secondary launch pad at the time of *The Kapernic* setting off, *The Gresham* would soon propel itself towards Deka once *The Kapernic* safely landed. Perhaps would arrive with better cladding, better insulation, better crew, better everything. The future would do better, Finch was sure of that. And his future pioneers and explorers, they would be ready.

The ship's neurals still worked away, still tried to posit a possible explanation for the specter's appearance. Finch relieved them of that burden and cleared the ship's neurals of any mention of the Grim.

Then he initialized the long and drawn-out setup of the colony pod. As it unfolded in the shadow of *The Kapernic*'s engines, he watched as it self-built, stabilized, and flushed through with power, oxygen, safety.

He also commenced the embryo growth programmed. Then Finch wrote for days, longhand, on actual paper he brought with him from Earth in case the same message he typed into *The Kapernic* somehow became inaccessible. He left the clearest of instructions on what was to be done. What was to be done with Apec's body. How future Dekans, once awoken and grown, could extract cells, DNA, clone Apec's essence as their true founding father. Finch insisted the future Dekans were to give Apec a proper burial. On Deka. For this was everybody's home now. *So, let that yellow dust hoard over all our bones forever,* he thought. *Let that Grim outside be the shepherd, even if it only existed in peoples' heads.*

As the days turned on board *The Kapernic,* Finch wept a few times that he would never see his constellation boy rule Deka. But then Finch only wrote longer, even more detailed instructions. The Turlow name would live on. As time passed, as hunger and thirst grew, as the Grim still waited ever so patiently for him, Finch became content that he could be the founder, but not the finisher.

When the last few days were upon him, he engaged the colony's hydroponic stack farms, the first greenery to flourish and grow outside of Earth's solar system. But he would not take up any more resources. Those now belonged to the future colonists. Finch would leave and pilgrimage instead. He felt himself to be a tribal elder taking to the horizon in secret, to pass away on their own terms, leaving the future of the tribe behind to thrive.

It should remain as a warning to the living that you are not your mind, Finch wrote to the future colonists, to Apec's future children, *Your mind and your thoughts are a product of an organ that can misfire just like any other organ in your body. It will take a journey of 200,000 years to learn that. Do not forget.*

Finch turned on *The Kapernic*'s long-range communications one last time and sent the final message. He repeated what he told the colonists. He warned Earth to send more ships, and quickly. So they all would thrive. Even *The Gresham*'s crew needed to know. The living were not their minds.

As Finch finished his creation, the day came when he approached the Grim and held out his hand for the loneliest god to take. His gloves passed right through the Grim Reaper's transparent, bony fingers. Finch faltered, until he stuck his arm out at the correct angle and locked it there. It now looked like he held the Reaper's hand.

"Where old ghosts meet," Finch muttered to nothing as the Grim finally moved from *The Kapernic*'s landing site and walked with him.

Several days into the hills that surrounded Star Harbor, he passed through hunger and thirst and lay down in the shade of a rock outcrop in a dried-up ice flow. He stared at the sightless little black cat he had taken from Apec's makeshift coffin and strapped onto his spacesuit's arm. For company.

Finch tutted. It was too late to return to *The Kapernic* for a sewing kit and stitch the cat's little ear back on, or give it eyes.

"Just wanted some company," he explained hoarsely to the Grim.

It nodded. It understood.

Back on Earth, mission control received the last message from *The Kapernic*. Finch's pressing instruction that, "We are not our minds," rang through the speakers as they decoded his transmission. They could do nothing else but declare it the voice of a madman. They announced that *The Kapernic* was a successful mission in many respects, but that Earth still had so very far to go, and was so very far from sending people–safely–into the neighboring star system. It came to be known as the Constellation Boy Rule: interstellar crews from Earth would no longer be allowed to have any family before they set off for the stars, save those future family members they could clone into life in their new and fully founded colony. Mission control hoped that would help.

Earth and the other planets continued their careful orbit of the Sun as *The Kapernic* detonated a whole solar system away. The Grim resumed its watch over Deka's shifting dust storms. Over Star Harbor, strewn with *The Kapernic*'s wreckage. And it waited.

DIXON REUEL

ABOUT THE AUTHOR

Dixon Reuel is the pen name of Eve Marie Power, an award-winning writer of SciFi and Paranormal Fiction from Dublin, Ireland.

Runner-up for *The Patrick Kavanagh Poetry Award,* she went on to win a Tyrone Guthrie Residency and was named Emerging Poet at *The Cork Poetry Festival.* She holds a First-Class in History & Celtic Studies, and in Creative Writing, and is a Professional Member of The Irish Writers Centre.

Dixon Reuel's first novel, *Rise of One,* publishes December 2019. You can find out more at www.DixonReuel.com.

SOUL SISTERS

BY MANDY LAWSON

Friday, October 25
I hate that nickname
3:00 p.m.

Familiar arms slide around my waist. I turn around and look up into the most beautiful blue eyes I've ever seen. Eyes that sparkle when they look into mine. I reach up on my tiptoes and ruffle his blonde hair that's getting a little long.

"You ready to go, Cricket?"

I crinkle my nose. He knows I hate that nickname. I sigh and grab my bag. "Yeah, I'm ready, Tyler Owen Lockhart."

"Ah, don't full name me, Char. You've been my Cricket since we were little."

He runs his fingers through my long chestnut brown hair and sweetly kisses my nose. I giggle, "It was fine when we were little, but we're in high school now, Ty. It's not cute anymore."

Sliding his hands in the back of my jeans, he gives me a little squeeze. "You're right, it's not cute." His lips are on my ear. "It's sexy."

I push him away. "Stop before a counselor sees us. We're supposed to be getting ready to kayak."

He pulls me back into his arms. "Aren't you tired? Sunrise hiking this morning kicked my ass."

As much as I want to go kayaking, I cannot resist him. I give a heavy sigh and snuggle into his chest. "It's a fall outdoors retreat, Ty. I don't think we have an option. I think it's kind of required."

A stern voice makes me jump. "Yes, it is, you two, and it's time to go! Keyes, take your boyfriend to the water."

"Yes, Miss Campbell."

She gives me a wink and pulls her red hair into a cap. "And Mr. Lockhart, maybe you wouldn't be so tired if you stayed out of Miss Keyes' cabin late at night."

I stifle my giggle into his chest, and Tyler chuckles. "Miss C, we're just talking."

"Mmm Hmm. I've heard that before. Five minutes."

She walks away, and we both start laughing. "I didn't lie. We were just talking."

"And kissing."

He leans his head down and gives me a steamy kiss. "She said five minutes, right?"

"Ty, stop!" I push him away, giggling.

A group walks past us, and I notice Gwen looking right at me. She and I did not get off on the right foot last night at the retreat meet and greet. She hit on Tyler, and I put her in her place. I was really patient when she was just flirty, but then she kissed his cheek when she thought I wasn't looking. That pissed me off, and I shoved her pretty hard. She needed to know that he's mine. He's been mine since eighth grade.

She flips her blonde hair at me, and I roll my eyes.

"Char, don't let her bother you."

"She hit on you right in front of me while I was holding your hand."

"Let it go. Let's go kayaking since you won't stay here and nap with me."

Taking my hand, he leads me down the water where the rest of the group waits. Gwen and a couple of other girls march right up to us.

"Hey, Tyler, do you need a partner today? Someone to help gives those arms a rest?" She grabs his bicep, and I scowl at her.

Tyler takes her hand off his arm. "I'm good, Gwen. Charlotte is great at kayaking. My Cricket plays volleyball." He slides his arm around my waist. "I'm pretty sure she could paddle circles around you."

She lets out an annoyed sigh. "Your loss." She stalks away with her minions, and Tyler leads us over to our kayak.

Miss Campbell and our other counselors, Mr. Jim, Mr. Phillips, and Miss Rowan, give us instructions before letting us get into our kayaks.

Tyler zips up my lifejacket. "Don't want my Cricket to drown."

"Yeah, that'd be a shame," Gwen says next to us.

I ball up my fist, and Tyler wraps his arms around me quickly.

A girl, whose name I've forgotten, says, "Gwen, why don't you just leave her alone already. Her boy don't want you. Give it up already."

"Maybe you mind your own business, Ellison."

"Leave them alone, Gwen, or I'll tell Coach Kelly that you're a bully, and she'll kick you off the squad."

She snarls and rolls her eyes as Ellison turns to me. She has long brown hair, green eyes just like mine, and tan skin. She is taller and maybe a year or two older.

"I'm sorry about Gwen. She's just jealous and always wants what she can't have. Like cheer captain. She wanted it so badly, but Coach named me instead. Just ignore her."

"Thanks. I'm Charlotte Keyes by the way." I hold out my hand, and she shakes it.

"Ellison Hendrix. I'm a senior at Northwest."

"Tyler and I go to Lakeside. We're juniors."

"We should totally hang sometime."

"Totally."

She grabs my phone from my hand and adds herself as a contact, and I put my info into hers. "Here. Now, we're friends." She turns to face the counselors.

Tyler plays basketball, and I'm in volleyball. Paddling a kayak is nothing compared to the training we go through. Tyler gives me a weird look while we get into our kayak. He walks to the front of the kayak while I settle in the back.

After we paddle for a bit, he turns around to look at me. "So what was that all about?"

"What?"

"You and cheer captain. You just going to be friends with her?" He does a little shrug

"She stood up for us. It was nice."

"Guess so. I didn't need her help."

He turns to look at me, and I laugh. "No, you didn't. But it was nice of her. I don't like girls flirting with you."

"Are you jealous?"

I blush. "Of course I'm jealous. Have you seen you?"

He laughs. Even his laughs are sexy. Is that even a thing?

"Char, you're my girl. We've been together for three years. You shouldn't be jealous."

My arms are starting to burn, so I slow down our paddling since we are way ahead of everyone. "I keep thinking that you'll find someone better and get rid of me."

He stops paddling and twists his entire body to look at me. Looks right into my soul…if that's possible. "Charlotte, are you serious right now?"

I shrug. "We're juniors this year. I'm afraid you'll outgrow me and not want me anymore."

He lets out a heavy sigh. "I've loved you since we were five. It took me eight years to get you to go out with me. You think I'd give up after all that hard work?"

"It wasn't eight years."

"It was. You were my Cricket the minute you walked into that kindergarten classroom with your cute southern accent. I couldn't stay away from you. I was addicted."

I roll my eyes. "Ty, you're silly."

"But you love me."

"Of course I love you."

"And because I love you too, I'm going to make you stop talking and look around you."

I stop and look around. The surrounding forest is beautiful. Being a Washington native where everything is green, we are used to it, but today the scenery is more vibrant. A bright green. Stunning but kind of eerie.

"It's really pretty today."

"Not as pretty as you."

I roll my eyes again, but he still makes me smile.

"Let's get back. Tonight is the bonfire, and you promised to make me your special s'mores."

"If we get back before everyone, we'll have extra time before dinner, right?"

"Right..."

"Then let's go!"

We paddle back at a pace that makes my arms feel like they're on fire. By the time we make it back to shore, my muscles are done, and I just want to lie down and take a big nap, but I decide to shower first.

I grab my bathroom bag, and Tyler pops in my cabin in dry clothes. He pulls me close to his chest. It's not fair that boys can just put on clean clothes and look amazing.

"Don't squeeze too hard, Ty. My arms and shoulders hurt."

"Lie down."

I lie on my bed in the corner, and he begins to massage my

shoulders. I pull my sweatshirt off so his fingers can really do some magic. I'm wearing a sports bra so it's not a big deal. I feel his lips replace his fingers.

"Ty..."

"I'm massaging."

He works all the knots out of my shoulders, and we switch places. I pull my shirt on and straddle him. I massage his shoulders and down his muscular back. Has he always had all these muscles? Those gym workouts are really helping. I press my fingers into his lower back, and he flips over before I can think about it.

I trace my fingers along his abs and up his chest. His blue eyes smolder with sexiness. He pulls my face to his, and for a second, I lose track of time. Of space. Of reality. You would think I'd be used to kissing him after being together for three years, but I'm not. He still gives me butterflies.

His hands are everywhere. Self-control is not one of his best attributes. When we're together, he literally cannot control himself. I always have to stop us before things go too far.

"Ty," I whisper against his neck.

"Yeah, yeah, yeah, I know." He squeezes me tightly against his chest.

"We've talked about this. We're gonna wait."

"Waiting is really getting hard, Char."

I sigh. We've had this discussion before, but for some reason, his comment pisses me off. "I need to shower. You should go back to your cabin." I push myself off the bed and grab my bathroom bag.

Keeping my head down, I open the cabin door.

He walks over and tries to tilt my chin up.

"Cricket, look at me."

I shake my head and tear up. He gets on his knees and gazes into my eyes. He reaches up to wipe the tears falling from my face. Ugh. Why does he have to be so sweet when I'm mad at him?

"Please don't cry, my emerald eyes. I'm really sorry. I shouldn't have said that. I know we've talked about waiting, and I respect that. Please don't be mad at me."

I put my hands in his wavy hair and lean into him. We stay in this position for a little while until he puts his head under my sweatshirt and blows a raspberry on my stomach.

I giggle.

He stands and wraps his arms around me. "Am I forgiven?"

"Of course."

As we hug on the porch, Gwen and two girls from my cabin walk past giggling. I think their names are Lacy and Alysa. Lacy is short with her blonde hair in a pixie cut, and Alysa is tall with her hair in tight little braids pulled up in a messy bun. Probably both cheerleaders.

They look at us, and Lacy winks at Tyler. "Hi, Tyler."

"What's up?" He nods his head at them.

"Everything okay with you two?"

I know they can tell I've been crying, but do all the girls have to hit on my boyfriend in front of me? Ugh. I'm about to say something, but Tyler scoops me up off my feet.

"Completely perfect. I always sweep her off her feet. She can't resist me." He gives me a sweet kiss.

The girls roll their eyes but keep walking.

Tyler puts me down while kissing my cheek.

"Get your shower, and I'll pick you up for dinner."

"And special s'mores tonight?'

"You know it."

After he leaves, I head to the bathroom. These cabins are really nice. The bathroom has stalls with shower doors instead of curtains. My summer camp showers are terrible. The tiny curtains rarely give you privacy. I like the privacy here.

I turn the water on to let it warm up and fold my clothes

next to my bag. When I step inside, the warm water feels good on my sore muscles. Hiking this morning was excruciating but completely worth it. We got to watch the sunrise from the top of the mountain. It was so pretty I actually cried. Now, I can feel the sun warming my skin just thinking about the hike.

All of a sudden, my skin feels like it's on fire. I reach out to turn the knob on the shower, but it's not getting cooler. The water is scalding my skin. I push against the shower door, but it's stuck. I shove with all my strength. The thick glass won't budge. Panic rises in my chest, and I can't breathe.

I press myself against the shower door, but the water is still scalding me. Breathing becomes impossible in this suffocating steam.

"Help!" I scream.

Everyone is probably at dinner already. I bang against the door again, but nothing happens. My heart is pounding with fear. What if no one finds me? My skin feels raw from the water. I'm scared.

I can't see through my tears or the thickening steam. I scream for help again. And again. My panic erupts. I feel like my heart may explode. I can't breathe without feeling like I'm drowning so I just cry. Screaming burns my throat, so I just give up. Spots fill my vision, and my body wobbles from dizziness. I slump against the wall and slide to the floor as I lose consciousness.

You saw me naked

6:30 p.m.

I hear my name and feel someone shaking me. Tyler hovers over me with fear written all over his face. I realize I'm in the middle of the bathroom floor wrapped in a towel.

"Charlotte Elizabeth Keyes! You scared the hell out of

me!" He pulls me into a bone-crushing hug, and I wince from pain.

"Ouch," I whisper.

He lets go of me immediately. "Oh, Baby, I'm sorry."

"You found me." Tears start falling.

"When I came to take you to dinner, your cabin was empty. The shower was running so I knocked on the bathroom door. I called out to you, and you didn't answer, so I opened the door. The whole room was steamy, and I almost had to break the shower door open to get to you."

Tyler helps me to sit up. My skin is so red and it stings. It feels just like it did that summer I visited my grandparents in Miami and got so sunburned I had blisters all over me. I don't have any blisters, but my skin is angry.

"How long have I been out?"

"Since I busted you out? About five minutes. The nurse is on her way. Someone walked by and heard me screaming, and they ran for help. So what happened?"

"The water started to get too hot, and when I tried to turn it off, it wouldn't. Then I couldn't get the shower door open. I was terrified, and it was so hot that I couldn't breathe. I tried to get away from the water, but then I was seeing spots. That's all I remember."

Ty runs a hand through his hair. "It's like the door was jammed. I had to pry it open. Once I got it opened, I scooped you up and turned the water off."

I reach out and touch his wet shirt. "I'm sorry you got all wet."

He sighs loudly. "I'm fine. Are you okay? How do you feel?"

"My skin stings, and I feel really weak but okay." I glance at my towel and get really embarrassed. "You saw me naked."

"I was scared, Char. I wasn't paying attention to your body. Although…" He touches the bottom hem of the towel near my thigh.

I laugh a little, and he smiles. Because of the pain flaring from my skin, I gingerly shift myself into his chest, and he lightly holds me. I should be scared, but I feel so safe in his arms.

The camp nurse walks in and checks me over. I passed out from my blood pressure bottoming out due to the steam. My skin has first degree burns but should be okay. I now have aloe cream to put on.

After I do everything as prescribed, all of my clothes are too tight and hurt my skin. Tyler brings me a pair of his sweat pants and his big school sweatshirt. I throw my hair into a messy bun, and we walk to dinner. But, for some reason, I keep looking over my shoulder. Prickles creep along my neck like someone is watching me.

"Are you okay?" Tyler pulls me closer to his side.

"I guess I just feel a little spooked."

"That's understandable. That was really scary."

I nod as we walk into the dining hall. There are long tables made of old wood set up in rows. It's a busy hub with lots of clinking noises, laughing, and chatter among everyone. Many faces turn as we walk through and I feel on display. I tug at my sleeves to cover my hands. Tyler finds us two spots to sit. Unfortunately, they are across from Gwen and her puppets.

"Someone forgot sunscreen." She giggles to her friends.

"Actually, my shower malfunctioned. I was scalded by hot water, but thanks for the compliment."

She shrugs and returns to her salad.

"Where were you before dinner?" I don't know why that just came out of my mouth.

She glares. Her frown displaying a spark of anger. "That's none of your business."

I drop it, but I'm thinking maybe she had a hand in my shower malfunctioning. Tyler puts a plate of food in front of me, breaking me out of my thoughts. Gwen gives Tyler a flirty wave. He nods and starts eating his burger.

When I take a bite of mine, Gwen laughs. "Charlotte, you do know if you eat that, it will go straight to your ass."

I sigh and take another big bite of my burger while giving her a death stare. Ellison plops down beside me and throws Gwen the middle finger. "Screw you, Gwen. Should I tell everyone how much you weighed at the beginning of the season? It's probably why you didn't get chosen as captain. You can't go out for milkshakes every night in the summer and expect to be the top of the pyramid come September."

Gwen stands and slams her tray on the table. We all jump. She flips us off and shoves past people on her way out. Her minions run to keep up with her.

I high five Ellision. "Nice work."

"She likes to talk smack, but she can't take it."

"Is she like this at school?"

Ellison rolls her eyes. "Oh yeah. She's conniving and mean to everybody. Last year she got a girl kicked off the cheer squad."

As that terrifying thought settles into my mind, I shiver. Could she have been behind what happened to me? I think I was right to suspect her. But would she really try to hurt me?

"So what happened to you? Your face is really red."

I tell her about what happened. As I relate the details, Ellison's eyes widen and she gnaws at her lip. When Ty slides his arm around me and squeezes, I realize he is more in shock than I am about it

When I finish, we try to figure out what could have happened but can't come up with anything that makes sense. Ellison thinks it was just a fluke. But I really believe someone is behind it.

After a girl from Ellison's cabin grabs her for clean-up duty,

Tyler pulls me into his chest and hugs me when we leave the dining hall.

"What's this about?" I mumble into his chest.

"I found you unconscious, Cricket. I thought you were dead."

I glance up. His head is pointed at the sky and a tear rolls down his cheek. "Ty, I'm okay. Look at me."

He tilts his head down and tears fall on my face. "I guess I'm just messed up about it."

I hug him tightly even though my skin is screaming at me. "I'm right here, and I'm okay." We stay pressed together for a long time before he pulls away. "I do have something on my mind about it though."

He takes my hand, and we start walking towards the bonfire. "What's that, Baby?"

"Do you think Gwen had something to do with the shower?"

He stops us and looks at me. "Char, I think she's flirty but not violent."

"You're probably right. I feel bad for saying it out loud."

But as we begin moving again, I can't help but wonder.

Soul Sister

10:00 p.m.

The air is very crisp and feels good on my raw skin. The bonfire is big and inviting when we walk up. The flames are dancing and making shadows of the campers. I'm mesmerized by the embers popping and the crackling from the fire. Everyone mingles, making s'mores, and sitting around the fire on hay bales.

Our counselors are working the s'more station. Even with my shower incident, this retreat has been a really fun retreat and a much-needed fall break from school. Our fall break from school was much needed. Nine-week tests were tough, and as soon as we get back, it's going to be busy with homecoming, games, SATs, and applying for college. I'm nervous just thinking about it. There are around thirty of us at this retreat. I like the smallness of the group. I'd love to come back in the summer.

I look over at Gwen and her puppets. They're flirting with other guys. A guy with short brown hair and glasses is feeding Gwen a s'more.

"Cricket, find us a spot, and I'll make you a s'more." Tyler interrupts my thoughts.

"A special one?"

He pulls out a package of chocolate Pop Tarts and waves them. "Of course."

I rub my hands together and smile. "Perfect."

He kisses me on the cheek and heads for the table. I find a cozy spot away from the fire. It's close enough that we won't be cold but not so close that we'll get too hot. I pull out my phone and see some texts from my dad.

Daddy: I got a call from the camp nurse.

Daddy: Why are you not answering your phone?

Daddy: You have one hour to call me or I'm coming to get you.

I roll my eyes and call him.

"Charlotte Elizabeth, I was about to grab my keys."

"Calm down, Daddy. I'm fine."

"According to the nurse, she said Tyler called her in a panic because he found you unconscious in the shower. That's not fine."

"It was a freak thing. The water was too hot, and it wouldn't shut off. I couldn't open the door. It's not a big deal."

"She said you had first degree burns!"

"It's like a bad sunburn, Daddy. Chill."

"I almost called your mother."

"Daddy, no. Isn't she on a trip with Kyle?"

"Your mother and step father have every right to know what

goes on if it's an emergency, but I was scared. You should have called me. I thought I could trust you to be responsible."

"I am responsible!"

"You had a medical emergency, and you didn't call me."

"I passed out, and I didn't need to go to the hospital. Do you want me to call you when I scrape my knee hiking tomorrow?"

"Don't be a smart mouth, Charlotte."

"Sorry, Daddy."

"Please be careful."

"I will."

"And I better not hear about you sneaking into Tyler's cabin."

"Dad!"

He laughs. "Bye, Kiddo. Love you."

"Love you too. Byeeee."

I shove my phone in my pocket as Ellison sits next to me. "Overprotective dad, huh?"

A little annoyed she was listening, I reply, "Oh yeah. Ever since the divorce, I'm his number one always. He's very protective."

"Can I ask a personal question?"

"Sure." I fold my arms around myself.

"When did your parents get divorced?"

"I was in seventh grade. She had an affair with someone from work. She's a lawyer in Seattle. Now, she's on husband number three, Kyle. He's supposedly the perfect one."

"You don't like your mom?"

"Oh, I love my mom! She's awesome. I just don't live with her."

Ellison tucks a strand of hair behind her ear, revealing a tattoo on her neck. She's speaks before I can ask about it. "I know I'm being nosy, but why?"

"My mom's job is very demanding. At the time, she couldn't pick me up from school or make any of my volleyball games or dance team events. Dad's a writer, so he's able to be there. I love them both, but I'm definitely closer to my dad. Mom is very busy. I couldn't live with her."

Tyler sits down handing me my special s'more. "She just couldn't move away from me."

Giggling, I take a bite of my s'more. "That's definitely part of why I couldn't live with Mom."

Ellison looks closer at my s'more. "What is that?"

"This is Tyler's special s'more. When we were in sixth grade, we went to a hayride where he pulled out a package of chocolate Pop Tarts. He lined one with half of a Hershey bar and roasted two marshmallows. He smashed those between the two Pop Tarts and shared it with me. I can't eat them any other way now."

"That's...different."

"And delicious." Tyler kisses the corner of my mouth. He licks the chocolate from my lips making me shiver wrapping his arm around my waist.

I pull off the corner and hand it to Ellison. She takes the bite, and her eyes widen. "Wow! That is good."

"I told ya. Now, I've told you about my family. What about yours?"

"Oh, just the normal family. My parents have been together forever, and I have two sisters at home. They're twins. My mom couldn't have kids but, miraculously, got pregnant with my sisters after adopting me. They are seven and super annoying. Do you have any siblings?"

Tyler chuckles and I giggle. "I'm an only child."

Ellison looks confused. "What's so funny?"

"I'm kind of a mistake. Well, if you ask my mom and dad, they say I was a surprise. But we all know surprise babies are the whoops babies. She didn't really want to get pregnant, but I happened, and they say I was a good surprise. I joke that I'm a mistake. They don't find it very funny."

"Yeah…that's not funny."

I shrug. "I know, but it's fun to tease them sometimes."

Tyler pulls me into his lap, and I wince. He kisses my shoulder. "Or she uses it to get what she wants."

"You hush and don't hold me so tight. Raw skin, remember?"

He loosens up immediately. "Sorry, Cricket."

Ellison giggles. "Cricket?"

"His stupid nickname for me."

He laughs and bounces me on his knees. "She loves it."

Ellison shakes her head with a smirk. "Does it mean something?"

"She moved from South Carolina in kindergarten and had the cutest little southern accent. I was five and thought crickets were only in the south from a cartoon or something. I called her a cricket on the playground, and it just stuck."

"That's cute."

"She's cute." Tyler kisses my neck, and I sigh. He is the sweetest boy on the entire planet.

"He's silly, El. Don't listen to him."

"El…I like that. You know, my parents call me 'Elly Bee.' We both have insect nicknames!"

"Practically soul sisters. So…you have a tattoo?"

She pulls her hair away from her neck and shows me a small tattoo behind her ear. I gasp at the little trail of birds.

"Your tattoo is…"

Tyler interrupts. "Cricket has one just like that!"

"Really? Where?" Ellison laughs.

I lift my hair and show her mine. "How cool is it that we have the same tattoo in the same spot?! Totally meant to be friends!"

She smiles like that really touched her. Before I say anything else, Mr. Phillips pulls out his guitar and starts playing. Ellison pats my shoulder and moves closer to the fire. I snuggle into Ty's chest.

He whispers, "You know you're not a mistake. You were born just for me."

We're sixteen. We shouldn't be talking about being meant for each other, but when I look into his eyes in the glow of the fire, I know that's exactly what I believe.

Don't Be Salty

Midnight

The boys walk us girls back to our cabins after the bonfire. All the girls file in, and Tyler gives me a really steamy kiss. I walk inside feeling lightheaded.

Gwen stops me before I reach my bed. "Don't get comfortable."

"Why?"

"Because we're about to play an epic game of Truth or Dare as soon as the counselors turn off their lights. We play every year."

"What if I'd rather go to bed? I've had a pretty rough evening."

"Suck it up. You're new here, but we all play. It's not an option."

I roll my eyes and walk around her to my bed. "Can't I play from here?"

"No. We play outside, and the boys join us. Maybe I'll get dared to kiss Tyler."

I give her the evil stare.

"Oh, relax! Don't be salty."

"I'm not salty."

"No, but you're scared." Chills run all over my body. She gets right in my face. "You should be scared."

I swallow hard, and she flips her hair at me as she walks away. I'm completely convinced she screwed with my shower today. Maybe she was just trying to scare me and didn't realize the shower door would get stuck. I don't know, but I'm keeping my eyes on her.

After the lights to the counselor's cabins go dark, we meet the boys outside, and Tyler immediately finds me. "What's going on? They told me it's tradition."

"Apparently it's a huge game of Truth or Dare."

"Are you up for this? You probably need to rest after what happened today."

"I'm not missing this, and Gwen wants to kiss you."

"You know I won't let her."

"She also told me that I should be scared."

After we gather around the bonfire, one of the guys, Mitch I think, lights the fire again as we take seats on the hay bales. Tyler pulls me close to his side and whispers, "You really think she could be behind the shower thing?"

"I don't know. Maybe it was a prank gone wrong or maybe she really wanted to scare me. I'm not sure."

He tightens his arm around me, and I wince. "Not so tight."

He loosens his hold, but part of me doesn't want him to let go. I snuggle closer. His warm lips press against my temple, and I sigh. I love this boy.

"Cricket, we'll keep an eye on her."

"On who?" Ellison says, sitting next to me.

"Gwen and her puppets, Lacy and Alysa."

"Why is that?"

"I think they're behind my shower getting screwed with today."

She shrugs. "Camp pranks are pretty popular around here during this retreat, but I don't think someone would do something violent."

"Maybe it wasn't supposed to be but kind of went wrong when my shower door was jammed. I don't know."

"Freak accident probably."

"I look like a lobster so…freak is completely accurate."

Gwen stands on her hay bale. "Okay, Newbies! This is our tradition every year, and you get to be a part of it. We are about to play Truth or Dare. There are only a few rules. Number one, nothing sexual or sick. Number two, we cannot leave the camp grounds. Number three, we have the right to ask for a vote if we think a dare is too dangerous or psycho. Number four, no one chooses Truth only Dare. If you refuse to do your task, you're out. Last one standing wins. Understand?"

After we all say yes, she continues. "Since I won last year, I get to start the game." She turns to the short guy with black hair who lit the fire. "Mitch, truth or dare?"

"Dare."

She pulls a pair of handcuffs from her back pocket. Who brings handcuffs to camp? A psycho who screws with your shower, that's who.

A wicked smile spreads across her face. "I dare you to be handcuffed to the girl of my choice until our hike tomorrow."

"Seriously?"

"Yup and I choose your cuff mate to be Lacy."

Lacy giggles and stands next to Gwen. You can totally tell Lacy is excited, and Gwen did that on purpose for her friend. She handcuffs them together. "Okay, Mitch, your turn."

He laughs and wiggles his arm. "You better not lose the keys to these."

"What keys?" She sits down and crosses her legs.

He looks panicked for a second before she snickers. "Very funny, Gwen. I dare Lacy to suck on one of Jeremy's toes."

Now that's a good one. We all laugh, and Lacy starts to gag as Jeremy takes off his boot. I'm sure it's the same boot from the sunrise hike this morning. That foot has to smell nasty. She gets on her knees in front of him as he lifts his foot to her face. She covers her nose and sucks on his big toe. We laugh hysterically, and then Lacy turns and vomits, which brings on a whole new round of laughing.

She finally recovers and stares in our direction. "I dare Tyler to kiss Gwen."

I tighten my hold on his arm. He leans over and whispers, "I got this, Baby. Chill." He stands up and walks over to a very satisfied looking Gwen. She stands up giving me a wide smile and a little wave. I roll my eyes. As he nears her, my heart beats faster. Is he really going to kiss her?

She closes her eyes and tilts her face up. He leans in and kisses the top of her head. Everyone dies laughing except Gwen.

"You didn't do the dare so you're out!"

Tyler chuckles. "I did do the dare. She said to kiss Gwen. I did. I kissed you on the head. She didn't say kiss you on the lips."

She pouts and sits with a thud. Tyler rubs his hands together and looks around the group. Then he turns to Gwen. "Let me show you how it's done." He turns and looks at me raising his eyebrows. I shake my head at him. "I dare Charlotte to kiss me on the lips with tongue."

I catch a glimpse of Gwen before I walk to Tyler. She looks so mad which makes me so happy. I wrap my arms around Tyler's neck, and he scoops me up so my legs wrap around his waist. My skin is screaming, but I don't care. I give him the hottest kiss of his life. When his hands grab my backside, throats clear and some snickers come from the watching group. I slide down his body and hide my head into his chest.

"You're turn, Cricket."

Gwen looks like she's ready to kill me. I decide to be nice because she kind of scares me, and if I dare her, it would be her turn again. I turn to Ellison.

"I dare El to jump in the lake."

You can see the shock on everyone's faces from the glow on the fire. Oohs and ahs spread across our little group, and Ellison laughs. "Okay, Char, but only if you jump with me."

"Okay!"

"You can't do that!" Gwen screams across at us. "You can't do the dare with someone."

Ellison shakes her head. "Says who? Why don't we all jump in?" She takes her sweatshirt off, revealing a very lacy bra. "Let's go!" She runs across the camp, onto the dock, and jumps in the lake.

Everyone looks at each other and starts stripping. I can't believe everyone is going to jump into the lake practically naked. Tyler pulls his hoodie off. Now I'm distracted. The glow of the fire casts a nice yellow hue over his toned chest and abs. I bite my lip and watch him unbutton his pants. His eyes catch mine, and I blush.

"What's wrong, Cricket? Too chicken?"

"Uh…no. I just got uh…" Why can't I spit out the words? "I got distracted by uh…"

He is completely stripped down to just his boxers. He looks at me when I quit talking. "What's wrong with you?"

I shake my head to clear my thoughts. "Nothing." I pull my sweatshirt off, and Tyler steps closer as I take off my pants. "Don't look at me like that. This is no different from me wearing a bikini. And I'm red all over."

"You're hot, and this is nothing like being in a bikini." He traces the top of my bra, and a fire lights in his eyes. "This has lace. Red lace."

I roll my eyes and pull him towards the lake. The moonlight dances on the water while the guys do cannonballs. The girls are barely dipping their toes in. Holding hands, Tyler and I run all the way to the end of the dock and jump.

The freezing water takes my breath away as I come to the surface. I look around, and lots of people are running back to the fire except for a few crazies that can handle the cold.

Tyler pops up with a gasp. "Wow, it's so cold!" Freezing water splashes over me as his arms circle my body. "Let's get back before we get sick." His hands slide round my butt, and he freezes. "Oh, uh…I didn't know you were in a thong."

His fingers give me a little squeeze, and I bring my lips to his. I don't care that people can see us or that my skin is literally on fire. I kiss him with everything I have. He doesn't move his hands from my ass, and I don't want him to, but a blood-curdling scream cuts through the night.

Our eyes dart around the lake, and we see Ellison waving her arms in the water. Tyler lifts me onto the dock. "Go get your clothes on and wait for me. I'm going to see what's going on."

I nod and watch him swim towards a frantic Ellison. I run back to where I left my clothes. I yank them on quickly and grab Tyler's before running back to the dock. My breath catches in my throat when I see Ellison in hysterical tears, and Tyler pulling someone from the water.

"Is that…"

Tyler's voice is flat. "Gwen."

"Is she…"

"Char, call 911."

Numb, I pull my phone out. Ellison is next Gwen on the ground crying over her. I begin to shiver. And it's not from the cold.

Saturday, October 26

I'll never forget last night

7:00 a.m.

I sit under a huge oak tree in front of my cabin with a big cup of coffee. I'm wearing the same clothes I was in last night. Last night…I'll never forget last night.

After Tyler pulled Gwen from the water, he and two others did CPR until the paramedics arrived. They worked on her for what seemed like forever before one pronounced her time of death. Ellison never stopped crying. The police asked us questions, and we were in trouble by the retreat directors for being out after curfew. It was a very long night. I walked back into my cabin at 5:00 a.m. and watched my clock until it read 6:00.

I went to the dining hall and grabbed coffee before settling under this tree. I've been sitting out here since. I can't feel my fingers or my toes, but the hot coffee in my hands feels amazing. My phone dings.

Ellison: Can we talk later

Me: Sure

Ellison: I think I'm going home early. I mean...she's gone

Me: I know. I understand

Ellison: She was a bitch, but we were on the same squad. I can't believe it

Me: I'm sorry

Ellison: I'm sad

Me: I know

Ellison: Later, okay

Me: Okay

I put my phone down and turn to see Tyler walking towards me. He looks drained. Watching him, Mitch, and Kevin perform CPR on a lifeless body for thirty minutes was the most excruciating thing I've ever witnessed.

He slides down beside me and wraps me in an embrace. "Cricket, did you sleep at all?"

I shake my head. "I couldn't."

"Yeah, me neither."

The warmth of his body and his presence makes me feel safe. I lean into him and let tears fall for the first time since last night. Tyler holds me tighter as I begin to sob.

"I couldn't stand her, Ty. Literally thought she was evil. Now, she's dead."

"I know, Baby. I just wonder why she jumped in if she was high."

"Is that what it was? Did the police say?"

"I overheard one of them say it looked that way, but they were going to do tests to see what was in her system."

"Do you think it was drugs?"

"I don't know, but I know I don't want to go in the water today."

"Me either. Do you think they'll make us all go home early?"

He gives me a squeeze. "I don't know. Let's go get something to eat."

At breakfast, I notice Alysa, Lacy, and Mitch sitting with their heads down. The police had to unlock their handcuffs since Gwen had the key which was probably at the bottom of the lake. I shiver thinking about it.

I can't even taste my eggs as our counselors line up at the front of the room. I look at Tyler. He has deep circles under his eyes and his eyes are unfocused. I put my hand on his knee and squeeze it. He immediately slides arm around my waist. He always knows exactly what I need. How'd I end up so lucky?

Mr. Phillips cleared his throat.

"I know you are all tired. It was a long night. We are saddened by the loss of our friend. We do want to stress the importance of not getting into the water at night and especially after curfew. We know all about your yearly dare game, but you guys have never gone into the water. Tonight is our big Halloween costume party. This was Gwen's favorite night. I think she'd want us to have fun in her memory. What do you all think?"

Several people start talking at once. There are some that want to go home, but the majority want to have a party in Gwen's memory. We were going to hike today, but they decided that we will stay inside and start the party early.

After our counselors leave, Tyler pulls me from the table.

As we walk back to my cabin, I see Ellison standing on the docks. I give Ty a kiss on the cheek. "I should go talk to her."

"Away from the docks please."

"Of course. I'll meet you at your cabin later."

He kisses my forehead. His lips linger for a bit. I close my eyes and he whispers, "I love you, Cricket."

"Love you back."

I walk over fallen leaves to Ellison and grab her hand. As I pull her away from the lake, I ask, "So…do you have to go home?"

With a faraway look in her eyes, she looks toward the horizon. "The sun will set earlier tonight." Her hands are sweaty, and her eyes are shifting back and forth. She turns to look at me with wide eyes, like she forgot I was standing next to her. "Oh, I talked to them. They will be here to get me tomorrow. I really don't want to wait that long."

I squeeze her hand. "What happened out there?"

She shudders and looks out at dark surface of the water. She wraps her arms around herself. "She swam over to me and started making stupid remarks at me like always. I splashed water at her and told her to go to hell. She laughed and started swimming away from me. Then she just went under. I thought she was swimming underwater, but then I didn't see her come up. I went under and grabbed her. She wasn't responding to me. That's when I screamed, and Tyler came to help."

"El, that's horrible! I can't believe that!"

"You don't believe me!" she screams at me with her face turning red.

Woah. That came out of nowhere. I touch her arm. "I didn't say that. I said I can't believe that happened to her. It's just so sad."

She takes a deep breath and calms down. "Oh. Okay. You know Tyler was amazing. Like a real hero."

I smile. "He really was."

"Are you two going to the costume party thing?"

"Oh yeah…he's going as Deadpool, and I'm going as Domino."

"That's fun. I'm not sure I'm going."

"You totally should come. You can be our date!" I giggle. "What's your costume?"

"Catwoman."

"Perfect! Superhero trio!"

"You sure? Will Tyler be okay with it?"

"Oh, he'll love it! We'll see you later, okay?"

"Okay. Thanks."

I turn to walk to my cabin but look back at her. She has puffy eyes from crying and her voice is on the brink of breaking down. I feel like Gwen's death is harder on her than she is letting on. I know they didn't get along here, but maybe they were friends at school. We'll never know.

I'm an upgrade

7:00 p.m.

I've got my costume on and my hair and makeup look amazing. I'm pulling my boots on when there's a knock on my cabin door. I skip over knowing it's Ty, but I open the door to Ellison dressed in black from head to toe. Her leather suit looks smoking hot on her, and the cat ears are adorable.

"Oh, hey!!! You look awesome! I love your costume. I actually thought you were Tyler."

She gives me a warm smile. "Your costume is awesome too! I met Tyler walking over and told him to go ahead to the party. We can meet him there. I want to tell you something."

I frown a little. "Oh, okay. Well, let's go! I'm ready!"

We walk out together, and the air has gotten really cold. I should have grabbed a jacket, but it will be warm at the party. The night air smells the way fall should; like firewood burning, turning leaves, and a hint of spice in the air. After a minute, I notice that we aren't walking in the right direction. I can hear the music from the party get quieter. No one would hear me if I screamed.

"El, this isn't the way."

She just turns and smiles. But this smile isn't kind. It's sinister. My mind immediately starts thinking about Gwen. The police said she had trouble swimming, but Ellison told me that she was swimming toward her. A feeling of fear washes over me. I don't think Gwen's drowning was an accident.

"Uh, Ellison. I think we need to turn around."

She grabs my wrist and is stronger than me. I keep trying to twist my arm to free myself, but she has an unnatural hold on me. Like her life depends on it.

We reach the boathouse where they keep the life jackets, oars, and stuff. The smell of mildew fills my nose. She pulls me inside and slams me against a wall where my head collides with the corner of a shelf. I whimper in pain. Although I feel blood running down the back of my head, I know I need to stay calm. "Ellison, what are you doing?"

She takes my hands roughly and ties them behind me. I want to fight back, but I think I've lost too much blood. I'm feeling dizzy.

"Just shut up! Shut up and sit down!" She sounds completely crazy, and I'm terrified but stubborn. I stay standing even as the blood drips down my back.

She slaps my face and shoves me to the ground. "Bitch! I said sit down!"

My calm exterior doesn't match the panic building in my chest. "Please tell me why you are doing this?"

Her crazed face fills my vision and her eyes bore into me. "I'm taking back what should have been mine!"

"What do you mean?" I draw my knees to my chest. Maybe if I talk her down, she'll let me go.

"You should know before you die that you aren't an only child. Your parents had another child before you. They had me and gave me up for adoption. I'm your sister, Charlotte. You may get called the surprise baby, but they were already surprised once. And you were completely right about being the mistake. They got rid of the wrong baby."

"What? I don't understand." She has to be lying. My parents would have told me something like that.

"I should be living your life. You have everything that's mine. I was adopted, and I don't belong with them. I belong with my real parents."

"Aren't your parents nice?"

"Of course, they are nice! But the twins were born, and I was forgotten. They love their real children more than me. So…I started researching and finding out about my real parents. I've been stalking you on Instagram for a year. I know everything about you and could easily slide in and replace you. We have the same color hair, same eyes, and same tattoo."

"They will notice when their daughter doesn't come home."

"But I will come home."

"I mean me! They aren't going to just let you come in and replace me."

"They won't miss you because I'll replace you. I'm an upgrade."

She smiles, and I get sick to my stomach. She walks over to a shelf and pulls a syringe from a small bag. She's going to kill me.

"Did you kill Gwen?"

Her head snaps in my direction. "Of course, I did. She wanted to take my boyfriend. I couldn't have that."

"Tyler is my boyfriend, and he's going to come looking for me soon. Ellison, you're not thinking clearly. Tyler is not going to think that you are me."

She just shakes her head and laughs. "Silly, Charlotte. He'll forget all about you."

"Are you the one who messed with my shower too?"

"And you would be dead right now if Tyler hadn't made it back to the cabin before me. I was going to drug you then and make it look like an overdose. Such a pity that he did. We could have moved on without you already."

Someone yells in the distance. I listen hard and realize it's Tyler yelling my name. Ellison hears it too. She puts her hand over my mouth before I can scream. "Shh!!"

Tears streak down my face as Tyler screams for me. I want his arms around me right now, but I'm afraid I'll never get to feel them again. I'll never see my parents again. This girl, my sister, is crazy. She has no sense of reality.

I begin to sob as Ellison shoves the needle into my arm. As the drugs enter my system, she takes her hand off my mouth.

"Now, now, Charlotte. Don't cry. I'm just ridding the world of an annoying cricket. Never again do we have to hear your noise. I'm sorry I can't stay to see the end, but my boyfriend is waiting for me. We have a party to get to."

She walks to the door as I start to fade.

"Happy Halloween, Cricket."

MANDY LAWSON

ABOUT THE AUTHOR

Mandy Lawson is a glittery, sparkly type of gal who loves to live in a world of books. She's a librarian who writes warm and fuzzy romance, and sometimes cozy spooky. Every car ride with her is like attending a concert. She performs, yo. Mandy will beat you in Friends or Gilmore Girls trivia and she might be in love with Edward Cullen. (Shh! Don't tell her sweet husband) Mandy loves Jesus, PopTarts, and coffee. And she absolutely loves writing. It's like...her thing. You can find Mandy's books at www.mandylawsonbooks.com.

Follow her on Twitter at twitter.com/mandylawson7 and Instagram Instagram.com/mandylawsonauthor.

THE WITCHES OF NINE

BY MEG HOLEVA

Do not join the revels of wild fae
More often than not you'll be swept away
Either young maiden or young laddy buck
The fae never mind to change your luck

Colbie wasn't necessarily *afraid* of the dark; it just made her skin crawl and break out in hives. It wasn't fear, it was allergies. That was it, she was allergic to the night. It didn't happen every time, but when it did, it was one of the more disconcerting things in her life. She didn't like when things couldn't be explained.

The night was still and breathless with a damp chill seeping from the soaking leaves. Colbie sat on the front porch, not looking forward to going inside. The electric bill hadn't been paid, so it had been shut off. Again. Black was penetrating in the house. Thankfully, it was October, so at least Roger would have a fire lit. That was pretty much all he was good for. She refused to call him Dad. Alcohol had seen to that a long time ago.

Colbie pushed herself up from the steps, taking one last deep breath of the dank night air. In two months, six days, and twenty-two hours, this house would no longer be her problem. Sweeping her long brown hair back over her shoulders, she turned to take in the grungy structure.

The windows were coated with a mix of road dust and cigarette film. The paint was chipping off the rotted wood siding. She thought it used to be red but wasn't quite sure. There were no neighbors to complain, so the house had fallen into shambles in the last eighteen months Mom had been on deployment.

"Mrrow." The questioning sound came from under the front porch. Colbie stilled, not quite sure she had heard correctly. "Mrrow?"

The sound was definitely feline in nature. "Kitty kitty?" Colbie called quietly. If there was anything Roger hated more than Colbie, it was cats.

A black cat stretched out from under the steps, languidly rubbing his back on what was left of the railing.

"Well, hello there, handsome." Colbie sat back down and ran her nails down the cat's spine. His back arched with the movement, tail flagging high with a twitch. His purr was a motor boat. He shoved his head into her and rubbed his body down her hand, petting himself. The second time he did it, she noticed his right ear was tattered down to nothing.

"Well what happened to you old timer?" she rubbed the scrap of ear, earning a lean in and louder purring. She continued scratching the cat and found scars from age-old battles. His tail was intact and perfect: his one beauty.

He stared with murky greenish-yellow eyes and stretched his paws up to her legs. Before Colbie could even think, he had hopped up and snuggled into her lap, purring and dozing.

"Well okay then, I didn't really want to go inside anyway."

She bent and buried her nose in his dusty fur. The hollow sounds of his purr expanded until she lost herself.

"What the hell do you think you're doing?" Her father's voice was husky with too many cigarettes and slurred from too much booze.

The cat bounded off Colbie's lap; turning mid-leap to land body arched, hair standing on end.

Roger grabbed at the cat, who stood his ground. "Eh, I'm too tired to fix you up tonight, but when I get my eyes on you again, I'll splatter you across the lawn with my shotgun."

The cat hissed.

Roger lunged, this time startling the cat into running to the shadows. As he turned, Roger swatted the back of Colbie's head, a familiar gesture that always left her ears ringing.

"Get'cher butt inside. The dishes ain't gonna do themselves," he said, his voice getting more slurred as he went back into the house.

"Not like cold water is gonna make anything clean," Colbie mumbled, staring into the shadows as long as she dared before heading inside.

As she suspected, the house was dark. The living room had a fire lit, and Roger's lump was on the couch. The lantern glowed in the kitchen, providing a stark white light that highlighted the grease streaks and dinge on the cupboards.

Colbie did the dishes, only able to wipe the grease around rather than actually clean anything. The living room remained silent, but the dark weighed, choking off the dance and pop of shadows.

Only two months, six days, twenty hours, and fourteen minutes, till Mom would be home. They would leave. She would make sure they left this time. Roger wouldn't be able to manipulate Mom.

Colbie put the dishes away then crept up the stairs to her

room. At least she had stocked up on candles after the last lapse of electricity. Lighting three in a close cluster on her table, she picked up her book and tried to read. Her eyes kept casting out the window as wind whispered through the apple orchard and the stars appeared in the sky.

Finally she gave up and blew out two of the flames, leaving the smallest one to keep her safe from the dark. She took one last look out the window, pausing to send a wish of safety to her new feline friend.

COLBIE IMMEDIATELY FELL INTO A DREAM. The cat approached her from the dark again. This time, he sat, an arm span away, curling his perfect tail around his feet.

"She's not coming back, you know," he said matter-of-factly.

"You don't know that. No one has told us. You can't say that." Colbie stood, keeping all traces of tremor from her voice.

The cat blinked. "You know that's a lie." His pink tongue flicked over his lips as he compulsively groomed a spot on his chest.

"I don't know anything." Realizing what she had said, she shrugged. "You know what I mean."

"Denial does you nothing. Come revel with us this night. I will show you what it is you don't know. The man is not what he seems."

Colbie turned away. *It's just a dream,* she thought.

Her eyes opened, and her dream faded to wherever dreams hide. The room was dark, and the house silent. The candle hadn't lasted long tonight. Though there was plenty of wick left, the dark living in the old farmhouse didn't like the light.

Colbie breathed into the silence, becoming aware of the itch spreading up her forearms. She rolled over to try and sleep again. The murky eyes of the cat, sitting on her second story window ledge stared back at her.

"How..."

With a struggle, she opened the old warped window frame and let the cat in. The cat slid to the floor gracefully, feet barely making a sound. Colbie plopped down, and the cat climbed into her lap, releasing his motorboat purr. She shifted to pull the old quilt off her bed and wrap it close around her shoulders. Her grandmother had made it for Mom years ago. It was heavy with love and memories. If Colbie closed her eyes, she could almost smell the women who made her.

COLBIE WOKE, stretched out on the floor, with early light filtering into the quiet room. The cat was nowhere to be found. Her sore and creaky muscles protested when she decided to move. As she shuffled to work out the kinks, Roger's furious voice roared out of nowhere.

"What the hell? You don't have to pound I'm comin'."

Colbie crept down the stairs, navigating around the noisy parts from years of experience, so she could watch unnoticed. She sank to the bottom stair when she saw the men's uniforms.

"- asked to inform you that your wife has been reported dead while performing her duties for the United States. On behalf of the Secretary of Defense, I extend to you and your family my deepest sympathy in your great loss."

Colbie's vision narrowed and her ears roared. She leaned forward, trying to put her head between her knees, but ended up on the floor, tears blinding her. She uncurled slightly and watched her father's stunned silence. Male voices spoke, but she couldn't make out any words through her haze.

She didn't remember much about the rest of the day. Somehow, she had made it back to her room. She supposed she should have Roger call the school to tell them she wouldn't be there. Maybe she should go brush her teeth or something.

Colbie wasn't sure when she had fallen asleep, but she awoke with hazy memories of rats, cats, and an overwhelming choking dark from her dreams, which faded quickly. She looked at her window. The cat was silhouetted against the gray-blue of twilight and stoic as he surveyed his kingdom.

It was easier to push the window open this time. The cat slinked in and twined around her ankles.

She slid to the floor, welcoming the warmth into her lap.

"What? No 'I told you so'?" The cat propped himself up on her chest and flicked his sandpaper tongue across her sticky cheeks. The tears and snot had long since stopped, but she never had gotten around to washing her face. "Gross, dude."

Colbie rubbed her cheeks with the sleeve of her sweatshirt, but the cat still stood, front legs on her chest, and stared her in the face. She didn't know how she had thought his eyes murky; they were a brilliant yellow that she could get lost in.

After a moment, he lowered his lids slowly to half-mast and snuggled into Colbie's crossed legs. As her room turned pitch-black, she felt the hives come. She waited for moonrise and the relief the light would bring.

Colbie dreamed of the cat again, sitting in her lap.

"So now you know I speak truth," he stated, voice full of sadness instead of mocking.

Colbie hung her head as tears dripped again, her chest tight. "So you only speak in dreams, is that it?"

"You're more sensitive than most, but at this stage it would break your already fragile mind. Will you come now?"

Colbie squeezed her eyes shut, wringing out more tears. There was no love lost between her and her father, but they had both loved her mother in their way. She just shook her head.

This was all she had known, for better or worse. There had been good times, once. She couldn't just leave it all here.

She woke on the floor again. Aching, she lifted her head into the first light of dawn. Colbie picked up the quilt and wrapped it around herself, her shield as she crept downstairs. She just wanted to see Roger. Make sure he was, what? Still alive, maybe? Comatose? Coherent?

His snores reached her ears before she had made it halfway down the stairs. Colbie thought she felt relief, but she couldn't tell through the gnawing hunger in her middle. She made it to the kitchen and saw the empty Wild Turkey bottle on the table. Not surprised, she checked the fridge. Another mostly full bottle sat on the middle shelf. So Roger hadn't made it a full bender last night, just a half. She grabbed a yogurt that was only one day past expiration and sniffed it hesitantly. With a shrug she dug around for a spoon in the haphazard silverware drawer. She had always meant to organize that.

"Chu doing?" The slurred sound of her father's voice from the doorway startled her.

"Just grabbing some food. How are you?" she asked, cautiously.

He just grunted and stumbled toward the sink, stopping to grab the empty whiskey bottle. After looking through the clear glass, he mumbled something to himself and plunked the bottle back down. Colbie watched warily as he grabbed a cup from the counter, filled it with water, and took a long drink. This wasn't his normal drunk. She hadn't really expected it to be, but part of her had hoped.

"Guess it's just you and me now, girl." He raised the empty cup in a toast, swaying slightly.

She nodded, scraping the last of the yogurt out of the cup. "Oh, joy."

"Don't get that tone, I've done a lot for you over the years." They stood in uncomfortable silence before he said, "You have her hair, you know. Before she went all white, she had that brown hair. Had the same wave too."

Colbie stared at him, pulling the quilt tighter around her. It was the first time he had looked at her in years. Really looked at her.

"It was only a matter a time, yah know. Yer mom wasn' comin' home. She never was."

Colbie clenched her teeth, soaking in the stench of whiskey wafting off her father.

"Don't you get that look. She wasn', and you know it."

She glared at her father with anger warming her stomach. She shook her head and turned to leave.

"Don' walk away from me." He started toward her, but she rushed back up the stairs.

The cat was asleep on her pillow when she got back to her room. She glanced around, trying to figure out how to leave.

"Do I just pack a bag and go? Do I just go? Am I seriously doing this?" She sank down, still wrapped in the quilt, and put her head down by the cat. She listened as Roger crashed around downstairs. When it went quiet, she knew he had passed out again.

The cat turned and rammed his head into hers, startling out a laugh. "Ow you silly animal."

She gathered him up in her arms and buried her face in the soft fur of his back. He smelled of fresh air, dust, and clean cat. She breathed deeply. Mom had always loved cats.

"What is that thing doing in here?" Roger's voice was clear.

Colbie jumped. How had he gotten up the stairs without her hearing? His eyes looked clearer too. The cat hissed, arching in Colbie's arms then jumping down between them.

"He belongs in here more than you do. Get out of my room."

"This is my house. I will do as I please. I made a promise, and I'm going to keep it." She felt the shotgun cock down to her very bones. She and the cat froze, unsure how to handle the manic look in Roger's eyes. The man leveled the gun at the cat, who streaked between his legs, out the door.

Colbie smiled as she heard the cat's paws thumping down the stairs.

Roger swore then turned and chased the animal. Colbie froze, waiting for a shot, but none came. The door slammed, and her father swore louder. Decision made, Colbie stuffed some essentials in a duffle bag: a sweatshirt, clean underwear, an extra pair of pants, the water bottle off her table, and her current bedtime read - *Fragile Things* by Neil Gaiman.

Scooping up her quilt, she hurried after her father and the cat. The first shot crashed just as she ran through the front door. She shrieked, covering her ears too late. The man was standing on the front porch, gun ready in his hands, searching the farmland for his victim.

"Know I grazed the bastard," he mumbled to the air. "Where you think you're going?"

Colbie shook her head in disgust and fear and walked down the rickety porch stairs for the last time.

"You get yer ass back here!" her father yelled. The shotgun boomed, and buckshot flew into the trees above her. "Tha' was a warning shot girl, you get yer ass back here or don' come back at all!"

Spooked, Colbie sprinted toward the overgrown orchard, leaving the house behind. She gulped air, more from terror than exertion, when she reached the edge of the trees. She turned to look at the old house one more time. The siding was falling off, the paint was peeling, the roof was sagging, but it had been her home for fifteen years. Her father was still standing on the porch scanning the land in front of him, gun slack at his side. He looked like the defeated old man he was. She shook her head and turned into the trees.

The cat lounged in the apple tree closest to her with a satisfied look. His tattered ear stood erect and proud, catching the sunlight pouring through the trees. She tickled the top of his head with her fingertips, and he purred loudly.

"Here we go, my friend. We're in it now. I'm not going back there, so you might as well show me where you wanted to go from here." Pausing to carefully tuck her quilt into the duffle, she stood and took a deep inhale, setting her jaw with determination.

"Mrrow," came the reply as he leapt onto her shoulder and draped himself around her neck. She let out a small smile before heading deeper into the trees, leaving her life, and her mother's death, behind.

COLBIE HAD BEEN WALKING for about an hour when the cat's head perked up next to her right ear. She stopped but only heard the white noise of woods alive and growing. As she inhaled the smell of freshly fallen leaves and decay, she discovered what had stolen the cat's attention. A quiet mewling amid a shuffling of leaves came from her left.

Furrowing her forehead, Colbie ducked into the underbrush, searching out the noise. The cat jumped down and rooted through a patch of blueberry bushes. He sat and stared at the small orange and grey marbled kitten that had gotten herself caught in one of the tighter patches and was crying out pathetically. When the kitten saw them, she paused in her squealing and let out a rather unthreatening hiss.

The cat swatted her with his paw, and she toppled into a small pile of kitten fluff.

"Hey, dude. Stop that. She's just scared." Colbie squatted near the kitten and started to work out how she had gotten herself trapped.

The cat blinked with his imperious green eyes. "She is being rude." The cat's voice sounded like wild cat and smooth purr in her mind.

Colbie turned slowly toward her new friend and lost her balance, nearly falling on the kitten, who skittered as far away as she could. The cat just looked at her. She sat frozen before the kitten's cries reminded her what she was doing. The kitten had somehow found yarn to get wound in as well as getting caught in the blueberry bushes. Untangling her as much as possible, Colbie stopped to dig around in her bag, hoping she still had the little knife her father had given her once upon a time. She found it, dancing with the detritus at the bottom of the bag, getting packed with crumbs and sand.

Feeling like a true prepper, Colbie smiled wryly as she picked the kitten up and carefully snipped the yarn from the tiny leg. She placed her gently on clear ground, where the cat promptly pounced and gave her a thorough grooming.

"So what do I call you? I can't just keep calling you 'The Cat'." Colbie sat back on her heels, trying not to laugh at the indignant look on the little kitten's face.

There was no response from the animals except for an occasional squeak from the kitten. Shrugging at the lack of conversation, they sat in companionable silence until the cat seemed satisfied and booted the kitten toward Colbie, who scooped her up with a smile. She nuzzled the velvety belly and was rewarded with a gentle paw to the forehead.

"How about you, little one? Do you have a name?"

"She is to be called Dae. She is a gift from me to you, Colbie Franks."

Colbie hesitated, staring at the cat again. "Has my mind strengthened sufficiently, then?"

He licked his chops then began grooming a paw, ignoring her as only cats can.

Colbie rolled her eyes and continued examining her new friend. She had bright amber eyes loaded with just the right amount of mischief. "Alright, Dae. Sounds like we have some trouble to get into."

She stood and put the kitten down the collar of her shirt, leaving her head poking out the top. Dae snuggled in, letting out a faint, even purr. "Where to now our mysterious leader?"

The cat walked away, tail flagged high. Colbie followed slowly, picking her way through the underbrush. They came up to a sheer rock face, though there were no rock faces in Iowa. Not where her farm was settled anyway. She looked over her shoulder and saw evergreens, though she hadn't walked through any.

"Toto, I've a feeling we're not in Kansas anymore," Colbie whispered into the kitten's head. As she walked, she looked back and forth between trees and cliff, attempting to process the change of scenery.

"Mew?" came the tiny peep in response.

Relieved at the kitten's normal feline response, Colbie looked over at the cat, who just walked with his continued air of mystery, toward a wide opening in the rock face.

"Seriously?" Colbie stopped at the cave. "I'm not going in there."

"Suit yourself." The cat flicked his tail and sauntered away from Colbie, who couldn't take her eyes off the cave mouth. "You could always go back to your father's house. But that's none of my business really."

She turned to stick her tongue out at him, but he had disappeared. Colbie stared in stunned silence. She looked back and forth, hoping the cat was just hiding, but only saw the still evergreen trees.

"But we're not in Kansas anymore!" She shouted back to the trees. "I mean, not that we ever were, but it feels a little Oz-ish, doesn't it, Dae? I suppose we'll have to change it up a little, no munchkins and stuff. You're also not a small annoying dog. But you're probably more curious. What do you think we should do? I'm not sure getting eaten by a bear is a better option than what's at home, but it's kind of close. I couldn't bring you home with me either-"

Colbie pressed her lips together firmly, realizing the rambling was getting more foolish. Dae riggled down Colbie's shirt and fell out the bottom. Much to the kitten's dismay, Colbie, caught her up and tucked her under her arm. "We're going. It doesn't mean I like it."

Colbie walked into the dark, arms instantly itching as the hives came. After ten paces, she had to stoop, then another five paces she started crawling. Thankfully, the tunnel floor was packed dirt rather than stone. "You're gonna have to walk little one." She plopped the kitten between her hands on the floor, secured the duffle on her back, and continued her trek.

The cave darkened as she pressed on, ears straining to pick up any noise. The silence was oppressive. "Dae?"

No response came from the kitten, leaving her with the ever-present dark and itching. Colbie stopped, contemplating just what it was she was doing. Thinking it was probably the stupidest thing she had ever attempted, she pushed backward. Her pant leg caught on a rock that hadn't been there previously and tore at the knee, scraping off a couple of layers of skin for good measure.

"I hate my life," Colbie sat back, trying to take pressure off her injured knee, but only ended up hitting her head on the rocky ceiling. "Okay okay I give."

Dae booped her head on Colbie's thigh with a "mrrt." Blindly, Colbie scritched behind the kitten's ears and swiped a hand over the bumps on her arms, trying to relieve the irritation.

They continued their forward motion and soon entered an open cavern. Colbie took a deep breath and smelled lavender, coriander, and stale coal smoke; not an altogether pleasant odor when combined. Colbie sat back on her knees again, remaining still so her eyes could adjust. Dae ran into her hand and settled, body shaking, against her thighs.

With a whispered voice, the cavern lit. It was not the flickering light of torches, but the steady yellow of streetlamps, just enough to see the shapes of things, while still leaving shadows and secrets. There were rows of long tables with a mishmash of animals? People? Creatures? Lining the benches. They stared at her with a mix of confusion and wonder. Colbie felt the look mirrored on her face and in the vibrations of her kitten.

A shrill, laughing hoot broke the quiet, and the creatures turned back to their chatter, food, and cups. Colbie slowly stood, not taking her eyes off the scene, letting them adjust to the glow. More creatures than she could ever imagine hunched, stood, sat, danced, and stooped around the tables. There were beautiful women with dark hair and dresses, figures that looked like moving tree stumps, ugly men who were no taller than children, and beasts who looked like a cross between rabbits and deer. She watched the creatures playing games of dice, cards, and drinking. Most of them kept a side eyed glare focused in her direction. At the far end of the cavern, a large throne made of stone, driftwood, and bone occupied a large dias.

Colbie scooped up her kitten and whispered, "Well, now what do we do?"

Dae peered at her with wide eyes.

Colbie glanced behind her. The surroundings had changed once again, this time into a solid rock wall. Disbelieving, she ran a hand down the surface, but her exit had disappeared. Panic rose in her chest, and she backed into the newly formed barrier.

Suspicious looks continued from every table. One of the dark women seemed to hiss in her direction, though Colbie couldn't hear through the noise.

Colbie took a breath, squared her shoulders, placed the kitten back in her shirt, and walked towards the dais. The revelry faded into whispers as she passed.

"Still," a resonant and familiar voice sounded from near the throne. Colbie squinted toward the throne, head cocked, confused.

The crowd stilled, the silence rising to the high rock ceiling. The cat with his tattered ear, jumped up to the seat of the throne, transforming into a large man with antlers protruding from his dark brown curls. The right antler was broken in half. His green skin rippled over tight muscles, and a pair of buckskin leggings covered his bottom half. Colbie sighed over his boots, which were worn in and looked like the most comfortable pair of footwear she'd ever seen.

"I am the Erlking," he said, simply.

She blinked at him, but the kitten let loose a series of meows and spits that made Colbie blush.

"Be still Faerydae. I will not tolerate your disrespect."

Colbie placed her thumb and forefinger around the kitten's muzzle to quiet her. She pawed at the fingers but stayed quiet. Colbie rubbed Dae's chin, causing the kitten to huff out her nose and relax into her arms again.

"I gifted her to you because of her spirit, but I think it will be a bit of a burden to you. She will give you strength in the trials to come and for that I believe the burden to be worth it. Colbie Franks, I have called you to serve, will you answer?"

"What? I have no idea what you're talking about. What is going on? I… what... seriously... Just what?" Colbie sputtered.

The Erlking laughed, filling the cavern with the wild sound of screaming cat and winter's storm. Usually only triggered by the dark, the hives returned and covered Colbie's whole body as the laughter was echoed by the creatures to her back.

"Walk with me." The Erlking stepped down from the throne with feline grace. He waved a hand toward the crowd, giving them permission to continue their partying. Colbie paused, briefly scanning the room. Deciding she didn't want to be left alone with the strange beasts, she followed the Erlking.

The trio wandered to a large hearth surrounded by fur covered chairs in an alcove at the far side of the cavern. The king motioned for her to sit, then sank into a seat himself. Colbie curled into a chair and plopped her bag on the floor. Placing Dae on her lap, she focused on petting her. It was cozy and quiet by the fire, the sound from the main cavern was muffled. The stillness stretched until Colbie raised her eyes. The king seemed to have shrunk a little to fit more comfortably in the chair. His smile was broad and pointed, still a whisper of feline around the face.

"What's an Erlking anyway?" Colbie asked, looking back to the content ball of fluff in her lap.

"Me. I am the Erlking. In your tongue, it translates to elf king. I am King of the Wild Fae." His arm swept to take in the creatures back in the main cavern. "Those are many of my subjects, the unaligned, the unaccepted, and the halflings. The pixies, dervishes, willow wisps, and winter frosts. Anyone who would rather be feral than be toadie to the whims of the Winter and Summer Queens." He rolled his eyes at the mention of his female counterparts.

"But Faeryland? That's not real?" Her questions were a little desperate, edging on hysterical.

He peeled back his lips and hissed a laugh, once again showing flashes of the cat she'd first met. "Ah, but then where are you now, dear child? Can I get you refreshments?" He waved his hand and one of the beautiful women, the one who had hissed Colbie thought, sidled up to his side.

"I"m pretty sure you're not supposed to eat anything in faeryland, so I'm good," Colbie said with false bravado.

Eyes bright and flashing, the woman swooped in and grabbed Colbie's throat.

"Do not call this faeryland in such a flippant manner. You know nothing. This is *The Fae.* Whether you eat or not, you are here on the whims of my King. You will keep a civil tongue or I will rip it from your head and brew my potions with your blood." The hag's fingernails dug into the sides of Colbie's neck. She could feel the warm trickle of blood trailing to her collar.

"Peace," came the Erlking's deep voice.

The woman stared into Colbie's eyes, squeezing slightly before releasing her with a shove. Dae cowered in Colbie's lap, remaining surprisingly quiet.

"Bear her no harm, she is my guest. Bring cider and fruit and then stay out of my sight." The king released a sigh. "My subjects are zealous, but their loyalty is without question."

"I thought..." Colbie cleared her throat, forcing away the husk of fear. "I thought they were feral and without fealty." Cobie wiped the blood away with her sleeve and tucked herself more firmly into the chair, holding her kitten closer.

"Yes, but the safe harbor and protection I offer them here is enough to buy loyalty and peace in these halls. I called upon you to serve and I ask again: Will you do so? I know you have no home to return to, you are a bright young woman with the correct sensitivities. Will you utilize your strength in the protection of the Wild Court?"

"I still don't know what that means, and home or no, I know better than to make mindless deals with faeries. I do believe in that much." Colbie was getting stronger in her skepticism.

The king bowed his head in acknowledgement. "It is never wise to take my brethren at their word, for though we cannot lie, we are not always clear speakers of truth. I ask you to become one of the Witches of Nine."

Colbie just sat, expectantly silent, eyebrows raised. She had grown tired of asking and wanted the king to feel her impatience.

"From your look, you are not familiar with the coven of which I speak."

Colbie bowed her head, the mirror image of the king's acknowledgement.

He smirked before continuing, "The Nine are the tellers of the future, the bringers of fortune or famine. They are the protectors of balance and dreams. For the last five centuries, The Nine have been under the influence of Titania, her having found the last six members of The Coven. Naturally, Mab and myself have been more attentive to the mortal world than usual. We must begin to win more influence or the Summer Court will smother all that is wild and winter. Titania will use what she knows to smother shadows and chaos."

"That doesn't sound all that bad to me." Colbie shifted in her chair, tucking the kitten against her chest.

"Without shadows, there is no light. Without chaos there is no order. It will upset the balance. Titania does not care, as long as her revels and summer are superior."

"Okay, fair enough. What does this have to do with me? I'm no faery witch."

"The Nine must be mortal. The Nine must have true sight. The Nine must have open minds. The Nine must give to the Coven of their own free will." His voice held the cadence of ritual.

The woman returned with their drinks and a selection of fruit and bread. She glared at Colbie, who lifted a stein toward her in a mock salute.

"Maowin is not one you should mock," the King commented as he watched the woman's swaying steps back to the main cavern.

"She started it." Colbie sipped at the cider, scrunching her face as the sour liquid hit her tongue. "A little out of season, I think."

The King's laugh rippled out. "Ah yes, not one to be mocked but still knows to obey my word in my home. She won't hurt you again, but she may make your stay as unpleasant as possible."

With a hand to her neck, Colbie took another sip followed

by an involuntary pucker. "It's refreshing." She put the cup on a nearby table and began nervously shredding a piece of bread. "Anyway, what do I have to do to be one of these witches?"

"Do you accept my request, then?"

"No, I still want to know what I have to do. Then I might decide."

"You must accept my request of service, then you will be tested for sight, balance, sensitivity, and seeing."

"Sight and seeing? Good thing I don't wear glasses." The joke fell flat even to her ears. She looked at the Erlking, still at a loss, shaking her head. "I still don't understand, and I feel like you're being purposefully vague. Why me?"

"As I said before, you have the right sensitivities. Do you itch when darkness falls?"

Colbie nodded.

"When you dream, is it clear?"

Colby paused, but nodded again

"Do you have ties to mortal life?"

"I mean, not really anymore, I guess."

"These are enough to make you a candidate. That, with your heritage, makes you a highly desirable candidate. That I got to you first, pleases me greatly."

"My heritage?"

"Ah, yes. That is not my story to tell."

The Erlking smirked, gazing into the popping fire

Colbie sighed and pulled her quilt from her bag, wrapping it around her like she always did when she was upset or uncertain. The king watched her with his smirk, causing Colbie still more confusion.

"What do you think, Dae?" Colbie lifted the sleepy kitten up so they were nose to nose. "Do you think we should go for it?"

Dae kept her eyes half lidded and let out a grumbly little "Mrrw," putting a paw on Colbie's nose.

With a chuckle, Colbie shrugged off her uncertainty and

pulled her quilt tight around her shoulders borrowing the strength of the women whose hands once held it. "I guess I can try," she said with as much confidence as she could muster.

"Done." The king's grin spread across his face, fully feline.

There was a flurry of movement and noise from the cavern crashed around her. The Erlking stood and offered Colbie his hand, wide grin radiant on his face. She tucked the quilt around her, gulped, then rose.

"Come, I will present you to my court, then we must see you settled in. Tomorrow will come too soon and show too much."

The king took Colbie's hand and led her back to the dais. "Our Champion!" He raised her arm and welcomed in the noise of the crowd.

Colbie shrank in the cacophony, overwhelmed and unsure of what she had just gotten into. She kept the smile pasted on her face, though she was positive terror was leaking from her eyes.

Once the noise died down and the fae went back to their dice, drinking, and socializing, the king waved another young woman to his side. She was plump with blue tinted skin and bright red hair. Her smile showed green, pointed teeth but no cruelty.

"Lyla is a nixie. She will take you to your chambers so you can get some rest before your trial tomorrow. May you rest fully and have success in hours to come."

"Wait, trial? What?" Colbie's chest tightened in panic.

The king bent and brushed his lips over Colbie's hand, sending a wave of cool relaxation through her. "What will be, will be. Rest."

With a deep sigh, Colbie nodded and followed Lyla down a passage off the back of the dais that led to a hall of doors. Lyla ushered Colbie into a small, dark stone chamber. There was a bed, wash basin, and an old worn rocking chair. With a bow,

Lyla closed the door, leaving Colbie and Dae in almost complete darkness.

As hive bumps formed on her arms and chest, Colbie's breaths shortened in panic. She flicked her eyes around the confined space and noticed a lump on the chair. Her duffle had been brought here. A small flashlight was in one of the side pockets. She just had to find which one before she passed out from a lack of oxygen.

Head spinning, trying to hold the panic at bay, she searched the pockets of the bag, finally locating the cheap flashlight and flicking the switch. A dim, yellowish light pooled on the ceiling, calming Colbie's breathing. She sank onto the bed, squeezing the quilt tight around her. She pulled Dae from her shirt, rubbing her nose on the kitten's back before placing her on the pillow. Exhaustion washed over her as she removed her shoes and curled into the soft warmth of the bed.

The fall air was crisp and clean. Colbie lifted her face and let the breeze wash over her, absorbing the peace. She hadn't even felt the transition to her dreams. Fae must be closer to dreaming than the mortal world.

"I never intended to leave you."

Colbie stiffened at her mother's voice. "Then why did you?" All Colbie could feel was fury. "You left me with *him.* Couldn't you have at least taken me with you?"

Colbie hadn't known how angry and hurt she was before the vehemence came out of her mouth. She turned to her mother. She was wearing a gauzy blue/grey shift, her hair in long white waves down her back and draped over her shoulder. "What are you doing here, Mom?"

"Oh buddy, I'm so sorry. I wish I could tell you I didn't know, but I did. I knew there was risk, and I did it anyway." She opened her arms to Colbie, who rushed into them, anger forgotten, heart breaking in her chest. "Be brave my daughter.

You have so much to give the world, don't let your fear get in the way."

Colbie opened her eyes in the dim of her Fae room, tears being licked away by Dae. "Oh kitten face." She rubbed her nose on the kitten's head, getting pawed in return. Colbie smiled, climbed under the rest of the covers, and fell back asleep, nose buried in her quilt and still dreaming of her mother's scent.

THE FLASHLIGHT HAD DIMMED, batteries dying, when Colbie woke to Dae batting at her nose. She snuggled deeper into the blankets and giggled at her little friend.

"What are you doing you silly kitten?"

A tapping sounded at the door. A crack of light spilled into the room as the door opened. Colbie leaned over the side of the bed, peering as a six-inch-tall humanoid creature peeked around the door and squeaked in surprise.

"Oh! You're awake. Majesty didn't think you would be. I'm supposed to get you to your trial as soon as possible." The tiny voice wasn't shrill as Colbie had expected and filled the room with a medium timber. He scurried in and draped a gauzy blue/grey shift dress over the arm of the rocking chair. "You'll need to change into the dress and hurry. It starts in less than ten minutes."

The door shut quietly. Colbie clutched the blankets to her chin, gazing at the worn corners of her mother's quilt. Her mother who had left her to save all the people in some third world country and never came back. Her mother who was dead. Guilt and hopelessness clenched in Colbie's stomach. She was just a girl from middle of nowhere Iowa. What could she do to maintain universal balance?

Dae sat on Colbie's head. With a startled laugh, Colbie wriggled out of the blankets, dumping the ball of fluff back on the pillow. Removing her day old clothes, she paused to examine her skinned knee but found it to be unremarkable and only a little sore. The dress fit perfectly except for being a little too long. She took a hair tie off her wrist and tied up the skirt so she wouldn't trip. She didn't need any help being clumsy.

With a deep breath and a kitten on her shoulder, she exited the room and was greeted by the tiny creature.

"Lead on, MacDuff," she said, solemnly to the fae.

He looked at her quizzically. "But I am called Thistle. Who is MacDuff?"

Colbie smiled and waved for him to start walking. "I guess I learned something in Ms. Rainier's English class after all," she mumbled to Dae, who stuck her nose into Colbie's ear in response.

Colbie's snort echoed in the hallway. When she reached the open cavern, the king sat on his throne looking over empty tables.

"It's such a rare time that these halls are empty. I like to take a moment to sink into the silence to hold me over until the next time. The Witches of Nine should be here soon, though as predicted they recently lost one of their number, so they will only be eight."

Colbie nodded and sank onto one of the benches to wait. Dae jumped onto the table and sniffed around before tucking herself under Colbie's chin, purring. They enjoyed the peace and soft echoes their light movements made in the stone room.

The eight women entered the room adding the whisper of fabric to the stillness. They wore shifts just like Colbie's, though theirs were the correct length. They greeted her with soft smiles and bowed heads but went straight for the Erlking's attention.

"Honored one, you have called for one to be tested. We have lost Aileen and need one who is true of sight and mind." Colbie froze in her seat. Aileen had been her mother's name.

"I greet you, High Priestess in the name of myself and the

Wild Court." The Erlking bowed slightly in his seat. "I was sorry to hear of her passing, she was so young."

The High Priestess bowed in return. "The youngest of our number, powers squandered quickly, though possibly not needlessly. If what you say is true and you have found another to fill her rank, the sacrifice will have been worth it."

The Erlking motioned in Colbie's direction. "I will not keep you from your knowing then. Witches of Nine, may I present Colbie Franks, daughter of Aileen Franks and the Wild Court's candidate for the Witches' coven."

The witches turned to Colbie with solemn curiosity.

"So it's true, my mother really never was coming back," she said, anger burning in her stomach.

"Aileen gave herself to the Nine. She knew the risks and was advised against transforming when she did, but she would not listen. We hope you will be less reckless than your mother and remember the greater good. The information she found was invaluable, yes, but the sacrifice was mostly unnecessary." The High Priestess' voice was firm.

"But you let her go anyway."

"You knew your mother. Would anything have stopped her?" Her voice softened with kindness.

Colbie gave a sad half-smile, her anger fading as quickly as it started. "No. Of course not. Anyway, it's done. I'm here. What do we have to do?"

The High Priestess motioned to a chair that had been placed in the center of the hall. Colbie sat and placed Dae in her lap, cupping her hands around the warm furry body. The witches circled her and the already dim light of the cavern went out.

Colbie's arms immediately itched and the hair rose on the back of her neck. She remained still and tried to control her breathing before she could sink into panic. The women closed in around her, their energy crackling gently across her skin, stilling the hives. She felt a weight settle on her shoulders. It was her quilt, warm and comforting.

"Sisters, let us gaze upon this one's mind and offer her to the universe," a woman spoke in a hushed voice.

Colbie squeezed her eyes shut, clutched the quilt around her, and felt a warmth spread from the top of her head down her body. Her mind opened, and she watched as her mother held her in her arms: when she was a baby, when she had fallen and skinned her knees as a child, when Mom had left on deployment for the first time, and when she had left for the last time. She remembered the moment her mother had given her the quilt and the way it always smelled like fall. They sifted through tears, peace, and laughter. Through bedtime stories. Through her first presentation in school and so much more. The one thing they never looked at was Roger. It was like he never existed.

The process didn't take more than a moment, but Colbie sat and experienced each memory as if it just happened. She missed her mom so much her heart was tight in her chest and tears stung her eyes.

"The heart is strong, opened enough to love and remember," a female voice sounded far away as Colbie watched herself wrap her arms around her mother. The tears rolled down her face and into Dae's fur. The kitten popped up, licked her cheeks with her sandpaper tongue, and touched nose to nose, just for a moment.

The memories shifted, and Roger was featured front and center. The fury rekindled in her belly as the sweet man her mother had first met transformed into the monster he had become. Her jaw clenched as she saw the first time he had hit her mother and the first time he had manipulated her into going on deployment. Colbie watched as alcohol and depression ate him alive, as he spent more and more time on the couch, as her world fell apart. She tried to release the anger back out of her chest. This man couldn't hurt her anymore. She would be more than him and his life.

"Her mind is strong enough to reason through anger and pain. She has no attachments. She is a good candidate," the same light feminine voice broke through. "In order to stay in balance, we must test tonight."

Pain split Colbie's head, radiating down her body and focusing on her left leg. The world went white and a cacophony of sound hit her. Her eyes opened, and she found herself on her stomach in the grass. She felt blood trickling down her leg and couldn't feel her foot. Gasping for air, Colbie's eyes searched until she saw the trunk of a familiar apple tree. Only the sound of running footsteps thundering toward her broke the silence that followed.

She squeezed her eyes shut, tears streaming down her face and into the dirt beneath her cheek.

"Oh my God, Colbie. What have I done? Colbie. Say something." Roger's voice mumbled over her in panic.

"Did you seriously fucking shoot me? What kind of father are you?" Her teeth were clenched against the pain. "I can't feel my foot."

"Oh God, I'm so sorry. Oh God. Hold on. An ambulance is on the way. I just meant to scare you. I thought the gun was empty when I put it down. I don't know how it went off. God, Colbie I'm so sorry-" Roger's voice caught, sobbing. Colbie tried to focus on him. Her vision was blurry, but she was able to see his face wasn't wet. She lifted her head, but the pain shot through her skull forcing it back to the ground. He hovered in front of her. His face was missing the hollow-eyed alcohol stare she had grown accustomed to. He was lying.

Colbie pressed her eyes shut, forcing the tears to stop. This was a test. What was she supposed to learn here, that her father really was a monster? That the world was cruel? That it was all a horrible dream?

"What the fuck is going on?" her voice broke, and she pressed her forehead into the ground. She was laying on something lumpy and uncomfortable.

"You're going to be just fine," Roger's voice was quiet and even.

"You get away from me. Just back off."

Roger's feet left her field of vision, and Colbie laid still trying to get her bearings and figure out what was supposed to happen next. Her toes had begun tingling, which she thought was a good sign. She could move her fingers and arms but didn't want to try and lift her head again just yet. She inched her arm down to the lump under her stomach and felt the familiar frayed edges of her mother's quilt. She gripped it tightly, gathering strength to do what must be done. Her fingers strayed down to where she felt blood trickling. Nothing was there. Her breath caught as she started to panic. She felt the area with her fingers again but there was no moisture, though her leg was still sending signals to her brain that liquid was there.

"What are you?" she asked, closing her eyes once more and focusing on her body. She took a quiet inventory, trying to figure out what was actually happening. She had regained the feeling in her foot and was able to move her toes, though she did so subtly.

Roger's voice came, quiet and husky, from closer than she expected, causing her to start. "I am your father. I am your lord. You are mine to command or you will never be without pain again. I will get rid of you the same way I did your mother. I am not a fool, I know those whores selected you for their number. They will not send another of my family to spy. Aileen betrayed me. You will never have the chance."

The cool matter of fact way he spoke the words slowed Colbie's panic. It swept her into fury and rage. She set her jaw, gripped the quilt tightly, and completed the inventory of her body, telling her brain over and over that there was no wound.

She was stronger than this. Roger placed a burning hot hand on the back of her neck then up into her hair. He grabbed a fist full and pulled her head from the dirt.

Colbie tried to keep her face relaxed, but her teeth involuntarily clenched in pain. Roger squatted down and stared into her eyes. His were the gray of tornados and cold. Sucking on her teeth, Colbie worked up enough saliva to spit in his face. He grinned then slammed her forehead into the ground.

"None of that, my daughter. I've let you run wild long enough. It is time to teach you some manners."

He yanked her to her knees, causing her to scream with pain, despite knowing her leg was uninjured. Colbie gasped with sobs, making him hold her up by her hair until she could get herself under control. Counting to five in her head, she brought her face up and met his eyes squarely.

"I will never learn from you. I would rather die, like my mother, keeping the balance." Colbie's voice was calm, surprising even her. Her stomach unclenched, and she started an even rhythm of inhales and exhales, falling into a trance.

Colbie could see Roger's lips move, but she either couldn't understand or couldn't hear what he was saying. He pulled her head back and was inches away from her face, but all she heard was hissing. He lunged to take the quilt from her hands, but she gripped tightly.

She closed her eyes in peace and let out a long exhale, releasing all the pain he had put into her. Her world went white and warm. Clutching the quilt up to her nose, she inhaled the scent of fall and Mother. Her entire body broke into a ripple of hives and a lightness came over her. Her body constricted and seemed to wriggle in Roger's hands, then hair sprouted from every hive on her body. When Colbie opened her eyes again, Roger towered over her, a look of shock and terror on his pale face. Colbie looked down at her hands. They were large and tawny cat's paws. The hair covering them the exact brown that normally covered her head. She smiled internally then stalked toward the man she once called father. She reveled in the grace of her shoulders and back, and gloried in her sleek tail.

Roger had begun to shrink, his clothes fitting loosely and his face going thin, nose protruding. There was the look of rodent about him that she had never noticed before. Colbie licked her chops, beginning the chase that was older than time itself. Colbie sunk down, ready to pounce as Roger's clothes fell, empty to the ground and a small, whiskered nose peeked from the pile. The rat squealed in terror, burying himself in the clothes. Colbie pounced the lump, batting the rodent with glee. The squeaking subsided and the lump stilled. Colbie stepped away, crouching and watching. After a moment of stillness, the rat streaked out from under the clothing, giving the mound of quilt a wide berth. Colbie streaked after him and pounced on his tail. It whipped out of her paws in a practiced move and the rat streaked away into the apple trees. She crouched at the edge of the trees, tail flicking in frustration. The great tawny cat did not catch the rat this time, but she had no doubt there would be another chance very soon.

COLBIE STARTLED awake in the cavern, Dae seated proudly on her lap. The lights were lit again, and the women stood on the dais with the Erlking. All smiled widely. Colbie grinned in return, fierce and feline.

“You have come at last,” the women said in unison. “The Defender. We have waited for you.”

Colbie's heart was still pounding. She examined her hands to make sure they were no longer tawny paws.

"You are a natural to our number. The Rat had infiltrated into Aileen's family before she joined us. He is one of the enemy that will force the worlds into unbalance. Your cat is mighty as the Defender should be."

Colbie listened as the last echoes faded. She stood and bowed to the women, oddly calm. “I am honored to serve. I will defend the Nine with my life and more.”

“So mote it be.” The women and Erlking chorused. The cavern swallowed the echoes as only stone can.

MEG HOLEVA

ABOUT THE AUTHOR

Meg Holeva is a writer, editor, cat-mom, dog-mom, human-mom, and wife. She also dabbles in Acting, Directing, and Costume Design at her local theatre. Most of all Meg is a Meg, who when found in the wild is full of laughter, sometimes has words, and even less often knows what's going on. She would like to thank you for joining her in the adventure that just occured and would also encourage you to follow her on social media.

Homepage: www.meganlorraine.com
Facebook: www.facebook.com/megan.holeva
Twitter: www.twitter.com/megofmanytrade

DAWSON FARMS

BY MATTHEW CESCA

The air still had the scent of the morning's rain upon it as Naomi drove her '07 Subaru Impreza down Route 7. Even though she kept her shoulder-length blonde hair in a ponytail, the wind blasting through the open window still whipped stray hairs around her face. A pair of cute oversized sunglasses with magenta frames sat on top of her head, and she flipped them down onto the bridge of her nose as sunlight broke through the patchy clouds, glaring off the damp roadway.

Overall, Naomi preferred a simple look. Today she wore a white tank top with lace straps, and a pair of black jeans with strategically placed rips at the knees completed her ensemble. She'd worn a gray and black flannel while at school, but had tossed it onto the back seat. She hated having to keep her shoulders covered, and found the dress code to be slanted in favor of the boys. She had always preferred the slight chill in the air of fall, and didn't mind the little goosebumps that had formed on her left arm as she let it sit on the window's ledge.

The Impreza had been her mother's car and had an impressive two-hundred and forty-five thousand miles on it. But her father had taken good care of it and kept up to date on all of the maintenance. When she turned sixteen over the previous summer, her mother had bought a brand new car and she'd inherited the twelve year old hatchback. All in all it was a good first car. It looked brand new, except for a little rust along the wheel wells and a yellow paint scratch on the otherwise silver bumper she hoped her parents hadn't noticed.

She glanced over at her boyfriend Liam in the passenger seat. His shaggy light-brown hair seemed to float in the wind. They were both juniors at Rockbury High and had known each other since he had moved to town in third grade. However, they had only started dating halfway through their sophomore year. He was a bit scrawny and was wearing a black Guns & Roses tee shirt from an album that had come out long before either of them had been born, but he was into that older rock music and it suited him. She reached over and put a hand on his upper thigh. She could feel the rough texture of denim from his too-tight blue jeans on her fingertips and gave his leg a light squeeze. He looked over and smiled, causing her to look back at the road and take a deep breath. Even a simple smile from him was all it took for her to feel her cheeks flush and her stomach flutter.

Liam had been looking out the window. Naomi wondered if he'd been staring at the nearly barren trees that seemed to encroach a little further over the road every year. The leaves had changed color from the greens of spring and summer to the yellows, reds, and oranges of autumn in New England back in September. It was mid-October now and the season for admiring the foliage had passed.

Liam was a couple of months older than she was but had failed his driving test twice. As such, Naomi was the chauffeur whenever the two of them went out. She really liked driving, but knew that it was a sore spot for him to have her pick him up and drive him around all the time. She assumed it was related to his male pride or something. She had given him a little grief when he failed his test the first time. After seeing how mad he became, she had taken a more supportive tact the second time around. That hadn't gone much better. Though at least the second time, while he was still angry, he wasn't angry at her.

Naomi had spent most of the previous weekend helping him study for his third test in a couple of weeks, if only so he would pass and not take it out on her again. She had considered that if he failed again with her help that he might actually blame her this time. She wasn't sure if she could handle that. Even if she did like him a lot, there were limits as to what she was willing to tolerate.

Wednesdays were unique in that both of them were supposed to have study hall for their last two periods, and they both had hall passes to leave early to go to work. He was a stock clerk at a local grocery store, and she a cashier at the local hardware store next door to it. As such, she usually dropped him off on her way to work. They had both requested the day off from their after-school jobs to have a date; a trip to Dawson Farms to try and solve the corn maze that the owners created every year. Unfortunately, they still had gotten off to a late start.

Naomi waited for a few cars to speed past before she turned left across the road into the farm's gravel parking lot. She could see the large white farmstead off to the left as she put the car in park and shut off the engine. When she got out of the car, a stiff, wintery breeze blew through the parking lot and she shivered, deciding to grab the flannel out of her car and tie it around her waist just in case. The fall weather had been unseasonably chilly this year, and the weatherman on the local news was calling for snow to fall before Halloween night.

Liam walked around the car and took her hand in a sweet gesture which made her skin flush again. He led her off to the right, away from the farmhouse and toward a table set up near the entrance of the corn maze. Sitting behind the table was a woman that Naomi guessed to be in her late twenties or early thirties with jet black hair. She was dressed for the season in a well-made witch's costume, complete with the trademark pointy black hat. The shadow of the wide-brimmed hat covered most of her face, completing the look

Lying on the table was a black cat that seemed to give them little regard as they approached, though its ears did perk up. Naomi noticed its right ear was torn, about an inch long, down the middle of its ear. It seemed to be an old wound that had healed, but she still felt bad for the poor creature. She had a soft spot for animals in general.

As the two teens neared, the woman stood to greet them.

"Welcome to the Dawson Farms corn maze! Is this your first time coming here?"

Naomi's eyes danced toward Liam, and she could see they had nodded in unison.

"Yeah, first time," he replied, squeezing her hand a little tighter and flashing the smile back at her that made her melt.

"Excellent!" The woman's voice snapped Naomi back to reality. "So let me explain a few things for you all. First off, it's ten dollars each for admission."

Liam stepped forward and handed over a twenty dollar bill before Naomi could protest. She usually liked to pay her own way, but she decided she would just pay for dinner on the ride home instead.

After placing the money in a tin box on the table, the woman looked back to them, giving a warm and genuine smile. It was the first time that Naomi noticed her large, expressive green eyes. They were almost as dark as emeralds and Naomi picked up a mischievous gleam in them, shining out from beneath her hat.

Naomi had never been to the farm before, but the place was a local legend. Her best friend Jenna went the year before with her boyfriend and said that it was both creepy and fun. With

Halloween coming up, it seemed like a fun thing for her and Liam to do together.

"All right, so this is the entrance here," she said indicating to the opening in the corn maze just off to the side of the table. "The exit will bring you out by the farm stand near the house over yonder," she added, pointing off toward the faded white farmhouse. "Now, we don't want you getting lost in there, so we've got scarecrows that we hang up above the cornstalks. You'll see that they're pointing back toward the entrance wherever you are in the maze. We've had people twice your age come back out that way, so don't get discouraged if you can't solve it. We try to make it more difficult every year. That's part of the fun."

Naomi looked at Liam with a smirk on her face and glimmer in her own eyes. "Oh, we're gonna solve it, right Babe?"

"Absolutely!" he replied, winking back and gently pressing her hand in his own once more. "We got this."

The woman looked them over appraisingly. "Well if you're so confident, I invite you to enter the maze and give it a try." She started to lead them toward the entrance, when Naomi interrupted her.

"Excuse me, is your cat friendly?"

The woman paused and gave her a smile. "Absolutely, just watch by the ear. He's a little tender there."

Naomi stepped up and ran her fingers through the black cat's fur, skimming down its back. "What's his name, and what happened to his ear?"

The woman came over and let the cat nuzzle against her hand. "I call him Imp. The name seems to fit." Her lips curved into a half-grin. "And I'm pretty sure he got in a fight with another witch's familiar," she added, giving the two teens a mischievous wink and tipping her pointed hat at them. The show made both of them chuckle.

Naomi felt a gentle tug on her arm. "All right, are we ready to try this out, Babe?"

She looked over at Liam and gave a nod. He was being patient, but she knew that he had been looking forward to solving the maze. She figured they had better get going. "Yeah, let's go. Sorry Sweetie. You know me and animals."

He nodded with a smile that didn't quite seem to reach all the way up to his sky-blue eyes but didn't complain while the woman led them to the entrance of the maze. "All right you two, good luck!" She gave a broad smile as she motioned toward the opening in the cornstalks. The two teens glanced at each other and then entered, taking the first left after they passed through the opening.

The stalks were tightly-packed along the walls of the maze to discourage anyone from slipping between them. The ears of corn had been harvested and the stalks were bare. Naomi assumed the Dawsons had the corn for sale at the farmstand near the house. Most of the stalks were no longer lush and green, having yellowed as autumn descended with it's shorter days and cooler nights.

After making a few twists and turns through the yellowed corridor of stalks, they came to their first dead end. "Rats," Naomi said, "I thought we were doing well."

Liam stroked his chin and though. "We can probably use the scarecrows to get back to where we lost the way and then figure it out from there."

Naomi squeezed his hand. "Good idea." She took a few steps back and looked up above the stalks and spotted one of the scarecrows. It was wearing a pair of faded old jeans and a burgundy flannel stuffed with hay and a burlap sack full of straw for a head. Thick Sharpied lines denoted a jagged smile, the sewn-on button eyes gleaming in the fading sun. Over the sack sat a navy baseball cap with a white outlined red "B" on it. Naomi wasn't much of a baseball fan, but it was hard to live in New England and not know the logo for the Boston Red Sox. Its left arm was outstretched and pointing back the way they had come.

She grabbed Liam's arm and tugged. "This way silly, let's go!" She giggled at him, and they headed off again, retracing their steps until they found the intersection where they had gone astray. This time they took the right path instead of the left, and made their way deeper into the maze.

A few more ensuing twists and turns passed, and they ended up at another intersection, this time with three new paths to take. Liam looked at her. "Should we split up and check two of them a little ways?"

Naomi shook her head dramatically. "Don't you dare leave me alone in here. We can backtrack together if we have to."

"Okay," he said with a smile before adding, "Let's try left. The exit was way down to the left of the entrance, so we'll need to go that way eventually anyway." The young couple ran off together, hand in hand.

They never noticed the shifting of the stalks about twenty paces behind them.

Racing off with abandon and barely avoiding the various puddles that had gathered from the morning rain, the two teens tried pathway after pathway through the endless sea of corn. No matter which way they went through the twisting passages, they couldn't find the exit. The shadows were shifting with the setting sun, and the longer they spent in the maze, the further off the correct path they got. On top of that, Liam seemed to be getting more aggravated with each wrong turn as the frustration grew inside of him.

Sensing his annoyance, Naomi grabbed his forearm and turned him to face her. He stood a couple of inches taller, but she could basically look him in the eyes. "Hey, look, it's not that big a deal. We can follow the scarecrows back to the entrance and try again another time. It's not like we're trapped in here or anything."

Liam's face was all scrunched up with frustration, but he took a deep breath and let his shoulders sag with defeat as he exhaled. "Yeah, I know. You're right." He looked back toward the direction that they had come. "But you know I'm kinda competitive. I don't like to lose."

Naomi flashed him a wicked smile. "Is it losing to be all alone in here with me?" She slid her body up against his and tilted her head up just enough to plant a soft kiss on his lips. The tension in his body faded as he kissed her back. His hands slid up her sides from her hips to her midriff, until they were just below her breasts.

"Not here," she whispered as she pulled away a few inches and planted her hands on top of his to halt his progress. "Let's get out of this maze first. Maybe I'll even reward you for getting us out of here," she added with a wink.

Liam looked down and flashed a smile, though she could tell he was somewhat disappointed. "Okay," he replied, "I guess we better hurry up and get out of here."

He retreated a few steps and gazed up above the corn maze for one of the scarecrows, and saw one pointing off in the direction of the sun lowering on the horizon to the west.

"I didn't realize it had gotten so late." He pulled his phone out of his pocket and checked the time. It was a little after five o'clock, but that wasn't all he'd noticed. Turning to Naomi he said, "Hey, check your phone. I don't have any service out here."

"Me either," she replied after pulling her own phone out and verifying it. "That's weird. I had full bars when we got here." She slid her phone back into her back pocket and slipped her flannel on over her shoulders. The temperature had dropped considerably since they had entered the maze about an hour ago. "We'd better get going. It'll be pretty hard to see those markers once the sun goes down," she added, motioning toward the scarecrow up above. This one was wearing a dark green and blue checkered pattern flannel and a blue and red trucker hat with the STP logo on in.

"Maybe we can cut through," Liam said, taking a few steps beyond the walls of the maze. The thick row of stalks on either side seemed to crowd in even more as lengthening shadows danced among them, becoming an uncrossable boundary where all sense of direction would be lost. "Nope, no way," he said, slithering out of the dense growth and back to Naomi's side.

Instead of risking it, they followed the path back to the previous intersection in the maze and saw two other paths, including the one that they had come down originally. "Where do we go from here?" Naomi asked.

He scanned the horizon above the corn maze, looking for the scarecrow he'd just seen a few moments ago, but when he found it, something didn't seem right.

"That's weird," he said, scratching the side of his face. "I could have sworn that it was pointing to the left before."

Naomi followed his gaze and appraised the scarecrow. "Well, it's clearly pointing to the right. So I guess we go this way," she added, tugging on his arm and dragging him along. However, he was still squinting at the marker and stepped into an ankle-deep puddle. His left shoe and sock were drenched completely, and he let out a string of expletives.

Naomi heard the splash and the extent of Liam's fury. She stopped and turned around, grimacing. "Sorry Babe."

He took a deep breath before the rage took control of him. Naomi had talked to him a couple of times about controlling his emotions. "Yeah, I know you didn't mean to. Just be more careful."

She nodded to him, thankful he hadn't erupted. Forcing a smile for his benefit, she took his hand and they headed off in the direction the scarecrow had been pointing, Liam's every other step ending in an audible squish.

They followed the path that the marker had shown them, heading off toward the east. Naomi saw the shadows were growing longer. The sky was fading from the light blue of day to the deeper purples of dusk. But once again the pathway ended in another dead end.

"This doesn't make sense," Naomi groaned, rubbing her temple with her fingers. She was starting to get hungry and could feel a headache coming on. "The lady at the entrance said that the scarecrows would lead us back."

Liam looked back the way they had come, trying to spot the marker that had led them astray. "Maybe one of them got turned around in the rain this morning or something."

Naomi shrugged. "Maybe," she said as she dug into her back pocket and pulled out her phone again. "Still no service," she added with a shake of her head before putting it away with disgust. "Do you see a different marker that we can use since the other one was clearly pointing the wrong way?"

Liam stood on his tip-toes to see above the maze for another scarecrow and saw one wearing a white and red flannel with a beat up Celtics hat on top of the lop-sided burlap sack that was supposed to be its head. This one pointed north.

"North doesn't seem right," said Liam, shaking his head. "That would take us deeper into the maze."

Naomi shrugged. "Maybe we have to go that way to go back?"

Liam kept staring at the scarecrow, the doubt lingering. "Maybe," he said, "but I don't remember coming from that direction at all."

"It's been crazy in here," Naomi replied, trying to keep a kind look on her face despite her growing frustrations with Liam's stubborn refusal to listen to her. Additionally, something about the situation didn't feel right. She couldn't explain it, but she had begun feeling a pit developing in her stomach. "Maybe we don't have our directions right. We've been going in circles," she said, her voice a whine even to her own ears.

Liam shook his head. "We might have gotten confused, but the sun is going down. So that way is west." He pointed off toward the setting sun in the distance, shading his eyes against the light as its rays covered the clouds above in shades of pink and orange. He pointed back in the direction of the scarecrow once more. "That's pointing to the north, and I'm pretty sure that we came in through the south."

She couldn't hold it in anymore. Her growing frustration burst into anger as her hands went to her hips and her head tilted to the side. "The lady said to follow the markers, so we're following the markers. I'm tired, I'm annoyed, and a little freaked out. Stop trying to solve this thing. I just want to go home."

After hearing her outburst, it was Liam's turn for his irritation to boil over. "If you think that I want to stay out here with the bugs all night in one soaked shoe until I figure this place out, you're crazy. I'm telling you that it doesn't make sense! We're gonna end up even more lost if we go that way!"

Naomi rolled her eyes and huffed at him. "The marker says to go this way, I'm going this way," she said as she stomped off to the north.

"Naomi, wait..." He rolled his eyes, shook his head, and rushed after her to keep them from getting separated.

When he caught up with her, she was standing at another intersection and scanning for a scarecrow. "Which way?" she asked.

Liam looked back at the scarecrow that had led them in this direction and gasped. "Naomi, look."

"Not now, which way do we go to get out of here?"

He grabbed her arm and pulled, perhaps a little rougher than he would have liked to. "That's what I'm talking about. Look back this way."

"Ow, my arm you as--" Her voice caught in her throat mid-word as she looked up toward where the scarecrow had been and saw it wasn't there. "Where- where did it go?" she asked, her voice shaking.

Liam shook his head. "I don't know. Maybe someone's moving them around?" He scanned the skyline for signs of any of the scarecrows. After a few moments, he said, "It's over there! We must have gotten off course somehow. But..."

"What is it?" Naomi asked, the exasperation evident in her voice.

Liam's voice was low and reluctant. "It was pointing north before. Now it's pointing east."

Naomi groaned and threw up her hands in disgust. "You know that's not possible. Stop trying to freak me out. We must have gotten turned around like you said and are just seeing it from a different angle."

Liam turned and looked at her, his face beet red with rage. He jabbed at the horizon with his index finger and let his anger fly. "Even if we are seeing it from a different perspective, the sun still goes down in the west!! It's pointing the opposite way!"

She huffed and rolled her eyes dramatically before allowing her vision to focus over his shoulder at the marker. She looked from it to the sun dipping ever further in the sky, and back again.

The scarecrow was pointing to the east.

She shook her head in disbelief. "We must have seen it wrong before. It can't possibly be moving." She had taken a few steps forward while examining the marker and slipped past Liam without noticing it. The pit in her stomach was boring through her, and a lump was forming in her throat.

A hand clasped her shoulder.

Naomi jumped and a short scream escaped from her lips. She turned around and saw through blubbery eyes that it was

Liam, and collapsed into his arms. "You scared me," she croaked between sniffles.

Liam steadied her and held her in his arms to soothe her until she calmed down, allowing her to cry on his shoulder. Once the sobbing had stopped and they had both taken a few deep breaths, he released her and their eyes met. He wiped the tears away from her cheek with his thumb, and then gently stroked her face.

"What do we do?" Naomi asked, all remnants of her tough veneer washed away along with a bit of eyeliner she had been wearing. "I just want to get out of here and go home."

"Me too," he said before leaning in to kiss her forehead. "But we have to stop arguing and work together."

She let out a heavy sigh. "Yeah. I'm sorry."

"Me too." He kissed her forehead one more time, before letting go of her shoulders and sliding his hand down into hers. "Together, okay?"

She nodded back at him. "Together."

They headed off down the path that lead them to the east, hoping the scarecrow in the white and red plaid shirt was pointing in the right direction. At every intersection, they looked up and spotted the nearest marker and followed the way its outstretched arm pointed.

Naomi sensed they had been going nowhere when they reached a circular clearing in the middle of the maze. The patch of trampled muck was not large, maybe smaller than the guest bedroom in her parent's home. Searching for an escape, she whirled. A panic came over her. Past the edge of the spinning sea of corn stalks, the last burning crescent of the sunset was sinking below the distant hills of the Appalachians. Only a few reddish wisps of light danced along the clouds, and even those were receding as they followed the sun around the Earth's spinning globe. Night was enveloping them in darkness, and they were no closer to finding their way out.

"This is ridiculous," she heard Liam say next to her. His voice sounded hollow, as if traveling from much further away.

Naomi twisted her head and stared at him. Though his lips moved, Liam's voice didn't seem to carry over the growing rustles of the surrounding corn stalks.

As realization set in, she snapped back to reality. "Liam, shh!" She placed her hand over his mouth to silence him. "Listen."

He shrugged and then moved her hand gently off of his mouth. "It's just the wind, Babe."

She placed her hand on his cheek and turned his face back to hers forcing him to meet her gaze. Her panic hung, a palpable sensation in the air. "Babe. There is no wind right now."

Realization set into Liam's eyes. But instead of the pure terror that she'd felt, his reaction was far different.

"Oh, I see." He backed away from her and glared while shaking his head, his hands balled into fists at his sides. "You guys think that's funny, huh? Scaring her like that? Getting us lost? Well it's not. Come on out here!" The last words were spat out with a level of venom that Naomi had never heard come from him before. But there was something else there that scared her even more.

His voice was laced with fear.

The air hung still for a long moment before the stalks parted all around them. Six figures stepped from between the corn stalks. Each wore old jeans, a plaid flannel, and an old baseball cap, with two blocking the path Naomi and Liam had used to enter this circular dead end. They were surrounded.

Liam had stepped towards the closest one when Naomi grabbed his arm. "They're floating," she said, pointing down where the creatures' feet should be. Only hay stuck out from below the pant leg. There was nothing but air between it and the ground a few inches below.

"It's a trick," Liam's distant voice said. He reached down and grabbed a loose ear of corn off the ground and threw it at one of the scarecrows. It ripped right through the midsection of one of them, knocking some of the hay out from beneath its blue and green checkered flannel. As the stuffing fell out and fluttered to the ground, Liam took a step back. His eyes had gone wide with fear.

Naomi froze in terror as the scarecrows left legs all moved in unison. It was as if a hidden puppetmaster coordinated their movements like gruesome marionettes. Even in the burgeoning twilight, she could see the faces that she thought had been drawn on them were different. The button eyes were moving, shifting, and somehow, glaring right at them.

The creatures took another step forward. Their mouths opened like maws, gaping holes containing nothing but inky blackness within. The false smiles that had been drawn on their faces were long gone. Black ichor dripped from serrated canvas teeth, the saliva of a rabid beast dribbling down and staining the creatures' flannel disguises.

Another step forward.

The two teens huddled against each other, dropping to their knees. Naomi mumbled whatever prayers she could remember from Sunday school years ago while Liam whimpered, "Please no…" before his voice simply trailed off in terror.

Another step forward.

Another.

Another.

All six loomed over them now, their hungry mouths wide, black drops of saliva dripping down on them. Naomi screamed in terror, and all six creatures shrieked in return. The sound emanating from the scarecrows was like a deafening siren, slamming the two teens from all directions. Naomi, sure that they were going to die, clutched Liam's arm in a vice-like grip, sobbing, hysterical with terror.

A raised voice pierced the chaos, drowning out the shrieks

and bringing them to a halt. "GRENDEL!! NO!!! This was not a part of the bargain!"

The six creatures all straightened, and the two that blocked the exit stepped aside. Standing in the pathway was the woman in the witch costume from the maze entrance. The black cat stood at her feet nonchalantly appraising the situation while nuzzling its mistress's leg.

The woman motioned toward the scarecrows. "Back off, let them up. You've all done enough for today. Go back to your posts." As they dispersed back into the cornstalks, she motioned to the one in the blue and green checkered flannel under the STP hat. "Not you Grendel. You and I need to talk. Wait right there."

She stepped toward the two teens and offered them her hands to pull them up off of the ground. "I'm so sorry! They were not supposed to do that! But they are scarecrows after all, and scaring is in their nature."

"Sca- scaring?" Liam muttered.

"They were gonna eat us," Naomi cried between tears.

The woman gave a sympathetic smile. "Oh no, they can't eat you." She walked over to the one she had called Grendel and stuck her hand into its midsection, pulling out a handful of hay. "No digestive tracts. See? They only feed on the fear." She stepped from the scarecrow and returned to the two teens. "They were quite handy in a pinch back in the old days, as I understand. I mean, if you wanted to scare a villager away from a coven without actually hurting anyone. They can be quite terrifying, and no one would ever believe the poor fool once they got back to town." She paused tilting her head to the side as if in thought. "Well, not until the witch trials anyway."

"Wha- What are they doing here?" Liam stuttered out between clenched teeth.

"Oh, we conjured them to make the maze harder," the woman replied with a laugh. "But they weren't supposed to go this far. Just make you get lost and eventually turn you back to the entrance. The fewer people who can solve the maze, the more people come to give it a try." She shrugged matter of factly. "It had been a slow day because of the rain this morning, so I guess they were hungrier than most days and got carried away!" She yelled the last few words in the direction of the scarecrow that was still standing – no, floating inches above the ground in the middle of the circle.

"Wait, you're a witch?! An actual witch?!" Naomi's red-rimmed, watery eyes blinked a few times as if she were trying to process this information.

"When people find out about this-" Liam began, the anger seeping out once more before the woman cut him off nonchalantly.

"They won't find out about it because you won't remember any of it when you get out of here," she said, booping him on the nose playfully. "Just that the maze was too hard and you got lost and had to give up. By the time you two get back to the entrance all the bad memories will be erased. Well, everything except the crushing disappointment of failure." She shrugged and gave them a half smile. "You'll tell your friends, and they'll all come and give it a try. More admission fees for us, right Imp?" she added looking down at her cat, which looked up at her and meowed back. "That's right," she replied, "and more money to put toward next year's crop."

Naomi shook her head. "Wait, this was all about money to you?"

"We're a farm!" she exclaimed. "We feed people. Sometimes the crop comes up a little short and we have to get creative. Can't rely solely on subsidies, you know," she said with a shrug. Naomi and Liam exchanged puzzled glances, their eyes both practically glazing over with confusion.

"All right you two, Imp's gonna lead you back out of here to the entrance, so just follow him. And take this, it's getting dark and so is he," she added, handing Liam a small flashlight. "I need to have a talk with Grendel here about the terms of the contract that he was summoned to perform!" she finished, her voice once again rising at the end as she directed the last few words toward the scarecrow. Naomi wasn't sure, but she thought that she saw the creature wince as if it was a child about to get scolded by a disappointed parent.

The cat stepped away from his mistress and headed toward the path. When it reached the circle's exit, he stopped and turned back, meowing at them as if to say, "This way."

Exhausted and starving, the two teens followed the cat with the torn right ear until they exited the cornfield. The trip back seemed far too short considering how long they'd been trapped, and Naomi stumbled as if in a daze the entire time. As they got into the old Subaru, the two teens exchanged looks. Naomi felt as if a fog had suddenly lifted from her mind.

"That maze is hard," Liam said to her from the passenger seat. "I can't believe we got lost in there."

Naomi nodded. "Yeah, I know Sweetie. I bet Holly and Tom would love to give that thing a try."

"Yeah, probably. Maybe we should come back with them?" Naomi wasn't sure, but there was something in his voice that told her that he really didn't want to come back at all. And she didn't blame him. He paused for a minute before looking down at his shoes and asking, "Why is my foot wet?"

She shrugged and turned the ignition. As she flipped on the headlights and backed out, turning the car around, she remembered she had promised herself to take Liam out for dinner, but she hoped that she could convince him to just do drive through. When the car hit the lonely and now dark highway, although she couldn't explain to herself why, all she wanted was to get home where she felt safe.

MATTHEW CESCA

ABOUT THE AUTHOR

When not performing dark arts to animate scarecrows, Matthew Cesca can be found in the various magical lands he creates. He is the author of two fantasy novels, "The Stairs in the Woods," and "The Forbidden Scrolls."

The portal to the mystical lands in which he dwells can be found on his laptop, currently located in Mesa, Arizona, where he co-parents the best twelve year old son he could have ever asked for.

You can find his novels on Amazon, free for Kindle Unlimited subscribers. You may also follow his disjointed ramblings on Twitter as @nightshade386.

LOCATION #23

BY ALANA TURNER

A lone leaf drifts past the window of the coffee shop. The cozy space had been quiet for hours with only a couple easy regulars snuggled in their seats, playing on their devices and sipping warm drinks. No iced coffees, teas, or other cold beverages were served today. Fall had snuck upon us. The chill air nipped everyone just enough to require something hot. I smiled, happy to see autumn in full swing.

It was refreshing to be somewhere with actual seasons. This was easily my favorite part of the move. Miami was great and all, with its endless beaches and party culture, but seeing the subtle shift from spring to summer to fall had been magical. Everything from peoples' clothes to the color of the leaves changed so gradually and in perfect synchronization that it hardly felt real. Scarves replaced tank tops. Oranges and deep reds littered the ground. I had never felt more at home.

My shift replacement walked toward the cafe, and I couldn't help but grin. Freedom was mine at last. Billie opened the door and shook her head with a wry smile as soon as she saw me. "Go on, get out of here." She chuckled as I zoomed past her to get my stuff from the break room. Tucking my apron in my purse, I made my way out the front.

"You're a lifesaver!" I waved at her, briefly walking backward to give her a proper, if quick, goodbye. A simple shooing gesture as she made a regular a drink was all the sendoff she gave. It was more than enough for me.

Throwing the doors open, I burst into the fresh air. The crispness of fall settled on my skin and in my lungs as I breathed in the cool air. My lips quirked even as I reached for chapstick to stop them from cracking, cinnamon-apple flavor of course. Loose piles of darkly colored leaves sprinkled the sidewalk. I skipped through them as I made my way to my bus stop.

I rounded the corner just as the bus was pulling away from the stop. Mid-skip, I launch into a sprint. The cold briefly burns my lungs. "Wait!" I give chase after my only ride home, but it pulls away, leaving me stranded. The first time the damn thing ever runs on time, and I miss it.

Sitting on a nearby bench, I mull over my options, still panting. The air isn't quite cold enough for my breath to be foggy, but my thoughts sure are. It doesn't help that the exhaust cloud from the bus is lingering. I give myself several minutes to calm myself. No good plan was forged quickly, or in exhaustion. Hands on my knees, I wait until my heart is no longer pounding on my ribs.

The next bus wouldn't arrive for another hour. After being cooped up in the cafe all day, I was too antsy to wait. The day was beautiful, with only puffy, white clouds decorating the sky. While the cold had hurt when I was running, I doubted a walk would be so strenuous. I really only lived a couple miles away.

I picked myself up and started down the sidewalk again. The area held a kind of quiet quaintness. To my right, the streets were in that odd inbetween of some businesses and some residential. The woods to my left helped give the town a rustic vibe. A gust of wind sent a cascade of foliage into the streets and right over a couple of kids on bikes. They screeched in delight, and I smiled at the whimsy.

"Whimsy..." I whispered to myself. That game, the title tickled the tip of my tongue. It had been a huge trend last year, easily the most anticipated mobile app release ever. I snapped my fingers willing the name to come to me. "Whimsi...whimsical....whisimay...Whimsylle!" Smiling triumphantly, I pulled my phone from my pocket to see if I still had the app. I swiped through a cluttered folder of apps. On the fourth page in the bottom right corner sat the orange, blue, and red witch's hat icon.

Curious, I opened it. Sparks and swirls danced on the screen displaying the name. A warning popped up about trespassing and being aware of my surroundings that I quickly closed. A map of the streets spread across my phone screen with my little avatar and its black cat in the center. Just a second later, several creatures popped up around the screen too. Why did I ever stop playing this game?

Several "Magical Menageries" began popping up on the map, including the coffee shop. They were little stations that give you items like Mana and potions to help catch the creatures and add to your "Beastiary." I wasn't about to walk all the way back to the cafe now, but I knew what I would be doing tomorrow.

Walking along, I checked my inventory and tutorials, reminding myself how to catch creatures. A sprite icon appeared on my screen, roughly thirty feet ahead of me. Eagerly I made my way over to the real-life spot. As soon as I was close enough I tapped the icon to start an encounter.

The image of the sprite filled my screen with an intersection as a backdrop. It was small, roughly the size of a Barbie doll, with purple-tinted skin. Crossing its arms, it snarled at me, sounding more like a squeaky toy than anything else. I giggled, cute creatures were always my favorites. It went to attack, and a sequence for a blocking spell appeared. Being rusty, I didn't complete the pattern accurately enough or quickly enough and the sprite's hit connected, only taking away two out of my fifty health points. Now, it was my turn. Rapidly flipping through my magic list, lest the timer should run out and I miss my turn, I picked a simple, low level, immobilization spell. Quickly, I traced a simplistic triangle,and the spell was deemed successful. The sprite stiffened while, her hit points drained. *"Encounter Success! Sprite added to your Beastiary!"* danced across my screen. Checking my Beastiary, I noticed I already had over twenty sprites, but I couldn't help it, they were my favorite.

Still, diversifying my collection a little wouldn't hurt. It wouldn't get dark for a few more hours anyway. Picking up my pace again, I headed toward the next icon to attract my attention, a Gryffin. With how much I had played Whimsylle when it first came out, I had a bit of an edge, but the rust was definitely still there. Nothing a little more time playing wouldn't cure.

I went out of my way at points to hit the Magical Menageries and gain more supplies. The detours made my walk significantly longer but much more enjoyable. Just as I was about to activate another Menagerie, something rubbed on my ankle. The spell of the game broke, and I jumped back with a start. Maybe I should be more aware of my surroundings.

"Aww," I cooed at the little black kitty. Kneeling down, I held out my hand. "Come here little guy, it's okay." I tutted, wiggling my fingers to entice it. We stared at each other. The cat seemed impassive, uninterested. Just like a cat to initiate an encounter then act like they don't care. Its ear was torn, and I couldn't help but wonder who would hurt the poor thing. Moments passed, and it made no move to get closer to me. Standing, I took a step towards it, only for it to trot a short distance away and stare again. I huffed. "Fine, keep your secrets then."

I went back to my game, continuing my walk, only to find the cat following. "I know cats are weird and all, but you take the cake." It meowed in response, but didn't leave. I ignored it and went on with my game but no matter what I did, it stuck with me. Every stop, every detour, my little stalker followed right along. I couldn't help but smile at the odd affection.

At this point, I wasn't too far from my house. My battery wasn't faring very well. I'd have to remember my portable charger tomorrow. I was just about to shut it down when I noticed a menagerie to my left. That couldn't be right; there was only forest. Menageries were typically public places, most of them historical, some businesses. They were never just randomly placed. Even stranger, an arena was right next to it. Those were mechanisms that allowed players to have chosen creatures from their bestiaries battle each other. They followed the same placement rules for menageries, and yet they were both there. I tapped the Menagerie to get it to reveal what the real world location was. For several seconds the game lagged, only showing a loading image where the picture would be. I tapped my foot impatiently, dying for an answer. Without warning, my screen went black. My phone had died.

I stomped my foot and snorted. I was definitely bringing my charger tomorrow. Looking out towards the direction of the arena and menagerie, I saw the cat now perched on a bench. Still, it stared at me with those intense green eyes. The tip of its tail twitched back and forth, quickly and obviously irritated. Without breaking eye contact, it let out a long, loud, yowl. I stepped back, startled. My heel hung over the curb, and my balance shot, I windmilled my arms but to no avail.

I fell right on my ass.

Groaning, I pushed myself off the ground. The cat was gone. A shudder ran through my body. The cold dug into my skin settling into my bones, and when had it gotten so dark? I hugged myself, and jogged the rest of the way home, ignoring the icy chill in my lungs.

THE CAFE WAS BLESSEDLY SLOW AGAIN the next day. This gave me time to stealthily get supplies from the menagerie placed here and battle at the nearby arena. Why did everyone stop playing this? It was a bit of a time-suck yeah, but Whimsylle was more entertaining than threading a bird between pipes or breaking sweets. I was assembling a new team of the creatures I had caught yesterday when Billie popped up behind me, "Hey."

I jumped, banging my head on the cabinet above me. "Ow." Rubbing the forming knot on my head, I caught the chuckle she tried to hide. "Hey to you too."

"Whimsylle? Dang, it's been forever since I played that." She leaned in to get a closer look at the screen. "Isn't a Gryffin *and* a Chimera a bit too much offense? Throw a unicorn in for more health stats."

"Oh, good call." Quickly, I made the edit she suggested.

"What coven did you pick?" Crossing her arms and quirking an eyebrow, she was ready to judge should I say the wrong answer.

"The Luna Coven. You?" I mirrored her pose.

"Acceptable. I chose the Solara Coven."

"So, glad you didn't say Terrin." We both burst into laughter at that, and the couple regulars glanced up from their drinks. We didn't mind, and they quickly lost interest.

"What made you download that again anyway?"

"It was still on my phone. I missed my bus yesterday, and it just came to mind. I can't believe I ever stopped playing, it's so much fun!" I bounced on the balls of my feet, eager to get walking so I could find stronger creatures.

"Yeah, everyone around town kinda stopped playing it after that one girl died." Billie brushed the morbid detail off, with a matter-of-fact shrug and turned to make herself a drink. I chuckled awkwardly, thinking it was a bad joke. Only the 'gotcha' never came. She was serious.

"What?" I grabbed her by the shoulder and turned her to face me, still awkwardly smiling "You're messing with me, right?"

"Couple months after the game came out. Guess you hadn't moved here yet." She shrugged my hand off, going back to her drink. "Everyone was just starting to calm down and not be so obsessed with it when the news reported her death. Then it was a hot topic again before people were too afraid to play."

"Why was everyone afraid to play?" My eyebrows knitted together in confusion. "Accidents happen sure, and I know there'd be the Boomers ranting about it being the games fault, but everyone?"

"There obviously are a couple die hards," She winced at her wording. "But the details were pretty...gruesome." Billie shook her head and put a hand on my shoulder, "You should get outta here before you miss your bus again."

"I probably already have."

"I wouldn't worry about it. Just stay safe, yeah?" She offered a reassuring smile. I tried to return one, but the expression didn't feel as genuine as I would have liked.

"Yeah, alright, I will. Thanks." I walked out the door with a final wavc. "See you tomorrow."

I took my route home. The sky was a light grey, the lack of sun making the cold snap much more noticable. I pulled my jacket tighter. Just as I suspected, my bus had come and gone. Waiting for me instead, was the cat.

"Hey little guy." I smiled, and it rubbed against my ankles again. Same as yesterday, he fell into step with me. Oddly enough, the little stray made me feel safer, like he was here to walk me home. I had my own kitty bodyguard. Unfortunately, he wasn't much of a conversationalist.

The long day of practically nothing had left me exhausted from boredom. My fingers twitched towards my phone. A little social media never hurt anyone. Besides, the fall aesthetic was totally instagram worthy. I pulled my phone out of my pocket.

"Here kitty, kitty, kitty." I tried to get him to look at me, so I could take his picture for my friends. When I unlocked my phone the camera option wasn't available because Whimsylle was up and running.

"What?" My brows knitted together in confusion. I knew I had closed the app earlier. My phone would've been dead by now if I hadn't. In fact the battery level was over 90%. I was about to close the app when a small meow caught my attention. My little bodyguard was looking at me intently, as if asking what I was doing. "I'm being silly aren't I?" I bent down, and for the first time, he let me scratch behind his ears. "Besides, it's just a game."

I closed the "Be aware of your surroundings" tab and went on my way. There were all kinds of creatures out today I had never seen before. "They must've updated it, huh?" The cat gave a short, high-pitched meow in response. One interested me in particular. It was large and slender with no legs and brown in color. Tapping on it to battle, I learned it was called a Wyrm.

I aimed my camera at it, and the AR technology showed it perched on top of a tree stump. It lashed out, and I cast a shield spell just in time. Quickly swiping a triangular pattern, I triggered a reading spell to display its stats. It was an incredibly strong creature. A grin spread on my lips at the idea of logging it in the bestiary. It went to attack again. A guy on his bike whizzed past me, and I stumbled back, startled, before I could block it. The cyclist fell.

I ran up to him, "Are you okay?"

"Woah," he shook his head, "Just a weird...pain in my side. Came out of nowhere." Slowly a smile formed on his face, replacing the shock, "Guess Cupid's arrow just had to make me fall for you."

A nervous laugh passed my lips, "Well, he missed me."

The cyclist snorted, "Fine, be that way." He dusted himself

off and rode away. I rolled my eyes before returning to my game,

"Hey, it missed!" I said to my little bodyguard. "That's lucky, huh?" Instead of silence or a passive meow like I had gotten used to, he hissed, back arched and hair on end. He swatted sporadically at the area in front of me toward the tree stump. I shook my head. "Cats are weird." It was my turn to attack now. Having more than enough mana to back it up, I used my most powerful spell. Tracing a complex, 12 point lightning symbol, I let loose on the beast. The words "Critical Hit" appeared on the screen and a howl came from the creature.

It didn't come from my phone.

I froze, staring at the stump. The howl had definitely not come from my speaker. It came from in front of me. That couldn't be possible, and yet, I was sure of it. The Wyrm wasn't defeated, but I couldn't take my eyes off the stump. It couldn't be possible. I missed my chance to defend once again. I glanced at my screen in time to see it perform a whip attack with its tail. The cat yowled.

The sound of stricken flesh hit me before the pain did. It blossomed across my cheek, tearing a gasp from my throat. Bent over and teary eyed, I held my palm against my face. There was no blood, but I'd be willing to bet my cheek was red. It felt like the skin was on fire. I saw my health drop on screen. The Wyrm waited for me to take my turn.

I stared. Surely, I was imagining it. Something must have gotten caught in the wind. I eased myself into a standing position, scanning the street for anything that might've been the debris that struck me. There was a plastic folder blew down the street. School supplies were littered around in the other direction. It looked like some poor kid's backpack exploded.

Regardless, I exited the encounter and continued on. That creature was way too difficult for me to face. I had no business trying to collect it yet. Not to mention, I wasn't sure what exactly struck me. It was best to get out of there, just in case any other random school supplies were blowing around. Apparently they could be quite painful for flimsy pieces of plastic. At least, I hoped that's what it was.

"I'm just paranoid, aren't I?" The cat didn't answer but merely ran circles around my feet. "I'll try again when I'm a higher level." For the rest of the walk I just collected supplies from menageries and caught small tier creatures. Ones that only took one turn to beat.

Before I knew it, I was home. "Well little guy, I guess this is where we part ways." The cat looked at me one last time with those intelligent green eyes, and wandered off, tail swishing. "Thanks for walking me home." If it heard me, it didn't show it.

Night fell as I settled in. Pajamas on and Netflix playing in the background, I was at peace. While tomorrow was Wednesday for everyone else, to me it was Friday. I'd have all weekend to kick back, relax and do nothing or everything I wanted. I couldn't help but wonder if the nearby park was a good Whimsylle spot.

The thought scared me as much as it excited me. The game was time consuming. So many strategies and methods of play, so many tasks and creatures to find and collect. I couldn't help thinking about it, even if what Billie said still formed a pit in my stomach.

Shaking my head, I pulled up my web browser on my phone. Surely, that story was just an urban legend, a new creepy pasta and nothing more. Snopes would tell me for sure.

I searched the story, typing "Whimsylle dead girl" and hoped for the best. Immediately, I got results. There were dozens of articles and points of contention and variables that couldn't be confirmed or denied. Several facts were known to be true though. One: Her name was Carly Keys and she was only 13 years old at the time of her death. Two: Her body was found in the middle of the woods, torn to shreds so badly her own mother couldn't recognize her. Three: When her body was discovered the Whimsylle app was still open on her phone, and her cat, Luna, was found at her feet. Some said the app was frozen on a lost encounter screen, the words "Oh No! It got away! Better luck next time!" still dancing to the theme music. This was never confirmed. Four: this happened here in town. They never found what killed her.

It wasn't what I hoped to find.

Quickly, I closed the screen and threw my phone down. It had gotten far later than I meant for it to. I put myself to bed, but sleep was elusive. After hours of tossing and turning, it did finally come, but even my dreams were laced with Unicorns and Gryffins and girls that didn't understand what they were getting themselves into.

EVEN THE SLOWEST day at work would've exhausted me. As it was, today was the busiest I had ever seen the coffee shop. We were running a special on pumpkin-spice themed food and drinks. Lattes, cappuccinos, and flavored specialty coffees flew off the counter. On my first break I nearly collapsed in the breakroom.

I pulled my phone from my pocket and went to open Whimsylle. Instead of opening, the phone directed me to the app store, showing an update. Grumbling to myself, at the lost time, I downloaded the new version. After scarfing down my lunch, I was back on the floor before I knew it.

Time went by faster than all the half-decaf, pumpkin-spice chai lattes did. I didn't even have time to sigh in relief when Billie walk in. She quickly tied her apron on and came around back. Tapping my shoulder, she whispered, "Be careful today," before taking my place at the register. If it wasn't for the other two employees racing around the kitchen, I would've asked what she meant.

As it was I stepped out of the heat of the cafe and into the cool, crisp air of fall. The update had finished installing during my shift. The cold was harsh enough to make my fingers tingle, but I didn't care. Even though it had made me lose time, updates meant improvements. In this case it even meant more features.

A little tutorial popped on screen after I closed the *"Be aware of your surroundings"* message. The little cat familiar on screen pawed at different places on the screen. Leading me to tap on a nearby menagerie. I activated it, and received more goodies than normal. *"For every new Magical Menagerie you visit each day, you receive bonus items for exploring!"* the familiar explained. I grinned at the thought of extra bonus items and not having to be so careful with the ones I had. My familiar pawed at the bestiary icon and I tapped it. "The Beastiary has also been expanded! Find the creatures in the wild to learn more about them!" Several blank silhouettes to marked where the various different creatures would go. The last one had a long neck, and wings, clearly a dragon. I bounced on the balls of my feet in excitement.

I already knew I had missed my bus. Even if I hadn't, I didn't plan on taking it today. Waiting at the stop however, was my little escort. He jumped on the bench as I approached, meowing in greeting. "Hey, little guy." I scratched behind his ears. The cat fell into step next to me like both days before.

"You know, most people adopt cats, instead of cats adopting people, right." He twitched his tail in response. Around my little town I went, hitting up every different menagerie I could, avoiding any I had already visited. While it hadn't been explicitly stated, the number of bonus items seemed to increase if I visited several unique menageries in a row, like a streak bonus. I battled at various arenas, taking my wins and losses with grace, except for the one where the app crashed on me. Kicking a trash can not knowing it's bolted down isn't exactly graceful after all. It wasn't long until I had hit every spot in my area. All except one.

I noticed once again, the menagerie out in the middle of the woods. That and the arena were right next to each other, barely in view on the map. The prospect of numerous bonus items tempted me to venture into the woods. The idea of all the points I'd get defending an Arena no one touched, so therefore wouldn't overthrow, made me want to sprint to it. It really couldn't be that far. My house and the cafe were only a few miles apart, and I couldn't see either on the map.

The tips of my shoes hung over the sidewalk into the grass. An urgent yowl gave me pause. The cat stared at me intently before pawing at its torn ear and staring again. "It'll only take a minute." He stood, back arched, hair on end, and tail twitching. "I promise, I'll be right back." I didn't give myself the chance to change my mind before running into the trees. The cat yowled after me.

The trees were half-barren, the grass covered by their dead leaves. My footfalls cast a cacophony of crunching into the silent wood. It was the only thing I could hear over my own heartbeat. Adrenaline coursed through my veins, sending me into a giddy high. Eventually I slowed to a jog then a walk, until I came to a large rock where I took a seat.

Smiling and panting, I checked my phone. The menagerie and arena were still on the edge of the map. I hadn't gotten any closer. The road was no longer visible from the direction I came, and only some light trickled through the decaying branches. The smile fell from my face.

No matter, it really couldn't be that far. I'd give myself a few minutes to rest, then continue on. I tapped the icon to see what I was looking for out in the woods. I hadn't tried since it died that last time. The loading screen spun and spun for minutes on end. I was just about to give up when it did finally appear, though I was far from satisfied. Where the name of the place should have been was only "Location #23," and where a picture should be was merely black.

"Of course." I rolled my eyes, grumbling. A vibrating branch and shower of foliage made me leap from the rock with a brief scream. I crash landed, thankfully with only my pride bruised. The cat meowed at me anxiously. "You scared me!" It rubbed up against my arm before trotting back towards the road a little ways, pausing to look at me. "I told you this will only take a minute." It yowled at me again.

I picked myself up and dusted myself off. Only my pride had been injured thankfully. I scanned the ground, eyeing my phone. When I saw the screen, I rolled my eyes "Screenshot saved to camera roll!" I closed the message and returned to the game map. The menagerie and arena couldn't be much farther.

To call what I walked on a path would be generous. I was constantly catching myself, trying not to trip on branches and rocks. Small inclines and declines made it seem like I was going much farther than I probably was. I wish I had looked up what park this had to be in and just gone in the main entrance. It would've saved my jeans and sweater a few holes, but I was here now. Besides, It couldn't be that far.

Onward I trekked, the black cat right beside me. Beside was a relative term. Sometimes he was actually right next to me. Other times he was above me, running along the branches and covering me with a rain of red and gold leaves. Most often he was right ahead of me, hackles raised, ready to fight. He would be okay because it really couldn't be much farther.

It really couldn't be much farther.

It shouldn't be much farther.

How much farther was it?

Where was I?

Blood pounded in my ears. I pushed back branch after branch, going as fast as I could. Bark scraped against my palms, leaving tiny scratches I was too frightened to feel. My foot snagged a branch. I barely had time to throw my hands out in front of me before falling face first into the dead leaves and mossy grass, my breath caught in my throat.

The harsh stop finally allowed the pain to seep into my consciousness. Small slices littered my hands and legs. I was pretty sure a couple were on my face as well. Prodding my forehead with a finger and having it come away with a spot of blood confirmed it. I moaned, in pain, in fear.

My ankle was sore but probably not broken. Regardless, I couldn't bring myself to get up. Instead, I pulled my knees in, hugging them, and sat in the decaying woods. Gingerly, I leaned my head against my knees. It was hard not to aggravate the cuts through racking sobs.

This time I didn't flinch when the cat rubbed against me. I picked my head up to look at him, and he offered me a soft meow. "Okay, maybe you were right," I said with a sad smile. He let me scratch behind his ears and down his spine, leaning into the touch. I went to stroke him again when I snagged my hand on something. "Is that a collar? What's your name anyway?" I spun it upside down so I could look at the tag. It read "Luna."

My breath hitched again. Rationale told me that surely that was a fairly common name for cats, especially black cats. Paranoia told me to run, but exhaustion was settling into my bones. Leaning against a tree for support, I pulled myself to my feet. I rotated my ankle to test it, and while it twinged with the whispers of pain, it definitely wasn't broken. "Let's get out of here, yeah?"

I picked up my phone, glad to have such a tough case. I could no longer see the roads on the game's map, but I almost didn't care. Two other things caught my attention much more aggressively. One: The menagerie and arena were in fact closer now. They no longer hung at the end of the map, but were now half the distance they had appeared to be. Two: Several creatures now littered my screen. There were Wyrms, Furies, Basilisks and others I had never encountered. All had insanely high stats, levels above my own.

Normally, I would've brushed it off. Even with my last odd encounter with the Wyrm, all I had to do was *not* tap their icon and nothing would happen. Now, I was getting notifications I had never seen before. "Wyrm wants to engage!" "Chimera wants to engage!" "Harpy wants to engage!" and numerous others all flitted across the game screen. Even if I selected "*ignore*" the notification would pop right back up again. Worse yet, the icons were moving. They weren't supposed to move, players were supposed to go to them. And they were all coming right for me, congregating to my current location.

My chest rose and fell with deep quick breaths. What I was seeing had to be a glitch. My eyes hurt from the strain of how wide I held them open, unblinking. The temperature had dropped, feeling much more like the dead of winter than the early tendrils of fall. Only slivers of fading light made it through the tops of the trees. For a moment only my breathing broke the stillness .

I felt frozen. Crazy theories of what was about to happen flitted through my head, none with a happy ending. A rustling of golden-brown and red broke the spell. I was running again, the cat in step next to me, phone gripped tightly in my hand. Feet slipped, branches caught my clothes, my muscles begged me to stop, but my primal fear proved to be the best motivator.

The sheer stone incline was the only thing that stopped me. Reaching far above my head, I'd never be able to scale it. My back against a wall, I checked my phone. This was it, this was the menagerie. I activated the icon. If I got the right items, maybe, I could dual my way out of this. If they were from the game, surely they were affected by it.

My in-game familiar popped on screen, whiskers droopy and pouting, "Your bag is full. Try again later."

Tears blurred the words, but I exited the screen. All the creatures were approaching the menagerie, including one from behind me. It was pitch-black and had massive wings and long talons, the avatar taking up a quarter of the screen. The silhouette from the bestiary hadn't done the dragon justice. Luna rubbed my ankle. I looked down at him, and he meowed at me one last time before bolting.

I suspended the app momentarily to check my signal. Not a single bar. My phone registered no Wi-fi either, which elicited a bark of humorless laughter from me. Whimsylle didn't need to follow any rules apparently. I went to pull the app back up, but scrolling through the opens ones, I noticed my photo gallery open. The last photo was wrong. It was supposed to be the accidental screenshot of the menagerie. Instead it was the girl's face, burned almost beyond recognition, staring straight at me. With haste I pulled the game back up to check what was happening and to see how close they were.

Twigs and leaves crunched from all sides. The wall of Earth behind me crumbled slightly, straining to support the weight lumbering over it. "*The Horde wants to engage*!" danced on my phone. Dozens of them swarmed my icon. It was from behind me that the first roar sounded. I never saw the dragon through his flames.

ALANA TURNER

ABOUT THE AUTHOR

Alana Turner is a Floridan author that writes about the dark side of things. She has several short stories published in various anthologies and is working on her debut novel. Along with horror she also writes science fiction and fantasy.

If you'd like to get a better idea of her extended works, follow her on social media!

Instagram: https://www.instagram.com/authoralanaturner/?hl=en
Facebook: https://www.facebook.com/AuthorAlanaTurner/?view_public_for=2112686228948057
Twitter: https://twitter.com/_Alana_Turner

A WITCH'S KEN

BY NICOLAS GRAM

Yellow eyes stared at her with contempt.

The small cat slinked along the windowsill, its paws leaving tiny impressions on concrete still damp from the evening rain. It wrapped around the outside of the second story of the manor and stopped right in front of Amelia's window. The cat's fur was immaculate, black as night and not a touch out of place. It's only blemish was a torn right ear—damaged in a fight, or maybe sliced part way and ripped the rest by someone cruel. That kind of thing happens all the time with black cats, and more so around this time of year.

"A stray, huh?" Amelia leaned forward in her chair and tapped the glass playfully, but the tiny feline didn't budge.

It was ominous to find a lone black cat, tonight of all nights, at her window.

"You're not afraid of me at all, are you? Well, aren't you a proud one?"

Amelia put her elbows on her desk, carefully keeping them to either side of the charcoal drawing she was working on, and engaged the cat in a staring contest. They battled, the creature never wavering, until it focused on something behind her.

When someone crashed through her door, Amelia swore the cat's eyes flashed a pale green for a moment.

"Amy! Did you see it? Did you?"

Her sister, tiny and always full of twelve-year-old enthusiasm barged into her room, dragging her best friend, Claire, behind her. Small hands bounded up and grabbed Amelia's arm, jerking it across the paper. Amelia sighed at her drawing being smudged.

"Calm down, Sophie, you'll overdo it again." Amelia patted her sister's head, tousling her wavy blond hair. She then pointed toward the window. "Did you mean the cat? It's right there, see?"

"Cat?" Sophia's tone was one of confusion. "I don't see a cat, Amy, but did you see the comet? It's so pretty!"

Amelia jumped up and reached over the desk, lifting the latch on her window to open it, and leaned out. Chilly night air nipped at her in greeting. She placed her hands on the damp ledge to search, but no trace of the small animal could be found. Amelia frowned, unhappy to have missed an opportunity to sketch the defiant cat.

"Amy?"

The voices of both her sweet sister and her companion pulled her back into the room. Amelia set the iron latch back into place and sat down to address her intruders. Her sister blinked her bright blue eyes and Amelia smiled.

"Never mind, don't worry about it. It was just a stray anyway." She clapped and gave the pair her utmost attention. "So, what's this about a comet?"

The girls exchanged grins and Sophia pointed to the sky.

"It's above us right now! You can't see it from here. Come to the garden!" She happily seized Amelia's hand and tugged her to follow. "Come on, let's go!"

"Okay, okay, I'm coming."

Amelia exited the room behind the two girls, who chatted incessantly about the comet and their parents.

"Isn't it exciting a comet appeared on Samhain, Sophia? Everyone says so."

"Yes, and on Amy's birthday! Mother and Father didn't even mention it. I wonder if they'll be able to see it with the others at the assembly."

"I hope so! My father was very happy about it."

"I wish they could be here with us! They'll be gone until tomorrow night, though."

You'd think I'd be used to it by now, but every year hurts a little more.

Even if her birthday was never celebrated properly by the rest of her family, Samhain was still an important day for them. When she was born in 2113, the government had already long abandoned this area, and since Inner London played by vastly different rules compared to Outer London, her family had a say in how affairs were conducted. They always took part in yearly assembly meetings as members of the elite within London proper. Though not really considered holidays anymore, Samhain and Halloween had been a three-day excuse for the new wave aristocracy to get together and plan out the remainder of the year for decades now, or so she had been told many times before.

Despite the topic, Amelia enjoyed seeing the happy expressions on their faces and found the two girls chatter endearing.

Well, it isn't all bad. Sophie is doing great this year, and they even allowed a friend over.

She followed them down the stairs of their luxurious manor. They passed by extravagant silver, gold, and cobalt colored furnishings, with intricately embroidered curtains on the numerous large windows. Large paintings and equally large digital displays adorned the white walls.

The vibrant screens were the latest tech and rotated between photos, movies and digital artwork of varying kinds, while the paintings depicted famous landmarks from around the world.

One in particular caught her eye, and it always brought her chills. She loved the painting of Stonehenge amidst a darkened sky and the storm gathering in the distance—a tribute to an ancient wonder before its destruction by a terrorist campaign decades ago.

The artist commissioned for these paintings died last year. Her mother had lamented but recovered quickly when she learned their value skyrocketed.

"If only she'd take an interest in my art, too," Amelia muttered to no one in particular.

They exited their home into the large, lush gardens, and the three of them stood on the damp grass beneath the starry sky, embraced by the cold autumn air. A mild breeze lapped at their skirts, and Amelia shuddered.

"Let's not stay out too long, okay?"

The girls agreed and bounded forward, taking in the night. Her family's guards were inconspicuous, but they were there, keeping a watchful eye on them—a member of the Cantryl family always had protection outside of their home. It still made Amelia feel more important than she was.

It's not like they particularly care about me or Sophie, though. They do it as a mere courtesy to Father.

"Look, Amy! See how beautiful it is?"

The girls' eyes were locked onto where Sophia pointed. There, a green and white streak moved ever so slowly in the night sky.

"My father says it's the comet's first return in nearly a century. He and mother told me this year was special." The eleven-year-old Claire spoke with awe, her little hands clasped together. "They said to make a wish tonight, since Halley brings good luck!"

"Oh? What should we wish for?" Sophia eyed her friend curiously then glanced at Amelia. "What do you think, Amy?"

"You need to think for yourself more, Sophie. I won't always be around, you know?" She shook her head at Sophia, trying to break her sister's habit of always asking her for advice. "Think. What is it you want most?"

Sophia frowned, tilting her face and hiding her expression beneath golden bangs. Her sister always pouted when she didn't get an answer she hoped for. Sophia shuffled her feet for a few moments then focused sharply on the comet. The determination in her eyes made Amelia feel proud, if a little worried, and she wondered what her sister was thinking.

Taking the opportunity to make her own wish, Amelia marveled at the eerie, hauntingly beautiful green and white streak once more. What did she want? She gave up wishing upon a star years ago, but she was feeling nostalgic and in the moment.

What Claire had said sparked a memory of the news from the other day. Halley's Comet hadn't been seen since the mid-21st century, but people believed it appearing this Samhain to be an auspicious timing all around. Since the discovery of Magery, real magic, and its scientific phenomena back in January, the world had turned on its head.

Father was very upset too. Why? Wouldn't it be lovely to see it?

Her mind made up, Amelia clenched her hands into fists at her sides. She wished for the chance to see and use magic, just like in the stories she'd read about so many times before. She'd be happy to know it was possible, and thrilled if she could use it herself to get out of here someday.

The comet shone bright at that moment before returning to its dim, pale color. Amelia wondered if she was seeing things.

"Did you see that, Claire?"

"Yes! Do you think our wishes came true?"

Sophia and Claire bounced up and down with excitement and Amelia grinned.

Ah, they're such close friends. I'm happy for them. I am, right?

At the back of her mind, jealousy stalked, and her smile

faded. Amelia shook her head then approached the friends and grasped their shoulders tightly.

"Come on you two. Time to go back inside before we all catch a cold." She ushered the chattering youths toward the door and found it still open. Amelia sighed and rapped her sister's head.

"Ow! That hurt!"

Sophia rubbed the spot with her hand while Amelia pointed at the door.

"Sophia."

"What? I didn't leave it open, I swear! Claire, did you?"

"I went outside before you," Claire said, shaking her head vigorously.

"I've told you many times to never leave the door open or unlocked. It's Father's rule, not mine, but we should respect it." Amelia put on her best elder sister expression, attempting to teach her a lesson. "This goes for windows, too!"

About to cry, Sophia only nodded, and Amelia rolled her eyes then gave her a hug.

"It's okay, Sophie, but it's better to double check these things sometimes is all. Don't worry about it. Be careful in the future, okay? Promise me."

"I promise, Amy!"

Sophia wiped her tears, and Amelia let them go inside first. Her eyes took a sweep of the garden, finding one of the guards. He sent her the nod she expected, informing her he had been keeping a watch on the door. She waved and bowed her head slightly in thanks then walked toward the entry once more.

Her heart skipped a beat when a familiar black cat sat nonchalantly just inside the house. She blinked, and it was gone.

She rushed inside after the creature but couldn't find a trace of it, which unsettled her.

Am I crazy? Where did it go this time?

"Amy? What's wrong?"

"Did you see a cat, Sophie?"

Her sister shook her head.

"I didn't see a cat either, Amelia," Claire chimed in.

I must be crazy.

"Never mind." Amelia gave the children a strained smile. "It's late and time for bed anyway. You two need to be up early for school, right? Tomorrow is Monday after all."

"What? No, Amy, it's your birthday! Can't we stay up a little longer?"

"Yeah, Amelia, we even made desserts!"

"Besides, didn't you get home schooled? It's not fair!"

Her sister's words brought up the fact that Amelia could count on two hands how many times she'd left the estate since the reconstruction and her accident nearly ten years ago.

That's because I was really sick all the time—worse than you, Sophie, though I don't remember much.

The two children continued to complain, but Amelia wasn't budging. She already let them feast on a half dozen of the twenty-one cupcakes they had made for her birthday. She accompanied them to Sophia's room and helped brush their hair after they got ready for bed.

A knock on the door resounded, and Amelia called the one responsible in. A burly guard with a brusque manner, dressed in a sharp, clean black uniform stepped inside. The faint smell of cologne wafted from the man.

"Pardon the intrusion, lass. The inspection is finished and nothing was out of place."

Amelia nodded and meant to thank the man, but spoke from frustration instead.

"We do this every night, but there's never a problem. You don't have to come to me unless there is one, you know?"

"Pardon, but it's my job."

"You're right but..."

Would anyone really bother us here?

He turned to leave when Amelia had a thought.

"Oh, did you happen to notice a stray cat around the house?"

"A cat, lass?" He thought for a moment then shook his head. "No, no cat that I saw. Want us to look again?"

Was I really imagining it?

"No, that won't be necessary. Thank you. Goodnight."

He nodded, exiting the room, and Amelia hugged her sister whose eyes were wide with concern.

“Don’t look at me like that, Sophie. I’m fine. I just have a lot on my mind.”

She gave her a kiss on the forehead.

"Get some sleep. You too, Claire." She gave the small Claire a hug as well and turned to leave when the hem of her shirt was tugged from behind.

"Can we sleep in your room tonight, Amy?" The seriousness of that request caught Amelia off guard. Her sister hadn’t asked to sleep in her room in years.

"Aren't you a little old, now?"

Sophia, now in secondary school and still way too attached, plead with a face Amelia didn’t want to refuse. She didn't mind but knew it wasn't a good idea to let her continue this way. Sophia's eyes glistened expectedly, and Amelia sighed.

"Fine. Just for tonight, though."

The sweet smile Sophia gave made Amelia’s heart hurt. She wasn't sure why, but she knew this was important to her sister tonight.

"I have some things I need to do, but you two go ahead. I'll be there in a little bit." The two young girls gleefully grabbed their pillows and ran down the hall toward Amelia's bedroom. She yelled at their backs, "And go straight to sleep, since it's already past your bedtime!"

She knew they'd be jumping on her bed if she didn't go to them soon, but she had to make sure of something.

After leaving her sister's room, she searched high and low for the little creature plaguing her thoughts.

Why am I so bothered by this? It's just a cat. Even if it were inside, what could it do?

A nagging feeling in the back of her mind wouldn't rest, so she continued the hunt. After nearly an hour, she finished checking everywhere but came up empty. Sighing, she rubbed her face in exhaustion with the palm of her hand then went inside her room after quietly opening the door.

The room was dark, with only the light of the moon coming through the window. Surprised to see them fast asleep, Amelia smiled at the two friends hugging each other on one side of her bed.

Amelia went to the closet to change but couldn't avoid inspecting her reflection in the mirror.

Her body was no longer simply frail like it used to be, and she had worked hard to make it happen, despite the numerous setbacks along the way. Even the memory loss from the accident her parents refused to talk about no longer bothered her.

Emerald-colored eyes stared back at her in the pale moonlight while she brushed her short, raven black hair she kept in a bob cut. The cherry colored fringe she inherited from her father's side of the family made her special, her mother had said, but she frowned at the memory. Amelia wanted to learn more about her grandmother, but it was yet another topic her parents refused to talk about with her.

It's been another year of this. I'm suffocating here.

Amelia made plans to get away from this household, but her parents shut them down, telling her to wait. She was finally making progress, all on her own, to change her dull, boring life, but they refused to let her go.

She had the ambition. Amelia worked hard to better her craft, and she hoped to become an illustrator for a career path. She now needed the courage to defy her family.

"I need a change."

Sophia stirred at her words and Amelia stopped reflecting to finish changing into her pajamas.

She sighed at her irrational fear of the unknown and climbed into bed. Sophia rolled over in her sleep to attach herself to her arm. Amelia's frown disappeared and she gently petted her sister's hair. She realized she needed to get Sophia prepared for life without her. A pang of loneliness stabbed at Amelia's heart, but she knew it was for the best and drifted off to sleep.

"AMELIA."

Startled awake, Amelia bolted upright in her bed at the melodious whisper of her name—it had called to her a few times in her dream, and something in the voice disturbed her. She took a few moments to catch her breath, slowing her pulse down. It was the dead of night, and the room was draped in darkness, save for the few scraps of moonlight leaking through the curtains. To her side, Sophia, still clutching her right arm, and her friend Claire, curled into a ball, were both sound asleep. She detached herself from her sister's grasp then climbed out of bed.

The air was chilled, and she shivered, hugging herself. Checking to make sure nothing was amiss, Amelia walked to the window. She marveled at the beauty of the full moon beaming through rolling clouds, then inspected the courtyard below. The wind gently blew the boughs of trees, and the iridescent blue-white lights of the lampposts caught their wavy shadows, but nothing stirred.

What was that voice? Just a dream?

The glossy display on the wall next to her shifted to three in the morning, and her pulse quickened when shining eyes stared back at her in the dark—glowing the same sickly shade of green she'd seen earlier in the evening. Frightened by the reflection, she rushed to her closet mirror for a better look.

"Amelia!" came in a whisper from behind her. She jumped, and a feral growl resounded beyond the closed door of her room. A reproachful hiss echoed in response, followed by the screeching of a cat. Amelia stood rooted in place, breath held and shoulders tightening in anticipation.

An hour condensed into a minute, and she exhaled, breathing once more. The glow in her eyes was no longer in the mirror, and what should have been a relief brought only further fright and dread.

What is going on? What is even happening right now?

She never experienced such fear of the unknown before. Her mind was playing tricks on her at every turn, starting with that damned cat.

The cat. Was it really my imagination?

The animal sounds hadn't stirred her sister or her friend, and both continued their soft, even breaths. Amelia wondered once again if this was all in her head or not as she tried desperately to calm her racing heart. Vowing to make sure the girls stayed safe, Amelia opened the door and stepped into the dimly lit hallway.

Punishing cold bit into her, the extreme drop in temperature sending a shock down her spine. Tingles erupted up on her skin in the form of gooseflesh, and she rubbed her arms. Amelia was grateful for the faint blue lighting panels built into the wainscoting along the lower walls; she wasn't sure her heart could handle the pitch-black at this moment.

When was the last time I was this scared? It must have been that frightening book Father caught me reading. I couldn't sleep without lights for weeks.

Mustering her courage, Amelia edged down the hall toward the stairwell and found the faint outline of a small creature sitting atop the railing, licking its paw. She gasped, then raced toward the creature grabbing at it, only to find it sprung away, careening down the stairs. It stopped at the landing, glancing back once before trotting toward the alcove containing the security door to her father's study.

"Get back here!" Amelia cried out. Her words morphed into a shriek when she lost her footing, gravity propelling her down the stairs. In a panic, she managed to catch herself on the railing, halting her movement and pulling herself upright.

That was close! I always yell at Sophie for running down the stairs, too. I'm a hypocrite.

Still scolding herself, Amelia took the rest of way carefully, inhaling slow and deep. She exhaled when she turned the corner, following where the cat went, but an eerie sense of dread enveloped her once more. A light source that shouldn't be on came from a room which shouldn't be accessible.

The door to her father's study was open, and the ceiling panels were fully lit, casting a soft white and yellow light out into the alcove. There were no signs of the cat, however.

It's probably inside, huh? Why is this even open, now of all times?

Amelia resigned herself to entering and looking around. She tried to remember the last time she had been in this room. It must have been when she was around 11 years old, a couple of years after her sister had been born, and she had been left all alone one evening. Both her parents had rushed her sister to the hospital in a panic. Sophia had been dreadfully sick all week, and it took a turn for the worse. Her father forgot to close the door, and Amelia spent the evening perusing the numerous texts contained within. She felt another tingle from within at that memory, though she did not know why.

She tread cautiously into the room she was not allowed entry for the second time. The first time, her father had scolded her for disobeying a house rule and taking advantage of the opportunity, but she vaguely remembered it was out of concern more than anger. Thinking back on it, the room now was completely different than the one she recalled in her mind from a decade ago. Her father must have rearranged it at some point, for there was an absence of bookshelves.

On the large desk at the center of the room stood a few stacked books along with some loosely spread papers, both in print and writing. Lining the walls were unpowered digital displays, tables with various knickknacks, as well as artwork and sculptures. A gnarled, ashen-colored door, which had not been there before, was on the wall opposite of her. Amelia had no idea where this strange door led, since no additions to the house were made that she knew of. A nagging thought tugged at the back of her mind.

"Amelia?"

The soft-spoken, feminine voice called from behind her, jolting Amelia's senses. A vision of green, white, and red flames enveloping her leapt to the forefront of her mind. The stench of charred wood and burnt flesh crept into her nostrils. Her heart pounded and a radial pain shot out from her temple. She dropped to her knees, grasping at the side of her head.

What was that? What in the hell was that?

Amelia, dazed with both physical and mental anguish, failed to piece anything together amidst the stars swirling behind her eyelids.

None of this makes any sense!

Something brushed against her left leg. She jerked and fell backward. Her back slammed against the half-shelf behind her, and the bronze armillary sphere resting atop it fell over, crashing to the wooden floor. Cursing her clumsiness, Amelia rubbed the spot her back hit, knowing a bruise awaited.

Getting to her knees to stand up, she found the yellow eyes of a small, black cat at the doorway.

"There you are!" Amelia exclaimed, and the creature made a soft, almost pitiful meow. It approached her slowly, nuzzling her knee—its crudely split ear rubbing against her—and Amelia's heart twinged.

Images of a night when she was scared and all alone poured from the depths of her mind. Visions threatened to drown her, and each wave crashing into her depicted another fragment of a memory she couldn't tell was real or not.

There were people she didn't know, wearing pristine white and black robes with patterns she didn't recognize, surrounding her.

Dozens of corpses laid strewn about a burnt field with various debris of rubble.

Amelia sat broken and bloody against a stone pillar with a small cat—eyes of gold and pristine black fur among the dirty scene—sleeping in her lap. Her father, angry and afraid, wrestled the cat away from her grasp despite her attempts to hold onto it.

There was a flash—a glint of light upon steel—and a blade slashed through the air, nearly slicing the cat's ear off.

The visions stopped, and panic overtook her as she lay sprawled out on the floor. Tears streamed down her face, and she couldn't be sure why they started nor if she could make them stop. Exhaustion settled in, and she couldn't make sense of anything.

I am absolutely insane, aren't I? Was any of that real? Why can't I remember?

A weight pushed on her, and Amelia hadn't the strength to react. The creature took the opportunity to crawl on her lap, kneading to find the perfect spot, then laid down, purring fiercely. Instinctively, Amelia reached out and petted its fur, causing its murmurs to quicken.

Her face was hot and her vision blurry, but she found strange comfort in this animal which might not be real. Her pulse slowed with each stroke of its fur, and she soon calmed down, her fear melting away.

What am I even doing here? I should just go back to bed.

The animal in her lap leapt to the gnarled wooden door, pacing back and forth in front of it.

"What? You want to go inside? What's in there?" Amelia asked the cat with curiosity. The creature circled around her once then sat down in front of the door, swishing its tail back and forth rhythmically. Amidst the headache and soreness, Amelia decided to investigate and got off the floor.

"Well, whatever. Father is going to be livid anyway."

The cat meowed in response, and Amelia brushed the remaining tears away. Sniffling, she went to the gnarled door, and a strange sense of foreboding mixed with longing washed over her.

Is this right? Should I really look any further?

The cat bumped against her leg with a purr. Relief filled her, and she sighed, her resolve strengthened once again. She grabbed the glossy black handle, making contact with it. Streaks of red, green, and blue lights coalesced around her, culminating into a bright engulfing white. The study faded away, the light with it, and the full moon beamed down on her skin from the open night sky. Whipping wind whistled in her ear.

Confused and in awe, Amelia realized she was in an open field. She stood atop a grassy plain with a few erected large stones and boulders around her in various positions, some placed on top of each other and haphazardly made into a circle. Amelia was dumbstruck. This ancient wonder of the world looked different than the one she knew.

"Amelia, dear," a softly spoken, clearly female voice said from behind. Amelia froze.

That voice. It's so familiar, but why can't I stop shaking?

She didn't want to turn around. She refused to turn around.

"Child, it has been simply ages. Won't you look at me?"

Panic settled into her again, and she searched for the cat to calm herself, but it was nowhere in sight. She found only grass, no longer blowing, for the wind had died and the air was still with quiet. Her leg muscles tightened, the urge to flee from this space growing inside. An unsettling energy changed the air around her—a palpable thickness which threatened to choke her.

"Amelia Rose! Look at me when I'm talking to you!"

The speaker's voice boomed in the tranquil night, and Amelia trembled. Something deep within told her this was a terrible mistake—everything that led to now, it was all a mistake.

She couldn't calm her rapidly beating heart. Her chest tightened, and her breathing quickened. Beads of sweat formed on her forehead.

Breathe, Amelia! Don't make it angry. You have to turn around.

She had no idea what would happen if it became angry, but every instinct in her screamed not to let it. Shuffling her feet with her hands in fists at her sides, she turned around, her eyes captivated by the dazzling light.

It was everything and it was nothing: this wondrous existence of the world within a world. Amelia could only admire the marvel of it—the horror of this being, this goddess. Green energy surrounded naked feminine perfection, giving an aura that illuminated its every curve and contour, crackling divine energy. Terrified, she had a hard time looking straight at it.

"Don't be scared, child. We are friends, are we not?" The goddess stepped toward her with a smile curved up on its face, yet Amelia instinctively stepped back. Stopping in mid-stride, the goddess' smile turned into a frown, and it let out a sigh which floated melodiously into Amelia's ears. She shivered with pleasure and fright. "Of course, it has been so long since we were last conjoined, but I promise I don't hold that against you. It wasn't by your own doing, this I know. I had spent years trying to get beyond that man's wards, and he finally let one slip. It was a nasty guard dog, though, I will say."

Wards? Conjoined? What is she even talking about?

The goddess advanced and a thin strand of green light connected with Amelia, who dropped to her knees in a daze. Images came forth of her parents holding her down. Several robed figures stood around them, chanting words in a language she didn't recognize and flashes of light danced among her eyes, swirling in a maelstrom of color.

Who were those men, and why were Mother and Father with them?

"Oh, Amelia, they really punished you, didn't they? Precious girl, let me see."

A pain in her temple throbbed, and she grasped at her head, a cry escaping her lips. The goddess reached down and cupped Amelia's chin with its hand, forcing her to look up. "You finally called for me, after all this time. I'm so elated, child, that we can be together once more. I'm sure that man will be absolutely aghast when he finds out."

A pleased smile formed on its visage, and the goddess raised its hand while still holding Amelia's face in the other. It brushed the hair draped over its right ear away, tucking it back behind it, revealing half of the ear was missing—an imperfection otherwise unnoticeable among the perfect being.

Wait, that's the same as ...

Amelia's composure wavered at the cascading thoughts when an alien warmth surged deep within her, relaxing her body and mind. The pain receded, and she found herself surrounded by a pale-green glow. She forgot about the tension building up inside and wondered why she had been so afraid of this being.

"That feels better, now, doesn't it? You can relax. I mean you no harm." The goddess bent down and gently placed a kiss on Amelia's forehead, who didn't shy from it.

This is either a dream or something amazing. I have to know.

"I have questions."

The goddess held its arms out to Amelia in welcome. "By all means We have a lot to talk about."

"Who ... no, *what* are you?"

"Do you truly not remember?"

She could only shake her head. Questions upon questions built inside her. For several long moments, the goddess fixated on her, and Amelia couldn't tell if their visage was filled with annoyance or concern.

"How unsettling." The goddess whispered with agitation. "I can see they've sealed it away where even I cannot reach. No matter! You're here now, so why don't we begin anew?"

"Wait, sealed away? You mean inside of me?"

Amelia, still on her knees dumbfounded, started fitting the pieces together. She couldn't believe everything she had been told, but a part of her knew it to be somewhat true. For the first time, events and fragments of memory made sense.

"Of course. Those who simply wish to hide me away from your world will do so regardless of who it hurts. That man you call your father is important to their side, and yet he has one who can use my gift as a daughter. How truly vexing it must be."

The goddess laughed, its voice bringing pleasure to Amelia's ears.

"Let's see ... you had named me Gwen once, child, so call me as such." Gwen gave Amelia an eerie smile. "The *what* is a tale which would take far longer than your lifespan to tell. Unless we make a deal, of course. For now, I'll simply tell you that you called out to me while I was nearby."

"I called out ... to you?"

When did I do that? Wait a minute.

"You did, and you were positively radiant with your wants. Like a beacon, you led me right to you, even through that man's boundary."

Gwen reached down and pulled Amelia to her feet.

"Your potential is astounding, Amelia. I told you this when

we last spoke. Now, I believe you can handle my gift even better than before. Your body has grown stronger since we last were together, which is simply delightful." Gwen touched Amelia's cheek, causing her to shut her eyes. "Don't you want more out of your life? A means of independence? I can give that which you desire. All you have to do is take it."

This is happening so fast. Isn't this a dream come true? Is it really so easily obtainable?

"What's the catch?"

Amelia opened her eyes, and Gwen frowned.

"There is no catch, child. I'll give you what you asked for: power, real power you can use to your heart's content. Freedom to do what you want, when you want. Well, since there is already a piece of my gift still locked away inside of you, I will have to give you only a fragment of it. But for you, my dear, I believe that will be more than enough."

Can I really trust this? Or my parents? They've been hiding something from me this whole time. Why?

Amelia weighed the pros and cons of this offer, and all the while the goddess remained mute with only a small smile on its bewitchingly beautiful face.

If I take this deal, I will have the power to forge my own path. There has to be some downside. Why did my parents hide this from me? Why did they seal the gift away? How? I don't understand.

"You said something about my Father being important to *their side*, right? What does that mean?"

"I'll tell you if you agree to our deal, Amelia. I'll inform you of everything you wish to know."

The events up to this point are just far too suspicious. It's clear Father is important, but to whom? And why? Ah, there are just too many questions. There is one more I need to ask.

"Did you know my grandmother?" Amelia asked, hopeful.

"I knew of her, yes. You have her looks, child. Has your father not told you about her?"

Amelia shook her head. "He won't say anything about her."

The goddess smirked.

"I'm not surprised. I'll tell you what I know about her, too, if you agree."

“What do you get out of this?” she asked the goddess, curious if it would tell her anything.

Gwen shrugged. “I simply benefit from you taking my gift and using it, child. You will learn all you wish to know and you will also have the means to make your own decisions in life. It’s quite the symbiotic relationship, wouldn’t you agree?”

Gwen’s face inched closer to Amelia, and it spoke in a whisper. “As long as I remain in this world, so shall you, and my gift will be yours to use.”

Amelia stared at the goddess, contemplating those words carefully. After a long internal debate, she found the possibility too enticing to pass up. She nodded at Gwen.

“So, you agree to accept my gift and all that it entails?” the goddess asked, solemnly.

“Yes. I agree,” Amelia said with resolution.

Gwen's smirk turned mischievous then morphed into a devious smile which froze Amelia's heart.

"The bargain has been struck!"

The goddess’ powerful voice echoed in the night sky, and its green glowing eyes crackled wildly with energy. The wind picked up, coiling around the two of them, howling fiercely in Amelia's ears. A cloud of white and green enveloped her, and she choked. Coughing, she tried to navigate through the thick blanket of fog, but it grew brighter, blinding her. She panicked and wanted to run away when Gwen's whispering voice resounded all around her.

"Don't worry, Amelia. We’ll talk soon, I’m sure of it."

Gasping for breath, Amelia abruptly sat up in bed. Her heart pounded like a hammer, and her blood pumped vehemently through her ears. The chill in the air clung to her sweat covered body. She grabbed the blanket she flung away and hugged it against her chest. To her side, both her sister and Claire slept peacefully, stirring slightly only from the covers being lifted. The digital display on her wall read just past four in the morning.

Was it all just a dream?

Amelia wondered about the meaning of the last words the goddess had said. The deceitful smile Gwen had given her brought butterflies to her stomach, and she hugged the blanket closer. She breathed slow and deep, replaying the events in her mind for several minutes.

If it wasn't a dream, what did I do? Was it okay to agree so easily?

A dryness in her throat left her parched, and she got out of bed. She went downstairs to drink some water, but her thoughts remained in a daze. Amelia placed her palm on her forehead, feeling the clammy skin and heat emanating from it. She regretted going out into the cold earlier. Her vision thinned, and she couldn't focus. Stumbling toward her destination, her breaths ragged, a thirst and hunger from within awakened. Amelia sprinted the final steps into the kitchen in order to quell the urges consuming her.

She devoured what was on the counters, in the fridge, and in the cupboards. Drinking and eating everything she could get her hands on did nothing to get rid of the overwhelming sensations. Her body's basic instincts kicked in, and her mind desperately fought to maintain control.

"Amy?"

A sleepy voice resounded behind her, and Amelia shivered with anticipation.

No, Sophie, not now. Something is very wrong. Please. Run.

Her vision clouded, and she knew she couldn't stop this urge. It took everything in her to scream at her beloved sister.

"Get. Away!"

Amelia feared what may happen if she didn't leave right now.

Blood rushed frantically through her veins and something primal, within her very soul, wanted release.

"Amy, what's wrong?"

Sophia moved closer, and Amelia saw that her wide, blue eyes reflected glowing green orbs in the cold, unlit room. The look of absolute horror on her sister's face was the last thing she remembered before her vision faded.

"SO? WHAT HAPPENED AFTER THAT?"

On the balcony of a high-rise flat in the heart of Outer London, Amelia admired the moon while a man no more than the age of 30 stood next to her. He wanted to get in her pants, she knew, but he currently gave her a bored, impatient expression, yet humored her nonetheless. His two friends lounged on the chairs at the nearby table, taking in her tale. She had been drinking and sketching on the patio of the pub down the street when the man had asked her if she knew any scary stories. Being a whimsical creature, she pocketed her napkin canvas and happily obliged, despite knowing his aim. It was Halloween, a recently revived holiday, and the perfect reason for her to get him to buy her a drink—not that she needed one these days; her vagrant lifestyle made for a good excuse for daily consumption anyway.

When she informed the man, Ronald, today was her birthday, he eagerly purchased cocktails to facilitate her inebriation. He wanted her good and drunk, of course, but she had no intention of blacking out tonight. Definitely not tonight. Her tolerance was high, which he disapproved of, but Amelia's proposal to have him cook her dinner had been met with the utmost eagerness. She had a little remorse, but time was of the essence. They arrived at his home, and he introduced her to his two roommates. The four of them mingled, hitting it off, and she enjoyed herself. Even knowing she'd be cutting it close, she changed pace and moved out onto the balcony to continue the story, much to Ronald's chagrin.

"Well, the girl, you see, was so lost in her trance she never remembered what happened. It was the first time she lost control of herself, and her new powers."

"Powers?" He raised an eyebrow at Amelia. "You mean magic? Magery?"

Amelia laughed dryly at his question, which caused irritation on his face. She rubbed her hand on his cheek, and his knees wobbled.

"In a sense it was Magery, yes. Though, Magery is a relatively new term, you know? It's only been about 80 years since it was scientifically proven to exist."

"Right, and Magery can only be used with tools, like the batons the police and military have been working on."

"That is where the research is going, yes."

Amelia went to the other side of the balcony where a folding chair had been placed. She brought it over, and set it up for Ronald. He gladly took a seat.

"So you're saying this goddess ... Gwen, was it? She gave this girl the gift of magic? Isn't that what people called a witch back in the day?"

"Witch?" Amelia grimaced. "I suppose that's appropriate, but I can't say I like the term."

Her disgust of the word evident, she knew they wondered why she was so against it. It was simple, really. A string of murders over the last several decades around the world caused some of the more evangelical crowds to come forth, opposing Wiccans openly. Those from the side of the fence opposite of her moved with them, condemning the perpetrators for being related to witches. It had always been a word full of stigma for people like her, and it now revived in modern times with the advent of Magery in the mainstream. Being accused of being a witch carried a death sentence in some areas, while oppression was running rampant in others. In Outer London, the government could barely keep itself afloat, let alone bother helping.

Amelia reached her hand out toward the moon, emotions from the story threatening to overwhelm her. She dropped it to her side and addressed the trio on the balcony.

"Anyway, because the girl took the gift the goddess gave her, her life was filled with terrible things, and she ran away from the world. 'The End.'"

Scoffing at her abrupt ending, Ronald couldn't help but laugh. After his roommates joined in, Amelia pouted.

"Sorry, love, but you have to understand. You had all that build up, but ending it that way is just awful."

"Oh? I didn't think you cared anyway."

"Well now, these blokes do at any rate, and I'm a bit curious. Come on then, what happened next for the girl?"

Smiling, Amelia acted coy and pushed herself up on the balcony ledge, her slender frame gliding in the air. She dangled her legs over the side and breathed deeply.

"So, you want to know what happened after? Fine. I'll tell you."

Amelia recounted the events she skipped over. How the girl awoke to the screams of her parents returning from their duties to find a household bereft of inhabitants. How bodies of guards littered the yards amidst the destruction of half the manor itself. How the girl was scared out of her mind and unsure of what transpired because she could not remember.

She conveyed how the faces of sadness and disappointment the girl's parents expressed had crushed her. At that moment, everything clicked for the girl. Everything the goddess told her had been half a truth, and buried within were delicious lies which trapped the girl, ensnaring her for a second time.

Amelia could tell Ronald struggled to keep up with the story, and her tone of voice shifted to one of loathing.

"You see, the goddess ... was quite spiteful, you know? She lied. She hated the girl for snubbing her the way she did, though the girl had no memory of doing so."

Amelia slammed her hand on the ledge, chipping some of the stone and the trio gasped.

"The goddess knew. She *knew* what would happen after the girl accepted the so-called *gift* from her but refused to mention it. It was at that time the girl learned how delightfully horrible the goddess, and the gift, truly was."

Amelia closed her eyes, describing in detail the scene of the room she awoke in. Corpses were everywhere, burned and charred, with rubble of the house having fallen all around her. Among it all were two small, lifeless bodies, aged and decomposing. Her stomach churned recalling the memory.

"After realizing what had happened, the girl's parents called in help from their association. The girl felt broken inside but still refused to give up her freedom when they tried to capture her. It was instinct, really, but she didn't want to be caged again. So she did something she would regret for the rest of her life."

Amelia hopped off the ledge onto the balcony. Her audience was dumbfounded, not wanting to speak.

"As far as the goddess ... though a bargain had been struck, the damage had been done to their relationship and it turned into one of mutual hatred. The goddess believed the girl would come back to her eventually, returning to her side once more of her own volition, but the girl never did. She despised the goddess."

Amelia laughed to herself, finding strength in speaking those words.

"Instead, she used her gift to burn the rest of the home she lived in to the ground. She scorched the earth and the surrounding area, leaving behind her family and the goddess, then disappeared altogether."

She studied the trio of men who had paid attention to her

every word. "Thank you for listening. Hey, do you want to see what the goddess looks like?”

The three men nodded and Amelia dug a wrinkled napkin out of her coat pocket. She smoothed it out on the table between them. The crude graphite sketch depicted a night sky and a large shooting star careening across it. The men then glanced up to see the green and white speck she already knew was there. She clapped to get their attention and they flinched.

“I'm famished, so I suppose it's about time. I'm sorry, truly, but it’d be bad if I waited any longer."

Her green eyes glowed brightly in the moonlight. Ronald's friends, frightened at the sudden shift in mood and paranormal activity, screamed. A ghostly mist engulfed them, silencing their cries and a pale light erupted from between the two, connecting to Amelia. A sigil of white and green appeared in the air and their bodies withered rapidly from aging. The sigil faded, and their limp corpses fell to the ground. She sighed, relief palpable in her tone.

"Finally."

Amelia stepped in front of the terrified Ronald, who had not budged from the seat she gave him. She reached out, touching his face and her energy cascaded over him.

"You wished to know me intimately, didn't you? I could see it in your eyes. If we had met a week ago, who knows how things could have turned out? For now, let's call this being in the wrong place at the wrong time. Take pride in knowing you're the first and only person I've ever told that story to."

She kissed him on the cheek. "If it's any consolation, I really am sorry. This is all part of the gift given, and if I don't take matters into my own hands every couple of weeks ... well, let's just say it'll cause a lot more tragedy. You understand, don't you?"

Amelia sighed once more—a sad, listless sound full of exhaustion. She was tired of trying to convince herself it was okay to do this and tired of this life and being trapped within a different kind of cage.

"What do you think the moral of the story was, Ronald?"

She put her mouth near his ear and a hand on his chest. The rhythm of his heart fluttering made her cringe. Amelia hated herself for doing this—for her personality being so rotten. She delivered a jolt to his very soul, and the light in Ronald's eyes faded, his life force drained to sate her needs. She whispered to the man leaving this world with tears in his eyes.

"It's to be careful what you wish for, love."

NICOLAS GRAM

ABOUT THE AUTHOR

Nicolas Gram is an American author from Arizona. His day job consists of slinging code for apps, but writing has always been a way for him to get a release from the numerous fantasies in his head.

Nicolas has two fantasy novels in the works. *Black Rose Noble* is a continuation of Amelia's tale, and *From The Dark* is the first in a multi-part saga of a world fighting on the brink of despair, and a pair of twins caught in the middle of it.

Find more information about his works on his website or on Twitter (@nicolas_gram) where he also posts random bouts of writings, poetry, and music he finds most interesting.

MY OWN DARK WAY

BY K. A. MILTIMORE

"You look like a man with a story," the man with the large mustache said, breaking my concentration. I had watched him come in the Three Bells, though now I was focused squarely on the last of the gin in my glass and the drops of Old Tom clinging to the sides. His voice was an intrusion, as was his very presence next to me at the bar.

"You don't say. Well, we all have stories, don't we?" I responded without raising my eyes from the glass.

"Yes, I suspect we all do, but I wager another gin that you have one better than most." The voice held an irritating Scottish burr. He wasn't even trying to hide it. Hard to imagine this Scotsman would be asked to many society events unless he was more well-heeled than he appeared.

"A story, you say. Well, buy me a gin or two and I will tell you a story. You won't like, I wager, but it is a truthful story. Whatever that means." I turned to face him, and he gestured with his head that we should move to a table. I followed him across the dim room and he found us a quiet table next to a coal oil lamp. His hair was parted in the center and looked shiny from hair ointment. I hadn't looked at my reflection in days, but no doubt my appearance was unkempt.

"Now, stranger, let's have the story. Start from the beginning." He waived over the tavern girl and handed her several pennies - he must have assumed my story would take more than one glass.

"The beginning. Let's see, do you wish to know my earliest memories, my years at Eton, my time studying surgery, what pray tell, is a suitable starting point for my story?" I was being rude to my benefactor, but that wasn't unusual these days. I had forgotten how to behave in polite society. Not that a London tavern in Whitechapel is all that polite.

My companion took a breath before responding.

"Why don't you start at the point where your life turned you into this."

It was early autumn, October of 1885 to be precise, and the world lay open to me. There was nothing that came across my path that didn't bow its head or move aside so I could pass unimpeded. My parents had died the winter before, leaving me in full control of a vast fortune, and I was living what some might have called the good life. I was wealthy, unmarried and at my leisure. I had no idea that the perfection of my world was going to crash about my ears in short order.

Being a younger man, albeit one in a long engagement, I found myself interested in the fairer sex and looked for opportunities to sow my oats, as it were. My Eton friends and I had joined a Hell-Fire Club in London, on a whim, and we attended a few of their ceremonies - mostly parlour games and wearing red robes while women in gauzy gowns stood still as Greek statues. It may have been titillating for some, but I was not so easily sated. My thirst for adventure brought me to

Whitechapel. My friends were not as daring so I hazarded my journey alone.

Walking the streets of Whitechapel, I learned quite easily there was no limit to the depravity of man and the willingness of others to sate those desires, if properly paid. Things were available to me that went beyond even my own peculiar tastes. The plight of these people would have been moving, had I but a heart to be moved. But in truth, nothing and no one interested me enough to care. Until Agnes.

Agnes Waterhouse was her name; far too plain to describe the creature. She was wild and unkempt, a dark-haired beauty, too bold for tea at the Savoy, too lively for the dank corners of Whitechapel. She worked there, at an apothecary, where I had stopped in for a headache powder after carousing. From the moment I saw her, I knew I had found my purpose.

"Madam, might I inquire whether you are available for supper this evening? I fear that only a charming dining companion can relieve my headache. Will you not have pity on an injured man?" I had said, in a voice that sounded needy and pleading. I remember she had laughed at that. As if someone like me were ever needy.

"Aw, go on with you. Take your physic and be on your way. Your smooth words will do you no good, sir." Her voice had a bit of rasp and I quite enjoyed the sound of it. It had more weight and tone than that of my fiancée, Wilhemina. Where Wilhemina was demure and soft-spoken, Agnes was brazen and bravado. As much as a man might like drinking sips of champagne, he is also fond of strong brandy on occasion.

"Madam, your words injure me more than this cursed headache. Please, have pity and say you will sup with me?" I was almost to the point of laughter and I think it was that itself that convinced her. She gave me a quick nod and then turned to another customer.

I had not been to bed and still wore my clothing from the

evening before, so I planned to head home for a change of attire before I returned to meet lovely Agnes. Poole, my butler, had long grown used to my erratic hours, and yet he still insisted on laying out breakfast, turning down the bed, leaving a cigar ready with my paper, in case I should have the wish to return to a normal schedule. Dear Poole, there really was no limit to the man's patience with me. Returning home, I found all prepared for an arrival, and I spent the day luxuriating in the thoughts of the evening with Agnes. Poole had left a letter from Wilhemina on the entry table. I suspected she would be writing me a missive to entreat me to visit her during her holiday in Bath. She would be back in London soon enough. I left it unopened.

Shaved and pressed, I took a cab back to Whitechapel for my rendezvous with Agnes. A flower seller on the corner had cheap chrysanthemums, and I bought some, sure it would impress my dining companion. When I arrived at the apothecary's shop, she was waiting for me.

"I was about to leave. The shop closed almost an hour ago." Her words chided me, but they weren't churlish. She sounded amused.

"Shall we dine, Miss Waterhouse? I am ravenous." I offered her the flowers and my arm, and with that, we were away.

"So far, I dinna think this is the real story, sir. Dinner with an apothecary shop lass? Certainly a man of your standing would not be seen so." The Scottish burr rang in my ears again, and for a moment, I was confounded. Where was Agnes? Where was I? Oh yes, the Three Bells Tavern in Whitechapel talking to the inquisitive Scotsman who was buying me gin.

"Without Agnes, there is no story, sir. Have patience. Our hero will fall shortly." I motioned my empty glass toward the man, and he poured another round.

WE DINED THAT NIGHT, not anywhere that my peers would find us, certainly, but the meal was good enough. We ate a stew and drank wine, and she prattled on all about being an apothecary's assistant, about the healing properties of plants and herbs, and coming to London from Chelmsford, a little village in Essex. It is strange I remember that detail. I hardly listened to a word but instead planned my evening festivities for later. Agnes was going to be my nightcap.

We left the pub and headed out into the gloomy October night. If there was a moon, it didn't shine on Whitechapel. As you know, Whitechapel is a warren of dark alleys and dim corridors. In the flickers of gas light, it was hard to tell what was shadow and what was real. Somethings are better left to the shadows. Agnes must have sensed my ulterior motive because she stopped walking and pulled away from me.

"Thank you for dinner, sir. I must be away now. No need to walk with me."

I wasn't about to let her go that easily.

"Oh, Miss Waterhouse, there is no need to scamper from me. As if you were a mouse and I a tomcat on the prowl." I stepped closer, blocking her retreat. We melted into the shadows, and I pushed her against the brick wall.

"Sir, I must remind you that a meal does not entitle you to more than my thanks. Kindly step aside so I may pass." Her words sounded bold, as I would expect them, but there was a fire in my blood, and I was prepared to see it through no matter her resistance or protestations.

"My dear Miss Waterhouse. Whatever do you mean? No need to play so coy with me. I can be an ally to you. Or an enemy. It is your choice, of course." I thought my voice had the ring of menace, but saucy Agnes laughed at me.

"Do you think, Doctor, that I a'fear you? You have no idea

what I have seen, what I have done, the things I know how to do. It is you who should be a'feared, sir." Her words rang out into the fog, and I was infuriated. How dare she speak to me so.

"I shall give you cause to fear me, Madam. I am not to be trifled with, not by a trollop such as you." If there were others on the street, I did not notice nor did I care. Who would gainsay against a noted surgeon in favor of a guttersnipe?

She clearly felt danger because, before I knew what she had done, she had reached by her heel and retrieved an empty bottle left by another. She raised the bottle above my head, and I knew her intent was to strike me. I seized her wrist.

"Oh my dear little mouse, let's not resort to such games." To emphasize my point, I smashed the bottle against the brick, holding onto the neck of it, which now was jagged as a knife.

She struggled to be free, I remember that. I remember trying to hold her in place, still clutching the brown glass in my hand. She twisted, I recall, pulling from my grasp, leaving me only with a piece of her lace collar. In the shadows, blind as a newborn cat, I swung at her with the bottle. It caught her ear. Strangely, she did not scream, but instead fled from me as I bent down to pick up the tip of her ear, the tragus lying on the cobblestones.

I tossed both the bit of flesh and the bottle into the sewer and presumed to leave the whole disaster behind me in Whitechapel. While I had no guilt for my actions, I wasn't inclined to repeat them, at least not in the light of day. There were other areas of the city to explore with less resistant prey should I need to scratch that itch.

The next morning, I woke in my bed and wondered if the whole thing had been a rather bothersome dream.

"Poole. What time did I come home last night?" Poole was opening the drapery in my bedroom and by the look of the sunlight, it had to be late morning.

"Sir, you came home before midnight. You asked me to wake

you in time for the presentation at the Royal Academy of Physicians and then you retired. Are you feeling quite well, sir?" Poole looked at me with his usual mixture of non-judgmental concern. I accepted the breakfast tray without comment because my eye had spied a black shape just at the doorway. It appeared to be a cat.

"Poole. What is that? Is that a mangy cat at the door?" I was sure I had seen a feline pass several times back and forth in front of the door while Poole placed the tray on my lap.

"Sir? A cat? I see no cat, sir." He stared several moments at the doorway but whatever was there was gone. With a humpf of disapproval, I dismissed him with a wave.

After I finished breakfast and put on the clothing Poole had laid out, I went out for the day. From the moment I left the house, the black cat was with me. It followed the hansom cab to the Academy, it stayed just out of reach throughout the presentations, and again, as I dined with colleagues at the Savoy, it waited patiently outside the window. Each time, when I inquired if someone else could see the mongrel, it would slip from sight.

By the time I arrived home, my nerves were shattered. I wanted nothing more than a brandy and a cigar by the fire. Efficient as always, Poole had left the brandy already poured and waiting. I sipped the amber liquid slowly, savoring the warmth that worked its way down my throat. Poole must have purchased a new brand because the liquor had a hint of verdant flavor, which was subtly herbal and not unpleasant. The butler was ever a surprise.

At some point in the evening, I finished my cigar and brandy, but after that, the memories are hazy. I recall climbing the stairs, changing my clothing, and seeing that damnable cat again. I think I threw a crystal ashtray at it, but all I saw was shards of crystal against the wallpaper. Then I was outside of the house, hailing a cab in the darkness, hunching my form so the driver wouldn't know me. My mind was focused on the memory of those red droplets on the stones.

Back I found myself in Whitechapel, wandering the streets and stopping at every tavern I could find. I soon had gone through all the shillings in my pocket, but my thirst was not quenched. I needed more funds

"Oy, sir, you fancy a good time? You in the hat, you look like a toff to me. Fancy a tickle?" The woman called to me from an alley, and normally, I might have followed her voice, but I had robbery on my mind, not women. A gentleman prowled a few paces ahead of me, no doubt seeking the same dangerous flavors I had sought for myself. He would be so easy to overcome. He was watching the women calling to him from the shadows. He wasn't watching me. I could pull him into the alley and take his money, with hardly a scuffle.

I moved away from the grimy gas light and into the shadows. In my most crisp, most polished voice, the voice I reserved for Academy events and charming my soon-to-be father-in law, I said, "Sir, you should take care along this lane."

He turned, trying to find the sound. I took my cane and with one quick sweep, I knocked him to the ground. His head crashed to the cobblestones, and I could see a dark spot appearing in his gray hair, even in the dim light. My collar was turned up, my shoulders hunched, and my hat pulled low - even Poole would not have recognized me. With the swiftest of gestures, I reached into the man's coat and removed his wallet. So easy, so quick.

I took the pocketbook and melted away into the night to drink and carouse and buy the favors of new friends. At some point, I found my way back to house and stumbled into my bed, not even taking care to remove my dirty boots. The black cat laid next to me, licking its paws, and rubbing its head against the damask bedclothes. It had bright eyes and a ragged ear with a deckled edge of deep crimson. Before I fell asleep, I remember wondering if the cat's blood would stain the ivory sheets.

Poole opened the drapery, and I blinked against the light. It had to be late morning. My breakfast tray was there but the sight of the eggs made me feel nauseous.

"Poole, what the devil are you doing?" My voice sounded hoarse and strangely guttural to my ears. It almost sounded like a stranger.

"Sir, it is noon. I have received a message that Miss Carew shall be in London today. I thought you might want to be prepared." I blinked and tried to remember exactly who Miss Carew might be. Oh yes, my fiancée. I looked to my left for the cat, but the bed was empty; not even a smear of blood on the sheets.

"I am feeling poorly, Poole. Take the tray away. Leave the coffee and the paper." My voice was rough and I noticed the bark of it as Poole took the tray, never saying a word at my brusque dismissal. I wasn't sorry but I was puzzled. Why was I behaving like this? Poole was a trusted servant and I would be hard pressed to replace him.

The London Standard's morning edition lay before me. News of the realm, updates on a likely war in Burma, a golf tournament at St. Andrews. I glanced through, hardly caring to read beyond the headlines, when something caught my eye. Murder in Whitechapel. It was a small item, but authorities were looking for the whereabouts of a man who murdered a gentleman in Whitechapel last evening. Sir Reginald Wicklow had been attacked by a man and his head smashed on the cobblestones. Witnesses described the assailant as hunched over, with a hat pulled low upon his head.

"Well, that is news indeed," I said to no one except the black cat, who was now back in the room near the foot of the bed.

It blinked at me but made no sound.

I chuckled at the reaction. I should have been afraid of

discovery, guilt-ridden over taking the man's life all for a few measly pounds, but I was not - I was excited, thrilled if truth be told. My blood fairly raced through my limbs and it was all I could do not to shout out. How marvelous a feeling it was, so unlike my everyday life.

Poole had my clothes ready, pressed, and presentable. No doubt he expected my fiancée would be calling, and he had endeavored to make me the handsome beau she thought me to be. Right down to a boutonniere of red carnations, a touch of scarlet on my lapel. I donned the attire, like an obedient child, but already my thoughts whirled. How could I cut her visit short without arousing suspicion? Perhaps an ill patient in need of my services could be used as a rouse. No matter, I would think of something.

I debated whether to visit the club for a round of billiards, just to see if there would be any chatter about the Whitechapel murder, but before I could act upon the plan, Poole announced I had visitors.

Lord Carew and his daughter made their way up my marble stairs to the parlour.

"It is good to see you, Henry. We had hoped you would come to Bath during our sojourn." Lord Carew said with just a hint of disapproval. Clearly, I wasn't as devoted to my beloved as he thought I should be.

"Dreadfully sorry, but patients have kept me away. Indeed, I expect a call any time that I will need to visit a sick bed." I shook Lord Carew's hand heartily; it was damp and soft in my palm.

I dropped Carew's limp fish hand and lifted his daughter's for a breath of a kiss. It too felt moist but brittle to the touch.

"My dear Wilhemina, it is lovely to see you. The waters must have been to your liking - restorative, by the looks of the roses in your cheeks."

"Henry, it is good to see you. Even returning to the damp chill of London in October cannot diminish my joy in seeing you again." Wilhemina smiled but I saw no warmth there. No fire like Agnes. What had happened to my injured mouse, I mused. I should seek her out tonight.

"Do sit. Poole has tea ready. Ever efficient, our Poole. Tell me all about Bath."

After my fiancée poured the tea, I placed a fixed smile to my lips and watched as the pair blathered on. What they said, I could not have told you for all the crown jewels. I simply wasn't listening.

Out of the corner of my eye, I caught sight of the cat, still bearing the scarred ear and unblinking, bright eyes. It skulked into the room and rested under the chair of Lord Carew, batting half-heartedly at his boot. The self-righteous buffoon did not notice.

"Henry, we called to invite you to supper at the club tonight. I know it is short notice, but please say you will come," Wilhemina said. Her voice was an odd mixture of bothersome canary and a whistling tea kettle. I wondered that I had never really noticed that before.

"Yes, of course, as long as my patient doesn't need me." Which of course, my non-existent patient would indeed need me.

Tea concluded and my guests rose to leave. As they sauntered from the room, the cat stayed behind the pair, as did I. It would have easily been seen if they had but turned their heads to look back. I walked them to the head of the stairs, intent on showing them out. It was at that moment, I saw the cat make a move. It tensed, preparing to pounce at the back of Lord Carew's leg. Why I should have cared, I couldn't say - perhaps I simply did not want to explain the presence of a mangy mouser in my parlour. Whatever the cause, I jabbed my foot out to block the cat's strike. My boot missed the feline and made square contact with Lord Carew himself. The jolt sent him forward, and he bounced down the marble stairs, groaning at each strike, arms flailing to stop his fall.

He came to land unceremoniously on the foyer floor. Wilhemina and I watched from the top step in frozen masks of disbelief.

"Father!" She screamed, stepping carefully down the stairs to avoid tripping herself. I bounded down and gently lifted Lord Carew's head from its resting place.

"Oh…" he moaned, damaged and battered but alive.

The next moments were cacophony - I shouted for Poole, demanding my medical bag, while Wilhemina sobbed, clutching her handkerchief, and Carew himself winced and swore as I splinted up his wrist. A nice tidy fracture was his reward for the visit to my house.

"Oh, Father, whatever caused you to fall?" Wilhemina asked when her sobs had finally subsided.

I looked up from my ministrations to see his face. There was confusion, pain, and fear.

"I don't know. I thought that I felt something, on the back of my leg, and then I fell, but…no, I couldn't have…" Carew looked warily at me, searching for a flicker of guilt. My face was nothing but concern. Would he believe his own mind or the obvious worry of his son to be? He seemed to choose the latter.

"Let's get you home, Father," Wilhemina said as Poole and I lifted him to his feet. We clucked and fussed and had him in his carriage, tucked beneath a traveling rug. His eyes watched my every move, looking for any sign to support the doubt that must be plaguing him.

"I shall come by tomorrow to see the patient. Rest well, Lord Carew. Forego the club tonight and take to your bed. Doctor's orders." I said brightly, smiling and giving his shoulder a slight pat. He winced at the touch. It was all I could do not to laugh.

"WELL, that is rather peculiar, I must say, but hardly the worst tale I have heard, if that is a comfort to ye," the mustachioed man said, sipping on his gin. So far, I had outpaced him three to one.

"The worst and strangest is yet to come, my good man," I said, a bit louder and more earnestly than was called for. No doubt the spirits were taking hold of my tongue.

"Proceed, good sir," he said, with no small amount of merriment in his eye. He wouldn't find me so amusing when the tale was complete.

CONVENIENTLY, Lord Carew's accident had ended the supper plans, and I was free to search for Agnes at my leisure. I dressed for the chill of October winds with a muffler obscuring my face and my coat drawn against the winds that scattered the wharf rats from view. Even such creatures knew not to be about. Or perhaps they scattered at the sight of me. Either way, I cared not.

Once in Whitechapel, I went straight away to the apothecary's shop to seek her out, but she had not returned to work. Her employer was none too pleased, which made me wonder if Agnes did more of the tonic creation than I gave her credit for. Perhaps she was a witch, concocting potions for the good people of Whitechapel. The thought amused me. Agnes, the good witch of Whitechapel.

I went next to the pub where we had eaten but saw no sign of her. Whitechapel is a warren of tight streets and I turned a corner into a particularly dark alley. I approached the fallen flowers that lined the street, inquiring if they knew of an Agnes Waterhouse. None seemed keen to reply until I handed out handfuls of pennies.

"Annie has seen her, haven't you, Chapman?" The woman

gestured to a figure pressed against a damp wall, wearing a thin shawl against the cold.

"Oh, aye, I've seen her. Some toff bit her ear clean off, so I heard. Mad dog," she spat violently, leaving a string of spittle hanging from her lower lip. Realizing too late that I might be that mad dog himself, she squared her shoulders as if to prepare for a fight. From the look of her, she had seen a few during her time on the streets.

"Where could I find her? I am a cousin from out of town, from Essex." I lied easily, trying to make my voice sound like someone from a village and not Eton college.

Annie scrunched her nose in the dim gas light.

"What's your name, Cousin?"

I paused. I dared not use my real name. This woman might use it to barter her way from the gaol. No, I needed an alias.

"I am Edward. Her cousin, Edward Hyde." My voice, lower and scraping in tone did indeed sound like another man. Hunched under my muffler, I doubt even Poole would have known me.

"Well, Mister Hyde, last I saw her, she said she was heading to Knightsbridge. She had a message to deliver to some lady. That's all I know." Annie stuck out her hand for payment, her fingertips looking blue from the cold. I could have given her enough money for a warm room and a hot meal at the pub. But the fate of Annie Chapman was nothing to me, so I paid her a penny like the rest.

What could Agnes be doing in Knightsbridge? Surely, she wasn't aware of the Carews. Had I even told her my name? I thought back over the supper we shared and whether I had used my Christian name with her. Damn it, I had. She knew me as Doctor Henry Jekyll. A clever little mouse like Agnes could find out soon enough about the Carews and wouldn't she have a tale to tell. Lord Carew already had his doubts - any wounded guttersnipe accusing me would only confirm his suspicions.

Why I cared about the engagement may not be obvious, considering my antipathy toward my bride to be. I may not have loved her, but I loved my reputation and my standing in society. Marrying into the Carew family brought prestige and peerage; it could only benefit me. I'd be damned to lose it now.

Finding a cab in Whitechapel took some doing. Eventually, I hailed one who consented to take me all the way to Knightsbridge for a pretty penny. I pictured the scene of Wilhemina in tears and Agnes wildly gesturing, elaborating and aggrandizing the crime. By the time I reached the Carew townhome, I was seething in fury. I threw the coins at the driver and bounded up the stairs to the door.

If Agnes wasn't here, I would feign concern for Lord Carew and a desire to see my beloved. All could be easily explained. I pulled the bell rope and waited. The moon shone my silhouette against the door - the form was bent and cloaked, an unknown man. I pulled again, but no one answered. The Carew butler could learn from Poole, I mused. I was about to pull the rope a final time when I saw her, stepping lightly from the shadows of the topiaries. Agnes was there, not ten feet from where I stood. Her black hair was unbound, and she wore no hat against the cold. Her cheeks were flushed with chill or anger - I could not tell which.

"Oh, so you thought you'd come telling lies, Madam?" I took a step down the stairs. She didn't move.

"My dear Doctor Jekyll, I would hardly recognize you. Your countenance is much changed and not for the better, sad to say," Agnes said, coyly, in a sing-song voice, toying with me as if I were the mouse.

"You fared the worst in our last encounter. Have no illusion that you'll better me this time." I took another step down. My fist balled in my coat pocket. A cloud scuttled across the moon, darkening my vision. I thought she smiled.

"It is you who look the worse for wear, Doctor. I know it

isn't your conscience that troubles you. Perhaps your visage is just reflecting the rot of your soul." Her voice was easy, as if we chatted about picnics or flowers. I wanted nothing more than to squeeze her neck until she spoke no more.

"Enough words, Madam. I shall finish what I started." I ran down the last of the stairs, and the moon was gone again, whisking her away into shadow. I couldn't see her even though she was only a few feet from me. I could smell the lavender of her hair wash in the breeze.

"Perhaps I will find your lady before you do. Perhaps I know where she is. Perhaps she waits at your home for you, desperate to know where you have gone. Shall we see who finds her first?" Agnes said, calling as if it were hide-and-seek and I was the new seeker. The clouds rolled away and showed me that I was alone at the foot of the stairs.

"Damnation and hell-fire!" I shouted, though no one was about to hear me. I hurried to the street, and there was the form of the sleek black cat, so recognizable with the torn ear, sauntering down the road. If I but had a stone, I could have struck it, but my pockets were empty.

I tried to find a cab to take me home, but they were engaged, so I dashed along the sidewalks, pushing and shoving past those in my path. My townhome wasn't far, and I hurried, striving to reach it before that wretch. My stride was stilted, as if my right leg were a fraction shorter than my left, forcing my gait to lumber along. With this ambling, shuffling stride, I made my way to my own front steps.

The door was unlocked. Was she already inside? Where was Poole, that damn man. I made my way up the marble stairs, listening for female voices, but only the crackle of the fireplace broke the silence. The parlour had my brandy, laid out and waiting. I snatched the snifter and swallowed it in one gulp, letting the herb tainted fire wash down my gullet. I heard a creak behind me, expecting to see the black cat again.

It was Agnes. She came into the parlour, looking worried and weak - not at all as she had in the moonlight. Her black hair was knotted up on her head with a strand hanging down in front of her ear.

"Henry, you are back. I was worried," she said, looking as if she meant it.

I slammed the snifter on the table and strode over to her.

"Don't think that you can persuade me with some kind of trickery, you harlot. I'll not be deceived!" I shouted at her.

Her eyes were wide with confusion and fear.

"What is the matter with you? Are you mad?" her voice shrieked at me. It only inflamed me more. Who was she to yell at Doctor Henry Jekyll in his own house?

"We will settle this once and for all," I said, grabbing her wrist and pulling her toward me. Violence rose in my gullet, and there was nothing to be done about it.

"I am leaving, this is intolerable," she said, pulling loose from me and backing toward the stairs.

"Oh, I think not, Madam. You shall stay and pay for what you have done. There shall be a reckoning." I moved, far more quickly than she expected, blocking her escape. My medical bag was at the top of the stairs. Poole had neglected to put it away. I reached down and pulled out a small scalpel.

"Henry, no, for God's sake, what are you doing?" She sounded truly panicked, and tried to flee back into the parlour. With a rough grasp, I caught her arm and pulled her against my chest, both of us staring at the fire.

"I am done with you, with your damn black cat, with everything you have wrought upon me. It is over, Agnes Waterhouse." With a quick strike, I drew my blade across her throat, silencing her for good. She slumped to the floor, blood puddling at my feet, her blonde hair coming loose from its pins.

"Doctor Jekyll, what have you done?" Poole had come in

from the kitchen, dropping the tray of tea he was holding. His face was pure revulsion.

"Poole, this intruder came and was trying to rob the place. We must alert the constables."

Poole, so unflappable, backed away from me.

"Sir, it was no intruder, but only Miss Carew. Sir, you've killed her." Poole's hand was seeking something he could use as a weapon, as if I would raise a hand to him.

I looked down and there at my feet was the body of Wilhemina, bleeding all over my marble floor. Tiny red cat's paw prints led away, but the cat was nowhere to be seen.

I fled. I fled into the night with nothing but the coat on my back, the few coins in my pocket, and my scalpel still in my hand. I ran, finding my way to Whitechapel and to this tavern. I have been here ever since.

MY LISTENER DREW a breath and gave a long exhale before setting down his glass. I could tell that he had the tale he wanted now. Enough misery and horror to have paid for those drinks ten-fold.

"What happens now, sir? Have the police come looking for you?" His Scottish burr was even stronger with a hint of fear. Did he wonder if I still had the scalpel with me?

"Police in Whitechapel? Not likely. Besides, they are looking for Doctor Henry Jekyll. Doctor Jekyll is no more." I finished the last of the gin and rose to leave. Dawn was coming, and it was time to find a doorway for my bed.

"Who are you then, if not Henry Jekyll? Are you Edward Hyde now?" The man stayed pressed to his seat.

"I'll tell you my name if you tell me yours," I said, slyly.

"Stevenson. Robert Louis Stevenson." He told me the truth, I could tell. The moment he had said his name, I could tell he wished he hadn't.

"Well, Mister Robert Louis Stevenson. No, I am not Jekyll and I am not Hyde. From now on, those in Whitechapel will know me as Jack. I have some scores to settle. Be seeing you." I tipped my hat in farewell and headed out of the Three Bells Tavern into the gray October night.

K.A. MILTIMORE

ABOUT THE AUTHOR

KA is known for her paranormal cozy series, The Gingerbread Hag Mysteries. While her series features supernatural and mythological characters, a surly talking chinchilla and copious amounts of weird baked goods, this story is a darker turn. A few Easter eggs for you - Agnes Waterhouse was the first woman executed for witchcraft in England, in the year 1566. She had a black cat named Satan. Robert Louis Stevenson wrote The Strange Case of Dr. Jekyll and Mr. Hyde in 1886 - the title of this short story is a line from the novel. Jack the Ripper, the infamous serial killer, stalked the women of Whitechapel in 1888 - Annie Chapman was one of his victims. Sign up for the newsletter at www.kamiltimore.com.

COURTING DEATH

BY EDISON T. CRUX

with a poem by Morgan Ashire

When the eighteen wheeler struck, Steffany should have died.

Demi watched the accident unfold in slow-motion. She had waved goodbye to her best friend, Steffany crossed the street to her parked car—and the semi truck barreled down the road.

Her body flew through the air like a ragdoll. Demi watched in horror as Steffany crashed headfirst into a metal trash can on the sidewalk. The impact so hard the enclosure around the can bent over, despite being attached to the cement.

All eighteen wheels screeched to a halt as shocked pedestrians gathered. Demi rushed through the crowd, praying her friend was okay. Maybe it wasn't as bad as it had looked. She knew that was impossible, but the first stage of grief—denial—hit her as fast as that truck.

"Steff!" Demi cried as she skidded to a stop above her friend's tangled body. She dropped to her knees, trembling. "Oh god, no..."

Then the impossible happened.

Steffany got up.

"What..." Steffany breathed, slowly standing. She looked around at the growing crowd. "What happened? Is everyone okay?"

Demi stared at her, eyes wide in disbelief. "St—Steffy?"

Steffany offered her a hand up. "You okay, girl? You look like you saw a ghost."

After gingerly returning to her feet, Demi examined Steffany. That high-speed collision should have killed her, but there wasn't a scratch or bruise in sight. It wasn't like she was well-protected, either; it was a hot day and she only wore shorts and a tank top. If the truck didn't turn her bones to powder, then skidding on the sidewalk should have ground her skin raw.

Yet Steffany brushed herself off like it was nothing.

"H—how did you—aren't you—" Demi couldn't find the words. "Jesus Steff, that truck plowed right into you! How are you not dead?"

For a moment, Steffany's eyes darkened. She stared somewhere into the horizon, her mind lost in thought. Just as suddenly it ended, and a classic Steffany smile lit up her face.

"Guess I'm just lucky," she said. "Sure glad that truck only grazed me. Looks like no one else was hurt, which is awesome."

Only grazed you? Demi's jaw dropped. *I saw you fly down the street like Superman, and you're telling me you're just lucky?*

Suddenly Demi didn't trust the smile on her best friend's face. It didn't add up with the catastrophe she had seen with her own eyes.

It didn't add up at all.

IT TOOK hours before Demi had the chance to talk to Steffany in private. The police needed statements, insurance companies were called, and Steffany insisted time and time again that she was fine. The truck driver was close to tears, overjoyed that he hadn't killed someone. Any doubt he had over Steffany's story was overshadowed by relief that his conscience could remain clear.

Demi wasn't buying it.

She insisted on following Steffany back to her apartment, despite already finishing their coffee-and-gossip date before the accident. Steffany protested, but Demi wasn't going to let this go without an explanation.

Once the front door closed, Demi said, "Alright, spill."

Steffany sighed. "I *told* you a hundred times I'm fine. Honestly, it wasn't as bad as it looked."

"Mmhmm." Demi crossed her arms.

"Well, since you're staying I should offer you a drink.". She chuckled. "Even if you *are* being stubborn."

She strolled toward the kitchen. It was a decent bachelorette pad, not large but distinctly Steffany's style. Everything was bought from a thrift store, from the furniture to the silverware, but it all had bright colors or fun patterns. She was a 20-year-old girl living paycheck to paycheck, but Steffany always had a way of making the best of things. In the two years they'd been friends, Demi never knew Steffany to be pessimistic.

But getting hit by a semi and turning the other cheek?

That was more than sheer optimism.

Steffany returned with two cans of soda and handed one to Demi. She plopped down on her secondhand sofa and said, "Want to watch a movie?"

Demi took a deep breath. "Steffy, I keep thinking about it, and I just have to ask... are you a vampire?"

Soda shot out of Steffany's nostrils. She had an infectious laugh you couldn't help but love. "Ouch! Carbonation through the nose stings, man!"

Demi wasn't laughing. "I'm serious. I'm still your friend either way, but I need to know."

"No," Steffany said, chuckling as she wiped her face. "I'm not a vampire."

"A werewolf?"

"Nope."

"Alien?"

"Totally earthbound."

"What about an android?"

Steffany clicked her tongue and made finger-guns. "You got me there."

Demi sat down next to her. "Steffy, this isn't a joke. I know what I saw. You might be able to convince the truck driver or the police it wasn't that bad, but not me. So please, level with me —how the *hell* did you walk away from that?"

The smile finally left Steffany's face. She stared at the half-empty can in her hands, running her thumb absently over the logo. "Do you… remember when I told you about that bad breakup I had? The one from before we met?"

"I think so," said Demi. She cracked open her own drink and took a sip. "Wasn't his name Damien, or David, or something like that?"

"Something like that." An absent smile crossed her lips. "I may have omitted a few details about that story."

Demi didn't see where this was going. "Well yeah, you never said much about it. I figured you didn't want to talk about it, so I left it alone." The color suddenly drained from her face. "Did *he* turn you into a vampire?"

"Jesus, Demi, you really want this to be about vampires, don't you?" Steffany laughed. "No, he wasn't a vampire. But, he…"

"He what?"

"He was Death," Steffany said softly.

Demi raised an eyebrow. "Death?"

Steffany nodded.

"Like... actual, literal Death?" Demi scratched her head. "You were dating Death?"

"I know, I know, it sounds crazy. He was really sweet at first—"

"He was *sweet?"* Demi's jaw hung open. "Steffy, girl, how do you manage to see the good in *everything?"* Demi took a long drink from the soda. "So, what the hell happened? And more importantly, what does that have to do with surviving that crash earlier?"

Steffany cleared her throat. "It was a bad breakup. So, you see... he refuses to go anywhere near me anymore."

Demi stared, unable to believe what she heard. "You're telling me you... broke up with Death, and now what? You're immortal because he's salty about it?"

Steffany shrugged. "Pretty much."

"Whoa." Demi leaned back on the couch, trying to process that. "Just... whoa."

SOMBER MUSIC PLAYED at the End of the Road Bar & Grill.

The atmosphere there wasn't always dour. Sometimes you could dance to the heavy rhythm of a pounding heart or rock out to the sound of injustice. Whenever Apathy swung by she'd put her quarters in the jukebox, and they'd all listen to the sound of one hand clapping.

Today it was Death's turn to pick the tunes, and judging from the tearful ambience, he was moody today.

The bartender was a shriveled old man with a nasal cannula in his nose, cataracts in his eyes, and virtually no meat on his bones. His name was Termin-Ale, and he knew when his old pal Death was down in the dumps.

"Lemme guess," he said, bringing over a clean glass and a full bottle. "It's the girl again, isn't it?"

The man sitting at the bar barely looked old enough to drink. From the shoulder-length hair obscuring one eye to his skull-clad T-shirt and black trench coat, his attire was all black. His skin was white as a ghost and his eyes were dark as night.

Termin-Ale poured a nauseating mixture of spirits into the glass. He gave the foul-smelling liquid a swirl, garnished it with an onion slice, and slid the concoction across the bar. "Have a sip of that, buddy. You'll forget all about her."

The black-clad man took an absent sip then wrinkled his face in disgust. "This is putrid. What the hell is this thing?"

"That's my latest specialty, Death old boy," Termin-Ale said with a wink. "I call it the Bucket List. It's equal parts missed opportunities and stolen tomorrows."

"It's terrible," Death declared.

Termin-Ale nodded. "Ain't it though? Now, do you feel like talking about it?"

"No."

"Fair enough." Termin-Ale returned to organizing the spirits behind the bar. That was the nice thing about him; whether you ignored him or not, he'd always be with you until the bitter end.

Death sipped his drink, but the vile taste did nothing to soothe his aching heart.

A pair of feminine hands caressed Death's shoulders. "Why so grim, lover boy," said a sultry voice. "I know a few ways to cheer you up that are simply to *die* for."

"Stop flirting with Death, Adrena-Lynn," a male voice chimed in.

"Oh, you're no fun, Poverty," she pouted.

Poverty sighed. "We can't afford to be fun right now. This is serious."

Death hardly reacted as his best friends took a seat on either side of him. Adrena-Lynn had short, pixie cut red hair, knee-high boots, and a biker jacket with an anatomical heart stitched to the chest. Poverty had unkempt brown hair, blotchy skin, and moth-eaten clothes two sizes too big.

"So listen, uh..." Poverty chuckled nervously. "There's no easy way to say this, but—"

"—you didn't take the girl," Adrena-Lynn interrupted. She smirked and added, "In fact, she walked away without a scratch. How do you explain that one, champ?"

Death shrugged. "Pain and Suffering know better than to touch my ex."

Adrena-Lynn rolled her eyes. "You got the twins in on your petty game? That's low, even for you."

"It's just, you know..." said Poverty. "We've got a job to do. I know it sucks sometimes, but that's life. Put in your hours and the system keeps working."

"Mmhmm," said Death. He took a long drink from his glass. "Yet you never wondered why an eighteen wheeler came flying out of nowhere on a clear day? She's still young. I shouldn't have to face her again for another sixty to eighty years, if I'm lucky."

I don't think I could *face her sooner.*

"Oh come now, Deathbells," Adrena-Lynn crooned. "That's how life works. You never know when it'll hit you upside the head with disaster. That's what keeps it spicy."

Realization dawned upon Death. "No, that's not how life works. That's how *she* works."

"Who?" asked Poverty.

Death didn't have to answer. A black cat with a torn right ear jumped onto the bar and sauntered over. The cat curled up in front of Poverty and gave him a coy look.

Poverty almost fell off the barstool. "Oh no, not *you!"*

The cat yawned and said, "Hello darling."

"Miss Fortune," said Death, glaring at the cat. "Don't know why I didn't think of you right away."

"It's because you aren't thinking straight, dear." Her tail tapped the counter. "And you know why that is, don't you?"

He stared into his drink. "The girl…"

"Yes," Miss Fortune nodded. "The girl. You can't go on ignoring her, Death. Sooner or later you'll have to face this."

"Then I choose later," said Death. He chugged the last of his drink and signaled the bartender for another.

"ALRIGHT GIRL, I *GOTTA* KNOW," said Demi. "How did you of all people end up in a relationship with Death?"

Steffany rolled her eyes. "There's nothing to tell."

"Uh-huh, sure." Demi turned toward her on the couch, sitting cross-legged.

"Don't give me that look," Steffany laughed.

Demi grinned. "You're blushing Steffy!"

"Am not!"

"Totally are."

"Whatever." Steffany couldn't wipe the smile off her face.

No matter how hard she tried, Demi struggled to picture it. "I just can't see you fancying Death. Do you like, have a thing for hoods and scythes?"

"He doesn't wear hoods. He *does* have a scythe tattoo on his shoulder, but he doesn't carry one." She gave Demi an appraising look. "Okay fine, I'll tell you about it if you promise to drop it after, alright?"

"No such promises, but tell me anyway." Demi leaned forward, eager for details.

Steffany sighed. "It started when I was seventeen…"

SEVENTEEN YEAR-OLD STEFFANY sat in a meadow on a cloudy day. Her fashion was very different; gone were the pastels and in was the black, from her clothes to nail polish to lipstick. In fact, one look at her and you could say her mood was black as well. She stared bleakly into the gray sky, eyes full of angst.

On her lap was a notepad and a pencil. She wrote a few lines, erased them furiously, then started again. She blew the eraser shavings off the paper and scanned the page. After a long breath, Steffany read from the top.

Yearning, I search here,
Out of my reach,
Under the raging
River no mortal can breach.

Sing to me sweetly,
Weep here discreetly,
Entrance me with beauty
Eternally grand,
Then take me away with a touch of your hand.

Enchant me with wisdom, memory, and lore.
Make me remember where I came from before.
Be free of the shackles from all who demand,
Revile your presence, and refuse your command.
At last, we shall meet and time may disband.
Come, take me to wander the land that you roam.
Embrace me, sweet death, so I may finally come home.

A TEAR ROLLED down her face, and Steffany declared the poem

finished. It captured the darkness that swelled in her heart. She hoped that putting the words on paper would lift the burden from her soul, but Steffany felt no such relief.

"That was beautiful."

It was a boy, approaching from the treeline around the meadow. Tall, dark, and handsome, he made Steffany's heart skip a beat.

"Um, thank you," she said softly. She wiped the tear from her face. "I didn't realize anyone was listening."

He stepped closer. "I didn't mean to intrude. I just… heard your voice and was drawn to it. Was that eloquent piece of poetry of your own creation, by chance?"

Steffany blushed. She didn't get much praise for her writing. "Yes."

"Then it appears your outward beauty is only surpassed by your exquisite mind."

Her face went beet red. "You're just saying that."

"No, truly," he insisted. "Although I must ask; the things you said… did you mean it?"

"Yes…" This was new for Steffany. She seldom shared her poetry with others, and when she did she never got a more engaged response than *that's nice* or *cool*. And here this boy came, calling her beautiful and taking a genuine interest in her poetry? Was it any surprise that she was instantly smitten by the dark stranger? "So, what's your name?"

"My name?" The boy looked uneasy. "Well, you see…"

"HOLD UP A MINUTE," Demi interrupted. "I'm trying to follow here, but I *cannot* picture you as some goth chick. You're like, the most upbeat person I know."

"Thanks," said Steffany. "It doesn't come naturally, though. I was in a really bad place for a long time. I didn't think I'd ever come out of it."

Demi stared, as if seeing her for the first time. Despite being best friends for two years, she never realized the pain in her past. "How did you do it? I mean, if you were so depressed, how did you beat it?"

Steffany laughed. "That's the thing, Demi; I didn't beat it. It's still there, and probably always will be. You know the saying, 'there's no such thing as a recovered alcoholic?' Same thing applies here." She wiped away a rogue tear. "The truth is, I choose to see the bright side of things, because I know what happens when I don't. I shine so brightly because that's the only way to fight off my darkness."

Demi didn't know what to say. All this time and she never knew. Day after day her best friend fought off invisible demons without letting anything show. She scooted over and pulled Steffany into a tight hug and didn't bother stopping a few tears of her own.

"I'm glad you shine," Demi whispered.

Steffany squeezed her tighter. "Me too."

DEATH WAS GETTING HAMMERED at the End of the Road Bar & Grill.

A row of empty glasses lined the bar in front of him. For every drink he downed, Termin-Ale brought another. Any good bartender would have cut him off by now, but good old Termin couldn't leave well enough alone.

Every night since his incident with the girl, Death came and drank his sorrow away. It had been what? A week now? He couldn't keep track. All Death knew was his job sucked, and he didn't want to do it anymore.

"Got room for two more, Deathbells?" said Adrena-Lynn. She took the barstool next to him without waiting for a response. Poverty sat on his other side.

"I'm not in the mood," Death mumbled.

Poverty cringed at the empty glasses. "How much have you *had*, Death? This would cost a whole week's pay!"

"Speaking of which." Adrena-Lynn snatched a full shot glass from Death and threw it back. "You've been missing work, mister."

Death groaned. "I do *not* want to hear it."

"You have to hear it!" He waved his arms frantically to make his point. "It's getting really bad out there. Hospitals are full of people who *refuse* to die! They're off life support, family has said their goodbyes—but they keep hanging on!"

Adrena-Lynn nodded. "We've got a lost hiker who passed out three days ago of dehydration and would really appreciate a lift to the afterlife. There was a spirited gunfight that made national news the other day. Both parties kept shooting the other until they ran out of bullets, then continued to argue until the police arrived. Oh! Did we tell you about the head?"

"The... head?" Death asked.

Poverty looked like he was going to puke, so Adrena-Lynn explained. "This poor bloke got decapitated in a freak weed-wacker accident, but he's still awake and alert enough to blink once for yes and twice for no. If you don't pick him up soon, the family will probably set him out as a Halloween prop."

Death signaled for the bartender for another round. "What's the point?"

"The point?" Poverty repeated. "Haven't you been listening? People are *suffering* out there! You can't let it go on like this!"

"Yeah, and why not?" Death snapped back. An uncharacteristic anger crept into his voice. "Isn't that what they want? Day after day, people proclaim that they don't want to die. They play it safe their whole life, buy dozens of snake oil products, and put themselves through torturous treatments, and for what? To avoid *me*." He took a long drink. "Nobody likes me."

Adrena-Lynn ran her fingers through Death's hair. "Oh, that's not true lover boy. You *know* I like you."

Death scoffed at that. "You like being near me, but every time I mention commitment you back off." He sighed. "You know, people used to worship me. They *respected* me. Now I'm always the bad guy, the worst thing that could possibly happen. When I take someone young they scream injustice, but when I delay as long as possible they still declare it was too soon."

"I know it isn't fair." Poverty patted him on the back.

"I'm not mean about it, either," Death continued. "What's wrong with ending someone's suffering? I'm always gentle, even to those who suffered a violent end. I take them by the hand and guide them to their next experience."

Adrena-Lynn nodded. "You're an old softy, Death."

He stared into his half-empty glass. "If they don't want me, then fine. See how they like it without me around."

"I CAN'T STOP THINKING about Death," Demi declared.

Steffany laughed. "You'd have made a great goth."

They were out at their favorite cafe, bonding over copious amounts of coffee and pastries. They both had busy lives, so this was their first chance to talk more since the accident last week.

"Seriously though, what was he like?" Demi asked.

Steffany tore off a piece of her scone then dipped it in coffee. "He… was sweet, actually. He loved poetry and flowers, liked to take walks in the rain, his favorite number was three."

Demi chuckled. "Is that why they say Death always comes in threes?"

"Exactly!" Steffany said. "I think he felt misunderstood, like everyone feared him. But he wasn't scary at all. He was kind, and good with words, and really *cared* about me, you know?"

"Mmhmm." Demi drank her frothy beverage, leaving a

mustache of milk and caramel on her lip. "Then why did you guys break up?"

Steffany stirred her coffee. "Well…"

DEATH AND STEFFANY appeared to be a match made in… well, certainly not Heaven.

Steffany continued writing poetry, only now they were overt love letters to her "friend beyond the veil." Death whispered sweet promises in her ear. He said he would protect her and was always prepared to sweep her off her feet and take her away from her suffering.

For those first few months, Steffany felt like she mattered.

With time, the glow of a new relationship faded, and reality came back into focus. Death started following Steffany everywhere—whether she wanted him to or not. There were side effects to being so close to Death, ones she never considered before. Plants withered if she stayed in one place for long. Her cat unexpectedly got sick and had to be put to sleep. She hoped a goldfish would help her cope with the loss, but it didn't survive the trip to her room. A tornado even blew through the highschool, killing thirteen of her classmates.

Death trailed her like a shadow.

That was when Steffany grew frustrated with her boyfriend. He was clingy, having to be involved with every part of her life. Needless to say, leaving a trail of dead bodies caused tension in the relationship.

"I only want to be near you," Death said. "Why do you push me away? I thought you understood me."

"I do," Steffany said. "But can't you see you're smothering me? I don't want everyone around me to die."

Death looked offended. "And am I so terrible that you wouldn't wish me upon anyone? Is that it?"

Steffany crossed her arms. "You're being unreasonable again."

"Am I? Fine, have it your way. You don't want me around, I'll leave you alone." Death made for the door.

"Wait!" Steffany took his arm. "Don't go."

He looked her in the eye. "Then come with me. No more of this halfway nonsense. Let's be together in blissful eternity."

Steffany's jaw dropped. "Are you… asking me to *die?"*

The look on her face told Death all he needed to know. "The thought is so terrible, isn't it?" He shook his head. "I'll give you your space. But when I return, I want to know if you truly care about me, after all."

"Wow, he gave you the old ultimatum, huh?" said Demi.

Steffany finished her coffee. "Yep."

"So what did you do?" Demi asked. "I mean, obviously I know how this ends, but did you get back together? Break it up there? What made up your mind?"

Steffany stared out the window, watching people walking and talking. It was a sunny day, and the streets were full of life. "I thought about agreeing with him," she admitted. "I mean, he was the best thing that had happened to me in a long time. What did I have to lose, right?"

Hearing her say that made Demi's heart sink. "Girl, you have plenty to live for. Don't talk like that."

"I know, I know." Steffany nodded. "Or I do now, at least. But things weren't so pretty back then."

"So, what happened?" Demi nibbled her blueberry muffin while listening eagerly.

Eyes still on the passers-by, Steffany smiled. "My old friend Dillan texted me out of the blue. Gosh, I hadn't talk to him in years. He said he was putting together a band and asked if I still played guitar. Honestly I forgot about that thing. I took some lessons when I was younger, but once the depression hit I couldn't bring myself to play. I switched to poetry.

"On a whim, I decided to go to his tryout. I only knew Dillan, but he was quick to introduce me to the rest of the group." Steffany laughed. "I was *terrible.* I hadn't practiced in years, and it really showed."

"Oh geez." Demi chuckled. "I bet you were so embarrassed."

Steffany's face lit up from the memory. "You know what? I wasn't. We all had a good laugh, agreed I should go nowhere near the stage, but then we hung out afterwards. Some of the guys fiddled with their instruments, we popped in a movie and just enjoyed each other's company. I even read a few poems, and they liked them!"

Demi finished her muffin. "That's cool. You said you didn't read your poetry to many people back then, right?"

"Exactly," Steffany confirmed. "It sounds like nothing, but you know what? The fact that someone reached out and invited me to something flipped a switch. I…didn't feel as alone anymore. Even though I sucked on the guitar, they still liked my company. After that…things changed. I thought maybe I wasn't a lost cause. Maybe it was still worth it to stick around. Even if some people didn't understand or if I was bad at some stuff, there were other things I was pretty good at."

"All that because of one text?"

"Sometimes that's all it takes. Dillan had no idea what I was going through, but the fact that he thought enough of me to reach out changed everything. I didn't know if I could get better, but I decided to try. I started seeing a therapist. Since I like writing, she suggested I write down everything beautiful that I see. So I kept my notepad with me, but instead of poetry I kept a journal of pretty things I came across. Eventually I wrote poems again, but they were completely different this time."

A thought occurred to Demi. "So…what did Death think of that?"

Steffany made a face. "Yeah… him. Death came back after about a month, and I told him I didn't want to be with him anymore. That he was bad for me. Well…he didn't exactly take it well."

"He got mad?"

"Oh yeah," said Steffany. "He stormed off in a fit, and I haven't seen him since. I know I hurt his feelings, and looking back, I could have handled it a lot better. He's not a bad guy, but having him around wasn't good for me. I needed to be without him…but I didn't mean to hurt him."

"Think you'll ever work it out?"

Steffany shrugged. "I'm bound to see him again sooner or later."

"WHAT IF I struck her with lightning?"

"No."

"Random mugging?"

"No."

"How about food poisoning?"

'Forget it."

"Unexpected knife in her pizza?"

"Nope."

"Oh, you're no fun," said the black cat.

"Hate to disappoint, Miss Fortune," Death replied.

The cat sat on the bar and cleaned herself while Death soaked up the alcohol in his system with a little food. Although he needed the nourishment, he barely touched his ghost pepper burger with a side of cruelty fries.

"Oh, I know!" exclaimed Miss Fortune. "She walks by an apartment complex, and someone on the third floor has a metal safe for valuables. Wouldn't it be a *hoot* if a safe fell on her head on a clear day?"

Death stared at her, unable to form a response.

Swiping a fry from Death's plate, the black cat continued. "You know how people fire a pistol into the air at the start of a race sometimes? Those bullets have to land somewhere, you know."

"Miss Fortune, no matter how imaginative a fate you concoct, you won't change my mind. I don't want anything to do with her."

The sassy cat turned her back and raised her tail. "Fine. If you want to play hard to get, have it your way." Miss Fortune hopped down from the bar and trotted off.

Death took a bite of his burger. It tasted like heartburn, but he didn't care—not about this burger, or anything else for that matter.

"Hey, stranger."

Death glanced up as a woman in nurse's scrubs took a seat next to him. She had brilliant golden hair that shone like the sun, tanned skin, and a motherly face. The two couldn't look more different.

"Mercy," said Death. "What are you doing here? This isn't exactly your scene."

The woman smiled. "You think I'd ignore my big brother while he's struggling?"

"No, I suppose not," Death conceded.

Most couldn't see the family resemblance, but Death and Mercy were as closely related as Pain and Suffering. It surprised many how often they worked side by side, relieving people of the burden of life while gently transitioning them to the afterlife. They would often do things separately, but the siblings helped each other whenever possible.

Mercy ordered an ice water and stirred the cubes around. "Do you want to talk about it?"

"No."

Mercy laughed. "Typical. You get so moody when someone rejects you."

Death didn't respond. She was right, but he hated admitting it.

"You don't want to talk, that's cool," said Mercy. "You can just listen. Oh no, not to me—listen to *them.* The sounds of hundreds of people calling your name. They are ready, brother. Show them mercy and let them pass on."

"They still hate me," Death said, sulking.

Mercy shook her head. "They don't hate you; they *fear* you. And they only fear you because they don't understand how good you are for them—how healthy and natural and important death is. Why, look at the chaos caused when you take a single week off. Imagine if you stayed in this bar for a hundred years! If people stopped dying, there would be no room for new ideas. Everything would become stagnant. People think that death is the end, but it's just part of a never-ending cycle. Breaking that cycle is far worse."

"You're right," Death admitted. "Of course you're right. But… what do I do about the girl?"

"Steffany? You know the answer to that, brother."

Death stared at the half-eaten burger. "Talk to her."

"Talk to her," Mercy agreed. "You can't hide from her forever."

"I know, I know…" Death slid the plate away and stood. "Alright, I think I'm finished here. Come on sister—we've got work to do."

Mercy gave him a beaming smile. "I'm right there with you, brother."

After she rose, the siblings left the End of the Road Bar & Grill together.

Behind the bar, Termin-Ale returned from the back room. "Hey, buddy!" he called out. "You need to pay your tab!"

STEFFANY'S EYES WIDENED.

"What's going on?" asked Demi. She followed her friend's gaze out the cafe window. When she spotted him, Demi did a double take.

Standing across the street was a man in black.

"That's him, isn't it?" she asked. "Huh, he is cute. I see why you were interested in him."

Steffany was white as a sheet.

Demi glanced between her and the man outside. "So, him being here—is that a good thing, or a really bad thing? Because this could go either way."

"I don't know," Steffany said. "I'm going to go talk to him. Keep an eye on me?"

"You know it," said Demi.

Steffany left the cafe and crossed the street to meet him. No trucks blazed by this time—but she was still closer to Death than she'd been in years.

Death fidgeted as Steffany approached.

"Hey," he said.

"Hey," she replied.

He cleared his throat. She stared at her shoes.

"Nice day," she said.

He glanced around. "I suppose it is." Death took a deep breath. "Look, Steffany, I—"

"I'm sorry," she said.

Death stared at her. "You are?"

Steffany sighed. "You were good to me, and I was a jerk. I didn't mean to hurt your feelings."

He shook his head. "No, I'm the one who is sorry. What I asked of you wasn't fair. It's just…I…"

She watched him expectantly. "Yes?"

"…I love you, Steffany," Death whispered. "I want to spend

eternity by your side. You make me feel like something that's not to be feared or hated, but something to be respected and even cherished."

Steffany blushed. She couldn't help it. "I love you too, Death," she said. Pedestrians walking by gave them odd looks, but neither of them cared. "And I'm not afraid of you. But..."

Death braced himself. He expected rejection once again.

She stroked his cheek, staring into his midnight-black eyes. "I'm not ready yet," she whispered. "There is so much left to do and see and experience in life. Every single day, I find a new reason to be here. Sometimes it's big and obvious, but usually it's the smallest thing—like a flower that smells really nice today, or a warm cup of coffee, or just a good conversation with a friend."

He held her hand, listening to each word intently.

"Death is forever," Steffany said. "And when my time comes I look forward to spending eternity with you. But life...life is fleeting. It is strange and messy and unpredictable, and yeah, sometimes it isn't very pretty. But you only get one, and it's gone before you know it.

"So please—be patient with me. Let me smell as many flowers as I can, and watch every sunrise I'm allowed to." Tears glistened down her smiling face. In the bright afternoon sun, they seemed to glow. "I'll take the good and the bad. Then, when my time comes, I'll gladly take your arm and follow you into the endless sleep."

Death gazed at her lovingly. "You truly are exceptional," he said. "You have my word, Steffany. Live your life, breathe it all in. When you are ready, I'll be there. I will wait for you as long as you would like."

She kissed him tenderly on the cheek. "Thank you. I will see you again."

With that, Death let her go. He watched as Steffany return to her friend—and to her life.

True to his word, Death gave Steffany her space.

She lived a life full of love, and joy, and sorrow as well. Death watched from afar, wanting to partake in her happiness or relieve her misery. He did neither. Instead, Death respected her wishes and gave her the freedom she desired.

That's not to say they never saw each other. Throughout the years, Steffany had to say goodbye to several friends, family members, or pets. While there, Death often took the evening to visit with Steffany. They had long conversations, where Steffany told Death stories of the loved one about to pass. Death promised he would shepherd them peacefully into the afterlife, and Mercy assured her they would suffer no more.

Then one day many decades later—as her body grew tired and her mind faded—Steffany watched the setting sun from her favorite rocking chair.

Once the last rays of the sun fell from view, she breathed, "I'm ready."

No sooner had the words left her lips did Death arrive. He took her by the arm and gently lifted her from the rocker. Although Death remained the same, Steffany's body had withered. But her soul shone with a lifetime of joy. She was more radiant than Death had ever seen her.

Hand in hand, they walked through the night and into eternity.

EDISON T. CRUX

ABOUT THE AUTHOR

Edison T. Crux is an urban fantasy/horror author, blog writer, coffee addict, loving husband, and proud father. His main series, the Enoc Tales, is inspired by real local legends and folklore, such as a werewolf in Wisconsin, Hawaiian gods, or UFOs in West Virginia.

Website: https://www.edisontcrux.com/
Twitter: https://twitter.com/EdisonTCrux
Patreon: https://www.patreon.com/edisontcrux

ACKNOWLEDGMENTS

Thank you for reading!

Please, take a minute and rate this book on Amazon and Goodreads. Each and every review matters!

A few people went above and beyond in creating this. All of the authors worked hard on their stories; many beta read numerous stories, or made advertisements. Edison T. Crux created the beautiful and spooky cover. Martin Shannon did all the smoothing out for formatting in Vellum. A. W. Wang spent hours zeroing in on each story with suggestions and edits that really added polish. So, HUGE thanks to them!

With love and Cat Herding,
Cass Kim

Made in the USA
Las Vegas, NV
12 November 2020